THUNDER

Hell's Handlers Book 10

Lilly Atlas

Table Of Contents

Prologue   1

Chapter One   14

Chapter Two   26

Chapter Three   37

Chapter Four   48

Chapter Five   64

Chapter Six   77

Chapter Seven   87

Chapter Eight   98

Chapter Nine   111

Chapter Ten   125

Chapter Eleven   135

Chapter Twelve   153

Chapter Thirteen   164

Chapter Fourteen   178

Chapter Fifteen   185

Chapter Sixteen   199

Chapter Seventeen   207

Chapter Eighteen   222

Chapter Nineteen   233

Chapter Twenty   242

Chapter Twenty-One   252
Chapter Twenty-Two   266
Chapter Twenty-Three   271
Chapter Twenty-Four   280
Chapter Twenty-Five   289
Chapter Twenty-Six   297
Chapter Twenty-Seven   308
Chapter Twenty-Eight   316
Chapter Twenty-Nine   325
Chapter Thirty   335
Chapter Thirty-One   343
Chapter Thirty-Two   352
Epilogue   365
Bonus Epilogue   373

Makenna has a past she'd rather bury deep in her mind. Unfortunately, as the sole guardian for her five siblings, forgetting where they came from isn't possible. All she can hope for is to provide her loved ones the kind of untroubled childhood she'd always dreamed of and keep them far away from where she grew up. Friendships and relationships, especially the romantic variety, don't rank on her priority list. That is until she's introduced to a hot biker whose playful personality and mesmerizing smile would make any woman perk up and take notice, even one with more responsibilities than sense.

Thunder has seen it all, done it all, and has no interest in the high maintenance, in-your-face, party girls. Give him a no-frills woman, like the diner's adorable new waitress, who doesn't play games rather than a scantily clad bimbo who manipulates men for sport. Makenna is precisely the kind of fun he needs to celebrate patching with the Hell's Handlers MC. Only he quickly discovers Makenna is a package deal with more baggage than a carefree guy like him can handle.

With each passing day, Thunder finds himself increasingly drawn to Makenna despite her mountain of responsibilities and his distrust of relationships. Even crazier is how some of her siblings are working their way under his skin and into his heart, as is Makenna.

Just as Thunder starts thinking about dates and promises, the CDMC roars back into his life. They're responsible for his beloved club brother's death, and he wants nothing more than to make them suffer.

When the threats start coming, and Makenna finds herself caught in the crossfire, Thunder will discover exactly the kind of man he is, and how far he's willing to go to keep Makenna and her siblings in his life.

For all of you.
Thank you for giving a home to the men and women
born in my imagination.

THUNDER

Lilly Atlas

Prologue

If she'd known the vital act of breathing could be so excruciating, Delilah might have thought twice about her actions.

No.

That wasn't true.

Despite the chilly temperature, stomach-cramping hunger, days of isolation, and the fists that had pummeled her, she'd do it again because she refused to get pregnant by *that man*.

Nothing in the world could make her conceive his child willingly.

Her husband.

The man she'd never wanted to marry, but who cared what she had in mind for her own life?

No one.

Delilah huffed out a self-deprecating laugh, which turned into a wince when a shock of fire streaked across her chest.

"Ohhh," she groaned, as she attempted to settle into a more bearable position on the hard floor of an abandoned shed at the very back of her community's property.

The fact she'd been successful in deceiving her husband for such a long time was a miracle in itself. For two years, her ruse had flown under the radar. For the seven hundred and fifty-two days she'd been married to a man more than three times her age, she'd managed to sneak a birth control pill down her throat.

She'd never missed a dose.

Never.

Members of their sheltered, brainwashed community pitied her husband, Roger. When he walked by, whispers trailed him, as did side glances and head shakes. As the man who'd married the girl considered by many in the compound to be the most desired, he should have been strutting like the prize rooster. She was the first of their founder's daughters, slated to produce near-royal children for years to come. Progeny with her father's founding blood who would one day lead the community with the same iron fist and deluded ideals her father currently did.

Unfortunately for old Roger, her tendency to be defiant, obstinate, and vocal in her opinions often overshadowed her reputation as a young fertile prize.

Especially those opinions which went against the values of their people. Nearly everything she believed in or desired flouted what she'd been taught.

She did not believe the world would end in her lifetime.

She did not believe they'd make use of the hundred-person bomb shelter the community members had spent nearly three decades building and stocking.

She did not believe they needed to form an army, prepared to rise up during the inevitable violent degradation of society.

She could not understand why the community leaders taught hatred and intense distrust of everyone with a lifestyle different from theirs.

She absolutely did not believe young children needed hours of physical and military training daily, followed by hard labor farming or working in their sewing shop.

No one questioned. No one had an independent thought. Every man, woman, and child she lived with seemed perfectly content to exist in their sheltered, fear-fueled world.

Thunder

Everyone except her, which had made for a difficult upbringing. The majority of her belief system came from her mother, who'd whispered tales of a life away from the community. One where women had free choice, men respected those they loved, and children spent their days playing frivolous games and laughing. Delilah loved those lessons disguised as stories, and when her mother had disappeared years ago, she'd kept them alive in her mind and with her actions, which led to many punishments. As a teen, she'd rebelled against the idea of military training, she'd vocally expressed her disinterest in an arranged marriage, and she'd flat out refused to work at times. None of it had ended well for her, but no matter how many beatings and punishments she'd endured, her desire for a different life persisted.

Poor Roger had been saddled with the black sheep, but she was young, pretty enough, and would provide numerous healthy offspring he could mold into little clones of himself.

Or so everyone had thought.

They had no idea that when she was in town on errands, she'd been sneaking off to meet up with a woman she'd encountered by chance years ago. The woman who worked at a Planned Parenthood. The very same woman who'd provided her the oral contraceptives when Delilah spilled her story in a fit of hysterics after finding out she'd be marrying a sixty-two-year-old man at the tender age of nineteen.

Actually, eighteen years and eleven months.

When she'd been thirteen, Delilah vowed she'd never bring a child into the world. At least not while living in the para-military community where she'd been raised. And since she'd had no hope of leaving, she'd pretty much resigned herself to the fact she'd never reproduce. Not that it mattered. The compound had so many children, it was practically overrun. She'd had a hand raising kids since she was in the single digits herself.

Roger, we all thought she'd give you many strapping sons and precious daughters to carry on her father's legacy. How could this have happened? She's so pretty.

How many times had she heard a version of the sentiment?

Because *that's* how it worked.

She may not have been formally educated, but she wasn't an idiot. General attractiveness had nothing to do with the ability to conceive a child. Of course, no one ever wondered if *he* was the problem. No, the defect had to lie with the woman.

She'd been so close to her goal. Within touching distance, really. Four more months and she and her brother would have finally saved enough to run away with the rest of their siblings. Every penny she'd found, bribed, or won, she'd stashed away. Most of the money came from her sixteen-year-old brother, Eric. Once boys became men at thirteen, they began earning a small wage for their farming duties. Her work as a seamstress had never been and would never be compensated. All in all, the meager amount they'd managed to scrimp together over the years was laughable, but enough to leave.

In four months, her youngest sister, Rae, would turn six months old. While not ideal, a six-month-old baby would be easier to care for on the run than a newborn.

But then, two days ago, Delilah's world had crashed down around her. They'd discovered her secret. A girl in her late teens had found the hidden stash of birth control pills and had immediately squealed to Delilah's husband. Didn't help that the brainwashed twit was hoping to slide into Delilah's position as Roger's wife when he wised up and tossed her aside. The bitch probably thought she'd struck gold.

Now that Delilah been caught with the worst kind of contraband possible, her husband was bound to search every inch of her measly personal property.

Would he find the money? The thought turned her stomach.

The cash was hidden well, but how thoroughly would he hunt?

Thunder

And what would he do to her once he found it? Maybe he'd finally kill her. It'd be the only way to stop her from finding a way to leave.

Delilah rotated her head to the side, wincing as her torso protested the small movement. Darkness waited behind a tiny rectangular window six feet off the ground of the tiny shed. Her husband had stuck her in here as punishment. That tiny window was the only glimpse of the outside world she'd had for the past three days. While minuscule, she might have been able to haul herself up, then squeeze through the little opening if her body didn't feel so broken.

She could still try.

It'd be agony, but freedom was worth any amount of pain. However, she'd only have the illusion of freedom. She couldn't leave the community. Not without her siblings. The bodily harm caused by attempting an escape wouldn't be worth it. The only option was to wait it out. Suffer through whatever additional punishment he had planned for her and hang on until he allowed her free rein of the compound again.

Then she would begin again. Because someday she'd get out.

If past behavior was predictive of what awaited her, Roger planned to keep her in the shack for a while. A solid number of days without food and only a scant amount of water, until she was too weak to defy him. She'd been in this same position, in this same shed many times before. Prior to her marriage, her father had been in charge of doling out discipline, and now the task fell to Roger. They shared a similar penchant for using their fists to express displeasure.

The shudder that coursed through her had nothing to do with physical pain this time.

She had to find a way to swallow her true nature, display sincere remorse, and play the role of meek, dutiful wife. Roger wanted her to suffer for her wrongdoings. As long as he was satisfied with her contrition and submission, there was a chance he'd keep his fists to himself even if he wouldn't release her for a bit longer.

Tap, tap, tap.

Delilah jumped then gasped as her ribs screamed.

Tap, tap, tap.

There it was again. A sound like someone was lightly rapping on the door. She struggled to a seated position on the floor, hissing and panting the entire time. Once she'd propped her back against the wall, she gave herself a moment to catch her breath and let the rush of blood in her ears calm.

Tap, tap, tap.

"Delilah?"

The low whisper barely met her ears. Either she'd gone mad from lack of food and water, or someone called her name through the door.

"Delilah?" A little louder this time.

Oh, my God. It was real. And it was Eric. "E-E?" she croaked. Could her throat get any drier?

Yes, it could—and would. She knew from personal experience.

"Oh, thank God," Eric said.

"Not so sure He's on my side, Eric," Delilah whispered.

Keys jangled, then two seconds later, her brother burst into the room.

Even as relief chased away much of her despair, Delilah frowned at him. "What are you doing here? Go! Do you have any idea what Roger will do to you if he catches you? And—oh, my God, is that Rae?" she said, staring at the bundle strapped to his chest.

"Shh, the only way they'll find me is if you keep squawking like that demented chicken in the coop." He dropped to his knees beside her, holding a water bottle to her lips, and she chuckled before taking a sip.

As the tepid liquid filled her mouth, she swished it before swallowing.

So good.

Thunder

"More, please," she said, still sounding like an animated frog.

Eric held the water for her again, and as he did, her gaze drifted to the fuzzy blonde head of their baby sister. The one whose mother was younger than Delilah herself. Barely eighteen to be exact. She'd recently married their father and lived a life no one would envy.

Eric gave her a small smile before stroking a tanned finger across the baby's head. "What are we dealing with here, Delilah? Can you walk?"

Her throat thickened as tears formed. She tried to pinch them off, but one escaped. As was his way, he patiently waited until she'd composed herself.

Her brother was a saint. The boy was huge with dark hair and dark eyes, like their father. At sixteen, he'd already passed six-foot-two and would continue to grow. Years of working on the farm and mandatory military-style training had honed his muscles as well. Eric could easily pass for older than she was.

No matter how many hundreds of hours her father had spent trying to mold his son into the perfect little soldier, Eric remained as gentle a giant that ever lived.

Until someone threatened those he loved. Then he could be as vicious as a junkyard dog—far more man than the boy he'd never been allowed to be.

Each of her five siblings had life beyond their years. All except little Rae, who, if everything went according to plan, would be the only one of them to experience an actual childhood. That thought, that hope for Rae's future, stoked the flame of defiance inside Delilah. Rae would have a life outside the gates of the community. So would the rest of her siblings.

"Roger discovered my birth control pills. He roughed me up pretty bad and hasn't fed me at all."

Eric nodded as he helped her drink another sip of water. "I thought it was something like that. Are you going to be able to walk out of here?" He was the only one who'd known her secret.

With a snort, she shrugged, then winced. "Haven't tried. It's been hours since Roger was last in here, and the most I've moved was from flat on the floor to against this wall when you knocked."

"We're ready to go, Delilah. The kids are packed and in position."

What?

"Eric," she breathed. She'd have grabbed him and shook him if the action wouldn't make her shout in agony. "We can't." Her heart kicked up, pounding against her aching ribs. This was insane. Pure madness. How could they pull it off? Rae was so young. So dependent on her mother for every second of her survival.

Even if this was the time to go, could Delilah's bruised and broken body cooperate enough to handle the physical demands of escape?

Madness.

"We have to," he said with panic in his voice. "Things are changing, Delilah. Roger is furious like I've never seen. I overheard him ranting like a madman in father's office. He was screaming about you being defective, and how he was promised offspring from the founder's bloodline, and he is demanding that promise be fulfilled."

"Oh, God, it's going to be impossible for me to protect myself from pregnancy after this." She tapped a hand to her aching forehead as though it would get her nerves firing more effectively. "I need to think, but I'm so hungry it's hard to concentrate."

"Delilah," he said in a severe tone that had her focusing on his face. "You don't understand."

Dread rolled through her empty stomach forcing bile up her esophagus. She swallowed, wincing as the acid burned. "What don't I?"

"H-he wants Cathryn," Eric whispered.

Thunder

She shook her head. His words struck a cold bolt of fear deep into her gut, yet at the same time, her brain rejected the statement as impossible. "She's fourteen. It's not—they've never —"

Eric nodded. "I know."

"Father said no, right? He's crazy, but even he's never gone that far off the deep end. Please tell me he said no." If she could have, she'd have crawled across the floor and knelt at Eric's feet, begging him to tell her their father refused Roger's demand.

"He agreed."

Delilah sagged. "Oh, my God. We have to get out of here. Now."

"First thing I did was grab the money and get the kids packed. They're ready to go. We need to leave tonight, but, God, Delilah, you look awful."

She let her eyes fall closed as she huffed out a painful laugh. "Thanks, Eric. You're sweet."

"You know what I mean. I've never seen you so bruised. How could he do this? I wish I could kill him. I'm not even kidding. If Roger or father walked in right now—"

"Shhh," she reached out as though to soothe him, grinding her teeth as her ribs protested. "Rae is right against your heart. She takes comfort in its strong, steady beat. You need to stay even. Okay?"

Eric blew out a breath. "Yeah, okay. I'm calm." He may have settled, but his eyes still held a violent hatred she'd never seen in him.

Delilah made her decision.

They'd be leaving that night. Right then. No matter how excruciating, she'd make it. They couldn't stay. She would die before allowing Roger to get his hands on her fourteen-year-old sister. And Eric's threats against their father and husband weren't idle. They were born of a desperation cultivated from years of torment and abuse. Though she was the community's black sheep and rebellious troublemaker, Eric had it even harder.

As a son of the community's founder, he was groomed to run the place one day. Everything he did and said reflected on their father, and Eric was never given a chance to forget that fact. He'd been mistreated his whole life not only by being hit, but powerful verbal abuse and violent, deadly training a young boy should never suffer through. He had the skills to carry through on his threat. Though she wouldn't mourn the bastard should Eric eliminate their father, she wouldn't survive without her beloved brother at her side either behind the walls of the community or in the real world.

"Help me up." She extended a hand, smiling through the pain.

Eric frowned and shook his head. Clearly, she'd fooled him about as well as she fooled herself. "Del—"

"Shh," she said, harsher this time. The exhaled sound rumbled through her chest as though a steam roller were crushing her ribs. "I-I'm all right. Just bruised and sore."

Lies. She was pretty sure Roger had broken at least one of her ribs.

Eric gripped her forearm, and she did the same to him, only her hand barely made it halfway around his bulging muscle.

"Okay, pull me up."

With a furrowed brow and eyes that spoke his disapproval, he hauled her to her feet in a swift, rip-off-the-Band-Aid move.

Delilah bit her lower lip as the pain in her chest stole her ability to breathe. Once upright, she grabbed Eric's sides and bowed her head as she puffed through the anguish. Shallow breaths were all she could manage. Each one made her dizzy.

"Jesus, Delilah, we can't—"

She lifted her head. "I'm okay," she said, though her strained voice sounded anything but.

Eric rolled his eyes in a move so typically teenager, it gave her hope a young man still lived inside the world-weary expressions and man's body Eric had.

"Here, give me Rae." She motioned to herself with her hands.

"What? No. Are you crazy? You can't carry the baby." He took a step back, shaking his head.

This was something she couldn't back down on. With her injured, Eric would end up doing more than his share of the work. She needed to carry her own weight and at least some of the others if they were to have any chance of success. "Eric, I'll be fine. She's tiny. I won't be able to help the others climb the fence. You'll need to do that. So hand Rae to me. I can manage her."

Hopefully.

He pressed his lips together in a look of pure displeasure. Sometimes, she wished he'd just tell her to fuck off if he disagreed with her. Though he was more willing to argue with her than anyone else, above all, they'd had obedience drilled into them with punishing efficiency. She'd been the only one who never thoroughly learned the lesson.

And she'd paid for it countless times throughout her twenty-one years.

But instead of fighting, Eric unstrapped the baby carrier and carefully helped transfer Rae to her chest.

"Shh, shh, shh," she crooned as she gently rocked back and forth. She'd handle this, pain and all. Women all around the world survived worse atrocities every day. "I-it's okay, baby girl. I've got y-you."

She closed her eyes and imagined life two years down the road. The younger kids happy and playing without fear. Her brother meeting a girl and dating like a normal teenage boy. Herself, working in a job she loved, surrounded by her happy siblings. None of them living under the feared thumb of the community. The visual strengthened her, overriding the worst of the pain. She could do this.

She had to.

The baby blinked up at her with sleepy eyes so full of innocence and trust before fading back out. Thankfully, this little girl had been a stellar sleeper since day one.

"You ready for an adventure, baby girl?" she whispered. Adventures had become her thing over the years. She'd discovered early on the easiest way to survive long days of physical training or work was to change the context in her mind. She'd drift off to faraway castles, the high seas, or a steamy jungle. Soon, it'd become a game she played with the younger children. A way of easing the stress of agonizing drills and grueling hours. What child didn't love an exciting adventure?

"Are *you* ready?" Eric asked.

She met her brother's gaze. This was it—the culmination of five years of plotting, saving, wishing, and waiting.

Was she ready? The answer to that question didn't matter. Escape was happening so, ready or not, she had to find her strength and make it happen. Five lives beside her own depended on her ability to keep them fed, sheltered, warm, safe, and off her father's radar.

"Let's do it," she said as she ignored the discomfort and gave Eric a smile that hopefully came across as confident.

After taking one step toward the door, fear rose sharp and swift, nearly swallowing her whole. Life was about to go from very hard to nearly impossible. At least for a while. Hopefully only for a little while. No matter how challenging day to day life was about to become, they'd be free. And that was all that mattered.

She inhaled, letting that terror motivate her to remain fierce and drive her determination. If they were discovered, they'd make her wish she was dead.

Or they might kill her outright this time.

She couldn't let that happen.

She had to continue forward with a single-minded focus, remain vigilant at all times, and protect her siblings with every ounce of fire in her blood.

"Take one final look around, Eric. We're never coming back." Not to mention that would be the last time she'd ever call him

Eric. The moment they stepped foot off the compound, they'd all assume new identities.

"Fuck that," he said with a snort.

As she hobbled out the door with as much hustle as she could muster, she heard Eric whisper, "There's not a damn thing here I want to see."

She couldn't agree more.

Chapter One

Thunder's chest rose and fell as he worked his final pose, which happened to be bent over, jiggling his ass in the air while a gaggle of sexually unsatisfied rich housewives screamed and chucked their husband's hard-earned dollar bills at him.

That's right, he was dancing at a bachelorette party for a ten-year vow renewal.

What the fuck would wealthy people come up with next?

Not that he was complaining, because these women were playing fast and loose when it came to shoving those crisp green bills down his shimmery black briefs. Hell, he'd even caught sight of more than one twenty getting stuffed in there. At this rate, he'd be upgrading his Harley in no time.

After suffering through a few moments of ear-piercing shrieks, the noise died down, and the money fluttered to the floor. Thunder straightened and faced the group of women trying to recapture their long-lost sorority days.

He wiped the back of his hand across his dripping forehead. Fuck, he needed some water. And a towel. Working his ass and grinding all over bored Stepford wives was thirsty work.

Clearly, the women were parched as well. They all but ignored him now that his performance had concluded, sucking back champagne like it would prevent their Botoxed faces from aging.

Thunder

Christ, he hated loaded, entitled women.

But at the same time, he was grateful for them because they'd been lining his pockets for years. Go-go dancing had been pretty much the only profession he'd known until he patched with the Hell's Handlers and began working at Zach's gym during the day.

Working in the daylight hours…who knew that was a thing?

After scooping the money off the floor—a degrading act he fucking hated—he slipped a pair of gray athletic pants over his briefs. No way was he leaving in the clichéd police officer getup he'd arrived wearing.

"Hey, Thunder." The syrupy, slightly slurred voice behind him had him rolling his eyes before he plastered a smile on his face and turned.

"Hey, Mrs. Henderson."

The short-haired, platinum-blonde in her Ralph Lauren dress and flats giggled. "Come on, how long have we known each other?"

Too fucking long.

"When are you going to start calling me Lisa?"

Never. These women got a naughty little thrill out of being called Mrs. Whoever while gawking at a nearly naked man who wasn't their husband. Hell, a few even liked it when he was fucking 'em. Just last month, some broad requested he shout "Mrs. Simpson" as he came down her throat. Whatever. He'd made a thousand bucks to get a blowjob then get her off with a dildo her husband bought her because he was having trouble getting it up.

The stories he could tell.

"I'll call you Lisa when you agree to leave your husband for me." A little flirting went a long way with these women and was the difference between a night of good tips and a night of fucking bank.

She tittered again, pink tinging her cheeks. The perfect little demure woman. Or so she wanted the world to think. In reality, she had a thing for deep throating a man twenty years her junior for cash.

He'd rather die than be chained to a gold digger like Lisa Henderson, not that it was a worry he'd ever have to give more than a second of thought. She may be in a bland, sexless marriage like most of these hoity-toity bitches, but she'd never leave. Who'd pay for her weekly spa trips and designer shoe collection?

To these ladies, he was damn good fantasy fodder, but not a single one of them would ever want a man like him on their arm at their next charity gala. To them, he was nothing more than a dirty biker and a male whore.

"It's too bad you're not working at *You've Got Male* anymore. We all miss your headlining act." She batted her false eyelashes as she stepped closer and ran a perfectly manicured fingernail down his sweaty chest.

His dick didn't so much as twitch.

"I hear ya, babe. Just couldn't swing the hours with my club commitments." That was the truth. Working at Zach's gym was great, really. Daytime hours, no one grabbing his ass, a regular salary. He loved it, but on a slow night when he'd been at YGM, he came home with an extra five hundred in cash. Though a rockin' boss, Zach sure as hell wasn't paying him that much. Still, he'd had to decide which club meant more to him because he couldn't swing both.

The Handlers had won out.

Easily.

Lisa pouted, projecting that glossy lower lip out in a move he'd grown immune to somewhere around the thousandth time it'd been used on him. Probably before he'd turned nineteen.

"You know," she said, as she traced a tattoo on his right pec, "I'm in the mood to keep having fun. How about you?"

Thunder bit back a sigh. He could really use the extra Benjamins she'd slip in his hand if he laid down and let her ride out her boredom. His dick's disinterest in her didn't mean shit.

Thunder

He'd spent enough time around professionals to know just how to get and keep it up no matter who was on the receiving end of his cock. After a few romps fucking women he had no interest in, he'd learned to disappear inside his head. To conjure up a vivid fantasy and fuck through it. All he had to do was call up an image of someone who tripped his trigger, and he'd be good to go for as long as necessary. Like that cute little waitress Toni had hired last week.

She was goddammed adorable.

There wasn't a soul in the club who'd believe he got hard for the plain Jane type, but after spending his entire life around prostitutes, strippers, and women sporting clubwear, he'd lost all interest in the painted-up party look. No, the cute, reserved, hardworking waitress was just the type he'd like to sink his dick into.

Look at that, he was hard.

And he was due at the clubhouse in exactly seventy minutes. At least an hour of that he'd spend on the road. So he really didn't have time for so much as a few thrusts with Lisa.

"Shit, babe, you know I'd love nothing more, but I gotta roll. I'm expected at the clubhouse soon."

"Oh, boo."

If that damn lip jutted out any farther, she'd be able to clean her eye makeup off with it.

"Next time, babe. Promise."

Her face brightened. "Oh, that's in two weeks when you dance for Betty's bachelorette party."

Betty being a forty-five-year-old shrew on her fourth marriage.

He winked. "Yes, ma'am. See you then." Lisa might be an annoying, stuck-up bitch, but she loved his act and hired him for the countless inane parties she wasted her life planning for her vast social circle. Worked for him. Even though he didn't have time to dance at YGM anymore, he did plenty of private events as a side hustle.

"Bye, Thunder."

As he walked away, she let her fingers trail down his torso, *accidentally* grazing his dick. Luckily, he was still half hard from thinking about the waitress. He had a rep to uphold, after all. Of course, Lisa assumed the chub was for her, and she hummed her approval.

He'd be a fool to correct her and lose that money train, so he just winked and strode out the door of the hall she'd rented out for the event.

Once outside in the crisp air, he finally took a cleansing breath. Time to shed one persona and step into another. He slipped into his cut, then mounted his bike. It'd warmed up enough to ride during the day, but nights still flirted with damn cold on occasion. He didn't care, though, and neither did most of his brothers. They'd chomped at the bit all winter, and all bikes were back on the road in full force.

Just as he was about to fire up his one-and-only, his phone rang.

"Sup?" he said into his helmet's Bluetooth.

"You on your way, Thunder?" Zach's voice filled his head.

"Yeah, man. You need me to stop anywhere on the way?"

"Nope. Just get your ass here. And try to keep from shaking it in front of my woman."

The line went dead.

Thunder laughed as he hit the throttle and shot out onto the highway. As he was overdue for a trim, the wind whipped his hair around his face beneath his dome. He fucking loved that feeling.

A few months ago, he'd busted in on the ol' ladies' girls' night only to find them watching a how-to twerking DVD. Buncha garbage. So, he'd turned that shit off and showed them how to get that shit done right. They'd ended up having an impromptu booty poppin' party. Of course, Izzy going into labor cut the fun short. Turned out, the ol' men of the club got a tad possessive when their women were in the presence of a little male ass shakin'. Who knew?

It'd become a running joke at his expense. One he had no choice but to bend over and take since he was still a prospect, and he wouldn't do a damn thing to jeopardize that. First time in his fucking life, he had people at his back. Brothers he could count on through thick and thin. Or at least they would be brothers once he'd patched in.

A solid hour later, he waltzed into the hoppin' clubhouse. Since it was only ten p.m., plenty of drinking hours remained. He strode up to the bar where Monty, another prospect, was slinging drinks. "Hey, T, you're here. Whatcha drinkin'?"

"Gimme a shot of tequila and a whiskey. I got some catching up to do."

"You got it," he said, as he pulled out a shot glass and set it in front of Thunder. Ten seconds later, it was full of tequila, and another two seconds after that, the liquor was sliding down Thunder's throat.

He sighed as he returned the shot glass to the bar. He was home. With his people. Men and women who understood blood didn't necessarily mean family, and who didn't judge a shady history. Hell, almost everyone here had a past that would make the outside world cringe and shy away. But between these walls and these brothers, acceptance ruled.

Time to relax and have some fucking fun.

Guys," Monty shouted over the pulse of music as he slid the whiskey to Thunder. "Thunder is here."

The music died, and the clubhouse fell eerily silent.

"Uh, what the hell, Mont?" he whispered, suddenly afraid to break the quiet. "It ain't my birthday. What's with the fucking spectacle?"

"Nah." Monty winked. "It's better."

What the fuck?

Copper emerged from the crowd and walked straight to him. People parted like he was fucking Moses, making a trail for the prez as their attention fell to Thunder.

A hard lump formed in the back of his throat. Oh shit. Had he fucked up?

He gulped down the whiskey in two painful swallows. After wiping his mouth with the back of his hand, he turned to face his president. Whatever happened next, he'd take it like a fucking man. He'd survived a beatdown before and could again. All he hoped was that whatever dipshit move he'd pulled wouldn't wreck his shot at a patch. He was so damn close to the end.

Lips in a flat line and eyes cold as steel in Antarctica, Copper didn't stop advancing until he was inches from Thunder.

He squared his shoulders and gave his president his eyes. Seconds ticked by as the formidable man Thunder respected above all stared him down. A bead of sweat trickled down his spine. His stomach cramped. The alcohol had been a mistake. It bubbled and burned like acid eating his insides.

"We had a vote tonight."

Fuck. Oh fuck. He was out.

Was he out?

He'd been a damn good prospect.

Hadn't he?

Hell, he'd done ever damn thing they asked of him without so much as a sigh of annoyance. Was it his past? The stripping? Occasional exchange of money for sex? No. This group wasn't prudish or judgmental.

Hell Jazz, Screw, and their newest member, Gumby, lived in a fucking triad, and nobody batted an eye.

The next thing he knew, his face slammed against Copper's massive chest. and a meaty palm slapped Thunder's back so hard, he nearly lost his breath.

What the hell kind of ass-kicking was this?

The guys screamed, stomped their boots, and clapped. Mav's shrill whistle pierced the air and cut through Thunder's fog.

Thunder

What the hell?

Copper released him with a laugh. "Did you even hear what I said, brother?"

Thunder blinked, glancing around at the grins on everyone's faces.

Wait…

Did he say, *brother?*

"No, I was freaking the fuck out in my head. Did you call me —?"

Finally, the man's beard split, revealing a huge amused grin. "Brother? Sure fucking did. You're in, *brother*. We voted tonight. Your patch-in is next Saturday followed by an epic fucking party." Copper whacked him on the back again then walked over to where his wife, Shell, stood with her adorable baby bump and tears in her eyes.

He'd done it. Found himself a place to land with people who fucking loved and understood him. Found himself brothers and sisters in chaos.

Thunder stood there, stunned as his new brothers began to congratulate him. It took a solid twenty minutes, but eventually he found himself alone at the bar with a drink in his hand. Now, he was grateful for the burn of alcohol to keep him from flying away.

"Hey, there, new patch-in," a flirty feminine voice whispered in his ear. "Why you sitting here drinking all by yourself?"

He glanced over his shoulder to find Bunny giving him the eye.

"Mind if I sit?" she gestured to the empty barstool next to him.

"Not at all." Thunder shot her his patented, panty-dropping smile. He was well aware of the power of a charming smile. Hell, he'd worked on the thing for years. On stage, before he revealed his body, that smile drew them in and made the ladies hungry for more. He often heard it was his best feature—even more of a draw than his tight ass, rippling abs, and mobile hips.

As expected, Bunny practically swooned as she slid onto the seat. Who knew if the name was real or a handle, but she wore it well. She looked exactly like the stereotypical Playboy Bunnies ol' Hugh loved. The ones on the magazines his mother and her friends had used as their Bible back in the day.

"Whatcha drinking, babe?" he asked as he flagged Monty.

Bunny tossed her long yellow-blond hair over her shoulder as she flashed him a glossy-lipped smile. "Well, aren't you the gentleman. Gin and tonic with two limes."

"You heard the lady," he said to Monty.

"Coming right up," Monty said, with a wink for Bunny.

As Monty set about making her drink, Bunny focused her attention back on Thunder. Her flat, tanned stomach was on full display thanks to a high-necked white crop top. Gave the perfect view of the bunny ears tattoo peeking out from her hip. Denim shorts, so itty-bitty, the pockets stuck out below the cutoff, and knee-high black leather boots completed the look of available and easy sex. She wasn't an official Handlers Honey but had been hanging around with them lately and would probably become formally affiliated with the club before long.

"How's it feel?" she asked, voice full of innuendo.

"Hasn't sunk in yet." He sipped his drink. "Still kinda in shock, I think. I knew it was coming up, but I had no idea they were votin' on me tonight. Thanks," he said to Monty, as the prospect delivered Bunny's drink.

Monty nodded before moving on.

She giggled then grabbed his hand, immediately placing it on her tit.

Okay…aggressive, this one.

"Well, of course it hasn't sunk in yet," she purred. "How can you tell me how it feels, if you haven't felt it yet?" She arched her back, pushing her tit into his hand, which she still held in place. Then she sucked that bottom lip in and sank her teeth in it.

Not an easy feat, but Thunder managed to avoid rolling his eyes. If she thought this routine new or irresistible, she had another think coming. This was his life. He dealt with a version of Bunny over and over. Every day for years and years. Only once he'd begun prospecting had he taken a step back from that world.

"So…" She dropped her voice to a throaty, sexy level. "How does it feel?"

Fake. It felt like a fake tit. Felt one, you felt 'em all.

"Feels like you're ready for a little fun tonight." He could play the damn game like a master.

"I am. Wanna play with me?" She lowered her hand, letting it rest on his thigh. Without any hesitation, she slid her hand up that thigh, straight to his uninterested dick.

Thunder caught her hand just before she discovered just how indifferent he was to this show, then lifted it to his mouth for a lingering kiss to her knuckles. "Babe, you have no fuckin' idea how interested I am. But, fuck, I need to take a rain check." It was the truth. Even thoughts of that cute waitress might not be enough to do it for him right then. Huh, second time he'd thought of her in one night.

"Well, that's no fun."

Christ, another pouting woman. If he never had to deal with one of them again, it'd be too soon. After dancing for a few hours and having the shit shocked out of him by his new brothers, he was tired as fuck and needed to head home to process the news.

"Sorry, gorgeous. Pretty sure Monty's off in an hour or so. Heard, he's a fucking beast in the sack." He winked, but she missed it, already turning her hungry gaze on the bald, muscular prospect behind the bar.

Easy come, easy go.

As he wormed his way through the crowd toward the exit, Thunder passed by a number of the happy couples that had gotten together since he'd started prospecting. Shell sat on Copper's lap while they chatted with Jazz and her men. The prez's hand rested over his wife's stomach, where their child grew. Whatever the prez just said had Shell's cheeks turning pink. He laughed, then turned her face to his, giving her a whopper of a kiss.

Would anyone believe him if he told them about the pang of jealously he experienced seeing all his brothers in love and sickeningly happy? Probably not. They all thought he lived this wild, uninhibited life of a sexy stripper, fucking his way through the world one pussy at a time.

If they only knew.

His fault for not being completely open with his new family, but some wounds took so long to heal the first time around, reopening them wasn't fathomable.

Across from Copper, Jazz sat on Screw's lap while their other man, Gumby, rested next to Screw with his arm around his shoulders. They looked so...perfect, breaking from social norms and expectations to be with who they loved.

Nice for them to be so comfortable in their collective skins.

Thunder only knew one world. The world of sex. He knew how to lure women in, give them the orgasm of their lives, tease them for hours, perform a lap dance like no other, whatever the hell they wanted. What he didn't know how to do was relate to them, to anyone really, on any other level. So he kept himself in the box he belonged in.

The one time he'd broken out of that box, he'd been ruthlessly shoved back in, and the lid nailed shut.

Ugh, pity party for one.

How pathetic.

He walked outside, breathing in the fresh mountain air. He had more than so many people. Freedom, family, cash in the bank, a sweet fucking bike, and women willing to drop to their knees any time he crooked a finger. A man with all that shouldn't have a damn thing to complain about.

As he made his way to his favorite lady, his phone chimed with a text.

Miss you. When are you coming for a visit?

His mother.

Thunder

At least the question was a simple one to answer.
Never.

Chapter Two

"Hey, Mak, can you drop this at table six for me?" Shell asked, holding out a bottle of hot sauce. "A few guys from the club can't eat unless the food is hot enough to burn their tongues off, and I forgot to take it with their plates." She balanced a full tray of dirty dishes on one hand with an ease Makenna might never master.

"Yeah, sure. Of course. Is that tray too heavy for you?" she asked the adorable pregnant woman as she accepted the condiment.

"Nah, I got it. Been doing this for years now. After a while, it's not even heavy anymore." Shell winked, demonstrating her point by raising and lowering the tray a few times.

"From your lips to God's ears." Mak smiled and took a step back. Just in case. Shell seemed to have it under control, but a bunch of filthy dishes falling on her wouldn't lead to a pleasant day.

"Hey." Shell snagged her arm with her free hand. "You're doing great. Especially for someone with no serving experience. I mean it."

"Thank you, Shell." She'd been working at Toni's Diner for exactly two weeks. Since the grand reopening. Apparently, someone had tossed a grenade through the window a month or so ago, and the entire dining room had to be reconstructed. Cassie's husband had died as well, a thought that flayed Mak's heart each and every time she recalled it, even though she'd never met the man. But she did know Cassie, and it hurt to think of how her new acquaintance had suffered such a terrible loss.

After hearing about the attack, she'd almost turned down the job. She'd had enough violence to last her a lifetime.

If they thought it weird that she didn't react with standard shock to the idea of a grenade explosion, thankfully, no one said anything. It wasn't as though she planned to announce she'd been brought up in a para-military camp where grenades were as common as toothbrushes.

The owner, Toni, and her handsome boyfriend, Zach had promised her she'd be safe. And it had been her only job prospect, so there she was.

She needed money. With six mouths to feed and six bodies to clothe and shelter, she needed the money desperately, and they'd been willing to pay her in cash, no questions asked—the benefit of working in a joint owned by an outlaw MC. People didn't blink when she made the unconventional request for cash payment. Not only did they pay in cash, they'd also been willing to take a chance on her despite her lack of waitressing experience. The only marketable skill she possessed was sewing, so in the last town they'd lived, she'd taken a seamstress job at a major clothing factory. But it was how Roger and her father found them six months ago. Now she needed to avoid that industry like the plague, which meant finding a job willing to train her from scratch.

At first, it had seemed hopeless. With so many qualified applicants looking for work, who the hell would hire a twenty-three-year-old woman with minimal job experience and no high school diploma? If it weren't for Cassie, the gem of a woman who'd crashed into Makenna with her cart in the grocery store, she wouldn't have had this opportunity at the diner. And she loved the job, even if waiting tables turned out to be more challenging than expected. If there was one thing Makenna knew, it was how to work hard and persevere, so she wasn't overly worried. She'd get the hang of it at some point.

"Excuse me, gentlemen," she said, face heating as she arrived at the booth full of seriously eye-catching and rugged men. Men like these—rough around the edges, muscular, dirty-mouthed, denim and leather wearing, sexy—well, they hadn't existed in her life prior to two years ago. She'd had no experience with this strong, protective type who also knew how to joke and play.

While the men she'd grown up with played at being alphas, they didn't have a tender bone in their bodies. Most were embittered by life, and were hateful, distrustful, bigoted, and downright nasty. Leaders of the community tried too hard to dominate their little slice of the world. They overcompensated for their internal weakness by being cruel to those they perceived even frailer than they were. The bikers at that table… well, authority oozed from their pores. They wore it like a second skin.

And wore it well.

Yet from what she's witnessed, they treated their women with a kind of respect, love, and caring she'd thought existed only in books and movies.

They were the most attractive group of men she'd ever been around. And they ate at the diner every day.

One of them, a very muscular, brown-haired man with his arm around a taller, more slender blond man, snorted. "Ain't nothing gentlemanly about those two," he said, pointing at the two bikers sitting across from him.

One was huge; absolutely enormous in height and width. She'd met him a few times since he was the boyfriend of her coworker, Holly. LJ looked like he could flick his finger and send her flying across the room. She suppressed a shudder of fear. After being on the receiving end of punches, kicks, and blows from men, wariness of those more physically powerful came with the territory. The guy next to him was smaller, not small, just smaller, and...gorgeous. So stunning that when he smiled, she clenched her teeth to keep her tongue from lolling out.

"Hey! Fuck you," LJ said. "Pretty sure you're the only one at this table who ain't a gentleman. Right, Gumby?"

The man he called Gumby glanced at the guy sitting next to him with an almost sappy grin. "Oh, I don't know. He was quite the gentleman last night when he let me come first while—"

"Ahh, Screw, make him, stop! Lalalalala." LJ stuck his fingers in his ears and hollered.

"Well, that I can do," the one she guessed was Screw said, right before kissing Gumby with some serious passion.

Makenna's mouth dropped open, and she stared at the men lost in each other. She wasn't completely naive, after living away from the sheltered community for two years. She knew men could be in a relationship with each other, but she'd never seen it up close and personal. If they'd lived in the community, they'd have been punished harshly, possibly even killed, so that kind of relationship just didn't exist. Hell, it was a demographic her father actively fought against.

Since she'd fled, she and her siblings had lived in small towns that weren't meccas of homosexuality either. Witnessing it up close and personal was one of many new experiences since meeting the men and women of the MC.

Once done kissing his guy, Screw laughed. "Bet you wouldn't have a problem hearing what he did to Jazz, though, would you, LJ?"

The one called LJ shrugged. "Well, no."

And then there was the fact that Jazmine, one of her bosses, was also involved with these two men. That just completely boggled her mind. In the community, men weren't faithful to one woman. They only married one at a time, but they prided themselves on having as many children as possible, so they spread their seed around. In fact, of the six of them, only she and her brother Lee shared a mother. According to Jazz, she and these two men were in a committed, loving relationship.

"Pretty sure our waitress doesn't want to hear the nasty shit you do to her boss, brother," the gorgeous man said, flashing her one of those brain-numbing smiles. She'd seen him around quite a few times but had never been formally introduced.

"Hi. We haven't officially met yet. I'm Thunder," he said as if reading her mind. He stuck out his hand.

Wow. No one man should be that good looking. With tanned skin, a sharply angled face, crystal blue eyes, and a dusting of light brown stubble across his chiseled jaw, he was lethally gorgeous. Then there were the full lips. And the longish, light coffee-colored hair. She needed to take a breath because she did not notice men like this. All the testosterone at the table must be scrambling her brain.

"Think you stunned her, brother."

He was so attractive, she'd swallowed her tongue. "Sorry." She took his hand, which was warm, strong, and just a little bit rough. "I'm Makenna. Most people call me Mak. I work here."

I work here? Wow...Mak...just wow.

Thunder kept giving her that magnetic smile as though she wasn't the dumbest person he'd spoken to all day. "Nice to meet you, Mak," he said with a wink. He indicated the hot sauce. "Thanks for dropping that off for us. Toni said you recently moved here?"

What? He'd talked to Toni about her? Holy crap. She wanted to dance around like a fifteen-year-old who'd just been asked to prom by a senior. Not that she had experience with that, but she heard things. Instead, she said, "Yes, a few weeks ago."

"What do you think of our little town so far?"

"Hey, guys. Hi, Thunder."

A low-pitched, sugar-soaked voice had Mak glancing over her shoulder as two women walked by with their ravenous gazes on Thunder. They wiggled their sparkly fingers as they flashed him perfectly straight and gleaming white teeth. Both were beautiful with long hair, heavy makeup, skinny jeans, tall boots, and tight tops that showed off impressive chests. Mak had never looked that glamorous on her best day, and these girls looked like they walked off a runway at nine in the morning at a diner. She didn't have a stitch of makeup on, and her black hair swung around her shoulders as it usually did. Her styling routine consisted of a brush and...well, that was it.

"Hey ladies, looking damn good today," Thunder said, shooting them the same smile he'd given Mak. He winked, which elicited a round of giggles that could have shattered Toni's brand-new windows.

Something dark and unpleasant twisted in Mak's stomach. Never before had she experienced jealousy, at least not regarding a man. But she'd felt it when being punished while her siblings and friends got to play or enjoy a rare treat, so she recognized the emotion.

Ridiculous.

She wiggled her hand out of his warm grasp.

"We'll see you at the clubhouse later, Thunder," one of them said as she practically drooled down her tight top.

Mak would be sure to drop extra napkins at that table.

"You know it, gorgeous." Thunder winked again then turned his attention back to her as the ladies walked off. Once again, she had his full focus, and the power of that enchanted smile aimed her way.

Ahh, she got it now. Silly her for thinking that was somehow a special expression for her. He gave that smile to everyone—well, everyone female. The man was dangerous, and she'd do well to remember that. Last thing she needed in her life was a guy who was going to bring drama or chaos. She had enough of that without trying to play the man-woman game.

She'd never win, so there was no point in signing up.

She had no use for men in general, so this little demonstration was a perfect reminder to stay in her lane. With a horde of siblings relying on her, dating couldn't be lower on the priority list.

"Nice to meet you, Thunder," she said with a polite smile. "I'll have Shell come refill your coffees in a few moments."

The other three men at the table snickered. As she turned her back and walked away, she heard one of the men say, "Strike one," but she didn't stick around to hear Thunder's reply.

The rest of her shift passed quickly and without incident as the diner stayed packed. She couldn't help risking an occasional glance in Thunder's direction. It wasn't often she found herself intrigued by a handsome man, but something about him kept drawing her attention. Twice, she'd caught him looking her way as well, which made no sense. Not while those 'Honeys'—as Jazz had called them—were around.

"Whew, today was nuts," Shell said, as she flopped down into a booth after the last patrons had left.

"Seriously," Toni agreed, also taking a seat. She slid a tall glass of water to Shell. "Hey, Mak, want to get off your feet for a few and sit with us?"

From where she stood behind the counter, she checked her phone. They still had to clean, but even then, she should have plenty of time before she had to pick Emmie up from Cassie, who'd offered to babysit since her other siblings had homeschool assignments.

"Sure. Though I'm not positive I'll ever be able to get up again if I sit. My legs are dead."

"I hear ya," Jazz said, also joining them. "Ever since we reopened, business has been insane."

"Hey!" Toni pointed a manicured finger at Jazz. "That's a good thing. And if you're tired, maybe you shouldn't stay up with your men all night, if you know what I mean."

Right. Jazz was the one with two boyfriends.

Mak studied the very slender woman with pixie hair and a satisfied grin.

"Pretty sure we all know what you mean." Shell rubbed her bump as she rolled her eyes.

"How does that even work? Being with two men?"

Thunder

Oh, crap.

"I—I'm sorry. That's none of my business at all." The question had tumbled from her lips before her brain had time to veto them. God, she barely knew these people, and now she was asking about one of their kinky relationships. How embarrassing.

But not for Jazz, who smiled while the other two laughed.

"Here we go," said Toni. "It's so wonderful. Every girl should be with two guys at once. The orgasms are incredible." She rolled her eyes, butchering the impression of Jazz's voice.

"Hey! I do not sound like that, bitch!" As she spoke, Jazz whacked Toni's arm with the back of her hand, but even she couldn't keep from chuckling.

Shell laughed as well. "Yeah, you sorta do. You're all kinds of braggy since you bagged Screw *and* Gumby."

"Well…" Jazz winked at her friend and coworker. "Can you blame me?"

Shell snorted. "Copper is more than enough man for me, thank you."

Makenna watched the back and forth with a smile on her face. She'd never had friends like these women. Not that they were friends, but they were a blast regardless. So comfortable and open with each other. They seemed more like cousins or even sisters than mere friends. Sometimes, like now, when they delved into the sex talk, she just smiled and nodded along as though she knew where they were coming from. Jumping into the conversation with talk of her sixty-two-year-old husband who needed little blue pills and smelled like BenGay probably wouldn't cut it, so she always stayed quiet.

"Seriously," Toni chimed in. "I think I'd die if I had to manage two bikers." She winked, and then all three of them were staring at Mak.

She blinked. "Uh, do I have something on my face?" She didn't feel anything when she ran a hand across her chin.

With a laugh, Toni shook her head. "Do you have a man?" she asked at the same time Jazz said, "You seeing anyone?"

Mak dropped her eyes. If they only knew. "Uh, no. No man." And no plans for a man. Her family was her focus.

With a shrug, Shell said, "Guys, she's only lived here a few weeks. Give her a hot second. Besides, we know plenty of men to set her up with."

"Oh, yes!" Toni clapped her hands. "This is a fabulous idea. Who are you thinking? Monty, maybe?"

She felt like she was watching a ping pong match with the way this conversation bounced back and forth across the table. Actually, she felt like the ping pong ball itself. "No, I'm good. Not looking for anything right now. I already have a lot on my plate." It wasn't a lie. With five younger family members to take care of, she was more than overtaxed. Besides, the possibility of Roger or her father finding them always lived at the forefront of her mind. She'd never subject a man to that fate.

"Ahh," Jazz said with a nod as though she understood Makenna's situation. "Bad breakup? Or bad relationship?"

As she scanned the understanding and compassionate faces, Mak found herself nodding and revealing more than she had... well, ever. "Something like that."

"Oh! That reminds me." Shell straightened and turned toward her. "Are you still looking for some extra cash?"

With a snort, Mak said, "Always."

"Well, the club is having a party for Thunder's patch-in on Saturday night. They could use an extra person to help out behind the bar."

What the heck was a patch-in? "Um, I've never worked as a bartender before."

With a wave of her hand, Shell said, "You'd really just be getting beer and pouring some straightforward drinks. You can totally handle it, and you won't be alone, so if there is something you don't know how to make, Monty can do it for you."

"I can show you anything you'd need to know before then," Jazz added.

"We'd need you for five hours, from nine to two, and it pays two hundred and fifty dollars,"
Shell said. "If that helps incentivize you."

If? Two hundred and fifty dollars for four hours of work? She cleared her throat. "Uh, yeah, that helps."

The three women chuckled. "We can practically hear your mind exploding," Shell said. "So, you're in?"

Emmie needed shoes, Rissa's jeans were about two inches too short, and she hadn't purchased a new bra in years. Yeah, she was in. "I'll do it. Just, uh, one thing?"

"Yeah?" Toni said.

"What's a patch-in?"

All the ladies' eyes widened. "Oh, boy," Jazz said with a laugh. "You're in for an education, girl."

Mak swallowed. The ladies began talking all at once about the parties at the Handlers' clubhouse. By the time she left, she'd laughed more at their stories and antics than she had in years.

A pit sat at the base of her stomach. Forming friendships beyond work acquaintances with these women would be as foolish as finding a boyfriend. She couldn't afford to divide her attention between friends and family. At all times, she needed to remain vigilant and on task. She also had the responsibility of protecting anyone she came in contact with from her father's wrath.

If her mother had known what Makenna knew about the community, would she have made different choices? If she'd known the community leaders would kill her for having an affair, or that her lover would become a brutal example for any woman in the community contemplating forming a relationship with a man outside their walls, would she have slept with him?

Makenna would never know the answers to those questions, but she'd internalized the ruthless lessons. She wouldn't allow anyone close enough to be harmed when Roger and her father inevitably caught up to them again.

Chapter Three

"How do I look?" Tex asked, as he smoothed his hands down his prospect's cut. He was a smart kid with a bit of Texas country swagger.

"You look like a fuckin' dirtbag, like always," Thunder said, hiding his grin with his coffee cup.

"Fuck you." Tex flipped him off, then checked his reflection in his goddammed spoon.

"Dude, what the fuck is wrong with you?"

Tex put the spoon down then shrugged. "Nothing's wrong. Just making sure I'm putting my best foot forward."

Best foot forward? What the...Thunder burst out laughing. "Fuck me, this is for Kristy, isn't it?"

"What? No! What the hell is wrong with a man wanting to look good?"

"Nothing. You do know she's not gonna strip in here, right?"

"Seriously, fuck you."

Thunder laughed. Tex was a trip. They were in a coffee shop, one town over, waiting on a friend of Thunder's. A friend who also happened to be a stripper Thunder had worked with in the past. After many years in the biz, he was well acquainted with all the entertainment in the area and then some. Though he knew them, he rarely associated with coworkers outside of the job. Not that he had any problems with his work peers, he just preferred to keep away from that world when not performing.

But this wasn't a social visit. This was strictly business. And he'd begged Copper to let him be the one to conduct this fact-finding mission. Ever since the day Viper had died, the urge to take the CDMC down had been clawing at him like a feral cat. He'd been there that day. Witnessed Viper's lifeless body broken and bleeding on the diner's floor. And while the club had eliminated the man who'd been personally responsible for tossing the grenade that killed Viper, it wasn't enough. Thunder wanted each and every CDMC motherfucker to pay.

Shit, if he thought about this much longer, he'd fucking cry as he'd done the day Viper died.

"Hey, there she is. There she is." Tex rested his hands on the table, then in his lap, then back on the table.

Thank God for the distraction. And what a distraction she was.

"Could you not act like you're gonna bust a nut the second she sits down?" Thunder asked, as he stood to greet Kristy.

"Shh, shut the fuck up," Tex whispered.

"Well, if it isn't the sexiest two men in the MC." Kristy strutted over on stilts with skintight leather pants, a bright red crop top, and her long brown hair in a sky-high ponytail.

"Hey, beautiful." He took her outstretched hands and accepted a kiss on his lips.

Tex cleared his throat in the most unsubtle way possible. With a roll of his eyes, Thunder said, "Kristy, this is Tex. Another prospect for the club."

Since she'd danced at several Handlers' parties, she probably already knew Tex by sight, but the two hadn't been formally introduced.

With a sly grin, Kristy extended a hand to Tex. "Hi, Tex," she purred. "I'm Kristy."

The woman was a shark. She'd been stripping for fifteen years and still had the same energetic, flexible, and tight body she'd had at eighteen. Having been married three times and engaged two more, as far as Thunder knew, the girl could play men like no other. She reeled 'em in, chewed 'em up, and spit them back out, never to be the same again.

Poor Tex had no idea what he was in for.

Kristy slid into the empty seat at their round table. After crossing her mile-long legs, she turned her attention to Tex. "I didn't realize you were bringing a toy, Thunder," she crooned. "You want to play with us, Tex?"

His eyes bugged, and Thunder nearly laughed. If he'd been a woman, he had no doubt Tex would be all over a threesome, but the kid seemed like he might hurl at the idea of getting naked with his fellow prospect.

"Simmer down there, tiger," Thunder said, drawing Kristy's attention. "This isn't that kind of visit."

She pouted. "Oh, that's too bad. We always had so much fun together."

They'd been together once, about five years ago. A woman who came to every single show he headlined asked to fuck him and another woman for her birthday. She'd paid serious coin for the experience. Thunder had barely touched Kristy and certainly hadn't fucked her since they'd focused the attention on their client. So technically, they hadn't been together at all.

Instead of rolling his eyes as he wanted, he winked. "You know it, baby."

Tex sat there gaping like he'd never seen someone with a set of tits before. The twenty-one-year-old cracked him up. Copper had wanted him to tag along with Thunder. He'd been accompanying different members on tasks recently to get more exposure and insight into the club's inner workings.

"So, if we're not here to test out my dick sucking technique, why're we here?" Kristy blinked those long, mahogany lashes as though she had an innocent cell in her body.

"Heard through the grapevine, you've been dancing at the Chrome Disciples parties the past few weekends."

Kristy pursed her full lips as she leaned back in her chair. "So, this *really* isn't a fun visit."

Thunder raised an eyebrow, which had her rolling her eyes and folding her arms under her double F tits in a move as practiced as her dance routines. No surprise, Tex's eyes drifted straight to those babies. Thunder was tempted to grab a napkin and wipe the guy's chin. Instead, he focused his gaze on Kristy's face.

She smirked, knowing she'd lost that round. "You always were a tough nut to crack, Thunder. Coulda had so much fun with so many girls over the years. Makes me sometimes wonder what's going on down there." As she spoke, she leaned over and cupped his dick.

Tex let out a strangled sound.

"Huh," she said with a frown. "Not much."

"Just cuz my dick doesn't want *you*, doesn't mean it's broken," he said. "Now, remove your fucking hand and tell me what I want to know."

As Kristy sat back in her chair with a huff, the back of Thunder's neck began to tingle. The sensation grew until he had no choice but to glance over his shoulder toward the line of patrons waiting for their beverage. Sure enough, Makenna stood there, gawking at him with a disgusted frown like he was some kind of deviant.

No doubt, she saw Kristy's hand groping his dick.

Fucking Kristy.

When her gaze met his, she startled and turned to face the counter. Damn, the girl looked so fucking adorable in simple black leggings, beat to hell converse sneakers, an oversized sweatshirt, and her shoulder-length hair in a messy pile on top of her head. Shorter strands hung free, giving her this tousled yet sexy casual appearance. Though he only had a quick peek, he was pretty sure that face of hers was completely makeup free. The girl couldn't be farther on the spectrum from Kristy if she tried.

Thunder

Sure, she'd probably be described as plain by most people he knew, but Thunder wasn't most people. The men and women he'd worked with for years were considered some of the most attractive due to their perfectly toned bodies, flawlessly made-up faces, skimpy outfits, and easy sexuality. To him, Makenna was refreshing and gorgeous in her natural state.

"So, you wanna ask me questions, or you just gonna stare at my neighbor all day?" Kristy asked.

"Huh?" His head snapped back around. "Makenna's your neighbor?"

Kristy's lips curled in a devilish grin. "She is. And let me tell you, baby, that girl is way too sweet for you." She laughed as she trailed a long, purple fingernail down his chest. "Don't even think about barking up that tree. Stick to the ones in our forest, baby."

"Yeah, I figured that out five seconds after meeting her." Which was why he'd stay away no matter how hard she made him. No one needed the fucked up that was in his brain when it came to relationships. After risking another glance at the back of Makenna's head—okay fine, and a quick peek at her pert but small ass—he put the ridiculous attraction on the shelf and got back to the task at hand.

"Enough bullshit. I need some details on the Disciples."

Kristy threw her arms in the air. "Come on, Thunder, you know I can't do that. I have no loyalty to that club. But a paycheck's a paycheck, and I can't risk losing this one because those bastards pay fucking well. Besides, you know they wouldn't tell me jack or shit about their business no matter how many of their faces I shake my tits in."

Fuck, she was right. A polite request would get him nowhere —time to break out the big guns. "I get it, babe, I really do. And I'm not trying to get you booted from your gig. But you do owe me, don't you?" About a year ago, Kristy had a piece of shit fiancé who knocked her around. She was one badass bitch, but even she wasn't a match for a two-hundred-fifty-pound pile of muscle. Lucky for her, the Handlers were. Thunder made sure the dude wouldn't be hitting a woman again.

Ever.

So yeah, she owed him.

With a sigh, she nodded, raking her long fingernails across her forearm in a nervous gesture he'd never seen from her. "Fuck you, Thunder." She looked at Tex for a moment as though hoping the prospect could somehow get her out of this, but Tex he kept his lips clamped. This wasn't his show. Finally, Kristy's shoulders slumped in defeat. "They're a bunch of assholes. Grabbiest motherfuckers. Not much for the word, no."

If those shitbags—

Kristy lifted a hand. "I can see you gearing up to play the hero. Don't bother. I can handle myself, and so can the girls I bring with me. I made sure of that after last year." She lifted one bare shoulder then let it drop. "Besides, I don't say no to much anyway."

Another one of those choked sounds came from Tex, who'd been quietly watching their byplay. Finally, he made himself useful. "Any idea how their business is going?"

Kristy studied him as though trying to decide if she trusted him. She'd been dancing at Handler's parties since long before Thunder's prospecting days began. She'd give Tex her trust by association.

Her eyes narrowed, and she hunched forward. "None of this shit came from me, you two understand? I'm dancing there the next three Saturdays, and I'll be fucked if I lose that cash."

Both he and Tex nodded. "Of course," he said.

"They're scrambling. Or at least they have been the past few weeks. Something happened a month or so ago with a delivery of whatever the fuck they move, and it cost them big time. I don't know any details, I swear. And ever since the diner blew up, I'm pretty sure there are Feds parking outside their clubhouse. Between the shipment fuck up and the investigation, they're partying all the time but doing very little business-wise."

Thunder

By the shrewd light in her eyes, she knew exactly what the CDMC transported. But she was too intelligent to voice it.

"What does *big time* mean?"

"A lotta money," she said with a shrug. "What else. It's all about the green shit, isn't it?"

For her, yes. For him? For so many years, also yes. He'd grown up with men and women willing to do anything and anyone for their next meal. It was only now that he had the Handlers in his life that he'd begun to realize there was more to life than selling one's body for a quick buck.

Kristy leaned in. "A couple of those guys get pretty fucking loose-lipped when they're trashed. Word is that Crank, their enforcer, is on a rampage. It's impossible to find a new way to transport his...product with all the interest from the cops. Two of their *customers* found alternate suppliers after the incident with the delivery trucks. Crank is an asshole on a good day, but he's been downright psychotic lately. You're lucky the cops are watching them so closely, and you better hope it stays that way for a good long while."

"Yeah? They talk about us?"

"Uh, yeah." Kristy laughed, leaning back in her seat. She toyed with the long necklace resting between her tits. Of course, Tex kept his focus glued to the very spot. "They talk about fucking you guys up all the time. All. The. Time. But I think it's mostly blowing off steam. They need an outlet for their anger, and it's you."

"You don't think they're planning something for when the Feds leave?"

She shrugged as though the thought didn't bother her in the least. Really, it probably didn't. Kristy was loyal as long as the money kept rolling in. She wasn't one for emotional entanglements. Hard to be in their line of business and have much faith in so-called love or even friendship.

"They're too fucking busy freaking out about their own shit."

"Good." He glanced Tex's way. "That's good." As much as Thunder and the rest of his club wanted the CDMC to pay, arrests would be so fucking unsatisfying. Good old MC justice would be a much better outcome, and that couldn't happen with federal agents crawling all over town.

She nodded. "I know they never found who blew up Toni's Diner," she said, and Thunder forced his face to remain neutral. "Guessing that's why the local PD and the Feds have been sniffing around so much. They assume it was the CDMC."

Just the mention of the man who killed Viper had guilt twisting Thunder's guts. His club knew exactly who'd blown up the diner and why. Hell, he'd been the one to chase the bomb-throwing motherfucker down and deliver his ass to Copper. But ever since that day, he'd been questioning his actions and wondering what he could have done differently to chase down the bomber but also keep Viper from dying.

He couldn't announce that the club had taken care of the fucker themselves, could he? Not to Kristy, who might turn around and vomit the information to the CDMC should they peel their wallets open for her.

"Well," she said as she examined her long, neon purple nails. "Whatever the fuck is going on, I'm pretty sure their hands are tied until the Feds get bored. Who knows how long that will be? Those fuckers have some stamina for this shit."

No fucking kidding.

Thunder leaned back, scratching his chin. Fuck, he'd forgotten to shave that morning, and his face itched like a motherfucker.

Kristy had given them a lot to think about. A lot to take back to Copper. The fact the prez trusted him with this intel gathering task before he'd officially patched in meant the fucking world to him. Copper understood how important it was for Thunder to be heavily involved in taking down the CDMC. He owed it to Viper and to Cassie, who he'd admittedly been avoiding since that fateful day.

"Thanks, Kristy."

"Yep," she said, popping the *p*. "Just keep me out of it, like I said, I got bills to pay."

"Will do, babe. You gonna be at my patch-in?"

Tex's eyes lit at the question. Poor guy was practically slobbering over the sexy stripper.

"No," Kristy said, the perfect amount of whine in her voice. Not enough to grate on the ears, but sufficient to make her glossy mouth look kissable. She was so damn practiced. If she wanted, she could have Tex eating out of her hand and acting as her manservant within minutes. The woman had some serious power. "I took a gig with the other club before I knew about it." She shifted her eyes to Tex. "Save me a dance for the next party, handsome?"

"Yeah, sure. Uh, fuck yeah." Tex grinned so big, his fucking cheeks were gonna crack.

Thunder rolled his eyes as he caught the mirth in Kristy's. She rose slowly, drawing every male eye in the place, just as she intended. Lived for. There was nothing the woman wanted more than the attention of all Y chromosomes.

Kristy was a prime example of why Thunder had never had a relationship in his life. How could anyone trust it? Lust and attraction? Sure, that was easy. Chemicals, needs, and physical urges could be easily satisfied. But the bullshit called love? Come on. Nothing but a game of one-upmanship, gold-digging, and emotional blackmail with some fucking thrown in, so the poor assholes in the relationship at least felt like they were getting something out of the deal.

A whole lotta time, effort, sacrifice, and compromise for what? Eventual heartbreak? Feeling like shit? Hurting each other in the deepest way possible?

Fuck that.

He'd grown up seeing the worst of the worst when it came to relationships. Men and women tearing each other down, beating each other up, and leaving the person they *loved* in complete ruins. So he'd done what his mother had done and taught himself not to give a shit and used the lessons learned to make a good life for himself.

Bodies were easy. Attraction was easy. Sex was easy. He looked good and knew how to work what his mama gave him to attract the opposite sex, get paid, and get out.

That was why he needed to refrain from acting on his attraction to Makenna. She wasn't just a body; wasn't an easy way to bust a nut. She was the type of girl that came with feelings, emotion, and fucking suffering.

Kristy bent forward, giving him an unobstructed view at her tits. Then she placed a wet one right on his mouth. She kissed as she did everything, with skill, practice, and an end goal in mind.

He let her slip her tongue in his mouth for a quick taste but ended it there. When she drew back, her attention wasn't even on him, but on Tex, who looked ready to hop across the table and get some for himself.

Thunder resisted rolling his eyes. She could kiss him like that all day long, and he'd never feel a thing and never want more.

"Bye, boys," she said with a wiggle of her fingers. She turned and strutted her way toward the exit with her long legs eating up the distance in no time. Her ass twitched each time those spiky heels hit the ground. Male gazes tracked every step she made.

"Damn, you're a lucky motherfucker. You know that?"

"Why? Cuz she stuck her tongue in my mouth?" The woman had probably kissed ten guys before him already that day. Tex had a lot to learn.

"Fuck yeah, man," Tex said. "A kiss like that? That woman wants you bad."

Thunder snorted, but his eyes fell to Kristy like every other schmuck in the coffeeshop. "That wasn't a kiss. It was a chess move."

"What the fuck are you talking about?" The guy had a home-grown sweetness about him. One a man-eater like Kristy would zero in on in no time. He'd have to remember to keep an eye out for Tex the next time Kristy was in house. He liked the guy and didn't want him ending up with a satisfied dick but an empty wallet.

No less than three men approached Kristy as she made her grand exit. She handed each one a card, no doubt for the strip club she worked at, before leaving the building.

Just as he was about to tell Tex they had to jet, he caught sight of Makenna watching him through the front window of the shop. She stood outside with a scrunched forehead and a frown on her pretty face, staring straight at him like she was trying to piece together a complicated puzzle.

Don't waste your time, sweetheart; nothing but cynicism in this head.

Kristy strode over to her, saying a few words that had Makenna nodding before the two of them walked off together. Shit, did they hang out?

What an odd pair.

What had Makenna thought of Kristy kissing him? Is that what had her mouth pulling down? Not that it mattered. She might as well see who he was from the get-go. Not like he was going to pursue her.

Still, she was fucking adorable, and it was in moments like this he wished he was as ignorant as his soon-to-be brothers. The ones with ol' ladies. The ones who didn't know what their futures held.

Pain. Disappointment. Heartbreak.

Loss.

Chapter Four

"I have nothing to wear," Mak grumbled as she frowned into her meager closet. "Nothing to wear, no girlfriends to borrow from, and my sisters are children." She glanced at the simple alarm clock on the plastic drawer system serving as her dresser. Seven was too late to bail. Some guy named Monty was expecting her behind the bar in ninety minutes.

"Why did I agree to do this?" she yelled to the ceiling.

"Mommy?" Emmie toddled into the room, her round little belly leading the way. Her two-year-old sister was the only one of her siblings who called her mom, probably because Mak was the only mother the child could recall knowing. Of all the kids, adjusting to calling Emmie by another name had been the hardest. For nearly a year, she'd had to consciously think to keep from calling her Rae.

"Hi, Mommy." Every time she heard the word uttered from those sweet and innocent lips, the heavy weight of all her responsibilities pressed down a little harder.

Mak's mother had engaged in an affair with an outsider when Mak was nine. Once her father found out, all hell had broken loose. The community publicly executed the man, and her mother disappeared, though no one believed that. Everyone in the community knew Mak's father had killed her mother.

Thunder

While Mak understood the all-consuming need for a life outside of the community, she couldn't understand why or how her mother hadn't considered what would happen to her children if she were to be caught. How they'd be raised only by the sadistic founder of their para-military community. It didn't take a psychologist to see her mother's actions were the reason Makenna refused to leave her siblings behind and was so willing to take on the massive responsibility of raising them all at such a young age.

"What's up, Ems?" This little peanut deserved more than a life in an itty-bitty overcrowded house with sparse furniture, damaged siblings, no parents, and barely enough money to scrape by. But their situation now was a million times superior to life in the community.

As had happened so many times over the past two years, seeing Emmie put everything into perspective. What she wore didn't matter. This was a job; she wasn't going to the Handlers' clubhouse to be eye-candy. She'd reserve that for if her life ever hit complete rock bottom and she was forced to strip.

The thought almost had her laughing out loud. Without a doubt, she'd be the worst stripper in existence.

"Kwisty here! Kwisty here!" She jumped up and down, clapping her little hands. Emmie loved their next-door neighbor, Kristy, who was, in fact, a stripper. The thirty-six-year-old beauty was utterly opposite of Mak. Kristy was loud, bright, ballsy, and she oozed sex in everything she did. Confidence should have been her middle name. But she was also sweet and accepting. Never once had she shown an ounce of judgment toward Makenna and her siblings. Since she worked nights, Kristy often watched Mak's youngest two sisters during the day for next to nothing.

Huh, maybe she did have one girlfriend. And one who would know what to wear to a biker party. She'd have to make sure to keep Kristy from getting too close in case her father or husband found them, but she could afford a casual friend.

"I'm in my room, Kristy!" she called out as she picked Emmie up and gently tossed her on the queen-sized bed. The toddler dissolved in a fit of baby giggles that never failed to bring a smile to Makenna's face. Being able to make the sweet child laugh with abandon was a fantastic gift.

"Is that my favorite monkey I hear?" Kristy asked as she burst into the room, carrying a hot pink duffle bag with the word "Diva," embroidered on the side.

"Oh, I knew I was your monkey, but I didn't know I was your favorite!" Mak said with a chuckle.

"Oh, you're a riot. Isn't she, sweet girl?" Kristy scooped Emmie up and blew on her chubby belly, making her squeal in delight. The way Kristy acted around the little girl never failed to amuse Makenna. Her neighbor claimed she didn't want children. Loudly and adamantly. There were six *nevers* if she recalled the conversation correctly, yet she was terrific with Emmie and Kara, Mak's seven-year-old sister.

"So, what brings you by?" Mak asked. She then realized she was standing before Kristy in nothing but a bra and her one pair of skinny jeans. "Oh, shit, sorry. I didn't realize I wasn't dressed."

Kristy burst out laughing. "Girl, please. You're wearing more than I see all shift sometimes. You're good. Besides, I'm here to dress you for your big night."

"My big night? I'm slinging drinks at a biker party, not strutting down a runway."

"Slinging drinks? Look at you, learning the lingo." Kristy arched a perfectly shaped eyebrow.

Mak's face heated. "I stole the phrase from Shell."

"Ahh, Queen of the Handlers." She curtseyed, which made Emmie laugh and try to copy the move only since she was standing on Mak's bed, she faceplanted into the comforter.

"You don't like her?" Shell seemed loved by everyone who met her. Mak included.

Thunder

Kristy waved a long-nailed hand. "No, she's great. Actually, all the ol' ladies in that club are. They're very secure in their relationships, which is a nice change for me. Usually, when I dance at a party where guys bring their women, I get death glares and bitchy comments all night. One time this fu—fudging B even yanked me by my hair, screeching about wanting to prove how fake I was by pulling off my wig." With a huff, she tossed her gorgeous mane of mahogany hair over her shoulder. "Please, this is all real. Now my tits on the other hand…" She laughed as she shrugged. "What can ya do?"

Mak just shook her head. Unlike any woman she'd been around in the past, Kristy's confidence and comfort in her own skin fascinated her. Emmie seemed just as captivated by the flashy woman. Thankfully, she was too young to ask what tits were. Though she was starting to repeat everything, so they needed to be a little more careful. After leaving the community, Mak vowed no one would censor her again, so she tended to be a bit rough with the language at times, though she seemed like a choir girl compared to the bikers.

"Kwisty, pwetty," Emmie said as she patted Kristy's shapely leg.

"Oh, thank you, sweet girl. I knew you were a smart one." She winked at Emmie, who tried to copy that move as well, but just ended up blinking her eyes.

Emmie might only be two, but she was dead on with the observation. How was it possible for Kristy to pull off glamorous in a pair of joggers and an oversized T-shirt hanging off one shoulder? Where she came across as some sort of casual wear model, Mak would look like a hobo in the same outfit. She'd been denied the chance to have girlfriends and play with her hair and makeup as a teen, and now she had far bigger worries on her plate. Yet she'd be lying if she didn't admit it'd be fun to get all done up every once in a while.

"All right," Kristy said as she set down her bag. "Let's get this show on the road. I brought you some goodies." With a slightly scary grin, she dug into the neon bag.

Mak eyed the duffle like it was a snake ready to strike. What the hell did she have in that thing? "Uh, Kris, I appreciate it and all, but we aren't exactly the same size." Kristy had a good six inches on her and an athletic, dancers' body. Mak was five-foot-four with some junk in the trunk and not the muscular variety.

"I went shopping!"

"Kristy! You didn't have to do that."

"Oh, please." She waved a hand as she continued to remove items from the bag like she was the Mary Poppins of clubwear. "After"—she cast a glance Emmie's way—"s-e-x, it's my favorite activity."

Dread began to wash over Mak as Kristy pulled item after item from the bag. "Uh, don't take this the wrong way, but we don't exactly have the same style."

With a snort, Kristy said, "As in I have style, and you don't?"

Well...yeah, okay, she'd give her that one. "Fair enough. I'm just a little less...flashy."

"If you mean you're boring, I know. And I took that into account. Don't worry. You'll look like a million bucks without feeling like a ho."

Mak's face burned. "Oh, God, I didn't mean—"

The laugh that bubbled out of Kristy was genuine and not at all forced or offended. Emmie viewed their exchange with wide, curious eyes until Kristy handed Emmie a few bangle bracelets. Then she oohed and aahed as she jangled them on her little wrist.

"I'm messing with you. Now shut up and try this on." She shoved an armful of clothes into Mak's hands.

"Here? Or should I go in the bathroom?"

"Jesus, you weren't kidding when you said you came from a conservative upbringing, huh? Just strip. We got all the same sh —uh stuff, girlfriend. And it's not like I'm going to be staring at you when I have this sweet girl to play with." She held her hand out with patience as Emmie slid the bracelets on and off Kristy's wrist again and again.

Right. Of course. They were all girls. Since her brother was due back soon, she shut the door, then held up the first article of clothing. "These pants look tiny. How is my big ass supposed to fit in them?"

Kristy looked at the ceiling. "Oh, you poor, sheltered dear. You need me in your life more than I realized." Abandoning Emmie, she strode over and put an arm around Mak's bare shoulders. "Okay, think of me as your fairy godmother. First of all, you do not have a big ass. You have the kind of ass that guys go nuts for. Trust me. A little bit of plump to your peach is a damn good thing. These are faux leather leggings," she said as she pulled the leggings off the store hanger. "They're the Spanx ones. They'll make that ass look like a million bucks, trust me. Put the damn things on."

Spanx? What the hell were Spanx? And did she want guys going nuts over her ass? After eyeing the leggings once again, Mak sighed and said, "Yes, ma'am."

"These first," Kristy said as she tossed something from the bag.

Mak caught the flying scrap of fabric with a frown. "Wait, is this underwear? You got me underwear? Why?"

Hands on her hips, Kristy said, "Because I guessed you didn't have a thong or a good push up bra. Shut up and put them on. You'll thank me. What's worse than panty lines?"

Uh...being twenty-three years old and trying to raise five siblings?

"Oookay. I'll shut up now and put it all on." As she listened to Emmie and Kristy chattering and giggling, she slipped into the closet and shut the door enough to keep Kristy from seeing her. There wasn't enough room or much light but she wasn't about to get totally naked in front of the other woman. Especially considering she'd never worn a thong. She lifted the tiny red thing to eye level. Seriously?

Here goes nothing.

She shimmied the minuscule panties up her legs. Next went the leggings, which did fit after all.

She stepped out of the closet. Huh, not only did they fit, they were comfortable, and made her ass look—

"Holy sh—wow!" Mak yelled as she checked her butt out in the mirror. "What kinda dark magic is in these things?"

"Told ya!" Kristy said, not even trying to hide the smug tone. "Sexy as hell, sister."

Now for the top. She held up the shirt, which was also black with a very subtle shimmer. It was cute but looked kinda small…

"Yes," Kristy said from behind her, smirking at her scrunched forehead. "It's a crop top. But it's not crazy short."

When Mak opened her mouth to protest, Kristy held up a hand.

"Honey, you're twenty-three, not eighty-three. I can't imagine how difficult it was for you to lose your parents in a car accident like you did. I get you have stuff you're still working through and responsibilities coming out that hot ass of yours, but you're young. It's okay to have fun and look good even while you're working. And it's okay to do it to catch the attention of a few sexy bikers in the process. If nothing else, it'll put a smile on your face for the night."

She'd given Kristy the standard cover story of having taken over guardianship of her siblings when their parents died in a tragic motor vehicle accident two years ago. As had been happening since she'd moved to Tennessee, guilt nearly had her cringing. Lying about her family had never been an issue—just a necessary evil to keep them safe. But lately, she'd begun to feel slimy about all the untruths she was forced to tell. But it couldn't be helped, so she'd have to learn to live with it because she refused to put her siblings or good people like Kristy and her coworkers at risk.

Thunder

As she stared at herself in the mirror, Mak worked the top over her head. Huh, it was actually…cute. Sleeveless, with wide straps she wouldn't have to worry would slip down her shoulders all night; the shirt was surprisingly conservative. A high-cut neckline assured her boobs wouldn't be popping out at some point. A wide band around the bottom trailed off into two long sashes Kristy tied in a bow at Mak's back. Yes, it was a crop top, but it only showed off an inch or so of skin in reality. When combined with the leather pants, the outfit made her look hot. Young, stylish, and dare she even say, sexy.

"Wow, Kris," she said as her throat thickened. "I look pretty good." Dressed this way, men might stare at her and want her. Desire her. Not because she'd make a good breed mule, but because she was just a woman they found attractive. Living in the community, women were forbidden from wearing anything that could be construed as enticing to men. Since she'd run, she'd been so focused on surviving and working, she'd never bothered to explore a more feminine or seductive side of herself. Who had time for that when there were so many kids counting on her? T-shirts and secondhand jeans had become her uniform, and while comfortable, she didn't exactly look like a sex kitten in them. She wasn't completely comfortable with the idea of attracting male attention all night, but she wanted to fit in and had to admit she was curious to find out if men could be drawn to her.

"You are gorgeous," Kristy said over her shoulder.

Makenna met her gaze in the chipped floor-length mirror that hung from the back of the door. "Thank you. It's perfect. I feel really comfy in this, too."

Kristy winked. "I know what I'm doing." She smiled and rubbed her hands together. "He's gonna lose his mind tonight."

"Huh? Who?"

"Oh, I just mean the guys there in general. You've got this whole innocent seductress thing going on. Men eat that shit up."

Makenna laughed so hard, her stomach ached. "Innocent seductress? You're crazy. I have nothing going on but bills, work, and responsibility. Oh, and diapers."

"You know, sweetie, it's okay to let yourself have some fun. Your siblings will be just fine if you take some time for yourself."

"They deserve so much more than what I've been able to give them, Kristy. How can I make that happen for them if I don't work a lot?"

"And what do you deserve?" Kristy asked with a tilt of her head. "You've put yourself sixth ever since your parents passed. You're allowed to have a life, Makenna. Parents all across the world, even single ones, learn to balance their own needs with their children's."

Makenna squirmed under the assessing gaze of her neighbor. What did she deserve? A harsh laugh almost escaped. Prison, probably. She'd technically kidnapped five minors and fled across state lines. The very last thing she deserved was fun and games. But Kristy didn't need that sob story. Kristy couldn't have her true history.

No one could.

Which was one of the reasons she never allowed herself to think beyond her siblings. Didn't look for love or relationships. Didn't dream. Didn't fantasize about more. At least not for herself. Her job was to provide more for those she loved. For her young siblings who still had a chance of dreaming and achieving those goals. They were innocent and worthy of a fulfilling life. She hadn't figured out what she was worthy of yet.

But Kristy knew none of that. So instead of laughing, Mak straightened her shoulders. "You're right. I do deserve some fun. Thank you for this." The appreciation was legit, even if she lied through her teeth about what the universe owed her.

"There ya go, girl." Kristy slapped her ass. Then she spent the next twenty minutes helping Mak with her makeup. After a fierce debate, they decided she'd just wear her hair in a high ponytail. She was bound to get heated, working the busy bar all night. Kristy still insisted on using her straightener on the locks, swearing a sleek ponytail made men fantasize about yanking it back as they "did her from behind." Once again, Makenna had bitten off her bark of disbelief. As if that would ever happen. To be honest, she barely understood the physics of it. Her experience consisted of lying flat on her back, staring at the ceiling, and praying her sixty-year-old husband's Viagra wouldn't make him last too long. Finding enjoyment in sex was a foreign concept.

"Okay, girl, I gotta bounce. I'm due at the Chrome Disciples clubhouse in an hour, and though I'll be wearing a lot less than you, it'll take me twice as long to get ready." With a wink, Kristy gathered up her mountain of beauty supplies. Emmie had fallen asleep a few moments ago on Makenna's bed, and she let out an adorable snore with each exhalation. "God, she's a cutie."

"She really is."

"You're lucky to have them," Kristy said, making Mak's jaw drop.

Though she loved her siblings with her entire heart and then some, it shocked her someone like Kristy, who had complete control over their life, would ever find her lucky. "You think I'm lucky? You can do whatever you want whenever you want to. You're totally free. I'm heavily shackled."

And constantly exhausted. Balancing a job, meals, schoolwork, babysitters, laundry, cleaning, and constant vigilance took everything she had and left her limp with fatigue most nights.

Kristy shrugged. "True, but I'm alone. You've gotta helluva lotta love in your life, honey. I've been married and engaged multiple times, trying to fill my life with love." Mak swore a flash of sadness passed through Kristy's eyes before she schooled her expression. "Anyway, have fun, serve drinks, get laid."

This time, she couldn't hold back her laughter. "Oh yeah," Mak said. "I can see it now. 'Hey, baby, wanna come back to my place? My two-year-old sister is asleep in my bed, and my four other siblings share walls with me. It'll be hot.'"

Laughing as she strode from the room, Kristy turned around. "Who said anything about bringing someone back here? Find a wall at the clubhouse and get fucked against it."

She swallowed a healthy gulp of nerves. A wall? What the hell? At the clubhouse? Did people do that?

And if so, what on earth kind of place was she walking in to?

A chaotic place, as she discovered an hour and a half later. The Handlers' clubhouse was booming, dark, sensory-overloading madness. Music with a deep base vibrated the walls, alcohol flowed, and men and women danced in ways she'd never been privy to before. Makenna didn't consider herself innocent; she'd been married for crying out loud, but she was finding out just how sheltered her life had been when it came to socializing.

"You're rocking this so far," Monty said as he popped the top off a beer, flipping the cap into a bin. He was around her age, bald with muscles galore, a light goatee, and teasing fair blue eyes. Thankfully, she'd studied about fifty YouTube videos on bartending, which gave her a leg up. Learning on the fly would have been impossible, given all the commotion around her. There were far too many distractions to focus solely on Monty's instructions.

Like the couple going at it against the wall, who kept drawing Mak's attention.

There they were, plastered against a wall in the clubhouse, just as Kristy had suggested. Right out in the open with their friends and strangers partying their asses off mere feet away.

Are they having sex?

"No, not yet. But give 'em a few minutes." Monty laughed near her ear.

Makenna jumped. Whoops, she'd meant the thought to stay in her head.

Monty seemed to get a kick out of the way she gawked and gaped at every lewd act. He stepped up next to her and slung an arm around her shoulders. "That's Maverick and his ol' lady, Stephanie. They're always going at it in one place or another. You'll get used to it."

Get used to the live sex show? "Yeah, I don't think so." As she'd learned from working with the girls at the diner, *ol' lady* was not, in fact, a term used to describe an elderly woman, but a term used to describe a biker's girlfriend or wife. It was used to denote a committed relationship within the club, or so they claimed.

"They're hot, huh?" Monty asked, still with his heavy arm across her shoulders.

"Huh?" Was it her imagination, or had his voice dropped a few octaves? It was then she realized she was still watching the couple, and her face heated. Hot? She was the one feeling hot. Didn't they have some air conditioning in the place? "Uh...I don't know. It's not like I'm staring at them or anything."

"Liar." He laughed. "Don't worry about it, babe. We've all been caught gawking at them a time or two. It's why they do it." His warm breath wafted over her ear, tickling the sensitive skin as he spoke. Instead of enjoying the feeling, she wanted to swat him away as she would a buzzing fly.

Why was he so close? He kept finding little ways to touch her and had been all night.

Oh, no. Her stomach flipped and not in a good way. Was Monty hitting on her? The guy was sweet and undoubtedly handsome, but she wasn't attracted to him in that way. In any way. Even if she was, she wouldn't have a clue how to handle one of these men. Plus, she didn't have the time or energy to learn—too many real-world problems to solve. Too many mouths to feed and bodies to clothe. Too many bad experiences with men to risk being anyone's possession ever again. Though none of the Handlers' women acted in the demure, beaten-down, dead-eyed way women in the community did. These men may be large, possessive, and growly, but the women with them appeared to revel in it instead of fear it, which led her to believe their experiences differed greatly from Mak's past.

His voice dropped low, seductive. "They like to be watched. Why do you think they don't just go upstairs to Mav's room?" He kissed her cheek, something she wasn't used to, but he often did, then said, "I'll grab the next few drinks. You enjoy the show."

"What? No. I'm not gonna do that," she said, tearing her gaze from the happy couple. But he was gone, and she'd already turned back to the pair who were so lost in each other, Mak had a feeling they'd forgotten they were in public.

As she watched, one of Maverick's hands crept its way up his ol' lady's denim skirt. He licked and sucked her neck as he did whatever he was doing under that skirt.

Beneath her new bra, her nipples tightened, becoming uncomfortable. Mak had the insane urge to press her palms to them and find some relief. She squirmed a pulsing feeling of... need throbbed between her legs. What the hell was happening to her? Was she getting turned on?

Oh, my God.

Mak glanced around, suddenly hyper-aware of being in public. To her relief, not a single person paid her any attention. Still, she needed to get herself under control.

Stephanie did nothing to hide her enjoyment of Maverick's attention on her body. She held her man close with one hand on his ass and one in the center of his back. Every few seconds, her fingers flexed, tensing.

With pleasure?

As Mak continued to stare at them, Stephanie's lips moved, the words "I love you," clearly identifiable. Mav lifted his head, making eye contact with his woman. They stayed that way, heated gazes locked until Stephanie bit her lower lip and trembled.

Holy crap, had the woman just orgasmed?

Thunder

Maverick kissed her, then they whispered back and forth, faces close and hands roaming lovingly over each other's bodies. The moment was so intimate, so much more than physical, she felt the need to look away and give them privacy, but she couldn't. Never before had she seen two people stare at each other like that outside of actors in a movie. Their gazes held pure, unconditional love and desire.

What would it be like to have a man look at her in such a way? Like she was the sole reason he woke in the morning?

Powerful. That's what it'd be.

Mak hadn't come close to experiencing anything like that. Hell, she'd barely felt true physical attraction. There'd been this boy she'd had a pull towards when she was an early teen, but knowing what her future held, she'd squashed the feelings and refused to allow them to occur again.

She'd certainly never felt so much as a flicker of attraction, want, or love for her husband. The thought of him made her shudder as it had from the moment she'd found out she would be forced to marry him and bear his children.

And now? Well, now she could identify a handsome, good-looking man, but nothing ever registered beyond that. She didn't feel what she'd read about in the romance novels she'd hidden between her mattress and box spring. None of the community's marriages were born of love or attraction, strictly the obligation to multiply. She'd begun to believe such a deep, primal desire for another person was nothing more than a myth, and those involved were consummate actors.

Yet, there was a real-life example of lust and love, staring her in the face.

Maybe it was her. Maybe she'd broken herself by suppressing her natural feelings and urges for so many years. Maybe the community had broken her by forcing her to endure the advances of a man three times her age.

What did it matter? Whatever the reason for her lacking libido, she didn't have the luxury of pursuing a man. Hell, the absence of those feelings was a gift. At least she didn't know what she was missing. Maybe Kristy had a point. She was lucky. The idea of cycling through man after man in search of some elusive perfect love seemed miserable.

Who the hell needed that in their lives?

Monty sauntered his way back over to her, a knowing smirk on his face. Once again, he circled her shoulders with his arm. The man was touchy as hell.

But she felt nothing. Not even a spark of heat for the sweet, funny, handsome man. Yeah, something had been destroyed in her all right.

"Good stuff, huh?" he asked as he wagged his eyebrows.

She shifted her gaze from Monty's grin back to Steph and Mav, only to find they'd migrated somewhere else. "Uh, yeah, sure."

Now, right where the couple had been, danced the guest of honor.

Thunder.

Three women surrounded him, all touching him and gyrating their bodies against his with moves that could have been choreographed. Thunder had his hands in the air, eyes closed as he swayed his body to the music. Mak didn't have a great view of him since his dance partners blocked most of his body, but he seemed to be a great dancer.

Monty laughed. "Now that one'll give you an education. Never met a man who could work the ladies quite like Thunder."

As though he sensed he'd become the topic of conversation, Thunder's eyes popped open, and his gaze locked with hers.

Her stomach flipped, different than before, and a strange flutter spread through her chest. She'd meant to ask Kristy about the kiss she'd witnessed at the coffee shop. About whether she was dating Thunder or not. From the handsy scene in front of her, she'd guess not.

"Is one of them his ol' lady?" she asked Monty, still maintaining eye contact with a dancing Thunder.

The prospect let out a booming laugh. "Thunder? Dating? Shit, babe, you're funny. Thunder doesn't date. He's a stripper and having too much fun banging any and every woman he can get his hands on. Which is pretty much all of them."

A stripper. That explained how he knew Kristy, but not why she'd kissed him as she had.

Thunder winked, and the gesture hit her straight between the legs with an unfamiliar tingling sensation.

Well, shit, maybe she wasn't broken after all, just pretty freaking bent.

Chapter Five

Thunder's arm throbbed with such intense, fiery agony, even the half bottle of moonshine he'd guzzled hadn't killed the torturous sensation. When he'd first learned of the Hell's Handlers tradition of branding their logo on the forearm of new patches, it had seemed like such a macho way to enter the brotherhood. Sear the symbol into his skin and be one with them forever. Endure the same pain all his brothers had before him. A bond in blood only a few understood.

Hell, he'd been fucking excited about it. Eager for the pain, even.

Until the moment Copper pulled the branding iron out of the bonfire, and the glowing tip careened toward his sensitive skin. Then all he'd wanted to do was puke and run screaming in the other direction. Somehow, he'd managed not to bawl like a little bitch when the red-hot metal turned his skin into barbecue. He'd also managed to stay on his feet, keep the contents of his stomach inside, and not scream. All requirements of the final test to be admitted into the club.

Now he got why Copper had him drink all that nasty shit right before branding him. And again after. The only thing keeping him from focusing on the ongoing discomfort was the fact his brain was sloshing around in the booze and unable to function.

So now, his arm screamed, and his head swam, but his body moved to the music like it was born to it. When you spent as many hours dancing as he had, no thought was required to get your groove on.

A few of the Honeys danced around him, or all up on him, really. He had no idea what the hell their names were. Hell, he couldn't even pick their faces out of a lineup. Didn't matter. All he wanted was to drink, dance, and enjoy his fucking night. For the first time in months, thoughts of Viper and questions over whether he'd failed a man he loved didn't dominate his consciousness.

Booze did.

He'd patched in.

God, it felt so damn amazing to finally belong to the club. To finally have a family he could be proud of. A family he could love. After what he'd grown up with…

Well, shit, thoughts like that were bound to kill his buzz in no time.

He could save that for a rainy day when he was in the mood to be depressed.

"You move like a dream," one of the girls whispered into his ear.

With his hands above his head and his eyes closed, he didn't know which one she was. Nor did he care. He rode the drunken wave, enjoying the feel of his body pumping to the music the way he always did. "Thanks, babe," he said on autopilot.

"I can only imagine how you work these hips in bed."

"Like a fucking pro, babe. Like a fucking pro."

She purred and ground her body against his; at least he assumed she was the grinder. Could have been one of the others, for all he knew.

"Any chance I'll get to do more than imagine?"

Fuck, no.

"Hell yeah, babe. Good fucking chance."

What were they talking about? The flirting rolled off his tongue without any effort from his wasted brain.

A tingle of awareness ran up the back of his neck as though one of the girls tickled him with her long nails, though none of them were touching him there. He opened his eyes only to lock onto the woman who'd been running through his thoughts far too much lately.

What the hell was Makenna doing here?

Behind the bar. With Monty's arm around her.

Were they fucking?

And why the hell did that idea bother him so much?

If there was one thing Thunder knew—besides dancing and how to fuck—it was body language. He was a master at reading it. Came with the territory.

Monty wanted Makenna, that was for damn sure. He was practically slobbering all over her. Thunder would bet his entire hard-earned savings account that the prospect sported some serious wood down below.

But Mak? Her stance was rigid, body angled away from Monty, and her gaze was one hundred percent on…well look at that, she was staring at him.

Little ol' Thunder.

Hmm, maybe a little test of the theory. He winked, and sure enough, her eyes flared, and she licked her lower lip—the lip with nothing more than a light sheen of gloss.

With her sexy yet understated outfit, subtle makeup, and big doe eyes, she was so out of her element, it was comical. She was also a welcome alternative to every single woman in the clubhouse.

And she wanted him. He'd put money on it.

For the first time in a while, he was considering a sexual encounter that didn't include an exchange of cash or obligation. It'd been a long time since he'd gone after a woman because he straight-up wanted inside her pussy. Maybe it was time to give himself a little treat. One night of no-strings fun to celebrate his shiny new patch.

Best part of it all? Now that he was a patched member, he could tell Monty to take a hike no matter what kind of claim the guy staked, or thought he'd staked. This was gonna be fucking fun.

One of the girls who was still dancing with him—yeah, he'd forgotten about them, sue him—rose up on her toes, bringing her lips level with his. Before she could go in for the kill, he shot her his most winning smile. "Hold that thought, gorgeous. Gotta take care of something real quick."

He wouldn't be back, but she'd have moved on to her next victim anyway, so who gave a fuck?

Ahh, out came the infamous pout he despised with such a passion. This one on lips that were decorated with a near-purple lipstick. It would look like she bruised the fuck outta whatever cock she ended up swallowing that night.

"Don't keep me waiting too long," the chick said, pressing a kiss to his cheek.

After a wink and a word of goodbye to the other two women, who seemed perfectly content to dance with each other once he was gone, he wormed his way toward the bar. Though only fifteen feet out, it took a few minutes since everyone he passed offered their congratulations.

He reached the bar just in time to see Monty kiss Mak on her smooth cheek. Her eyes narrowed, and if he hadn't been so obsessed with staring at her, he'd have missed the subtle gesture of annoyance.

"Take a hike, Monty."

The prospect clenched his teeth but didn't release Thunder's prize.

"Trouble with your ears tonight?"

Monty ran a hand over his smooth scalp as he sighed. "This seriously how it's gonna be? Patched in for five minutes, and you're a dick now?"

Wide eyes bouncing between the two of them, Mak opened her mouth, probably to try to defuse the situation, but Thunder beat her to it. "Nah, just want to be served a drink by a gorgeous woman, not a bald meathead."

With a laugh, Monty held up his hands. "Fair enough, man. Congrats, by the way." He meandered away, grabbing a bottle as someone called out an order.

"I'll take a beer, pretty girl, so he doesn't get on your case for slacking off." He winked, and the most adorable blush flushed her cheeks.

"Yeah, okay, sure," she said as she uncapped a bottle without asking what kind he wanted.

He didn't give a shit what beer she served him. The woman was so damn cute, all flustered and unpracticed in her response to him.

She cleared her throat. "Thanks for the save, by the way." Her smile was so sincere, Thunder wouldn't have believed it real if it wasn't directly in front of him. "Monty's nice, but a little…"

"That octopus was all the fuck over you."

With a tinkling laugh, she held out the dewy bottle. "Well, I wasn't going to say *that*, but he is a little friendly for my liking."

Instead of grabbing the bottle, he circled her wrist with his fingers. "You can tell him to back the fuck off if he's making you uncomfortable. Seriously, any guy here will respect that. And if they don't, I'll make sure they do."

Her gaze went to his hand on her as though to point out the fact he also was touching without being invited to do so. Instead of releasing her wrist, he just gave her his patented smile—the one he planned to work to its full potential to get her into his bed tonight.

She tilted her head, and a little puff of laughter left her lips.

"What's so funny?"

"Nothing." She shook her head.

"Hey, can I get a shot of vodka?" someone called out a few feet away.

Thunder

Mak extracted her hand. "Of course. Coming right up."

He stayed and watched as she poured the shot with slow but sure movements. "Hey, how'd you end up here tonight? Thought you worked at the diner."

"There you go." She slid the shot to a dude Thunder had seen at a few parties there in the past.

Not a bad guy, but he wanted her attention on him, not some other fucker.

"Uh, Shell and Toni told me you guys needed extra help tonight because it was going to be nuts." A nervous laugh escaped her, and she smoothed her hands down the front of her top. "They weren't wrong. This is nuts."

Just as he was about to respond with some snarky quip about nuts, her eyes popped wide and her mouth dropped into an O shape. "Oh! I can't believe I didn't congratulate you! I'm so sorry. I didn't mean to be rude. Congratulations!" She threw her hands in the air as though scoring a touchdown. "Now that I know what a patch-in ceremony is, I appreciate what a big deal tonight is for you."

Didn't want to be rude? Christ, she couldn't be rude if she was screaming obscenities at him. He hadn't realized they made women this cute and sweet anymore. At least not ones that came within a mile of the club. "Thanks, babe," he said, keeping the award-winning smile in place. Her authenticity unnerved him even as it made him want to rip off her clothes and see what kind of woman lay beneath the sweet veneer.

Even with copious amounts of alcohol muddling his brain, he picked up on Mak's serious take-home-to-mom vibe. Of course, his mom was a prostitute, so...

Those kinds of girls had needs, too. And he couldn't wait to satisfy hers.

She smiled back, hers seeming much less practiced than his. How come she hadn't flirted or invited him to her bed yet? Was he losing his touch? Maybe he needed to make his intentions explicitly clear with this one.

Just as he was about to make Makenna an offer she couldn't refuse, Izzy rushed him from behind. "Okay, hotshot," she said, drawing the attention of quite a few people around them. "Since it's been all about you tonight, it's only fair we get a little something too." She arched a jet-black eyebrow. "Get your ass up on that bar and give us a show. You're in for a treat, Mak. This guy can twerk like no other."

"Wha…I…uh…" Mak blinked, face bright pink.

"Speechless, huh?" he asked with a wink. Probably looked more like he had a tic with the amount of alcohol coursing through him.

When she shook her head and shrugged, he couldn't help but laugh. "Iz, pretty sure Copper will kick my ass if I start stripping in front of you all." Though a well-timed strip show with plenty of sultry looks sent Makenna's way was sure to get the message across far better than drunken words ever could.

This idea had merit.

If his prez was on board.

"Copper has given his full permission for this *one time and one time only*, to use his words." Izzy said with a roll of her eyes. "So get your ass up there and give us a treat. It's my birthday tomorrow, and I wanna see you shake it."

"Your woman is such a delicate flower, Jig," Thunder said as Izzy's ol' man and baby daddy strode up behind her.

"Don't I know it." Jig kissed her cheek and patted her ass, which earned him a scowl. "I find it's best to give her what she wants."

With a nod, Izzy said, "He's smart like that. It's why I'm so willing to keep his dick happy."

Mak made a choked sound that had Jig snickering though his eyes had grown heavy-lidded and dark for his woman.

The music changed, and Ginuwine's *Pony* blared through the speakers.

Thunder

"I even picked a song for you." Izzy did a shit job of masking her laughter. So shitty, in fact, her eyes twinkled, and she snorted, loud, which made Jig laugh.

Thunder rolled his eyes. "Seriously? This is the most stereotypical male stripper song ever. You disappoint me, Iz." Even as he spoke the words, the beat flowed through his blood, making his hips move in an unconscious rhythm. What could he say? He fucking loved to dance, cliché song, and all.

Izzy shrugged. "Long as *you* don't disappoint us ladies, it's all good."

By then, they'd drawn more than a crowd. Tipsy women yelled and hooted for him to get his ass on the bar and start dancing. Screw yelled something about being owed for voting his ass in. Though he couldn't see his horndog of a brother, he had a feeling his woman Jazz *and* his man Gumby were rolling their eyes.

Thunder peeked over his shoulder to find Mak observing the entire scene with a bit of slack-jawed shock and awe. Oh well, what the fuck? Might as well give her something to really drop her jaw over. She'd be begging for his dick in no time.

They always did.

Lifting his hands in defeat, he glanced at the gathered crowd. "You ladies want a show?"

A round of *hell yeahs*, and *fuck yeses* filled the clubhouse along with shrieks and whoops.

"I better not see your tiny fucking dick!" Mav screamed from across the clubhouse.

"You should be so lucky," he called back, really getting into it now. The years spent entertaining crowds left a substantial mark on him, and he quickly fell into the natural performance role. "All right, ladies, here we fucking go."

Feeling way soberer than he was, Thunder leaped on the bar in one powerful jump. Without hesitation, he ripped his cut off and tossed it to Mak, who caught it in one hand. "Keep that safe for me, babe."

She glanced down at the leather in her hands as if she'd never seen a piece of clothing before. Please, as cute as she was, she'd certainly had her fair share of offers. Look at Monty for fuck's sake. The guy had been practically humping her leg.

"Hey," he called down to her.

When her pretty blue eyes met his, he lifted his T-shirt and ran his hand down his washboard stomach. Having a good body was the number one job requirement. Even more important than impressive dance moves or charisma.

"This one's for you, baby." He winked and spun, snapping his hips with the *pop, pop, pop* of the music. Within seconds, he'd lost himself in the pounding pulse of the beat. His body moved on muscle memory, no thought necessary, twisting, thrusting, and generally driving the ladies wild. They screamed each time his pelvis popped and shouted how much they wanted to be his goddammed pony whenever he ran his hands over his sweaty torso.

Someone, a woman he'd never seen before, climbed up on the bar, dancing with some serious skill. When he crooked a finger her way, she shook her hips and shimmied her barely covered tits as she made her way closer.

Thunder shot her a smoldering look as he fingered the zipper of his jeans.

Bam, bam. Two more thrusts, then he lowered the zipper tooth by tooth. The woman licked her lips as she danced closer, clearly enjoying the show and the attention of being in everyone's line of sight. Once he'd loosened his jeans, Thunder spun, shoved the pants to the ground, then bent over, now clad only in his tight hunter-green boxer briefs.

The ladies, and even a few men, screamed.

Pop, pop.

A few bounces of his ass and more screams erupted.

Damn, Mak must be eating this shit up knowing she'd be on the receiving end of these thrusts before the night was over. As he continued twerking for his dance partner, he turned his head in Mak's direction. She stood watching with dull eyes and a frown on her face. His cut still dangled from her fingers, but limp at her side, not pressed to her nose as she inhaled his scent. Or held tight to her chest as she went gaga over his ass.

Yeah, he'd had both those fantasies a few seconds ago.

Before he had time to wonder if she was a prude who disapproved of a little skin, a sharp slap to his ass had him straightening. He spun, only to end up in the arms of his dance partner. Without missing a beat, he ground against her in a sensual rhythm that had the crowd going nuts.

Damn, this shit was fun as fuck.

She'd lost her top at some point, dancing in a lace bra that barely contained her massive tits. Now that the men of the club had something to stare at beside him, they were as into this as the ladies.

Hot skin pressed against his back.

Ahh, another horny, drunk chick looking for his cock. Too bad for these girls, it was spoken for that night.

Before long, at least four women had joined him on the bar. He gave them and the crowd what they wanted, lewdly dancing with each of the girls. Hands trailed all over his body, smoothing the perspiration into his skin. At one point, he was pretty sure he felt a tongue lick up his spine, but the combination of alcohol, many hands, and writhing bodies made it difficult to be sure.

At least his arm wasn't hurting for the moment.

With only twenty seconds left in the song, he turned his back on the crowd, bent over, and let his ass be the grand finale. The music ended, but the cheers continued until he faced the crowd with his hands in the air. Then the noise died down.

"Hey, everybody," he yelled. "Thanks for being here to celebrate with me. Hope you enjoyed that little show. If you did, find me, and I'll give you a business card." He winked as some of his brothers grumbled about hustling for cash.

"Holy shit, you can move," the ballsy woman who'd hijacked his dance said, batting her lashes his way.

"Thanks, babe. You've got some rhythm yourself." She smiled and shimmied closer, utterly comfortable with her near nudity. Though so was he. Hell, he'd seen more skin than she had on display flashed around since he was five years old. "How about a drink? You must have worked up a thirst."

"I sure fucking did. I'm gonna hop down, get dressed, then grab something cold. Hold on. I'll help you get off."

A sensual smile curved her glossy lips. "That's what I was hoping you'd say."

What?

Oh…shit, he must be off his game if he missed that one.

Thunder hopped off the bar, stuffed his legs into his jeans, then feet in his boots. "All right, babe," he said, straightening. He extended his arms to the woman. "Jump on down."

She did, making sure to rub her tits all over him as he lowered her to the floor.

With a smile to soften the blow, he said, "Thanks for the dance, but I already got some pussy lined up for tonight."

Wait for it…

And there it was. Pout central. Why did women do this? Did they somehow think he'd suddenly get hard as steel when their lower lip jutted out? Maybe it was supposed to remind him of getting sucked off?

Whatever. It sure as fuck didn't work on him.

"Next time?" She asked, a significant whine in her tone.

"You bet."

Nope.

"See you around, babe." Before he had the chance to turn away, she grabbed his shoulders, yanked him close, and laid a wet one right on his mouth. He kept his lips shut to avoid her tongue, but the move sure as hell didn't deter her.

When she pulled back, her blue eyes had darkened to a storm-sea gray. "Bye," she said, breathless. Then she spun and began searching for her discarded top. If he'd been more of a gentleman, he'd have lent a hand, but his attention had already diverted to his treat for the evening.

Mak stood behind the bar, watching every move he made with a pensive gleam in her eye, and lips pressed thin as though she was studying the behavior of a new species she didn't understand.

Huh, not exactly the heated, fuck-me-now vibes he'd been shooting for, but not a brush off, either. He could work with neutral. Hell, how long had it been since he'd had to put any effort into getting laid? Shit, had he ever? Could be fun.

"Were you talking about me?" She asked as she tilted her head. Most of the subtle gloss on her mouth had worn off her bottom lip as though she'd been gnawing at it recently—arousal from watching him dance, no doubt.

"Talking 'bout you when, babe?" He smiled at her. For some reason, her expression didn't change. The tense set of her shoulders didn't loosen, either. What the hell? Women always reacted to his smile. They lost their fucking minds. Maybe he was drunker than he'd thought, and the booze was making his face contort in an unsexy way.

"When you said you had some, uh, some p-pussy lined up for tonight." Her voice dropped to a near whisper on the word pussy. "Did you mean me?"

She didn't sound angry, disgusted, or appalled in any way. Then again, she sure as fuck didn't sound interested. She came across as…curious. Like he was some science project, she'd been assigned to work out.

Maybe she just needed another of his patented grins. This time he made sure her gaze was on his mouth before he shot it her way. "Sure did, babe. Wanna take off for a bit? Betcha Monty can handle the bar without you for thirty minutes or so."

Without so much as cracking a smile, she glanced at the other end of the bar where Monty stood, observing them with a frown. "Uh, thank you, but I'm good."

Thunder blinked. Surely, he'd misheard.

She's good?

She was good?

What the actual fuck? Sure, she was good now, but she'd be fucking great after he made her come a time or two in the next half hour.

For the first time in his entire fucking life, a female had rendered him speechless. His mouth opened, then closed again. Frankly, he had no idea how to respond. He didn't want to be an arrogant asshole, but women paid for the privilege of having his cock.

Literally paid money—lots of it every now and again.

He'd have understood more if she came across as disgusted by his dance. At least then he'd know she wasn't his type. Too pure, too prudish, too stuffy. But she just acted so...indifferent. As though she could take it or leave it. No skin off her back.

"Here." With a sweet smile that he wanted to fucking lick, she held out a large glass of ice water. "I'm sure you need this. Enjoy the rest of your night. And congratulations again, Thunder."

Then she walked down the bar, getting asked to serve up a drink almost immediately.

Thunder ran a hand through his damp hair. She'd been interested, dammit. He'd caught the goddamn attraction in her gaze not twenty minutes before. And she'd anticipated he'd be thirsty and brought him a drink.

Sweet, cute, and attracted to him.

But then, she'd turned her back on him and went about her job as though he didn't exist.

What. The. Fuck.

Maybe she didn't understand what he'd meant when he asked her to take thirty and leave with him.

Yeah, that had to be it.

What else could it be?

Chapter Six

It seemed as though every person in the clubhouse worked up as much of a thirst as Thunder had during his little...performance.

After he disappeared, the bar grew so busy, Mak barely had one second to obsess about Thunder's blatant and erotic offer. Could it even be called an offer? Really, it was an assumption. An arrogantly made assumption that she'd be in his bed...if he even wanted a bed. God, he'd told that half-naked woman he already had some *pussy* lined up for the evening.

He'd spoken with such confidence. As if it were a forgone conclusion she'd be sleeping with him. Sure, she was ignorant when it came to the whole hook-up game, as her brother called it, but...had she given him some sort of confirmation without knowing it?

Weirdest part of the whole encounter was how he didn't come off as an asshole. The guy wasn't a cocky jerk. He'd just been one hundred percent convinced she'd hop over the bar and run off with him for sex.

That was what he'd wanted, right?

Had she read the situation wrong?

Ugh. She'd been dying for a break from the insanity of the bar for the last hour and a half, and now that she had fifteen minutes to herself, all she wanted was to be busy enough to distract herself. Because, in reality, she'd wanted to say yes to Thunder, and that's what had her mind spiraling out of control. For the first time in her twenty-three years, she wanted to strip off her clothes and be touched by a man.

And a man she didn't even know, at that. The reaction was so unlike her. Perhaps watching the couple going at it earlier had scrambled her brain or unleashed a torrent of rogue hormones.

She'd only ever seen bodies like Thunder's in movies and read about in books. Muscles galore. Vivid tattoos. Metal bars through his nipples. Dazzling smile. And the way he moved? My God, it was the stuff fantasies were born of. One glance made her crave to know what all that smooth, firm skin would feel like under her fingertips. Or even more arousing, how would it feel to have his hands on her. Maybe even his mouth?

She'd always assumed there had to be more to sex than what she'd experienced. There *had* to be, right? Otherwise, why would people write all those steamy books where women screamed their man's name as they lost control of their bodies? Hell, why would Stephanie let Maverick finger her against the wall in public if it didn't feel incredible?

Her experiences with sex were less than pleasant, to put it in mild terms. Sex with her husband had been bland at best, painful at worst, but never, not even once, pleasurable. The act was committed for two purposes: to get her pregnant and to get her husband off the handful of times he'd come to her for that reason. She knew she was a little screwed in the head when it came to physical intimacy. Probably came with the territory.

If she were honest with herself, she did want to know what put that look of ecstasy on Stephanie's face. She ignored those thoughts because of her situation, but who wouldn't be curious?

She lingered behind the clubhouse in the mild evening, with the thrum of music in the background, and inhaled the fresh mountain air.

None of these thoughts of Thunder or her body's unfamiliar reaction to the man mattered.

Thunder

Her family mattered.

Keeping a roof over their heads and food in their bellies mattered.

Their safety mattered.

Their freedom mattered.

Her freedom mattered as her siblings' freedom depended on it.

So whatever happened, however many times Thunder flashed that potent grin her way, however curious her body grew, and however tempted her mind became, she couldn't let him divert her from her path. Her life wasn't about fun, frivolity, or games. It wasn't about drunk dancing on a bar or hooking up. Hell, that was a world she couldn't even comprehend. And it had to be the reason she felt drawn to Thunder. The way he lived fascinated her. The carefree attitude. The ease with which he connected to people, women especially. The free and blatant sexuality. The ability to have fun and behave irresponsibly.

The man was fascinating. All of the Handlers were. An incredible group of people who seemed to embody the phrase *work hard, play harder*.

The door opened, and as though she'd conjured him with her mind, Thunder stumbled out into the balmy moonlit night.

"Fuck," he muttered, holding his hands out like a circus performer wavering on a tightrope. Once steady, he took a sip of his beer then stared up at the cloudless night sky with a sigh.

Mak remained quiet, taking a second to observe him in a moment when he wasn't aware of the attention. The man was gorgeous. Hard, without being huge and bulky like LJ. So many fascinating tattoos without being overdone like Maverick. Capable of everything he did while having a magnetic personality, unlike his brother Rocket, who rarely spoke. He was a combination of so many of the best traits possessed by his brothers. Mak had spent quite a bit of time observing them all over the past few weeks whenever they ate in the diner.

Thunder's eyes fell closed, and he drew in a long inhale, much as she'd done. Something about the clean mountain air soothed the soul. Or at least, it did for her.

Was it the same for him? Did his soul need peace and serenity as hers did? If so, he hid it damn well, always smiling, laughing, flirting.

After watching him for a time, guilt wormed its way under her skin. He'd come outside for a private moment and didn't deserve her spying on him. Maybe she could sneak back in without him hearing.

She took one step toward the door. The crunch of leaves under her foot might as well have been a shotgun renting the quiet night.

Shit!

Mak winced and froze in place as Thunder's spine snapped straight. He turned slowly, and for one second, met her gaze with a startled vulnerability she'd have never expected from a man who oozed as much confidence as he did.

The open expression lasted all of three seconds before his eyes sparkled, and a smile slid onto those lips. "Looks like we ended up all alone after all." He stalked over to where she rested with her back against the building, still warm from the day's sun. Before she had a chance to scoot away—or maybe she hadn't wanted to move—he had his hands landed on either side of her head. "Must be a sign."

She'd been here before. Too many times to count. Dwarfed by a large man in a physical position of power and crowded against a wall, unable to escape. Thankfully, it had been years, so her body no longer reacted with a reflexive tremble of fear as it readied itself for whatever painful punishment was coming her way.

Instead, when she breathed and the combination of masculine body wash, liquor, and clean sweat invaded her senses, her knees nearly buckled.

Thunder

Holy crap, had a man ever smelled so good? Who the hell even knew the smell of a man could make her all tingly inside? Surely not her. The men in the community only ever smelled like tobacco, gunpowder, or hay.

"Do you agree?" he asked in a low, husky voice that made shivers run down her spine.

"Huh?" Agree? Her brain had short circuited the second he got too close, and she seemed to have lost all control over her body.

A deep chuckled rumbled from his chest. "Us. Outside. Alone. It's a sign."

Oh right. She gazed up into his sparkling eyes, blinking to clear the cobwebs. Didn't exactly work. The man needed to take about six giant steps back so she could think. "A sign of what?" she managed.

"That we need to fuck."

Her mouth dried up. Who spoke like that? She'd been away from the community for two years, and while not a social butterfly by any means, she'd been around people enough to be hit on and observe others in the same situation. No one spoke like that, with such a blatant offer of sex. Certainly not her husband.

The one she was still married to. Another reason to end this right now. She'd be legally married until the day Roger died. For one, she couldn't afford a divorce lawyer. Even if she could, the risk of discovery involved with sending divorce papers wasn't worth it. So on paper, she'd stay married though in her mind she never was.

More concerning than all of that was the thrill she experienced at his crude words, and the hungry way he licked his lips while staring at her.

What the hell was going on with her?

One of his eyebrows slowly rose while he continued to watch her as though waiting—

Oh shit! Waiting for her to respond.

"I…uh…we, um, I…"

Way to go, Mak. That oughta kill his attraction.

"I'll take that as agreement," he said, lowering his lips to her ear. "We taking this inside, or you good to go right here?"

What?

Right there…as in outside the clubhouse with a party raging on just one wall away? If her brain had been functioning, she'd have laughed out loud at the insanity of the question. He couldn't possibly have meant it how she'd taken it.

Could he?

When she didn't speak yet again, he pulled back and gave her a wolfish grin. "Out here it is, then."

Somehow, he'd taken her silence, rapidly rising chest, and racing pulse as an affirmative answer. With a nearly inaudible growl, he ran his nose along the column of her neck.

"You smell like fucking candy."

Mak gasped and flattened her palms against the building. If she could have, she'd have held on for dear life as it felt like she was about to fly off the surface of the earth.

"Shit," he whispered back near her ear. "This is gonna be fucking explosive." He captured her earlobe between his teeth and gave a little tug.

Mak squeaked as goosebumps erupted over her body. Ten seconds ago, if someone had told her a nip to her earlobe could make her entire being throb, she'd have laughed until she cried. She'd had sex countless times and never reacted as she'd just done to a split-second scrape of teeth against her ear.

"Th-thunder," she said, as she peeled her hands off the wall and pressed them to his chest. Her mind seemed to be at war with whether to push away or yank him closer.

He however, had no such conflict in his head.

"Shit, my name sounds good on your lips, babe," he said exactly half a second before he joined his mouth to hers. Flames licked at her skin, heating her until she felt near combusting. Her lips acted of their own accord, parting in surprise.

Thunder

With a groan, Thunder took full advantage and slipped his tongue inside. When it stroked against hers, she jolted at the unexpected clench between her legs. What the hell? He did it again, and she trembled, curling her fingers around the fabric of his T-shirt. Her legs shook, and her nipples ached. She had the insane urge to press them against his hard body to relieve the needy discomfort.

How many times had she had sex with her husband in the two years they were together? A lot. He'd been determined to have a child. In all the times she'd laid beneath him and endured his sweaty, uncoordinated rutting and shriveled body, she'd never felt even a fraction of the sensations Thunder's mouth evoked in her at that moment.

He groaned as he slid his hands into her hair and fisted the strands. His tense grip tugged on her scalp, not hurting, but riding the edge. If he pulled just a bit harder, his hold would tip into painful. But he didn't. He held her with just the right amount of pressure, not letting her have control. She was fully aware of his power, his presence, his ability to crush her if he dared.

But all he did was give her pleasure.

Everything but the boozy taste of him, the heat from his body, the tickle of his stubbled chin faded away. Mak was no longer a woman with a thousand responsibilities pressing down on her shoulders, she was just a woman.

For the first time in her life, her body overrode her mind and came to life in a way she'd only read about. It was real. The breathy, consuming pleasure that felt so wonderful it made a person greedy for more.

"Fuck," Thunder whispered against her mouth. "Knew you'd taste so goddammed sweet." He let out a little growl as he kissed her again, and the next thing she knew, something hard was grinding into her stomach.

Abort, abort, abort, her brain screamed at full internal volume while the throbbing between her legs seemed to shout *more, more, more.*

Something jingled in the distance, as though down a long tunnel. Too far away to concern her. All she wanted to focus on were the delicious shivers Thunder brought her.

"Ignore it," Thunder said with a groan, sliding his hands from her hair down to her back.

Huh?

Mak chased his lips as her fuzzy brain processed the ringing. Oh, shit. That was her phone. For one split second, she almost gave in. Almost let the ringing die out in favor of plunging back into the pool of erotic sensations. But at the very last second, something snapped to attention in her head.

"Shit!" she muttered as she wrenched out of Thunder's hold with a near-violent jerk.

"What the—"

"I need to see who it is." As she turned her back on Thunder, she pulled her phone from her back pocket. Leif's name flashed across the screen. "Shit," she mumbled again. Mak hit answer then held the phone to her ear as she put some distance between her and the man who almost made her ignore her family.

"Swear to God, Lee, if you're calling because you're sick of watching the kids, I'm gonna kick your ass," she said in a harsh whisper. Hopefully, Thunder couldn't hear her.

"Come on, Mak. It's been hours. I got this girl calling me. There's a party—"

"Absolutely not." She rubbed at an ache forming across her forehead. "Seriously, Lee, no. I have another two hours of work. I can't leave. We need this money. You know that."

When he groaned in annoyance, tears prickled at the corners of Mak's eyes. It was so easy to forget he was eighteen—still a kid. Just learning how to be a man. He'd had terrible male role models his entire life and now had none. His only "parent" was a twenty-three-year-old woman just as clueless about life as he was. He'd been robbed of a childhood and now, was saddled with the responsibility of being the man of the house. Mak tried not to put too much on him, but it was inevitable as the oldest male. All his life, he'd been responsible and serious beyond his years. Now he seemed to have taken a leap backward and turned into a rebellious teenage boy. Freedom had made him realize what he'd missed out on, and now he made up for lost time by partying and dating.

Could she blame him? No. Which was why she forced herself to keep from nagging him and overloading him with responsibility. But sometimes, like tonight, she just needed help. Sometimes doing it all on her own wasn't possible.

He'd survive a missed party.

Her eyes fell shut, and she shook her head. Whenever she thought about what must go on at those parties, her stomach hurt.

"Please, Lee," she said. In reality, he was an incredible brother. More mature than most eighteen-year-olds, but still...

"Fine," he grumbled. "But I'm going out as soon as you get home."

Geeze, it'd be after two by the time she got home. But what could she do? She wasn't his mother. He was technically old enough to do as he pleased, and if she ever pushed him to the point he left, she'd be completely screwed. "Fine."

She ended the call, straightened, and turned back to find Thunder leaning against the building with his arms folded across his chest and a smirk on his kiss-swollen lips.

"Boyfriend?" he asked, not sounding at all like he minded if she was in a relationship.

Should she say yes? Maybe it'd deter him. Send him sniffing around someone else. Lee's call had been a stark reminder that her life wasn't her own. Four other people, three of them helpless, depended on her and her ability to provide for them and keep them safe. Relationships, even just making out with an attractive man, wasn't in the cards for her.

She had way too much to lose.

So instead of throwing caution to the wind and picking up where they left off as he tempted her to do, she smiled at Thunder and said. "My break is over. Better get back inside."

If she hadn't felt so self-conscious and out of her element, she'd have laughed at the way his jaw hit the ground.

"You've gotta be kidding me." Usually, words rolled off his tongue like warm butter. Now, his tone had taken on a frosty note. He dropped his arms and scowled.

"Uh, no. Monty gave me fifteen minutes. Actually, I'm a few minutes late. I don't want to upset him." She shoved her hands in her pockets and stared at the ground. "Uh, thanks. That was fun."

Could she be any more awkward?

"Fun?" He laughed as he shook his head, but the harsh sound grated on her instead of making her join in. "Fucking fun would have been getting my dick sucked. Who the fuck knew you'd be nothing but a cock tease? Have *fun* working with fucking Monty."

Mak winced as he threw the door open and disappeared into the building. Of course, he didn't hold it for her, and it slammed shut so hard, she jumped.

For a moment, she stood there staring at the closed door with a frown on her face. What the hell had just happened to turn him from charming and seductive to a total jerk? For the life of her, she had no idea why her words had made him so angry.

Though his actions made her feel like garbage, maybe it was for the best. Clearly, she wasn't cut out to play in his world. The fantasy was nice, but just that—a little time spent playing make-believe.

From now on, she'd stick to books to get her fantasy fix.

Chapter Seven

It might be time to give a physician a call. Thunder was obviously sick and in serious need of medical attention. For the past two days, he'd been a complete fucking mess. His appetite had gone to shit, he'd tossed and turned each night, and for some unknown reason, every time he shut his eyes, Makenna's sweet face appeared, as did the feel of her soft, hungry mouth. And her slender fingers gathering up the fabric of his shirt. And, Christ, did he mention the throaty little whimper she'd made when he'd finally given in and pressed his erection into her soft belly? The one he heard echoing through his head all night?

Shit, that tiny sound nearly made him come on the spot and leave an embarrassing wet spot on her shirt.

She'd been liquid heat in his arms, nearly burning him to ash with her honeyed and seemingly innocent kisses. God, the woman had the good girl act down, and damn if it didn't crank his gears.

Then she'd gone and pulled the fucking plug after the mysterious phone call he was pretty sure came from a man. A man with whom she appeared to be in a close personal relationship, if the way she dropped her voice and wandered off to take the call was any indication.

The part that baffled him in this little tango they'd danced was how she'd all but told him to fuck off after ending the call.

What the hell?

She'd wanted him as much as he'd wanted her. He'd spent enough time around horny women who had their sights set on his dick to know what the hell he was talking about. And Makenna had eyes for his cock. But she'd turned him down cold.

Twice in one night.

What kind of game was she playing? Clearly, she caught on to how the good girl-next-door act did it for him but wasn't leaving him with blue balls on more than one occasion taking it too far?

Shit, he wanted a sweetheart, not a prude virgin.

Still, he could admit he'd been a bit of an ass, okay a total fucker in those last few moments. And the guilt of being less than his usual charming self had to be responsible for his Makenna perseverations over the rest of the weekend. His conscience, which seldom weighed in on his life choices, had been screaming at him for more than forty-eight hours.

Enough was enough.

"Hey, Thunder, the usual?" Shell asked as she sidled up to his table at the diner Tuesday morning.

"Yeah, babe, thanks."

"All right, a three-egg omelet with ham and cheddar, extra potatoes, and buttered white toast coming right up. I'll grab you a coffee refill, too."

"Thanks, hon. Copper's a lucky fucking man."

She grinned at that, a pretty pink blush flushing her cheeks. Rubbing the swell of her pregnant belly, she tilted her head and gave him an assessing once-over. "You know, I'm the one who's pregnant, and I still can't eat like you. Where the hell do you put it all?"

With a wink and his legendary smile, he flexed his right bicep. "Takes a lotta fuel to keep these babies running."

Thunder

Shell's eyes rolled back so far they nearly revolved in her head. "You're seriously demented," she said, but her giggle gave away the fact the insult held no weight.

"Hey," he said, grabbing her wrist as she began to turn away. "Mak working today?"

He'd been hoping to be seated in her section but didn't want to show his cards by requesting it. Still, Shell's eyes narrowed with a knowing gleam. "She's not. I swear that girl would never take a day off if Toni didn't force her to. She's worked here the last seven days straight, including Sunday morning after working at the clubhouse all night Saturday. Toni flat out refused to let her in the door today."

Huh. Thunder frowned. Was she hurting that badly for money? The thought of her working herself to exhaustion had him unable to react with his usual playful banter.

Shell cleared her throat, drawing him from his thoughts.

"What? Huh?"

She glanced at where he still held onto her and chuckled. "You gonna give me my hand back? I need that one to carry your food."

"Oh, shit, sorry." He released her at once, and she walked away with a chuckle as she shook her head and sent her blond curls bouncing.

Before he had the chance to dive back into obsessing, Screw slid into the booth opposite him. Gumby followed a second later.

"Well, well, well, if it isn't two-thirds of the happy throuple," Thunder said as he leaned back in the booth and folded his arms across his chest. "You here to ogle the pretty member of your relationship?" he asked with a smirk. Jazmine, the brave woman who lived with these two men, worked as the diner's general manager.

Screw flipped him off, while the more subtle Gumby snorted.

"Can't argue with you calling our Jazzy pretty, but you're still an asshole. And while seeing our girl is always a plus, she's actually not the reason I'm here," Screw said as he flipped his coffee mug over on its clean white saucer.

"She's why I'm here," Gumby announced. "And pretty doesn't even come close to describing how gorgeous that woman is." As he spoke, his gaze scanned the diner, no doubt searching for the woman in question.

Screw frowned at his lover, which made Thunder bit his lip to keep from laughing.

"I thought you were here because you wanted to have breakfast with me," Screw said, with the most pitiful pout Thunder had ever seen.

"Of course, I am, baby." Gumby stroked a hand over Screw's shoulder-length hair in an exaggerated and slightly patronizing caress. He winked at Thunder, then rolled his eyes.

"I don't even give a shit that you're making fun of me right now. I'll take your hands on me, and your time any way I can get them."

Gumby's eyes softened, and he grabbed the front of Screw's cut, yanking the man in for a less-than-chaste kiss.

Thunder didn't bother to look away. Instead, he studied the two lovers and tried to process the strange twisting in his gut.

What the hell did it mean? It was happening with more frequency lately when he witnessed his new brothers with their woman. An uncomfortable coil looped low in his stomach. One that had him both wanting to stare and turn away at the same time.

Thunder had had his fair share of threesomes in the past. Two girls, two guys, hell, he didn't care. He'd even been sucked off by a guy a time or two, and while it felt good—hell, it was a mouth on his dick—the fact it was attached to a dude didn't do much for him. His cock got hard for tits and pussy, and that was just the way nature had crafted him.

So, it wasn't the combination of Gumby and Screw getting to him, it was something else. And damned if he knew what the fuck that was.

Thunder

"Need a favor," Screw said, when they finally broke apart and after Shell had poured coffee for Gumby and refilled Thunder's. Screw waved her away when she tried to fill his mug.

"Anything," Thunder responded. It wasn't an empty promise, either. He'd do any damn thing his new brothers asked of him.

"You know the CDMC has been quiet lately. They took a huge financial hit after..." Screw lowered his voice. "After one of their shipments didn't make it to its destination. And ever since Jeremy tossed a grenade through the window of this place, the cops have been lodged so far up the CDMC's ass, they've been shitting gold shields."

His heart rate kicked up as did his guilt any time someone mentioned the day Viper died. He'd wanted to think of something other than Makenna, but this only brought on more discomfort and remorse.

Six weeks or so ago, the Handlers had gotten some sweet intel regarding where, when, and how the CDMC shipped weapons up and down the east coast. Screw had organized a swift and effective operation to fuck with the shipping company they used for transport. The effort was wildly successful, making the CDMC miss critical deliveries and lose tens, maybe even hundreds of thousands of dollars revenue. Only a few days later, Jeremy, a CDMC prospect who happened to live next door to Jazz and had mad hatred for the Handlers, tossed a grenade through the window of Toni's Diner.

The restaurant had been left in shambles.

And Viper had died.

He rubbed his chest as though it would relieve the ache Viper's absence created.

As Screw waited for Thunder to process what he'd said, he kept an arm across Gumby's shoulders. Every few seconds, Screw unconsciously played with the hair at the nape of Gumby's neck.

Once again, Thunder's stomach clenched, and this time, his chest constricted as well.

Maybe he did need to see a fucking doctor. Did heart disease run in his family? Fuck if he knew. STDs sure ran in his family, but those came from being whores, not genetics.

"Yeah," he said, flattening his palms on the table instead of giving in to the urge to press a fist to his chest. "I'm up on all that. What of it?" Suddenly, his omelet looked like one deadly hardened artery on a plate, so he shoved it to the center of the table.

"Well, we got word that the cops closed the case—straight-up lack of evidence. No one can find Jeremy. Looks like the fucker took off after he blew this place up," Screw said with a wicked gleam in his eyes.

"Chicken shit."

"Yep."

The day came back to him in a rush. The way Viper had told him he'd keep Jazz safe and that Thunder should chase down Jeremy. The way Viper had failed to mention he planned to throw his body over Jazz's right there in the diner, saving her, but getting his heroic fucking ass mortally wounded in the process.

Fuck, his chest couldn't take many more of these twinges.

He'd successfully caught up to Jeremy about a quarter mile from the diner as the fucker fled for his life. Damn, it would have been sweet to be in the room when Screw pulled the trigger on that guy. He owed that to Viper at the very least. If only he'd been patched in at the time.

He'd told all the guys not to worry about him. He was handling that shit fine, but truth be told, he'd had a few fucking nightmares where he was going about his typical day, and one of his brothers exploded right before his eyes.

Fuck, not the time for that shit. "So what do you need from me?" he asked before clearing his throat. Anything to keep from falling down the rabbit hole of bad memories.

"Got word that the CDMC will be celebrating this weekend. Getting rid of the pigs on their backs means time to party."

Thunder

"And what? You want eyes on the place?" He'd jump on any chance to be involved in eliminating the CDMC. Maybe then, he'd be able to rid his mind of the gruesome image of Viper's lifeless body. It had only been through sheer force of will he'd been able to enter the diner at all once the remodel had been complete, and each time he did, he had a moment of panic before stepping inside. Fuck yeah, he'd take on this task.

Screw nodded as he lifted Gumby's coffee cup to his lips. "Exactly," he said after taking a sip. "Knew you were quicker than you look."

With a roll of his eyes, Gumby slid the mug back in front of himself. "You can't insult the guy if you're trying to get him to do you a favor. And why the hell do you always decline coffee if you're just gonna drink mine?"

"Well, I called it a favor, but I was lying. It's an order," Screw said, with a smirk for Thunder and a kiss for Gumby's cheek.

Thunder grunted as he folded his arms across his chest. No surprise there. Screw was about a subtle as a bull.

"And I swipe your coffee because it tastes like you." He winked at Gumby whose gaze seemed to heat at the words.

"You do like the way I taste, don't you?" Gumby asked, his voice dropping a few octaves.

"Damn straight. Love the way Jazzy tastes too. Man, she went nuts when—"

Ohh, this is getting good.

Gumby cleared his throat and widened his eyes in Thunder's direction, which made Screw turn a scowl his way.

"What?" Thunder asked with a shrug. He tried to mash his lips together but couldn't keep the smirk from creeping across his face. "Don't pipe down on my account. I'd love to know what you two dirty dogs did to Jazzy last night. Or did you say this morning?"

Screw flipped him off again.

"Oh, come on, man, you used to be so much more fun before you went and put a shackle around each of your legs," he said around a laugh.

All that did was earn him another middle finger.

"Just tell me if you're in, fucker."

"Of course, I'm in. Whatever you need." He drained his coffee. "All kidding aside. You name it, I'm there. Any time, any place. Especially if it involves those fuckers."

Screw held out a fist. "Know it, brother. Feels good to call you that."

"Feels even better to hear it," Thunder said as he tapped his knuckles to Screw's then Gumby's.

"It's gonna be you and Mav. I'll have him get with you on the details before Saturday."

Thunder stood, then tossed a few bills, including a healthy tip, on the table. No criticism to the chef. The food rocked, as usual. He just wasn't in the mood to eat anymore.

As he walked toward the door, Shell crossed his path, carrying an empty coffee carafe. "Leaving already?" she asked, a wrinkle across her forehead.

"Yeah, got some business to attend to. Hey, you know Mak's address?"

Shell tilted her head and studied him.

After a good fifteen seconds, he couldn't ignore the urge to squirm. "What is it, Shell?"

"Why do you want her address?"

He raised an eyebrow. "Nosey ol' ladies," he muttered.

Shell shrugged, completely unrepentant. "She's dealing with a lot, Thunder. Just want to make sure you're not gonna jerk her around. I don't know if it's a good idea for you to head out to her place. It's...she's just got a lot on her plate already without having to deal with a womanizing biker on top of it all."

He ran a hand down his face. "What the fuck, Shell? It's not like I leave a trail of devastated hearts all across Tennessee. Not looking to make the chick fall in love with me. Just have some shit to talk to her about." Was that how they all saw him? A womanizing heartbreaker? It was almost laughable, considering he hadn't fucked a woman he'd pursued in nearly a year.

Jazz wandered up behind Shell and circled her arm around her friend, patting her baby bump.

Two on one, just what he fucking needed.

"I don't know, Shell, I think you should give him her address," Jazz said with a slightly evil grin. She rested her chin on Shell's shoulder.

"Thank you." He pointed to Jazz. "You should listen to your sister."

The two women shared a look that made no fucking sense to him, then Jazz snickered. "I'll text it to you." Then she pulled out her phone, and ten seconds later, his vibrated against his ass.

"Thank you," he said as he threw his hands in the air and glared at Shell. "That so hard?"

Shell's eyes narrowed, so he shut the fuck up before she got pissed, and he ended up with a visit from her unhappy ol' man —and his prez.

"Thunder," Jazz called as he strode toward the door.

Christ, what now? Hands on his hips, he turned back around.

"Have fun." She didn't even try to keep the obnoxious smirk off her face.

"Uhh, thanks?" What the hell did they know that he didn't? Did she live in some roach-infested one-room shack or some shit?

He shivered.

Fuck, she better not.

He'd had enough of that shit growing up.

After a long shift at the gym, his GPS led him out to the middle of fucking nowhere, partway up the mountains, looking at two small houses side by side without any other nearby neighbors. From the outside, the place was plain-as-fuck brown with no landscaping, tan doors, and a large rectangular window on each side of the door.

Far as he could tell, it looked like a normal fucking place to live, if a little underwhelming.

"Whatever," he mumbled to an imaginary Jazz as he climbed off his bike. He strode to the door with a large brass hook hanging crookedly from a nail and gave a firm knock.

Not ten seconds later, a deep voice called out, "Hold it right there, missy. What's the rule about opening the door?"

He frowned and missed the answer as he looked over his shoulder. Sure enough, the mailbox said nine-zero-six-three; same number Jazz had texted. Maybe she got it wrong?

The door opened, and a very tall, relatively muscular guy who looked like he couldn't have been more than twenty filled the space. Thunder's eyes immediately went to the toddler, balanced on the giant's hip. She had none of the same coloring as Makenna with blonde hair and pale skin, but her eyes were the exact same shade of blue. Same face shape, too.

His stomach dropped.

Was this her ol' man? The one who called Saturday night?

"Kristy lives in the other house," the guy said, as he began to back up and shut the door.

"Uh, wait." Thunder stuck his boot out, keeping the door from closing in his face.

"I'm looking for Makenna." He spoke the words to the guy but couldn't take his eyes off the little girl who looked so much like a young, blond Mak.

"Who the fuck are you?" the guy asked, voice now full of menace.

Thunder shifted his gaze. "Not your concern." Well, technically, it was his concern if Mak was his ol' lady. Shit. Was she shacked up with some barely out of his teens kid? And, fuck, did she have a kid?

The guy's eyes narrowed to displeased slits, but instead of slamming the door in Thunder's face like he probably wanted, he whispered in the little girl's ear. After she nodded with more enthusiasm than Thunder had ever shown for anything in his life, the guy set her down, and she ran off screaming, "Mommy! The man is here for you!"

Mommy?

Blood rushed blood from his face. His brain screamed at him to turn and book it the fuck outta there, but his feet stayed rooted to the ground. For some sick reason, he needed to lay eyes on her.

Mak was a goddammed mother, and she lived with a man who looked ready to rip Thunder's nuts off.

And he was there to apologize for acting like an ass after a hot and heavy makeout session. How the fuck was he gonna get out of this one?

No wonder Shell hesitated to share the address.

And damn Jazz for taking sick pleasure in his humiliation.

And damn him for thinking she was different than the cheating housewives who paid for his time.

Chapter Eight

"Dammit," Mak muttered as she frowned down at her sauce-stained T-shirt.

She wiped the blotch, smudging it instead of making the situation better, then huffed out a "Whatever," before returning her attention to the tomato sauce she'd set to simmer an hour ago. Not like she'd be seeing anyone.

One lick of the wooden spoon had her humming. "Mmm, that's good stuff." The only thing she'd learned from her father she appreciated was this tomato sauce. The man had a recipe that brought tears to the eyes. Actually, it'd been her grandmother's specialty. Her father deserved nothing from her, not even credit for passing down her favorite meal. It's not like he'd been the one to teach her to make it. Heaven forbid, he lifted a pinkie to help in the home.

"Mommy!" Emmie yelled two seconds before she came flying around the corner and into the kitchen. "The man is here for you!"

"Whoa!" Mak caught her, hoisting the squirming toddler up onto her hip. "Oh, my gosh, you're getting so heavy. What is the rule about running in the house, Miss Emilia?"

"No wunning," Emmie said with a pitiful jutted lip. Where the girl learned that move, Mak would never know, but it was dammed effective. One look at those chubby cheeks, downturned eyes, and protruding lower lip and every adult within a quarter mile was putty in her pudgy little hands.

All part of her plan for toddler world domination.

Mak pressed her lips together until the urge to grin faded. "That's right. No running in the house. Especially in the kitchen when I'm cooking. Got it? There is hot stuff in here, and I don't want these little piggies to get hurt," she said as she tickled Emmie's bare toes, eliciting a fit of giggles from her youngest sibling.

"The man is here," Emmie announced once she'd finished laughing.

"What man?" Mak peeked at her sauce then lowered the heat a smidge more. Another fifteen minutes and it'd be perfect.

"At the door."

"There's a man at the door?"

Emmie nodded, her attention now on the sauce. "Yook, bubbles!" she said as she clapped her hands.

"Did you open the door, Emmie?"

Her sister shook her head. "No. Lee opened it."

Well, crap. Then there really could be someone at the door, not just the ramblings of an imaginative two-year-old. Mak gave the sauce a quick stir then darted out of the kitchen. "Sorry, Lee," she called out. "I'm coming." Then, in a lower voice, she said, "Let's go," to Emmie as she set the toddler down.

Her brother's large form blocked the doorway, and as she approached, he didn't bother to move. "Okay, I'm here. Who is it?" He still didn't give her space, just did this grunting thing she'd noticed many of the MC members did. Must be a guy thing.

Emmie ran up behind him and latched onto the back of his leg.

"Lee, buddy, move over so I can see who it is." Once again, he didn't budge. Mak sighed as she rolled her eyes and wedged herself between Lee and the doorframe with a grunt. "Seriously," she said, hip checking him. Her brother was damn solid and didn't shift a millimeter with her effort. "Get outta my wa— Thunder!" She stopped trying to displace Lee and gaped at the man standing on her stoop with a half-smile.

His gaze shifted from her to Lee and back again. "Uh, hey, Mak."

"Wha-um, what are you doing here?" And why the hell did he have to look so good. Seriously? Shouldn't the cut over his olive-green T-shirt hide the way it fitted to his perfect chest?

"You know him?" Lee asked in a deeper voice than usual.

She rolled her eyes. "Yes, guard dog, I know him. Chill. He's in the club with Toni and Jazz's boyfriends."

Lee grunted again, and though his display of protectiveness bordered on ridiculous, warmth filled Mak's heart. Her brother might have been driving her nuts lately with his gross display of teenage stupidity, but he was still a good guy who'd always have her back.

Emmie tried to poke her head between Mak's legs, so she scooped her sister up once again.

Thunder cleared his throat. "Wanted to talk to you for a minute, but if this is a bad time…"

"What? No, it's fine. Why would this be a bad time?" Did either of them notice the unnatural high pitch to her voice? One quick peek at the way Lee was staring at her as though she had ten heads answered that question. Why the hell did this man make her so stupid?

Thunder scratched his chin then flicked his gaze between her and her brother a few times. Mak nearly burned up as the hot blast of embarrassment rushed her. Did he think…

"We're about to eat." Lee's curt statement had her face even hotter.

Right. She was standing there in a stained T-shirt, with a toddler on her hip and a man in the doorway looking like a possessive ape. Of course, he'd assume something inaccurate. Mak cleared her throat before gazing up at her scowling brother.

"Then maybe you should go put the pasta in the water, Lee," she said, giving him the fiercest get-the-hell-out-of-here glare she could muster. "It should be boiling by now." He frowned at Thunder for another few seconds before sauntering off. Had she been thinking properly, she'd have handed Emmie off, but as it was, Thunder's presence made her completely forget how to think.

"Sorry," she said with a shake of her head as she stepped out onto the stoop with him. "My brother can be a little intense at times, but he's a good kid. Uh, what was it you needed to talk to me about?"

"Brother?"

"Yeah, that was my brother, Lee."

The smile she'd become familiar with over the past week or so curled his lips in its usual fashion. "And this little princess?"

"Um, this is my sister, Emmie."

"Dis is my mommy," Emmie said, patting Mak's face with the non-gentle affection of an excited two-year-old.

"Mommy?" Thunder asked, eyebrows drawing down.

"Uhh..." She so did not want to get into any of that right now, or ever. Especially not with the sexiest man she'd ever met. She shifted Emmie to a more comfortable position on her hip. "So, what was it you wanted to talk to me about?"

"You sit next to me!" Emmie announced as she launched herself out of Mak's arms without warning.

"Oh, shit, I mean, crap, uh..fu—fumble!" Thunder shouted as his hands shot out on reflex. The poor guy had his arms full of a spirited toddler before he knew what hit him.

Makenna would have laughed at the look of complete and utter panic in his eyes if she wasn't already more embarrassed than she'd ever been in her life. "Emmie," she said, voice firm. "Come back, Mr., uh, Mr. Thunder"—God, how ridiculous—"didn't come here to play with you. Come on down."

Emmie's face screwed up, and she shook her head. Awesome, they'd be dealing with a full-on tantrum in no time.

"It's all right," Thunder said as he moved her sister to his hip, mimicking the position Mak had held her in. His wide, slightly wild eyes betrayed his calm words, but damn if the sight of the charming man holding her kid sister didn't make her insides all warm and squishy.

"You sit by me," Emmie proclaimed again.

"Uh, we kinda do a family thing for lunch on Sunday's, and we missed this week since I worked, so we're doing it for dinner tonight. Would you like to join us? It's nothing fancy," she rushed on. "Just spaghetti and meatballs. Garlic bread. Uh, and salad." She almost called Lee back so he could slap his hand over her mouth and keep her from word vomiting.

"Yucky, salad," Emmie said, wrinkling her nose.

"I'm with you, kid. Salad is yucky."

Emmie beamed and batted her lashes at Thunder. She was in full-on flirt-mode.

"So, dinner. We'd love you to join us."

Say no, say no, say no.

"Sure," he said, shifting his gaze to the happy toddler now squealing in his arms. The poor guy looked like he'd rather be anywhere but standing on Mak's stoop holding a child.

Well, if anything came from this mortifying debacle, it's that she wouldn't have to stress about fending off his advances anymore. This meal would pretty much guarantee he'd never see her as anything but an overworked charity case with too many mouths to feed.

IF ANYONE HAD asked him what his plans for the afternoon were, the dead last answer would have been sitting around a huge wobbly wooden table with six other people, five of them children. Well, maybe Lee didn't qualify as a child. The guy had to be seventeen or eighteen, maybe even nineteen.

It was as though he'd stepped into an episode of the Twilight Zone. The two younger kids stared as though he was a zoo animal. Lee glared at him, and the other two girls he'd been introduced to as Amy and Rissa concentrated on loading their plates. Apparently, the six of them were all siblings. They looked it, with their dark hair and blue eyes. Emmie was the only one whose coloring differed.

Makenna bustled about making sure the younger kids had food, drinks with lids, and napkins tucked into their shirts.

"Phew," she said as she finally took a seat, long after everyone else had begun to eat.

He cleared his throat.

Makenna's eyes popped when she looked at him, almost as though she'd forgotten he was there. "Are you not hungry?" she asked, gaze on his empty plate.

He lifted the giant bowl of spaghetti and held it out to her. The ceramic had chipped in multiple places, same with the plates, but no one seemed to notice or care. Not that he did. Hell, he knew firsthand what it meant to live without. "Ladies first," he said.

Makenna made a small sound of disbelief with her jaw hanging open then she gave him a smile that lit his insides. "Thank you," she said as she took the offered bowl. Her cheeks pinked and the two words held sincerity and a bit of awe. As if no one considered her or put her first.

Hell, taking care of all these kids, which it seemed was exactly her responsibility, had to be a thankless and draining job. If she did indeed have guardianship over all these kids, she was a twenty-three-year-old single mother of five. The stress and hardships she must deal with day to day boggled his mind. Suddenly he saw her in an entirely different light. Makenna was as unselfish as they came and absolutely incredible. The things she must sacrifice for her family...

Damn, he'd given away that houseplant Shell brought him when he rented his place. Keeping the thing alive had been more responsibility than he'd been willing to undertake. Hell, keeping himself breathing took all his energy some days, and here she was, younger than him and so together.

After dishing out about a third of the portion size he'd have taken for himself, Makenna passed the bowl back to him. "Please, eat as much as you want. I always make extra pasta."

After loading his plate, he gazed around the table at the happily eating children who spoke with their mouths full, giggled and teased each other. Now that they were eating, none of them seemed bothered by the stranger at the table, though the fifteen-year-old Amy sent him curious glances from the corner of her eye every so often.

The scene was so domestic it could have come straight from one of those made for TV movies. He shifted, tugging at the collar of his T-shirt. Felt like the damn thing was shrink-wrapped to his body and tightening down by the second. He could honestly say this was the first time in his twenty-five years that he'd ever sat through a family dinner. Hell, as a kid, he'd often eaten nothing but cereal and sandwiches for weeks on end. His mother had been too busy *entertaining* clients to come home for a meal, let alone cook one. Sure, the club got together for barbecues and meals on the regular, but that was more a loud, slightly less inappropriate than a typical party, not an intimate family gathering where people who loved each other talked about their day and shit.

Every few seconds, the urge to flee the table and run screaming out the door hit him full in the face. The only thing keeping his ass in the seat was fear over his club brother's wrath. Zach would beat him bloody if he ditched Makenna mid-meal, and she vented to Toni. Christ, and if she said something to Jazz, he'd have Gumby and Screw looking to pound him to dust. Not to mention if Shell caught wind of it. Last thing he needed was to get on his president's shit list five minutes after patching in. Even this family lovefest was preferable to an ass-chewing by Copper.

Makenna gave him a shy smile before holding up a bottle of wine. "You look like you could use some of this."

Fuck yes. Wine wasn't his thing, give him a beer or some vodka, and he was a happy man. But there was alcohol in that wine, and he needed it. "Thanks," he said.

She wouldn't meet his gaze as she picked up a plastic tumbler and filled it halfway with the yellowish wine. It was a white, not a red. That was about as much as he knew about the stuff.

"Sorry, I don't have wine glasses. But I've got the wine. Comes in handy after taking care of these crazies all day."

She probably meant it as a joke, something to ease the thick tension, but he didn't laugh. He couldn't. The real reason he didn't leave despite being way outside his comfort zone was Mak herself. She didn't deserve to have him act like a complete jerk and bail on her before he'd had a chance to eat the meal she'd probably spent hours pre—"Holy sh—shoot," he said, glancing at the child across from him who was far too busy shoveling spaghetti in her trap to have noticed his near slip-up. "Makenna, this is delicious." And it was. Easily the best meal he had in years, maybe ever.

"Thank you," she said, beaming as though he'd informed her she won the lottery.

"So nummy," Emmie chimed in from her booster seat on the other side of Mak.

"Mak, it's your turn to go first today," the little girl sitting across from him said. She glanced up, big blue eyes fixated on her sister. Thunder knew next to nothing about kids, but he'd spent enough time with Beth over the last year to guess this one was about the same age. Which would put her around five. And she was damned adorable with curly dark brown pigtails, a line of sauce across her cheek, and the buttons on her shirt out of sequence. Mak had said her name was Kelly...no Kira? Kim?

"Oh, I think we'll skip that tonight, Kara," Mak said before taking a small bite of her food.

Kara, right.

Her nose scrunched as she pursed her little lips. "But you always say it's very important." This kid was just adorable and acted like a serious little adult.

"Yeah, Mak," Lee said with a smirk. "You always tell us we can't skip it when it's our week to go first. So get to it."

Poor Makenna's face was so red, she might have been in danger of having a stroke. The color did nothing to detract from how cute she looked in her oversized-T-shirt and joggers with her hair in a lopsided ponytail.

"Okay." She cleared her throat as she gave him a half-smile. "We, uh, have this tradition of going around the table and saying one thing we are grateful for that happened during the week. It's silly," she said, shaking her head, "but I'm trying to instill a sense of gratitude in them for the life we have now...uh, I mean the life we have."

Well, shit. Not only was she a hardworking, responsible adult, she was a damn good parent. The only life lessons he'd learned from his mother was to wrap it up and how to lie to the cops. This was just...sweet and made an odd warmth fill his belly alongside the food.

He watched her as she faced her siblings and said, "Okay, let's see...I'm grateful Toni gave me the day off today because I was able to take Kara and Emmie to the park and play with them all day long." As she ended the sentence, she bopped Emmie on the nose setting off another round of those cute as fuck giggles the toddler gave out so freely. By now, her little face was splattered with sauce and her hands looked like she'd stuck them in red paint.

Makenna wasn't like anyone he'd ever met before. Admittedly his family was more of a shitshow than most, but many of the guys were drawn to club life because of shitty family situations, so he certainly wasn't alone. This set up here was something out of a movie, and he'd have thought they were living a fairytale life if it wasn't for the fact Makenna seemed to be raising all of these children alone. Somewhere along the way, this family endured hard times, maybe even tragedy, and Makenna had stepped up and into the role of parent.

She was pretty damned impressive.

He zoned out as the rest of her siblings said what they were grateful for, until Kara's turn. The seven-year-old smiled with a white milk mustache as she said, "I'm thankful Makenna had an extra job on Saturday night. Now I don't have to wear those shoes with the holes in them anymore." Once done with her announcement, she went back to eating as though she hadn't just shot a harpoon straight through Thunder's heart.

Christ, he hadn't even considered the money it must take to keep all these bodies clothed and mouths fed. No one seemed to think anything of Kara's comment, but he felt rocked to his core.

"I'm thankful for the new Justin Bieber song," Amy said with a wistful sigh.

Thunder couldn't help but laugh at that while Lee snorted.

"What?" Amy asked, glaring at her brother. Then she focused her narrowed eyes on Thunder. "Okay, Mr. Newbie, it's your turn."

Next to him, waves of discomfort rolled off Makenna. "No, Amy, he does not have to participate in our family ritual." She turned to him. "Seriously, you do not have to do this."

"Uh, if we have to, he does too, Mak. You're the one who always says, 'If you're alive and at this table to eat, you have at least one thing to be thankful for.'"

"Kill me now," Mak muttered.

Though he'd rather scalp himself then delve into his feelings in front of a horde of children, poor Mak needed to be put out of her misery. "Okay, I got this." He frowned. When was the last time he'd thought about or expressed gratitude for something? Been a damn long while. "Um, I'm thankful for my brothers—in the motorcycle club."

Kara stuffed a forkful of pasta in her mouth. "Why?" she asked around the food.

"Well, they accept me as I am, no matter where or what I came from."

"Well, duh," Risa said, attention on her food. "They're your brothers." She spoke as though having her family's back was a forgone conclusion. It made him smile to know this girl would never have to question her family's love or loyalty as he had his whole life.

Shit, this meal was making him downright sappy.

His gaze connected with Mak's, and when she gave him a soft smile of thanks, he felt it in his soul. She didn't speak through the remainder of the meal, letting her siblings carry the chaotic conversation. When nothing but crumbs of garlic bread and stuck-on sauce remained on the plates, Lee stood. "Up you go, Amy. We're on dish duty."

Makenna smiled at her brother. "Thanks, Lee." Then she stood. "Kara, let's go take your medicine. I'll be right back," she said to Thunder. "Don't worry about Emmie, she'll be fine there for a minute. She's strapped in the seat."

"Wha—" But Mak was gone with Kara two steps behind. The rest of the gang had disappeared as well, leaving him alone with the sauce-covered two-year-old who was now staring at him.

Christ, please let Makenna come back soon. Never had he felt more like a fish outta water than he did having to watch a small child, even for a few seconds. What was he supposed to do now? He sure as hell couldn't offer her a lap dance, and that's about all he had in his bag of tricks as far as providing entertainment.

The second Kira and Mak disappeared from sight, Emmie wiggled and began to climb out of her booster seat.

Thunder lurched forward, extending an arm though he had no chance of catching her if she fell. "Uh, kid, you allowed to do that?"

"No," Emmie said with an impish smile.

Naughty little shit. It took all he had not to laugh. Makenna probably wouldn't appreciate it if he reinforced the toddler's bad behavior. Looked like he was gonna have to get up and help her. "Here, kid," he said as he started to rise. "Let me get you."

"No!" Emmie said with such strength, he plopped back down without thinking. "I do it by my own self." And wouldn't ya know, she was on the ground and toddling her chubby self his way without so much as a stumble. "Up, peez," she said when she reached him.

He glanced around, but no one had returned.

Guess she's talking to me.

When he held out his arms, she immediately jumped up into them, then settled herself on his lap as though she belonged there. Her big blue eyes stared at him before she yawned so wide, she nearly toppled herself over. Thunder settled his hands on her back.

Was this okay? Was this right? There were rules about touching kids, right?

Shit, what if he was fucking it all up and somehow damaged her?

He was about to suggest she get down and go find Makenna when Emmie flopped forward, face-planting against his chest. "Oh, shi—shoot. Did you hurt yourself?"

Emmie giggled and said, "Gimme a hug."

Uhhh, was that allowed? Beth was big enough, she didn't ask anyone to pick her up and cart her around, and she only ever snuggled with Copper.

He didn't react fast enough. Emmie grabbed his arm and pulled it tighter around her.

Thunder tensed. What now? Were they just supposed to sit here like this?

"I tired," Emmie said. "Sing me a song."

What the fuck? Okay, this had gone too far. He didn't know any kid-appropriate songs like Old Mc Whoever the fuck. All he knew were dance beats he'd ripped his clothes off to.

"Peez," she said, blinking those blue eyes up at him.

He bit off a groan.

How did anyone ever say no to this child? She was like some kind of witch. God help him, he was going to hell for sure, but he began to hum the first song that came into mind. No one needed to know it was full of explicit, x-rated lyrics, hence the humming.

Emmie made a squeaking sound, then her body went lax against him as another giant yawn overtook her. Thunder forced himself to relax as he settled back in the chair with his arms around her. Within seconds, Emmie's back rose and fell in a deep, even rhythm against his arms.

Well, huh, this wasn't so bad. It was kinda nice. She was warm, soft, and smelled powdery. Emmie sighed, and damn if it wasn't the cutest sound he'd ever heard. This little witch had him firmly under her spell, and he might just walk out the door with her.

Okay, that would never happen, but he could enjoy a few moments of cuddles until Mak returned. Warmth spread through him as Emmie burrowed in closer in her sleep. He had a vision of Mak rocking the little girl to sleep every night. It made a smile curl his lips. No wonder she sacrificed and worked so hard for her family. This was surprisingly satisfying.

With a yawn of his own, Thunder rested his head on the back of the chair and closed his eyes. He should be panicking at all these unfamiliar feelings of domesticity.

And he would.

Later.

Chapter Nine

Returning to the dining room would take every ounce of strength Makenna possessed. Bizarre didn't come close to describing the past forty minutes of her life. Why the hell hadn't she politely told Thunder dinner was a family affair and sent him on his way?

He couldn't have more than a few years on her, yet based on their lifestyle discrepancies, they might as well reside on different planets. He was gorgeous, fun, and…free. He spent his time ripping off his clothes for money in clubs and at parties before going on to party even more with his MC brothers. She helped homeschool, wiped dirty butts, dried tears, and managed the mounting bills, all while working as many hours a day as possible.

The poor guy probably regretted his decision to stay the moment his very fine behind hit her shabby chair.

"Mak, I took it. Why are we still standing here?" Kara asked, holding the partly finished cup of water.

With a shake of her head to get her brain in gear, she gently pushed the glass back toward her most serious sister. "You know the drill, Kara, drink the whole thing."

She grumbled as any seven-year-old would, but did as asked. "Ugh," she said when she finished. "Water is so boring."

Mak laughed and kissed the top of her sister's head. "You need any help with schoolwork?" She stowed the empty cup and medication on the top shelf in the bathroom medicine cabinet.

"Nope," she said as she set the glass down on the vanity counter. "All I have is one more page of math. It's an easy one." All the kids were homeschooled using an official online curriculum. Sharing two older than dirt computers made it a mega challenge, but they managed. Amy kept their schedules running smoothly with her beyond-her-fifteen-years sense of responsibility, thank God. Maybe by the time Emmie was ready for Kindergarten, Mak would feel comfortable enough enrolling them in a brick and mortar school, but she'd always been too afraid her father would find her and snatch the kids from a schoolyard.

"All right. I need to head back in and check if Emmie is torturing Thunder. Holler if you need me."

Kara tilted her head. "He's nice."

"He is." Nice to look at. Nice to talk to. Nice to kiss…

"He's different than we are. I think we scared him. Did you see his face when we said what we were thankful for? It was kinda like this." She widened her eyes until they nearly popped from their sockets.

Makenna barked out a laugh. Truer words had never been spoken.

"And did you see all the tattoos on his arms?" Her eyes grew wide and curious. "I like them. I think I'll do that when I'm a grown up too."

Lord, save her from this one. Mak rolled her eyes. "How about we concentrate on the math homework right now, and we can plan your first tattoo sleeve later."

"Okay." As Kara scampered off, Mak sagged against the bathroom counter. As long as she kept moving, her energy level wouldn't peter out. It was times like this when she had a few seconds to slow down and rest against a solid surface, that fatigue overtook, and the weight resting on her shoulders felt heavier than she could bear.

For five seconds, she allowed herself a quick pity party in which she embraced a sliver of jealousy she felt for Thunder's life. For the lives of the women she worked with and their ol' men. They all seemed to not only have their shit together but came across so content. Then the guilt hit as it always did when those thoughts invaded her mind. She loved her siblings and wouldn't trade them for the world. But it sure would be nice to have someone to carry a portion of her load some days.

As incredible as the man was to fantasize about, Thunder wouldn't be looking to take on the role of partner to an overworked, underpaid, stressed-out woman whose only experiences with sex included pleasureless romps with her sixty-something-year-old husband. Add to it the fact she had *technically* kidnapped five minors, fled across multiple state lines, and assumed new identities... Yeah, it was time for her to hike up those big-girl panties and face facts. Thunder wouldn't be the only man to run screaming from her mess.

Any sane man would.

Not that his feelings about her situation mattered. Even if Thunder wanted in her life in a romantic way, she couldn't allow it. Not while her father and husband were out there searching for her. They'd murder him without blinking an eye.

With a hollowness in her chest Mak refused to acknowledge as loneliness, she shuffled her way out of the small bathroom. What right did she have to feel lonely? With five siblings around all the time, she was lucky to have ten minutes of alone time all day. So many people would kill for the family she had, well, the family she lived with, anyway. She was lucky, blessed to have such wonderful siblings in her life. This increasingly frequent battle with feelings of emptiness needed to stop. Since the emotions came entirely from within her, she was the one with the power to stop them.

Shaking her head at the clichéd internal pep talk, Makenna stepped back into the dining room and drew up short. She barely managed to keep an "aww," from escaping.

Where the vacancy in her chest had been seconds before, a warmth filled her to near bursting. Had she ever seen anything more adorable than the sight of Emmie curled up and snoozing away on the handsome biker's lap? Emmie's pudgy little cheek pooched her lips out where it was mashed against Thunder's chest. He'd tipped his head up, resting it against the high back of the chair.

Was he asleep as well?

As the question popped into her head, his big hand began a gentle glide up and down Emmie's back. The toddler sighed in her slumber and seemed to burrow deeper into his chest.

That's a nice chest, isn't it, Emmie?

Sure, Mak had been pressed up against it for entirely different reasons, but she'd enjoyed it just as much.

As she observed them, a flash of Thunder bandaging skinned knees, reading books, and tucking Emmie into bed invaded her psyche. Following that, she pictured him returning from a club meeting and walking up behind her while she prepared a meal similar to tonight's. He'd wrap his strong arms around her and draw her snug against that very chest Emmie occupied...

Mak squeezed her eyes tight, stopping those dangerous, dangerous thoughts of domestic bliss. Shaken to her core, she blew out a breath then opened her eyes to find Thunder still sitting there, rubbing Emmie's back.

As she lifted her gaze from his soothing hand, it connected with his startled eyes. "Uh, hey," she said.

Stunning display of communication, Mak.

He cleared his throat. "Hey."

She waved her hand in his direction. "Sorry about all this. She loves a good snuggle. I should have told her to leave you alone or taken her with me." Mak said, a notch above a whisper as she moved in Thunder's direction, arms outstretched. "Let me get her from you."

His eyes flared wide, and he looked down almost as though he'd forgotten Emmie had passed out all over him. "No, uh, she's okay. You don't need to disturb her. I hear it's never a good idea to wake 'em up."

With a chuckle, Makenna sank into the empty seat next to the cutest duo she'd ever seen. "Yeah, kids can be a bear if you wake them up from a deep sleep. Then again, so can most adults."

"Yeah, unless you come at me with a vat of coffee, don't even think of waking me early," he said with a low laugh.

Mak smiled, and then silence fell, thick and heavy with unease. She'd been mad at him the other night after he stormed off, basically slamming the door in her face. Now, she could barely resist the impulse to snuggle all over him like Emmie. She was also dying to ask him what he meant when he said his brothers accepted him no matter where or what he came from. She'd assumed his life was nothing but fun and games, but maybe this charming man had something in common with her. Maybe he had a past he loathed as well.

They looked at each other across the span of the table. Could this be more awkward? She didn't possess the skills to have a normal conversation with an attractive man, let alone flirt.

Wait, what? *Flirt*? Why the hell would she even think along those lines? Flirting should be dead last on her priority list. Way, way below feeding, clothing, sheltering, and educating the five humans in her care.

"So what—" she started at the same time he said, "Is everything—"

Ugh, this was painful.

He gave her a tight grin.

Why, yes, things could get more awkward.

"Please, go ahead," she said around a tense laugh.

"I was just gonna ask if Kara was okay. You mentioned medicine."

"Oh, yeah." Did he actually care, or was this a question to fill the time and make him seem interested in their drama? "She takes Tegretol for a seizure disorder." When his face turned horrified, she lifted a hand. "Don't worry, she's doing great. Hasn't had a seizure in a year." Since she'd started receiving proper medical care outside the community.

"Wow, that's a lot to deal with."

"It can be." Another uncomfortable laugh/grunt left her. Time to change the subject. "So what was it that brought you here? I assume it wasn't the idea of an amazing dinner party with me and my siblings."

He huffed out a laugh that had Emmie shifting against him. As though it was the most natural thing in the world, he made a shushing noise and rubbed her back. The man didn't even seem conscious of the actions. But Mak sure as hell was cognizant of it. Same way she was aware of the tightening low in her belly.

"No, can't say I expected to walk in on family night." He laughed again then raked his free hand through his hair. "Actually, I came to apologize to you."

Her eyes widened, and she found complete sentences impossible. "Apologize? Why?"

"Shit," he said, looking heavenward as he shook his head.

Mak waited. Resisting the temptation to peek at the ceiling grew near impossible, the longer he stared at it. What was he searching for?

"I was a dick to you the other night," he finally said. "I was trashed, flying high from patching in, and looking to fuck." He winced and glanced down at Emmie. "Sorry."

With a giggle, Mak said, "No worries, she's out."

"Right. Anyway, I was just...fired up, and you were there, and..." He shrugged.

Ouch.

He was drunk, horny, and she was there. What girl wanted to hear those words? Even with her dismal lack of experience, that rejection was evident enough to hurt. Mak swallowed a lump and plastered a smile on her face. This was for the best. Truly. Saved her any awkward conversation about her obligations and inability to start anything up right now—even a strictly physical relationship.

Especially that kind of relationship. It'd lead to nothing but embarrassment and force her to reveal too many secrets from her past.

So instead of letting the seed of his dismissal bloom into insult, she kept up the face smiling. "Don't worry about it. I, uh, figured it was something like that. You don't seem to have an enemy in the world, and I'm pretty sure everyone loves you, so I don't think you're a dick. Don't worry about it."

"All right," he said, flashing her the smile she'd grown accustomed to seeing on his face for the first time that evening. "Friends, then?"

She nodded, but the agreement lodged in her throat. "Friends." It took considerable effort to push that one word off her tongue. It tasted bitter.

"Seems like you have a lot going on," he said in a gentle manner as though he sensed her inner battle.

God, how embarrassing. Last thing she wanted was for him to think she was pining away and mourning the missed opportunity of being his...whatever.

Fling? One-night stand? Hook-up?

She'd lived in the real world long enough to understand that's how most operated, at least those around her age, but the notion was so ridiculous she almost laughed out loud. Instead of obsessing, which was what she didn't want him to think she was doing, she should be thanking him for the reminder of what her life was and wasn't.

"I do," she said with a firm nod. "Have a lot going on. I always do. And I can always use an extra friend. So, thank you. You didn't need to come all the way out here for this, but I'm glad you did. So is Emmie."

With a genuine laugh from Thunder, much of the tension in the room dissolved. "Hell, you won't hear me complaining about a free homecooked meal. It was delicious as fuck, by the way." He winked.

Mak's cheeks heated. This conversation seemed to lighten him back to his usual friendly, cheerful self. His mood was infectious, and she found herself grinning back at him.

"Shit," he said, glancing at the crooked clock on her wall. "I'm due at the clubhouse for church in an hour."

"Oh, okay, let me grab Em—"

Mak's cell rang from the kitchen. "Shit."

That freakin' smile of his was going to be the death of her. It made her want to lick his mouth, and never in a million years would she have expected that thought to cross her mind.

"Go grab it. I'm good for a few more minutes. I'll keep the princess."

"Okay, um, thanks," she said as she darted into the kitchen. Kristy's name shone from her face up, cheap, pay by the minute phone resting on the counter. "Hey, Kristy," she said as she answered.

"Hey, girl, I only have a minute before I gotta get my ass on stage, but I wanted to run something by you." Music pumped in the background, probably from the club where Kristy worked.

"Sure, what do you need?"

"I've got a bartending job for you, kinda like the one you did for the Handlers if you're interested."

If she was interested? Hell, she was always interested in extra cash. "Yes. Definitely interested. Where is it?"

"At another club a town over. Not too far."

"Awesome. Tell them I'm interested, and I can get all the details from you when you have more time."

"Mak, they're not exactly like the Handlers." Kristy's voice had taken on a note of caution.

Mak's forehead scrunched. "What do you mean?"

"They're a little…rougher around the edges. A little less respectful."

She chewed her lower lip. "But I'll just be bartending, right? That's all they want from me."

"Yes," her friend said with finality. "These guys like to drink and always have trouble keeping up with the demand. You'll be busy as hell working the bar, and they pay well. They'll give you five hundred dollars for a four-hour stint."

"Holy shit," she muttered. Five hundred? Five hundred? God, she could really use that extra cash. So what if she had to fend off a few aggressive advances? She'd dealt with far worse. "That's incredible. I'm in, Kristy. So, so in."

There was a long pause before Kristy finally said. "Okay, I'll let them know, and I'll pop over tomorrow with the deets."

"Thank you, Kristy. Seriously. You have no idea how much this will help."

"You're welcome, sweetie. Anytime."

They ended the call, and Mak practically bounced into the dining room.

"Good news?" Thunder asked.

"Uh, yeah, kinda. I got a bartending job for Saturday night that pays really, really well."

"All right, babe, that's awesome." He sounded so genuinely happy for her, she couldn't help but beam at him. As though he'd been around children his whole life, he stood and transferred the sleeping Emmie to her. Once her arms were full of her warm, sleeping sister, who she refused to acknowledge now smelled like Thunder, he leaned in close. "Thank you for dinner," he whispered against her ear. "I owe you one." Then he pressed a lingering kiss to her cheek, and her damn knees wobbled.

On shaky legs, she followed him to the door and watched him jog to his bike. Without looking back, he swung a leg over the beast of a machine, giving her a prime view of his exquisite ass. One quick wave and a wink later, and he was off like a shot.

"Ugh," Mak said to her sleeping sister. "Why, Emmie? Why?"

"Why what?" Lee said from directly behind her.

"Jesus!" Mak yelped, jumping so hard it was a miracle Emmie didn't wake. "You scared me."

"Sorry," he said in a tone that relayed otherwise. "You fucking him?"

Her mouth fell open. "Excuse me?"

Lee tilted his head and folded his arms across his chest, looking much older than his eighteen years. "I asked if you're fucking him."

"Yeah, I heard you. I just can't believe you asked me that." Especially with the way his social life had been going. Though she had no actual proof, she was pretty sure he'd been hooking up with random girls every chance he got. Another young adult experience he'd embraced to the max. And what the hell could she say about it? She sure as hell hadn't had any kind of normal dating life as a teenager. She'd been pure as the driven snow until her nineteenth birthday when she'd been married off and spent the night, legs spread while a sixty-year-old man tried his damnedest to knock her up. What kind of advice, warnings, or education could she impart on him? None he'd take seriously. So she made sure his stash of condoms never ran dry because the last thing they needed around the house was another mouth to feed.

Lee shrugged, then turned and began to walk back toward his bedroom.

"Wait, Lee, hold up," Mak said as she rubbed a hand across her forehead where an ache was firing up. "Um, I'm gonna need you to watch the kids again this Saturday night. I got a really great paying—"

"Seriously?" he asked with a roll of his eyes. "I can't this weekend, find someone else to be on babysitting duty."

"Are you working the closing shift at the pizza parlor?" Crap, she hadn't even considered his schedule before agreeing to the job. Still, the money was so good, maybe he could swap shifts with someone.

He dropped his gaze and kicked at the frayed edge of the shabby runner lining the front hallway. "Nah, I'm not working."

"Well, if it's a party, can you go late? Or skip it? Lee, it's five hundred dollars for four hours of work. That's insane, and we could really use it."

Still looking at the floor, he sighed. "Fucking sick of always needing money."

He didn't make a ton at his job, but it took so much pressure off her to have another earner in the house. She still paid the majority of the bills to allow him some spending money, but he definitely contributed. In fact, she'd thought he was feeling pretty good about his own money situation since getting the job.

"I know, Lee. It's why I've been taking more jobs." Having parental conversations with him never came easy. Whether it was the closeness in their ages, their size difference, or the fact she never felt like she had any idea what the hell she was doing, acting as a maternal figure to him proved a challenge. Having difficult conversations about his life made her feel like a fraud. "Um, I thought you were doing okay with the money you made at—"

"I'm not working there anymore."

She blinked. "What?"

"I lost the job. The freaking dictators who run the place said I was late too many times. Such bullshit."

Mak swallowed. Tread carefully. "Wow, ah, when did this happen?"

With a shrug, he leaned against the wall. "Dunno. A week ago, I guess."

A *week* ago? "Jesus, Lee, why didn't you say anything? And how have you been paying for stuff?"

He shrugged again. "Been using what I had saved up."

She pressed a hand to her suddenly queasy stomach. "Lee, that was the money you were starting to save for the future. To maybe get an apartment, or maybe go to college someday. To have...more." It'd been something she'd been adamant about when he started working in the last place they'd lived. No matter how much he made, she insisted he put a small percentage aside.

"Yeah, well, I got shit to do now."

Blowing out a breath, Mak willed herself not to get angry. That route never worked with Lee. As difficult as it was to feel like his guardian, he never seemed to see her that way either. If she got a little lecture happy, he would shut down. "So, are you gonna look for another job? I might be able to get you something at the diner."

His audible snort had her frowning. "No, thanks. Love you, sis, but I'm not interested in working with you and living with you. Too much togetherness."

Okay, well that kinda smarted, but again...eighteen-year-old boy. "Well, I'm sure there are plenty of places looking for help with the summer coming up soon. Tourist season and all that. And since school will be done soon, you'll be able to work more hours."

Finally, he lifted his gaze. "Ehh, not sure I want to work right now."

Say what?

What the hell did he think he was going to be doing all summer? And what happened to the mature, responsible, caring brother who'd rescued her, protected her, and supported her throughout their childhood? Was this just a normal period of rebellion or a symptom of a deeper problem?

"Look," he cut in before she was able to pursue the troubling statement, "I'll watch them this Saturday since it's so much money, but from now on, you gotta make other arrangements, okay?"

Forcing back a sigh of frustration, Makenna nodded. She couldn't afford a blow-up with him right now. "Sure."

"If it's far in advance, you can ask me, but not a few days out."

"Fair enough." But was it? No, none of it was fair. Hell, her whole life had been unfair. And when had she started thinking along the lines of fair anyway? Those thoughts led to nothing but bitterness and misery.

Because fair would be sharing an apartment with a group of girlfriends. Fair would be taking Thunder up on his offer the other night. Fair would be never having had to marry a man three times her age. It'd be fair if she'd been allowed to dream of a future. To make goals, work toward a satisfying career, to have a life of her own. Fair would be cutting her list of responsibilities down by about ninety percent.

Wasting brain power and time on *fair* was a fool's errand. Maybe that was the lesson Lee needed to learn.

"Great, thanks. Hey, I'm going out in a bit. Don't wait up," he said, then strode down the hall toward his bedroom.

What the hell had happened to her beloved brother? To the boy who helped her get the kids to bed every night? To the teen who snuck her icepacks after each punishment? To the young man who carried more than his share of the weight as they escaped the community? What happened to the boy who kept her sane when she feared they'd made a huge mistake in leaving? When she'd been too busy working every hour possible to properly take care of everyone, Lee had jumped in and kept the kids happy.

Where had that boy gone?

With a sigh, she stared down the empty hall. That boy had grown into a young man who realized all that had been stolen from him in his young life.

For a few moments tonight, while Emmie slept on Thunder's chest, she had a glimpse of what life would be like with a man. It'd be so easy to close her eyes tonight and run with that fantasy. Let it morph into a dream where Thunder played a starring role, her siblings had a father figure to look up to, and she had a partner to walk through life with. But she wouldn't allow herself to indulge in those domestic thoughts. Instead, she'd let the evening be what it was.

A beautiful illusion.

Chapter Ten

Days later, Thunder still couldn't get the time he spent at Makenna's out of his mind. He'd left, feeling...weird. Off-kilter, in a way he couldn't quite come to terms with. The following day at work, he'd been so distracted Zach had nearly kicked his ass out the door when he'd tried for the tenth time to get Thunder's attention. Throughout his shift, he continually zoned out, replaying every aspect of his conversations with Makenna.

The woman was incredible. How she made it through each day with a smile on her face knowing the height of responsibility piled on her plate baffled him. Despite all he'd glimpsed of her home life, he had a feeling it'd been the tip of the iceberg. Mak had a past. An ugly, dirty, grimy past that led her to become the mother to her five younger siblings. None of them had hinted at such a story, but bits and pieces of the Makenna-puzzle were starting to fall into place.

They'd popped up in town not long ago.

They had very limited funds.

She homeschooled the kids.

They didn't seem to have any extended family connections to speak of or friends from where they'd lived previously.

Little signs of someone who'd fled and didn't want their past catching up with them. He got that. He'd practically run from the small town in Kentucky where he'd been raised. In the years he'd been gone, he hadn't spoken to his mother, stepfather, or any of the people he'd grown up around. Growing up in a brothel with a mother who cared little for him and didn't shield him from her dysfunctional lifestyle ensured he had no desire to revisit his past.

Ever.

The urge to ask what set Makenna's life on its current trajectory grew each time he'd seen her over the past few days, which was often. What could he say? He was a single guy, living with a single roommate. Neither could cook for shit. Visiting the diner for breakfast daily just made sense. He had time to shoot the shit with his brothers and start the day with hot coffee and a delicious meal.

Okay, fine, sometimes he stopped by for lunch, as well.

He was a hungry guy. Had nothing to do with the genuine smile Makenna had for him whenever he walked through the jingling door. Nothing at all. And nothing to do with the way his dick got hard whenever he caught a glimpse of her round ass in those jeans she liked to wear.

True to his word, he acted like a friend; treated her the same he treated his brothers' ol' ladies. Only problem was, those women didn't get him to half chub whenever someone spoke their names. Whatever voodoo magic Mak possessed, it'd fucked something up inside him. He'd turned down three cash offers from bored housewives looking for a good time. Ones willing to compensate him greatly for the privilege of blowing him. Weird, but who the fuck was he to turn down extra cash on top of an orgasm? A man fucked in the head, that's who he was. All he could think of was Makenna. In the past, sleeping with one woman while wanting another had never been a problem. Actually, it'd been preferable for him to fantasize about a woman he actually wanted to fuck as it got him through banging some pretty unappealing broads. But this hold Makenna had over him wasn't the same. It wasn't just the desire to fuck her—which he had in spades, just ask his right hand—but he also wanted to hang out with her, ease her burdens, and make her laugh.

See those cute kids again.

Fucking insane.

"Hey, dude, what the fuck is up with you tonight?"

Thunder jolted then blinked at Maverick, who stood with his tattooed arms crossed over his thin chest. His eyebrow with a barbell through it had risen far into his forehead.

"Sorry, you say something to me?" Thunder asked, as he stretched his arms overhead. Anything to get his blood flowing and mind in the game.

"Yeah, brother, I've been talking at you for about three minutes. You're on another fucking planet." Maverick propped his hip against the bar and shook his head as Monty offered up a bottle of whiskey. "What gives?"

"No, thanks, Mont. We're rolling out in a few. And nothin's up. Just got some shit on my mind."

Mav cocked his head. "Shit you need the club's help with?" For someone who typically didn't speak without making a sexual innuendo, Mav could buckle down and be as serious as fuck when it came to club business.

"Nah, personal shit." Thunder waved a hand in front of his face. "For real, it's nothing, brother. Don't give it a thought. I'm done with the zombie routine."

For a moment, Maverick remained serious, then a shit-eating grin split his lips. "Personal, huh? That means one thing and one thing only. Pussy troubles. What's wrong, brother? Couldn't make the cat purr last night?"

The fuck? "You're a demented fucker, you know that, right?"

With a snort, Mav nodded. "So Steph tells me every day. Night, too." He winked. "It's what she loves most about me."

Shaking his head, Thunder snorted. "All right, what the fuck's our game plan for tonight?" He started walking toward a table, but Mav stopped him with a hand on his arm.

"You sure you're good for this? I need your head in the game. No one will fault you for having your own stress, but if I need to find someone to cover for you, I need to know now because we leave in ten."

Oh, he was good for it. Dying to get revenge for Viper. Time to table all thoughts of Makenna, his neglected dick, and his fucked-up head. Tonight, the club got one hundred percent of his focus. "I'm straight, Mav. Promise. You got my full attention."

With a nod, Mav slapped him on the back. "Good man," he said. "Let's go sit."

Thunder followed him to a square four-person table. Once settled, Mav pulled out a tablet. "Okay, I've got a few cameras positioned in some areas that give us a view of the CDMC's clubhouse. There aren't stellar angles, but they give us a good idea of how many people are coming and going and shit like that." He pulled up an app on the tablet that revealed a split-screen view of four camera angles.

One had a fairly solid view of the parking lot, one the rear of the warehouse the CDMC claimed as their clubhouse, one was too far to see much more than a grainy image of the building, and the fourth had a view of two doors on the side of the building.

"Where do these doors lead?" asked Thunder, pointing to the image of the side doors.

Mav shrugged. "Not sure. Haven't seen them used much. One might go to the main level, and my guess is a basement for the other."

"Hmm." Thunder scratched his chin as he focused on the screen.

"Whatcha thinking?" Mav sat back in his seat and gave Thunder his full attention.

"I'm wondering how close we can get to the place. I know it's too fucking risky to try to get inside, especially after what happened with Screw and his man, but once they're all trashed and distracted, we might be able to creep around outside. I'd fucking kill to know where that door goes. Shit, they could store all their guns in there if it goes underground."

About six weeks ago, Screw and Gumby had gone to a party at the CDMC's clubhouse. They'd hoped to gather some intel incognito, and the plan would have worked if it hadn't been for their ol' lady's neighbor who recognized them and outed the pair to the CDMC's enforcer, Crank. The night almost ended in disaster, but Gumby and Screw managed to get out with nothing more than shit in their pants and pounding hearts.

Well, that and a new set of assholes courtesy of a furious Copper. They might have failed to mention their plan to the prez before charging full speed ahead. Thunder hoped to avoid that foolish mistake. Only sanctioned actions for him.

Twisting his lower lip, Maverick seemed to consider their options. Thunder remained quiet, giving him a minute or two to think.

"Here's the thing," he said. "Their security is shit. It was when Screw and G went there, and even now, they haven't beefed it up. We can get damn close without being on their property, and no one will ever notice us. Let's stick to our side of the fence tonight. If we like what we see, we'll try to get beyond the gates another time. Sound like a plan?"

"Works for me," Thunder said with a nod. No point in arguing with the man who'd worked in the security biz for more than a decade. Mav knew surveillance like the back of his hand. What the hell did Thunder know beyond shaking his ass and making women come?

Maybe it was time to start thinking a little more seriously about a career. Working at the gym was great and all, but it wasn't exactly his passion. He worked out to stay fit and look good and training others to do the same paid the bills for now, but Thunder didn't envision a long future of coaching mildly motivated gym newbies or even fitness enthusiasts. Just wasn't for him.

Over the years, he'd had a few ideas of jobs he could turn into a career. One thought, in particular, kept creeping into his brain, but it was so ridiculous, he'd never given it more than a few moments of brainpower.

"Okay, let's roll," Mav said. "No bikes. We're taking a cage." He rose from the table and motioned for Thunder to follow.

"Figured as much," Thunder said, hopping up and jogging after his brother. "Quieter and easier to go unnoticed if we're not cruising in with roaring pipes."

"Yep. Gimme one second."

Thunder followed Mav with his gaze as the man bounded halfway up the staircase. On her way down, his ol' lady, Stephanie, met him halfway. They spoke a few low words back and forth before Mav shook his head. Steph frowned while planting her hands on her hips.

It took an enormous amount of effort for Thunder to keep from laughing. Without hearing a word, he knew exactly how that conversation was going. The petite, blond, former FBI agent was asking her tatted-up biker boyfriend why the fuck he wouldn't let her tag along. Mav would be throwing out some bullshit reasons having to do with him being unable to fully concentrate if she were there and had to worry about her.

Steph narrowed her eyes, clearly gearing up for a fight when Mav whispered something in her ear. The change in her was really something to see. She melted against her man, and then they were kissing like they'd been apart for months.

Instead of shifting his gaze, because this sure as fuck wasn't the first time he'd seen those two swapping spit, Thunder watched as he'd done with Gumby and Screw the other day. Sure, they were hot, sexy, fired up, and all that, but as with G and Screw, there existed an intimacy to their kiss that came from something deeper than mere physical attraction.

An ache pulsed low in Thunder's gut.

Christ, he needed to take a few dancing jobs, maybe get himself laid, and remember who he was and what kind of life he lived. If he kept on this ridiculous daydreaming path, he'd turn into a romantic sap in no time. He'd end up like his mother, tying himself to someone only to end up with holes in his heart and bitterness in his soul.

Thunder rolled his shoulders. "Yo, Mav, think you can try trying to crawl down your ol' lady's throat so we can get this shit done?"

They pulled apart without so much as a hint of embarrassment. Steph wiped Mav's mouth with her thumb then gave him a smile that absolutely did not pinch Thunder's heart. Then, after one final ass grab, Mav was jogging down the stairs.

"Stay safe out there, Thunder," Steph called out with a wave. "And keep his inked ass in line."

Thunder nodded and waved back. "You got ink on your ass, too, brother?"

Mav snorted and preceded Thunder out the door. "I got ink everywhere."

With a laugh, Thunder bumped Mav's shoulder. "Well, not *everywhere,* I'm sure."

Mav stopped walking and pierced Thunder with a mischievous look. "Everywhere."

No fucking way. "You telling me you inked your junk, brother?"

Walking once again, Mav nodded. "Yep. Wanna see?"

"I kinda do. I've never seen one as small as a baby carrot. I'm curious," he said, straight-faced.

Mav snorted. They reached a pick-up owned by the club, and Mav walked around toward the driver's side. Yanking it open, he said, "I'd drop trou right now, but we don't have time. Takes me a good fifteen minutes to pack this python back in my jeans."

"You fucking wish." With a laugh, Thunder slid into the passenger seat and removed his cut. Wearing that anywhere near the CDMC clubhouse was like a deer prancing in front of a hunter with a bright red target painted on their fur.

An hour later, they parked on the side of the road about half a mile down from the CDMC's clubhouse. The old warehouse sat about a mile off the highway. At one point, there had been three or four other businesses in the area, but all were long gone. One of the other buildings had suffered fire damage a few years ago. A few others remained in disrepair. The CDMCs warehouse-turned-clubhouse was set further behind the other buildings. The club put fifteen-foot chain-linked razor wire fencing around the entire perimeter, leaving only one way on and off the property. Most of the property immediately outside the fence consisted of overgrown brush and wooded areas.

The setup worked perfectly for Mav and Thunder, who didn't need to be on the property, just close enough to get a feel for what was happening, but if they found something worth the risk of scaling the fence, both could manage it. Barbed wire and all.

"Place is fucking hoppin'," Mav mumbled as they pushed aside branches to see through the fence.

They stood side by side in all black with matching dark skull caps behind two adjacent trees. This vantage point provided a clear view of the entrance to the clubhouse where hordes of thirsty partiers had been flowing in for the past five minutes.

"It is. The investigation sure didn't hurt their numbers."

Mav grunted.

"Where's that side door?" Thunder asked in a low voice. "I wanna lay eyes on it, see if it gets any action. If it's quiet, maybe we can hop this fucker and get a closer look."

Though it was dark as fuck in the area around the clubhouse, Thunder could make out the whites of Mav's eyes. "I don't know...you up for that climb?"

"Fuck yeah. I'm young and agile, brother. You, on the other hand, might need to wait here on the ground for me."

"Fucker," Mav whispered.

Chuckling to himself, Thunder turned his attention back to the entrance.

"Let's give it a bit until there aren't so many of these assholes hanging around outside," Mav said.

They watched in silence as the CDMC's members and their guests packed the place. Every time a biker in a CDMC cut strolled through his field of vision, Thunder found himself with curled fists and a clenched jaw.

Had that fucker laughed and cheered when he found out the news of Viper's death?

Had he given Jeremy the grenade that crashed through the window and destroyed the diner?

"You're fucking tense, man," Mav said after a few moments.

"Can't help it. Wondering how many of these fuckers partied when they heard about Viper's death." And fantasizing about setting fire to the whole damned compound. Oh, that would be sweet.

"I feel ya," Mav said. "But Viper would be the first one to tell you to hold steady and not do something rash. You charging out there and getting yourself fucking killed would only ensure Viper beats your ass in the afterlife. We'll get our revenge, brother. Every one of us wants it bad."

Thunder shook out his arms. Mav was right. Viper hadn't been one to act on blind emotion. He was rational and thought through his actions, and Thunder would be disrespecting his memory if he gave into his murderous impulse. So he rolled his shoulders and said, "I'm cool."

Women seemed to be the predominant attendees at this party. Beyond the club members, that was. Tall, short, thin, plump, blond, brunette; women of all kinds filed into the clubhouse. Some were accompanied by bikers in CDMC cuts, some solo, and some in groups with their friends. Distinguishing the difference between sweet butts and randoms from town wasn't easy as they all had two things in common: sky-high heels and itty-bitty clothes. Lots of jiggling assets were on full display tonight.

"Hey, I know her," Mav said about fifteen minutes later. "You worked with her, right? What's her name?"

"Who?" Thunder asked, scanning the mob the best he could, given the poor lighting. Unable to tell exactly where Mav pointed, he narrowed his eyes and examined each face approaching the door.

"Kristy. I think that's her name. Stripper you used to work with. Tall, long brown hair. She's danced at our clubhouse a buncha times."

"Oh, yeah," Thunder said as he continued to look for her. Now that he knew who he was trying to locate, he focused on the taller women. "She dances here a lot, too. Says they pay real good but ain't much on the word no. Think she might be fucking one of 'em. Maybe the prez, Blade."

"Jesus, why? I heard that guy's a sadistic fuck."

Thunder shrugged though he knew Mav couldn't see him well. "Job security, maybe. Who knows why she does half the shit she does? But Kristy can handle herself." Ahh, there she was, strutting in on pointy heels with a dress barely covering her fit ass. Next to her and about six inches shorter was the one and only woman he'd noticed wearing pants. Kristy's friend also had a wide strapped tank top that didn't even show off her tits. With her more conservative outfit, the woman stuck out like a sore thumb.

Wait a minute…

The way she dressed and her slightly stiff posture reminded him of—

"Oh, fuck," Thunder said on a sharp exhale as though he'd been socked in the gut. He grabbed the fence and shoved his face against the links as though it'd give him a closer view. His stomach lurched, and a red haze filled his field of vision.

What the fuck is she doing here?

"What's wrong?" Mav asked, body tensing and readying for action.

"That's Makenna."

Chapter Eleven

"Hey, thanks for riding with me, Kristy," Mak said as she put her rattletrap of a car in park in the lot of a vast warehouse.

"No problem." Kristy flipped the dome light on, tugged down the visor, and gave her face a good once-over. She must have decided the layers of makeup she already had on weren't enough because she reapplied her lipstick and freshened her mascara. The innocuous and probably routine moves had Makenna squirming in her seat. She wore a tinted moisturizer, a pale pink lip gloss, a light dusting of shimmery eyeshadow, and one coat of mascara. That was all, and it felt like gallons of goop on her face. Makeup was forbidden in the community—way too likely to make girls interested in the outside world or become sluts—and by the time she was out and taking care of five siblings, learning the subtle art of dressing up her face never became a priority. Now she wished she'd taken Kristy up on her offer of help.

Same with her clothes. After her bartending gig last weekend, she'd decided to go with comfort over style this time around, pairing dark skinny jeans with a conservative black tank top and flats.

Based on the hordes of women walking into the clubhouse, she was gonna stick out like a tan crayon in a box of hot pinks.

"You'll be okay to get yourself home without me, right?" Kristy asked before popping her pouty lips a final time in the mirror. She turned in her seat and gave Mak a dazzling smile. "I'll be dancing for a bit, but then I'll probably end up sticking around all night."

"Uh, yeah, I'm good. I appreciate you riding with me since I've never been out this way, but I got it from here."

"All right, girl, let's get on in there. Don't want you to be late." Kristy opened the door and stepped out of the thirteen-year-old Chevy Malibu as though emerging from a stretch limousine.

With a churning stomach and thumping heart, Mak stood from the driver's seat in time to catch Kristy adjusting her skintight, hot pink dress over her envy-inducing ass. With a little shimmy, she tugged the skirt down her hips only to have it ride right back up the moment she lifted her arms to plump her breasts. The thing fit so snug to Kristy's body, Mak had no idea how she could walk, let alone dance. However, clothes weren't exactly a requirement in her performance. Looked like the silver zipper running the length of Kristy's dress would come in handy. Especially since the thing already seemed to be halfway undone, giving the world a generous view of her cantaloupe-sized breasts.

Five hundred dollars. Five hundred dollars.

It'd become her mantra over the past few days, keeping her from canceling as she'd wished she could.

"Let's get this over with," she mumbled as she shuffled after her friend.

"What'd you say?" Kristy asked, but her attention diverted to the door where a burly man was checking over each person who entered the clubhouse.

"Nothing."

With each step closer to the entrance, Mak's stomach wound tighter. Truth of the matter was, she'd rather be anywhere else. The distinct smell of weed and booze permeated the air, increasing in strength as they neared the building. It brought back memories of living in the community when the men would get high and tromp out into a field to shoot beer bottles. Those nights had been the worst. Hours of sleeplessness, listening to hundreds of rounds of gunfire before Roger came home, ranting about her ineffectiveness as a wife. He'd fall on top of her stinking of marijuana and stale beer as he demanded she spread her legs.

Sighing, she shook off the memories. If she could survive those nights, she could make it through a few hours tending bar for this MC. Though, she had a feeling this wasn't going to be the same kind of fun and welcoming experience as last week's gig at the Handlers' clubhouse.

A low-pitched whistle had Mak's gaze snapping up to the huge man standing by the entrance to the clubhouse.

"Damn, woman," he said to Kristy. "You are smokin' tonight. Blade's gonna have you bent over for his cock within minutes of seeing you."

As Mak's jaw fell, Kristy let out a laugh and spun around her arms outstretched. "You think so?"

Seriously? She said it as though the idea of some guy screwing her in the middle of the clubhouse was a good thing.

"Know, so, babe. Hope you're ready for him. He's in a shit mood, so you'll be getting it good tonight," the giant said as he winked.

Kristy patted his massive chest as she sashayed by. "Pretty sure you remember how well I can handle myself, big boy."

The giant laughed then shifted his attention to Mak, who stood there gaping like she'd never seen a man talk to a woman before. "Well, well," he said, playful smile turning into more of a hungry leer. "Who do we have here?"

Kristy rested a fuchsia-tipped hand on his round shoulder. "This is Makenna," she said. "She'll be working the bar tonight with PeeWee and Level."

"Gotcha." He took a step forward. "Arms out, babe."

"Huh?" Mak looked at Kristy then back to the giant.

"No one comes in here without being checked for weapons first."

"Oh, uh, sure." She extended her arms. Made sense. He must not have checked Kristy because he knew her. Either that or he could sense there wasn't anywhere for her to hide anything bigger than a matchstick.

Two large paws landed on her hips then trailed down her legs in what seemed to be much more of a caress than a pat-down. She tensed as he began to trail up the insides of her thighs. The higher he coasted, the more uncomfortable she became until she yelped as he blatantly brushed a hand over her crotch.

Instead of apologizing, he winked and continued the search, cupping her breasts before Kristy finally cleared her throat and ended Mak's torture.

"Dude, seriously, if she's late, I'm blaming you." Kristy rolled her eyes and huffed.

Mak's face felt about a thousand degrees, and the second his hands left her body, she folded her arms over her breasts. If she could have curled into a ball and rolled away, she would have.

Five hundred dollars. Five hundred dollars.

"All right," he said with a chuckle. "She's clean. Though I don't know how long she'll stay that way in there." He jerked a thumb over his shoulder. "Fresh meat as pristine as her oughta be real popular."

Mak swallowed a rise of nausea.

Another eye-roll had Kristy slinging her arm across Mak's shoulders. "Pretty sure you won't be getting any from her," she snapped as she propelled Mak into the building. "Fucking inbred idiot," she muttered under her breath.

Mak's forehead scrunched. "If you think he's an idiot, why did you..."

Glancing down at her, Kristy's lips curved. "Let him fuck me?"

Mak nodded.

Thunder

Shrugging, Kristy said, "He's got big muscles and an even bigger dick. Plus, you'd never know it, but the asshole is loaded. Walked away with some serious cash the next morning."

Well, that answer certainly didn't clear up anything. Just as she was about to ask Kristy if she slept with many of the club members for money, the main room of the CDMC clubhouse came into view.

She stopped dead in her tracks.

Holy crap.

The place was packed wall to wall with bodies moving to the music. Based on the music alone, she could tell the vibe was completely different from that of the Hell's Handlers. Scream, heavy metal blared thought the speakers. Men leered at women, grabbing and groping all around them. A completely naked woman danced on a table ten feet away. Was that what Kristy was about to do?

Holy crap

Kristy laughed, and Mak looked at her. "What?"

"You look like a frightened deer. Tits up, girl. You need to wipe that expression off your face because, like BD said back there, the flies will swarm if they think you're fresh, tender meat."

Five hundred dollars. Five hundred dollars.

Mak trailed after Kristy, ignoring everyone who spoke to her neighbor as they made their way to the bar. What she couldn't ignore was everything happening on the perimeter of the room. The very first thing she saw as she turned her head was a man sitting on a ratty couch against the wall with his legs spread wide. A woman knelt between his thighs, clearly sucking his dick. His eyes were closed, head was thrown back in pleasure, and hand fisted in the woman's hair, jerking her up and down on his erection.

At the end of the very same couch, another woman lay bent over the armrest with her feet on the floor, hands braced on a cushion. She had a glazed-over shine in her eyes.

Was she even aware of her surroundings?

Behind her, a man with his pants around his knees fucked into her while making out with yet another girl.

Jesus.

Mak averted her eyes, turning her head forward. She'd seen enough. Last week she couldn't tear her gaze from Maverick and Stephanie going at it in the Handlers' clubhouse. This scene could not have differed more and turned her stomach.

The entire place smelled like marijuana and had a smoky haze to it. She had to hustle to keep up with Kristy, who'd stopped to talk to another man in a Chrome Disciples cut.

"Where's Blade?" Kristy asked.

The man shrugged. "Don't fucking know." He held a hand up toward Kristy's face. A trail of white powder ran from his thumb to his wrist. "You want?"

Kristy's eyes lit. "Yesss."

The guy jerked his hand away. "You gonna give me a shot at that pussy tonight?"

With a pout, Kristy shrugged. "Up to Blade. You know the drill, Crank."

The man with the crooked nose and messed up ear who Kristy referred to as Crank, fingered the silver zipper resting just below the center of her breasts. "You ain't his ol' lady," he said, voice thick.

If the floor could have opened up and swallowed her whole, Mak would have welcomed it. Since Kristy was the only other person she knew in the entire place, she had no choice but to stand there like a moron and wait until Kristy finished doing… whatever with this guy so her friend could introduce her to who she'd be working with.

A husky laugh left Kristy. "Like that matters? I'm being fucked by your president. You want a piece, you ask him."

A chill ran down Mak's spine. Her friend's statement reminded her way too much of life in the community. The parallel wasn't one she'd picked up on when hanging around the Handlers, but was this club life? Women viewed as property? Shell, Toni, Jazz, and Holly sure didn't act as though owned by their club. Hell, if anything, their men seemed owned by the women.

Well, maybe not, but each relationship she'd seen in the Handler's club spoke of a true partnership.

Not ownership.

She shuddered. Never again.

"I just might do that," Crank said, pulling the zipper down another inch.

All Kristy did was nod, as though this behavior was so familiar to her, it didn't even register. "You know where to find me."

It was then Crank turned his attention to Mak, and she couldn't help but take a step back at his assessing gaze. The once-over didn't come across as curious, but malicious. As though he was searching for some way to use her, regardless of her desires. "This our barmaid for tonight?" Crank asked with a raised eyebrow.

"Yep," Kristy said. "Makenna, this is Crank, the enforcer for the Disciples. If you think he seems like an asshole, you're wrong. He's much worse."

When Crank laughed so loud heads turned their way, Mak's eyes widened. "Changed my mind, Kristy," he said, licking his lower lip. Then he faced Makenna. "Two hours of work, then you get a break. Ask around for me then."

Uhh, what?

No, no, no. That would not be happening. She sent Kristy a panicked look.

Kristy frowned as she looped her arm through Mak's, but it only lasted a second before she replaced it with an overconfident smile. "Catch ya later, Crank." She dragged Makenna toward the bar, then stopped and spun. "Listen, Mak, whatever you do, do not end up alone with that man, do you hear me?"

"Um, yeah, I hear you." The warning wasn't necessary. She had no plans to wander off anywhere with Crank. Her hands shook, so she stuck them in her back pockets.

"I mean it, Mak. He's a sadistic fucker who'll eat you alive and spit out whatever's left, and I promise you it won't be much. You cannot handle him, and he senses it. It'll make him want you more. I don't care what you have to do, do not end up alone with him. Repeat it back to me because I'll be dancing soon and won't be able to keep an eye on you the whole night."

"Kristy, I won't end up alone with him. Promise. Trust me, I'm not looking for any kind of trouble. I'm here for one reason and one reason only."

Five hundred dollars. Five hundred dollars.

With a nod, Kristy delivered her to the end of the bar. "Level!" she yelled above the booming music.

A man around Mak's age with a three-inch blonde mohawk and no other hair turned their way. "Hey." He lifted his chin in their direction.

"Got your help for the night," Kristy said, tilting her head toward Mak.

"Fucking finally," he called as he uncapped a bottle of beer. "Send her on back."

"All right, girl. Good luck. Gotta get my ass up on one of the tables and start dancing. You good?"

Was she good? No, but, "Yeah, all good."

Kristy kissed her cheek then flounced her way into the crowd, stopping every two seconds to chat with someone new.

"Hey, babe," the man called Level said as he wandered her way. "Come on back." He gave her a blatant up and down assessment, lingering on her breasts. The brazen staring made her skin crawl until he wrinkled his nose. Then her cheeks heated, and she wished to sink through the floor. Guess she didn't quite pass muster.

"You party here before?" he asked.

She shook her head. "No. Not really my usual scene, to be honest."

He snorted. "Figured that shit out. Hope you can hack it; gonna get busy as fuck in here in a few."

"I'll be fine." Hopefully the words would convince him over the slight tremor in her voice.

With an unconvinced shrug, he turned away from her. Was she supposed to follow?

When he turned and whistled like she was a dog, she hurried to catch up.

He spent the next few minutes showing her the ropes while also managing to run the bar. She met their third counterpart for the evening, a short slender man with a shaved head named Pee Wee who sneered at her, and that was the extent of the acknowledgment. At least Level had come across somewhat personable even if he seemed completely unimpressed by her in every way.

"Hope you ain't one of those bitches who freaks out every time a guy asks her to suck his dick," he said as he pointed out where they stored the glasses. "Cuz it's gonna fuckin' happen, and I don't wanna hear shit about it. Suck it the fuck up and move on."

This was a mistake. A serious mistake. Her heart pounded. Maybe she should leave.

Kara needs shoes. Lee isn't working.

"It's n-no big deal," she said because what else was she supposed to say? That the thought of being propositioned made her skin crawl and her stomach bubble? Yeah, that'd be a surefire way to watch her cash fly out the window.

She could do this. She was strong, resilient, driven. Catcalls and propositions were merely words. A wooden bar separated her from the rest of the men. She'd be safe. She'd be fine.

Please let that be true.

"Right. You set? Can't hold your hand all night." he said, as he rubbed the back of his neck. With a silver spike through his left nostril, a dark bruise under one eye, and a tattoo of a giant spider making its way up his neck, he didn't make a comfortable picture to look at, so she stared out at the crowd.

"Yep, I got this." Hopefully, she sounded confident instead of terrified.

"Okay, let me know if you need somethin' but try not to bitch, too. I don't have time for that shit."

Right. She had about two seconds to continue feeling fear before someone signaled her to grab a beer and a shot of tequila. Within minutes she became so busy she barely had time to pull her hair up off her sweaty neck.

Two hours whizzed by in the blink of an eye. She kept her head down, ignored the lewd gesture and words, and served drinks like her life depended on it. By the time Level motioned for her to take a twenty-minute break, her feet ached, she stunk of booze, and she'd been asked no less than two dozen times if she'd like to suck some guy's dick or find him when she was done so he could, "dick her into next Tuesday."

Literally, three guys had used those exact words. These guys were as clever as they were appealing.

She needed a freakin' break.

"Bathroom?" she yelled to Pee Wee as she walked toward the end of the bar.

Of course, he didn't answer her with actual words, he'd not once uttered a sound her way, but he pointed a black-tipped finger toward a hallway in the far left corner of the clubhouse.

"So helpful," she muttered under her breath. Without wasting any time, Mak kept her head down and speed-walked in the general direction Pee Wee had pointed. Or at least, she thought she did. Weaving her way through a crowded room of huge, grabby-handed drunk bikers might have veered her off course. By the time she made it to the dim hallway, Mak was dying for a shower. Literally every guy she'd passed had put his hands on her in some fashion. What the hell was with them thinking they had the right to touch any woman in any way?

Bullshit.

For the life of her, she couldn't understand why any woman would willingly subject themselves to this life. She'd sacrificed everything to escape a scenario where she was treated like property.

The second she returned home, she'd be scrubbing off the top five layers of skin.

Five hundred dollars. Five hundred dollars.

The mantra was the only thing preventing her from turning toward the exit instead of the bathroom. Thankfully, the hallway leading to the restroom was momentarily deserted, which gave her a chance to lean against the wall and catch her breath, unobserved.

Tonight was the first and last time she'd be stepping foot in this clubhouse regardless of the cash. No amount of money was worth a repeat of fielding the disgusting comments and unwelcome groping that had been lobbed at her all night. She'd just beg Toni for extra shifts at the diner. Or maybe it was time to find a steadier second job.

As Makenna rested with her back against the wall and eyes closed, the sound of approaching male voices made her insides clench. One of them sounded like Crank, who she'd been unlucky enough to catch the eye of. If he found her alone on break, who knew what the hell he'd demand of her.

No, no, no. Her blood pressure spiked, making her dizzy as the need to flee pushed her into action.

"Shit," she whispered before darting across the hallway into the restroom. Hopefully, she'd made it before he realized who had been hanging in the hall. With the low lighting and her forgettable outfit, she might have pulled it off.

Heart racing and head spinning, Mak pressed her palms against the closed door of the bathroom and breathed. She closed her eyes and focused on evening out her choppy breaths.

Memories of being locked in the small shed and hearing her abuser approach assaulted her. The knowledge of what would happen and the anticipation of pain had her entire body trembling. She was supposed to have gotten away.

Beneath her feet, the floor began to undulate as though an earthquake ripped through the city.

How did she end up back here, at Roger's mercy?

She wasn't ever supposed to endure a beating again.

She'd escaped.

No! She bit her lower lip to keep from screaming.

Never let them see your fear.

The voices grew louder, snapping her back to her reality.

It wasn't Roger. It wasn't her father.

I'm not at the compound. I'm in Tennessee. I'm working in the CDMC clubhouse.

She trembled, breathing as quietly as possible. She had to get control of herself in case she was discovered. If she passed out, she'd be doomed.

The men seemed to stop moving directly outside the door. Her eyes flew open to find the knob jiggling as though one of the men placed their hand on it. She jammed a fist against her open mouth to hold back the screams.

Hide!

The room spun as she turned to scramble into a stall.

On a loud gasp, her heart leaped into her throat.

Holy shit, she wasn't in a bathroom.

"No, no, no," she whispered so low the words barely made a sound. With her heart lodged deep in her throat, she whipped her head around in frantic jerks of her head. How the hell could she have been so stupid as to end up in some kind of office? There wasn't anywhere to hide in the tiny room except under the desk, and she'd seen that movie. The psychotic killer discovered the girl every time.

Think. Think!

With silent steps, she backed up toward the desk, eyes glued to the door.

Thunder

"You sure this is the right time to act? We finally got the cops out of our asses." A voice she didn't recognize had her freezing.

Mak held her breath.

Don't open the door. Don't open the door.

"Since when do you give a fuck about the cops, Blade?" That was Crank.

"Since I haven't been able to take a shit without one of them joining me in the can."

Crank snorted. "We'd be fucking stupid to launch an all-out attack right now, but roughing up a Handlers ol' lady is perfect. Those pussies ain't gonna run to the pigs. We need to send a message. We ain't gone, and they better not fucking forget it."

Oh, my God. Mak's stomach roiled. She was going to be sick.

"Makes sense. So what're you thinking? You're the one who told me all their bitches are guarded now."

Mak could picture the evil grin curling the lips on Crank's craggily face. "Yeah, but I've had eyes on them. Every afternoon at around two, that slut fucking two Handlers takes the trash out back behind the diner."

Mak squeezed her eyes shut, shaking her head. She didn't want to hear this. Didn't want to be privy to a plan to hurt Jazmine. The urge to stick her fingers in her ears became near impossible to ignore, but she dug her fingernails into her palms and forced herself to keep listening. She might very well be the only person who could keep Jazz from being attacked, so she needed to memorize every detail spoken.

"Okay," Blade said, full of skepticism. Blade was the president if she recalled the quick rundown Kristy had given her on the way over.

"She takes it out alone. All we gotta do is have someone waiting there for her," Crank said, humor lacing his words.

The room spun. Mak released a silent breath in an attempt to keep from passing out. She'd noticed none of the ol' ladies were ever completely alone, but she'd assumed it was merely an overprotective macho biker thing. How the hell was she to have known the CDMC and HHMC were violent enemies? It's not like they ever mentioned club business around her.

Why the hell had Kristy let her come here? Why the hell was Kristy associating with these monsters?

"You planning to bring her back here or somewhere more off the grid?"

Crank laughed. "Nah, just want 'em to kick her ass a bit right then and there. Nothing that'll make her go to the hospital. Docs'll call the fucking cops. We do it right there, but be ready to split. Want 'em to know we're paying attention to 'em. Make 'em think we know their habits, schedules. Rattle the fuck outta those goddammed Handlers."

Blade's laugher sent a shiver down Mak's spine. "Can always count on you, Crank. That bitch has caused us a fuck ton of trouble. You choose who you want to get the job done. Lotta the guys will volunteer. They'll look forward to making that bitch ugly for a good long time."

She bit her lower lip so hard the metallic tinge of blood flooded her taste buds. She had to tell someone immediately. Thunder's face was the first that popped into her head, but she had no way to contact him. Shell would be the best bet since she had direct access to Copper at all times. Her hand went to her back pocket for her cheap, prepaid phone.

Shit! She'd left it on a shelf behind the bar. Having the bulky thing in her against her backside all night had been driving her nuts.

The voices grew muffled then stopped completely.

Mak blew out a breath as relief settled over her. Any need to use the restroom had long disappeared, and now all she wanted was to get to her phone and call Shell.

As she was about to reach for the rusty knob to peek into the hall, the door swung open, and she came face to face with an astonished Crank.

"Well, well, well, who do we have here?" His eyes lit like he'd won the freakin lottery.

Thunder

Her tongue locked up, preventing speech. All that came out was a croak.

"I did tell you to come find me on your break, didn't I?" His mouth curled into what was probably supposed to be a smile, but it only made him look like a predator—a hungry lion.

And she was the gazelle.

One about to be eaten if she didn't find her freakin' voice. "I-I was looking for the bathroom," she said with a forced laugh. "Got totally turned around." With a shrug, she took a step to the side to let him in the room. "I'll just go back out and see if I can find it."

He stalked forward, forcing her to shuffle back until she collided with the wall with a hard thump. "I'll tell you where it is."

Her eyes darted left and right. No chance of escape. She'd been here before, many times before. Waiting for the fists, unable to pretend they weren't coming, unable to run. Insane as it was, the rapid beat of her heart and the icy rush of fear in her veins wasn't the anticipation of pain. She'd been hit countless times, beaten on more than one occasion, and she'd endured it. She was far more afraid of—

"After." He moved so fast, she never saw it coming. Two strong hands shoved her to her knees. They hit the hard-concrete floor with a crack that had her crying out as agony shot up her thighs. In record time, he had his jeans unzipped and his hard cock out.

Yeah, that. That's what she'd been terrified of.

The pungent stench of body odor combined with weed and booze in a nauseating waft that made her stomach lurch. Right in front of her face, the ruddy head of his swollen dick bobbed and dripped.

Mak's entire body quaked, and she shook her head, clenching her teeth together so hard, they squeaked.

Crank smirked and grasped her jaw in a vise hold. Try as she might, she couldn't school her fear, and it must have shown on her face because he grew even harder. "Open up, slut." He squeezed her jaw so tight; she couldn't possibly fight against the prying hand.

As her lower jaw began to open, tears filled her eyes. This could not be happening.

"Crank?" Kristy's sultry voice preceded her in the room, and Mak could have wept in relief. "There you are," she said, tone full of sex and sin. "Been looking for you."

Crank stared down at Mak's for one more second before releasing her face. Immediately, her palms hit the floor, and she worked her aching jaw side to side.

"Oh, yeah?" He turned to face Kristy.

Mak wasted no time scrambling to her feet and as far from him as she could possibly manage, in the pea-sized office.

"Sure have." She sauntered into the room with a sexy smile on her painted lips. "Blade's getting his dick sucked by a sweet butt," she said without an ounce of jealousy. "Know what that means?"

Mak braced against the wall, biting her lip to keep her from sobbing out loud.

"Two for the price of one?" Crank said. His voice grew deeper the closer Kristy got. When she was within reach, he yanked her to him by the front of her dress.

She let out an indelicate snort. "No, it means you can ditch the naive little girl and fuck a real woman. A woman who will let you do whatever you want."

He tilted his head. "Whatever I want, huh?"

Kristy bit her lower lip and subtly thrust out her chest as she nodded. Her eyes grew heavy-lidded, and she nearly moaned. "Whatever and wherever."

Crank did groan as his hand curled around the back of Kristy's head. He yanked her face close to his. "Unless you want in, get your ugly ass back behind the fucking bar," he barked, right before taking Kristy's mouth in a brutal kiss.

Thunder

Keeping flush against the wall, Mak sidestepped her way around the pair, now devouring each other. As she passed them, Kristy's eyes opened and made contact with Mak's. She nodded at her neighbor. Any other time, she'd owe Kristy more than she could repay, but her friend had been the one to get her in this mess. Today, she owed no debt.

The moment her flats hit the hallway, Mak turned left instead of right, making her way toward a heavy steel door on unsteady legs. If that thing didn't lead to fresh air, she'd lose it right there in the hall; crazy bikers be damned.

Once she'd collected herself, she'd return to the bar and finish the job to avoid rousing anyone's suspicious, but the moment she left, she was driving to Jazz's. Showing up at two-thirty in the morning would probably give her friend a heart attack, but there was no way she could sit on this information until morning.

The closer she came to the door, the quicker she moved until she was flat out running. She rushed the door, slamming into the bar, and burst out into the night.

Thank God.

One lone streetlamp stood about twenty feet away, providing enough illumination to avoid pitch darkness, but not by much. Thankfully, she was the only person out on this side of the building—wherever she was.

As the door shut behind her, Mak slumped her back against it then doubled over with her hands on her knees. Her breath came in sharp pants, and the tears she'd managed to hold at bay leaked from the corners of her eyes.

Who knew how long she stayed out there, crouched over and crying like a child.

"Stand up and walk back inside," she whispered though her feet refused to unroot. "You can do this. You've survived worse."

"What the fuck are you doing here?" A heavy hand landed on her shoulder.

Mak's spine snapped straight as she screamed so loud, she'd earn a starring role in the next thrasher film. A palm slapped over her mouth.

Crank found her.

Just as she was about to sink her teeth into the hand over her mouth, her eyes landed on her captor, and overwhelming relief flowed through her.

Thunder.

Chapter Twelve

Two hours.

Two fucking hours he'd been rooted in one spot, monitoring the entrance to the CDMC clubhouse. Makenna had yet to reemerge. What the fuck was she doing in there? Drinking? Dancing? Fucking?

Fuck! He dragged a hand through his hair, almost ripping the strands out.

Had he pegged her wrong? Maybe this was her thing. Maybe she played the part of hardworking, doting big sister really well. Perhaps she had the innocent act down pat, reeling in schmucks like him who bought her performance while she was partying it up and fucking her way through a bunch of psychotic motherfuckers. Christ, was she like his mother, portraying a character she thought a man would want? He'd grown up with women like that and sworn one would never get the drop on him.

No. His gut rejected the idea with a violent lurch. Mak wasn't fake. He could recognize fake from a mile away, and she was as genuine as it came. No one could fake their personality that well. He'd spent enough time with her over the past few weeks to know she was the real deal. Authentic. Gorgeous. Sweet.

Which left one other option. She had no idea what the hell she walked into. And that meant she'd be fresh meat—a guppy in an ocean full of hungry sharks.

Christ, the thought of it had him nearly parting the chain-link fence with his bare hands and charging forward. He gripped the metallic rungs so hard, the metal bit into his finger joints, but he welcomed the discomfort. The ache fueled his growing rage.

The guys in the CDMC were straight-up assholes. Fuckers who had no problem using—and hurting—anyone man, woman, even a fucking child to advance their agenda.

But wait, hadn't she mentioned a high paying job for the night?

Oh, fuck. Was she working in there?

"Dude," Mav said as he strode back from where he'd been scoping out the rear side of the building since Thunder refused to leave his spot. "What the fuck is up with you?"

"Nothing," Thunder bit out, attention on the thug standing sentry at the entrance.

"T, you got it bad for this one, huh?"

"What?" He finally tore his gaze away and pinned Mav with it. "No. The fuck you talking about? She just works at the diner, and she's too fucking sweet for this shit. I'd feel this way about any of the ol' ladies."

"Uh-huh," Maverick said, and Thunder swore he could hear the smirk in his voice. "Look, she's been in there for two hours. Might as well face facts. She ain't coming out anytime soon. We're here to do a job, T. That side door has been clear all night. Now's the time if we wanna scope it out. Everyone's fucking wasted and too busy trying to find someone to suck their tiny dicks to pay attention to us. I don't wanna pull rank on you, brother, but…"

Shit. As much as he hated, *hated*, to move, Mav was right. Copper hadn't sent them to babysit Makenna, a full-grown woman who sure as hell didn't look as though she'd been dragged in there against her will. The prez had sent them on a fact-finding mission. The intel they collected would be used to avenge Viper. He needed to keep his head in the game.

Mak would be fine. Plus, she had Kristy with her, and if anyone could navigate that shit, Kristy was it.

Whatever you need to tell yourself, man.

Fuck.

With one last clench-jawed look at the entrance, Thunder nodded. "All right, let's do it." But he'd sure as hell be checking back before they left.

Together, they tromped around the perimeter of the building, not bothering to soften their steps or temper the noise. The loud music pumping from the CDMC clubhouse drowned out any ambient sounds their boots made. Hell, the volume would have drowned out a Category Five hurricane.

As they reached the spot Mav had chosen to ascend the fence, Maverick slowed down. On the other side of the fence, about fifty feet in waited the two closed doors they'd seen on the grainy surveillance videos.

"One on the right leads into the main level of the building. At least as far as I've been able to tell. The other one is a mystery. See those low windows?" Mav pointed to the left side of both doors, where somebody had blacked out three low to the ground rectangular windows.

"Yeah."

"Thinking that's a basement. And I'm thinking they got a damn good reason for darkening those windows."

Thunder ran a hand through his hair. "And you're hoping that door will get us there?"

"Mm-hmm." Mav nodded.

"What are the chances it's open?"

With a shrug, Mav said. "Slim to none. Never stopped me before."

Thunder smiled for the first time all night. "Well, that sounds fun. Okay, ready?" He glanced up with a wince. "Damn, that barbed wire is gonna suck."

"Made you wear that sweatshirt for a reason, brother," Mav said as he reached behind his neck and yanked his own sweatshirt over his head. "Lay it on top, and you can climb right over. Easy as fucking pie. Mmm, pie. Could go for some of that shit. Too bad the diner's not twenty-four hours. Guess I'll have to have a different kind of pie when I get home." He winked.

With a snort, Thunder began to move his hips as though dancing to music as he worked his sweatshirt up his torso. "Your technique sucks, Mav. You'd make shit for tips. This is how you take your clothes off. But I can give you a few pointers if you'd like. I'm sure Steph would appreciate it."

Mav's chin lifted as he barked out a laugh. "Fuck, bet she would. I might take you up on that."

"Last one to the top is a rotten egg," Thunder said, as he tossed the sweatshirt around his neck then began to scale the fence.

With a muffled curse, Mav shot after him.

When they were about halfway up the fifteen-foot fence, the heavy creak of a door opening had them both freezing solid.

"Of-fucking-course," Mav mumbled under his breath.

Thunder didn't so much as breathe as he hung suspended ten feet off the ground. One small-framed person ran from the building then sagged against the door after it closed. Two seconds later, a single harsh sob made it to his ear over the music. He had to strain to hear more, it was enough to have him squinting through the dark to make out the intruder.

"Mother fuck," he said as he doubled his speed to the top of the fence.

"Wait! Thunder, hold up," Mav whispered, as he too resumed climbing, probably in hopes of yanking Thunder down.

"It's Makenna," Thunder said.

"Oh, shit."

He reached the top before Mav, slung his sweatshirt atop the sharp barbs, then scrambled over the thick fabric barrier. In his haste, he sliced a long gash into his arm on one of the razors. The warm trickle of blood down his forearm barely registered beyond a minor annoyance. With a grunt, he wiped his arm on his jeans and scrambled halfway down the fence before jumping to the ground.

His boots hit the ground with a bone-jarring thump that he felt up his spine and into his teeth. But he shook it off and sprinted until he stood over Makenna, who was hunched forward with her hands on her knees. Her entire body shook, and her breath came in shuddered gasps. Anger rose in him, swift and violent in its intensity. Whoever caused this reaction from her would pay. Dearly.

He dropped his hand to her heaving shoulder. "What the fuck are you doing here?" he asked, voice like gravel.

Makenna straightened and screamed so loud he had no choice but to clamp a hand over her mouth.

"Jesus fucking Christ. You'll wake the dead in Texas."

Her eyes went wide and wild like that of a trapped animal, but the second her gaze landed on his face, she sagged as though all the air had been let out of her.

He caught her before she crumpled to the ground, then dragged her to his chest. Next time he'd give a warning. Not that there'd be a next time. He'd tie her to her bed before letting her anywhere near this fucking place again.

Fuck! Now he was thinking of her naked and tied to his bed as she begged him to let her come.

"Thunder." Her arms came around his back, tighter than he'd have expected, considering she hadn't touched him since the night she worked their bar. He held her just as close. Fuck, she felt good in his arms. Warm, safe...shaking.

"Shit, sorry, didn't mean to scare the life outta you. But, Mak, what the fuck are you doing here?" The desire he'd felt minutes ago transformed into a sharp need to keep her safe and get her off the property.

"I-I...uh...I'm working. The bar. L-like I did f-for y-you guys."

"Kristy set this up?" Maverick asked as he joined them.

Mak nodded against his chest. "Yeah."

"Why are you out here? Did something happen? Did they fucking touch you?" His voice rose with each question, and his hold on her tightened until she squeaked.

"Chill, brother," Mav said. "She's fucking crying."

"Fuck," Thunder mumbled against her hair. "It's okay, Mak," he whispered into her scalp. "Tell us what happened."

She shuddered then began to cry in earnest. Thunder just held her, rubbing his palm up and down her back in soothing strokes. He'd give anything for them to have been anywhere else with far fewer items of clothing between them

Mav kept an eye on their surroundings, but after a few minutes, he gave Thunder the side-eye. Every second they spent loitering on CDMC grounds, the risk of being discovered ramped up, especially if they expected Makenna inside working the bar.

"Mak, I need you to tell us what went down so we can get out of here. It's not safe for us to linger."

She lifted her head, meeting his gaze with her tearstained face. "What? No, I can't leave. I have two hours left." With her head shaking back and forth, she gave him a gentle shove. "You guys just leave, and I'll call when I'm finished."

"Fuck that," Mav said at the same time Thunder scoffed. "Are you out of your mind?"

"It's five hundred dollars," Makenna whispered in a voice full of shame. "I-I need it."

"I'll give you five hundred dollars to leave with us right now." If she didn't get moving, he was gonna toss her over his shoulder and make a run for it, her wishes be damned.

"Smooth, brother," Mav said with a roll of his eyes. He inched closer, pulling Makenna out of Thunder's reach.

Had Mav been anyone but a brother who had an ol' lady of his own, Thunder would have given him an up close and personal view of his knuckles.

Thunder

"Look, sweetheart," Mav said, all soothing and understanding in contrast to Thunder's snarling. "The club, our club, will compensate you for the money you lost tonight. We gotta get moving. We've been standing here way too long, and they catch Thunder or me, they'll take pleasure in making our lives hell."

Mak sucked in a breath, her troubled gaze bouncing between the two of them.

Smart man, Mav was, making her concerned for their safety over her own. He had Mak's number.

"Okay, I'll tell you once we're out of here," she said, then glanced over her shoulder at the building. "My phone…"

"Forget it. We'll get you a new one." Thunder guided her toward the fence with a hand on her lower back.

"Wait," she said, coming to a full stop. "How are we…" Her chin lifted as her gaze followed the fence up, up, up before she gaped at him. "Oh shit, you're gonna make me climb that, aren't you?"

"Hey." He wrapped a hand around her upper arm, drew her close once again, allowing the softness of her skin to penetrate his palms. For some reason, he couldn't get enough of her in his personal space. When he touched her, he could reassure himself of her safety. It was the only way to make his insides settle. "I'll be right behind you. You got this." He stroked the baby-smooth skin of her inner arm.

Her gaze shifted to the top of the fence then back to him. "I'm good," she said.

"Let's do it," Mav said from beside them. "Faster we get up there, the faster I get home and can fuck my woman."

He just laughed while Mak blinked at him, mouth hanging open.

"Sorry," Mav said with a shrug and grin that belied his words. "You'll get used to me."

"Yeah, he's a bit of an acquired taste." Thunder pressed his palm to Mak's lower back and nudged her to the fence.

"Hey! I'll have you know I taste damn delicious."

Mak's fingers curled around the links of the fence. Oblivious to their banter, she stared up and took a breath. "Nothing I haven't done before," she muttered.

"What was that?" Thunder stared down at her.

She shook her head. "Nothing. I'm ready."

He met Mav's surprised stare, and when his brother shrugged, Thunder made a mental note to ask about that comment at a later date. Mak had a past, and learning it grew more vital to him the more time he spent with her. All he could hope was her story wouldn't send him off on a murderous rage, searching for whoever hurt her, whoever forced her to become a mother to five children at such a young age.

Whoever had stolen her dreams.

"I'll be right behind you," Thunder said. "You don't need to go crazy fast, but we need to get outta here sooner than later. Kay?"

"Got it," Mak said as she reached up and hooked her fingers around fence wire. She blew out a breath. "Let's do it."

Then she was off, climbing at a sure, steady pace. Thunder ascended directly below her, heart pounding each time she wedged a small foot in the links and pushed up higher. Never in his life had it been a more inappropriate time to notice a woman's ass, but fuck if he couldn't help but enjoy the flex and pull of those tight jeans stretching across her ass every time she hiked a leg further up the fence.

The woman just did it for him, and the fact that she wasn't even trying to capture his attention made her all the more potent. Any woman could hike up her tits, slather on makeup, speak in a sex kitten voice, and turn on the charm. But a woman who got him hard as hell in a pair of worn jeans and t-shirts with barely any face goop? That was one he wanted.

And fuck, how he wanted Makenna.

Not a peep of complaint. No whining. No pouts. She did what she had to, even if the task proved unpleasant, which this climb certainly was. Thunder's finger joints ached and his arm throbbed where the barbed wire had sliced it.

Maverick kept pace with Makenna, whispering words of encouragement, the higher they climbed. "Okay," he said when they reached the top. "Careful going over, and keep your body over Thunder's sweatshirt. Hold the top of the fence under the razor wire. Like this." He demonstrated, swinging a long leg over the top and following it with the other.

Makenna watched with a nod. "Okay," she said, a waver in her voice, but still no grumbling. She didn't even ask to pause for a break though slightly breathless and huffing for air.

As she struggled her way over the top of the fence, she grew even more winded. Probably nerves combined with intense physical activity. Once she'd cleared the wire, she began the descent. After moving down a few links, she ended up face to face with Thunder. Through the fence, he met her anxious gaze. "You're quite the badass, Miss Makenna," he said, flashing her his famous grin.

It did the trick, relaxing the muscles in her face and drawing a small smile from her. Thunder couldn't help himself. He pressed a quick kiss to her upturned lips through the fence.

Fuck, she was just as sweet as he remembered, sweeter even.

She gasped, and her eyes popped wide.

"I'm gonna climb below you for the rest of the way down," Mav said, oblivious to the sparks crackling above him.

"Uh, yeah, thanks," Makenna called down.

"Just take it slow and steady."

After giving Thunder another sweet smile, she continued the descent, and he scaled the top of the fence without injury this time.

A few minutes later, all three of them had feet planted on solid ground. The moment his boots hit the dirt, Thunder sought Makenna out, pulling her to his side with an arm around her shoulders. After being so worried about her for the past two hours, he needed her close to ease his mind. His body didn't mind having her pressed up against him either.

"My car is here," she said as they hiked their way toward Maverick's truck.

"Shit." Thunder and Maverick both came to a stop.

Maverick rubbed his jaw. "We can't leave it. Mak, you're gonna have to drive out of here yourself. If anyone spots you in the lot, tell them you're grabbing something and will be right back in. Make a right out of the compound. Our navy-blue truck is parked about a half-mile down the road. Pull over when you see us. Thunder will hop in with you and drive your car the rest of the way back, okay?"

Thunder could see she wanted to argue at being ordered around, but she had a good head on her shoulders. The plan made sense. The night had rattled her. She didn't need to be driving with her nerves shot and gallons of adrenalin coursing through her. As fired up as he was, Thunder could get them back in one piece while Makenna tried to relax.

They began walking again until Makenna let out a loud gasp and froze.

Both he and Maverick tensed, ready for a fight. "What's wrong?" Thunder asked. "You see something?"

"No." Makenna shook her head as she pressed a fist to her mouth. "What happened with Crank freaked me out so badly, I forgot to tell you what I overheard. God, what the hell is wrong with me? I'm a horrible person."

Thunder's blood turned to ice.

"Hon," Mav said, as if talking to a frightened animal. "Pretty sure you couldn't be horrible if you tried. Just tell us what you heard. We'll take care of it."

Makenna dropped her arm and met his gaze with solemn eyes. "The CDMC is planning to attack Jazmine tomorrow."

Thunder knew they were talking. That Makenna was sharing important information, but, like a malfunctioning record player, his mind stuck on one detail, replaying it again and again.

Thunder

"What the fuck did Crank do to you?"

Chapter Thirteen

"Hey, Miss!"

Makenna rubbed her eyes as she stifled another yawn.

"Yo! Waitress!"

A hand slapped on a table, and she nearly jumped out of her skin.

"Sorry!" Mak scurried two tables over, holding out the mostly full carafe of coffee. "Refill?"

A middle-aged man with a stereotypical beer gut and eyebrows so bushy they were difficult not to stare at frowned her way. "What? No. This isn't what I ordered." As he scowled, he shoved a plate piled high with piping hot pancakes her way. "I wanted the Omelet Supreme."

Across the booth from him, a small woman who appeared the same age stared out the window as though embarrassed by her companion's behavior.

"I am so sorry, sir," Makenna said, snatching up the untouched plate. "I'll put a rush on that omelet, and your meal will be comped. Promise it will just be a few minutes." She turned and slogged toward the kitchen. Her legs were heavier than she could ever remember them being, and clearly, her brain was only functioning at about half capacity.

Thunder

That's what happened to a girl when she went to bed at three-thirty in the morning and had to be at work by six forty-five. For a hot second, she'd contemplated the glorious idea of calling out, but the money... After losing out on five hundred dollars last night, there was no way in hell she could afford a missed shift. So there she was, sleepwalking her way through the shift and screwing up every other order. And after almost seven hours of work, that added up to a lot of frustration.

Thank God Thunder hadn't come in at all this shift. She had no interest in him witnessing her humiliation.

"Hey, Ernesto," she said to the head cook as she pushed into the kitchen. "I goofed on table three. Gonna need a Supreme STAT."

"Again, *mija*?" he asked, shaking his spatula at her.

She winced. "Yes, again. I'm so sorry. I promise I'll get my head in the game."

With a snort, Ernesto said, "You're lucky I love you, *mija*."

"I know." She dropped a kiss on the older man's wrinkled cheek. "You're the best." After a quick loop, checking on her tables, and making sure no new patrons had been seated in her section, she dashed back to the kitchen for the omelet.

Just as Ernesto placed the hot plate on her tray, it disappeared. "What?" Mak spun around to see Toni sauntering off. "I've got this," she called over her shoulder.

Mak hurried out of the kitchen after her boss and the diner's owner. She also happened to be the ol' lady of the Handlers' vice president, Zach. Before Mak made it too far, someone grabbed her arm and hauled her behind the counter. Holly, Steph, and Jazz stood there, arms crossed, frowning at her.

"Uh, what's up, guys?" Mak said, taking a step back. Sometimes these ladies came across a million times tougher than their biker partners.

"What's up?" Jazz parroted, her eyes narrowing. "Why don't you tell us what's up?"

"Seriously," Holly said, her expression much softer than Jazz's. "You've been seriously off all day. Mixing up orders and stumbling around with bags under your eyes. I swear I caught you fall asleep standing in front of the coffee maker a little while ago."

Heat rushed to Mak's face. So much for successfully hiding her extreme fatigue from her coworkers.

"I'm so sorry. I had a late night. That's all. Didn't get nearly enough sleep." She ran a hand through the hair she hadn't had time to style since she'd grabbed every second of sleep possible before work. "I'll do better."

After they'd left the Chrome Disciples clubhouse last night, Thunder had driven her car to her house while Maverick tailed them. Lee didn't even question her arrival with two men in the middle of the night, he'd been so eager to "go out," whatever that meant. He'd practically flown out of the house and into his piece of junk car the second her tires rolled into the driveway. Thankfully, the rest of the kids were long asleep, because about five minutes later, Copper, Zach, Screw, and Gumby had shown up and grilled her about every second she'd been in that clubhouse.

Copper made it quite clear she was not to mention the threat against Jazz, or anything about being on CDMC property to any of the ol' ladies.

And now she had to find a way out of this interrogation.

Her stomach fluttered and not in a good way as all three women's eyes narrowed. If she hadn't known better, she'd have sworn they'd choreographed the move.

"Honey, we're not doing this because we're worried about the customers and want you to do better. We're worried about you and want to make sure you don't need help." Toni joined them, placing a hand on Mak's tense shoulder before moving to stand in line with the others.

"Here's what I know," Shell said, adding a foot tap to the unhappy posture. "I know my husband woke me up sometime after midnight to tell me he had to run out and take care of something important." She made air quotes for those last two words. "That is code for club business he can't or won't tell me about. I know he was gone for a few hours, and then this morning, I overheard him talking on the phone. Your name was dropped. So was Jazz's."

Oh, crap. Mak swallowed hard.

"And so was the Chrome Disciples."

"Um…" Her face heated until it felt like it might melt right off her body. How the hell was she supposed to get out of this?

"And here's what I know," Jazz cut in before Mak could formulate a believable response. "I know my men have been sitting in a booth all morning like two snarling junkyard dogs. I've been forbidden to 'step one goddammed foot' outside the building and told that if I took the trash out at the end of the day, I'd 'be sorrier than I've ever been in my life.'" She did the air quotes as well, accompanying it with a dramatic eye-roll. "Please, as if either of those men scare me."

"So," Shell continued. "We want to know what's going on."

As she spoke, the door to the diner opened, and Copper stepped into the building. Used to the jingle of bells announcing customers, none of the women reacted. In less than three seconds, Copper had zeroed in on his pregnant wife. Due to the way they stood, Mak was the one who witnessed his approach. "Uh, Shell…"

Shell held up a hand. "Nu-uh, don't even try to give us some bullshit answer my husband told you to say. Something is going on that involves you, Jazz, and the CDMC, and we want to know what it is."

"Shell." Mak squeaked out the word this time, her gaze on the huge, bearded man with his arms crossed over his massive chest and a scowl the size of Texas on his furry face.

Shell huffed. "What? What are you looking at?" She spun around and gasped. "Oh, hi, baby!"

"Oh, boy," Jazz whispered as all four of them took a collective step back. "Now him? He scares me. Yikes, he's mad. I'm gonna just go—"

"Don't even think about moving that gorgeous ass one step," Screw said, as he strolled up next to Copper.

Jazz froze in place and pursed her lips.

"So much for not being scared of him," Holly muttered.

"Shut up. I'm not scared. I'm only staying here for Shell's sake. Solidarity in sisterhood and all that shit."

Screw snorted.

Mak couldn't do anything but stand there wide-eyed, gawking at this group of intimidating men and ballsy women. Had she defied her husband so blatantly, or any of the men in the community, she'd have had a hell of a beating coming her way. She'd lived through those beatings more times than she cared to recall.

What would it be like to feel so secure and safe in a relationship that fear never entered the mind? To know that even though they'd angered their men, they were loved, and no one would ever raise a hand against them? What would it be like to live the dream Makenna would never achieve? These women knew their men would be angry if they were caught nosing around club business. Sure, they'd probably deal with a grumbling male for a few hours, but they never had to fear pain or punishment.

They were lucky.

They were loved.

"And what were you ladies talking about, Michelle?" Copper asked in full growl mode.

"Oooh." Jazz sucked in an audible breath before leaning closer to Mak. "Full first name. Never a good thing."

Screw narrowed his eyes at his woman, but his lips quirked. "You better watch all that sass, *Jazmine*."

"Yeah?" She tilted her head. "What are you gonna do about it?"

Just as Screw opened his mouth, the bell jangled over the door and in strode Thunder. He took one look at Mak and threw his hands in the air. "You gotta be fucking kidding me." He stormed straight over to her. "Knew I shoulda come by earlier this morning. What the hell are you doing here?"

"Uh…" Mak looked at the smirks on her coworkers' faces before focusing back on Thunder. "I'm working." Why on earth would he care?

"Seriously?" He turned to Copper. "Prez? A little help here."

Copper blew out a deep breath. "Let's not make more of a scene than we already have, huh? This place closes in thirty, right?" He continued after Shell nodded. "We'll have a chat once all the customers leave."

Everyone dispersed, Copper to the table with Screw where Gumby still sat, and the ladies back to their jobs. Only Thunder remained, blocking her exit when Makenna tried to leave the space behind the counter.

"Babe, why the hell didn't you call out today?" he asked with a frown as he stroked a thumb over what had to be a spectacular bag under her eye.

The urge to lean into him hit her hard. Wouldn't it feel amazing to have a man like him at her back? One strong and capable who could hold her up when the weight on her shoulders weakened her.

But Makenna didn't have the luxury of indulging in such fantasies because reality would still be waiting when Thunder removed his hand and stepped back. Her father and husband were still out there. They'd still destroy Thunder, and probably the rest of the Handlers should they find her. She still had five siblings to raise and protect from their past. Reality demanded she buck up, suck up, and stand strong for the little ones depending on her for survival.

So instead of begging him to hold her and make the big bad world disappear for a while, she shrugged. "You know why."

If it came out snippy, he'd just have to forgive her. The loss of last night's five hundred dollars forced her to restructure the entire next month's budget. The stress combined with a serious lack of sleep and now a horde of pissed off bikers had her on edge.

It would push anyone to their limit.

With a nod and a dazzling smile she probably didn't deserve, he took a few steps back. "Even exhausted, you're gorgeous." He winked. "Thirty minutes." Then he spun with a flourish and joined his brothers at the table of sinfully attractive men.

Mak groaned as she turned and mumbled, "Thirty minutes."

IF HE COULD kick his own ass, he'd make it so he couldn't sit for a week. Why the hell hadn't he come here first thing in the morning? Better yet, he should have swung by her house and blocked her goddammed driveway. Of course, stubborn and overly responsible Makenna wouldn't stay home. What was a night of trauma when there was work to be done? The money meant a great deal to her, not for herself, of course, she didn't have a selfish bone in her body, but because she had so many others to care for.

"Well, boys, what are you all in the mood for?" Shell asked, as she leaned her hip against her husband's large shoulder.

Copper slipped his arm around her waist and pulled her close. "Just coffee, please, baby," he said. The others nodded their agreement, so Thunder did as well even though he could have eaten the table he was so hungry. Last thing he wanted to do was hold up their ability to close up by submitting a late order.

Mak needed to get home so she could get some sleep. Though how restful would a house full of rowdy kids and teens be?

Hmm, the thought got him thinking…

"Hey, Shell, can I ask you a favor?"

"Of course, Thunder. What do you need?"

"It's kind of a huge one."

She shrugged. "You know if I can do it, I will."

He peeked at Copper, who'd raised an eyebrow as he watched the exchange. "Mak didn't get to bed until after three-thirty this morning, and I'm assuming she was here before seven. She's exhausted."

"Yeah, she's been dragging through the whole shift, making mistakes, and looking like a zombie. Completely out of character for her." Frowning, Shell shifted her concerned gaze to Mak as she walked a tray full of dirty dishes into the kitchen.

"She's trashed. But she's got all her siblings at home. Maybe the younger one or two could stay with you guys tonight, give her a chance to have some quiet time?" He gave Shell his most endearing smile, earning himself a kick from Copper under the table.

"Ow, fuck!"

Shell laughed, rubbing her husband's upper back. "Put away those pearly whites. You don't have to charm me, Romeo. It's a fantastic idea, and I'm embarrassed I didn't think of it first. Between Mama V and I, we can take both of them. You know Cassie loves spending time with the kids. It's good for her. Keeps her busy, and her mind occupied. It'll be fun. A big pajama party. Then Mak can have some alone time." As she spoke those final words, she flashed Thunder an impish grin.

What the hell was that supposed to mean?

"Jesus," Copper muttered. "Looks like I'm sleeping at the clubhouse." But there was no heat behind his words. The prez approved of the idea as much as his ol' lady did. Mak had no idea she'd already been tucked into the family fold, especially after she'd passed along information that prevented Jazz from being injured.

They sat around, sipping coffee and bullshitting until the women finished, and the last customers vacated the diner.

"All right," Jazz said as she dragged a table up alongside the booth. Toni joined her, pulling over empty chairs. They all shuffled around so each woman could sit by their respective ol' man.

Mak ended up next to him as though she was his to protect. Christ, were that the case, he'd be bound to fuck it up within the week. What the hell did he know about keeping a woman happy? Especially one who came with a pack of children.

Fuck. It'd be a disaster from day one. No, he needed to stick to what he understood. Dancing, fucking, and his club. Thoughts of the pressure and responsibility associated with making a woman his own had him breaking out in a cold sweat.

No matter how nice it felt to have Makenna's leg brush his under the table. Or how his chest puffed up when she looked at him with those big, trusting eyes. Or how hard his dick got when she licked that damn lower lip.

Once everyone was seated and had a full cup of steaming coffee, Copper dove right in. "Last night Makenna worked the bar for a CDMC party."

All the women gasped, and their heads whipped in Mak's direction.

"Seriously?" Toni asked, eyes wide.

Beside him, Mak squirmed, clearly uncomfortable with being singled out. "I didn't know," she whispered, staring at the table.

"She had no idea what the club's history with them was," he snapped at Toni, cringing at the defensiveness bite to his own voice.

Toni's face fell, and Zach opened his mouth, probably to blast him for being a dick to his VP's ol' lady.

"Of course, not," Copper cut in. "Why would she? We keep that shit wrapped up tight. She just assumed they were another club like ours. Let's get that straight from the start."

Thunder could have kissed his president at that moment. Makenna visibly relaxed.

"Mak, if you don't want to tell the story, I'll let Thunder take over."

She gazed at him, "Knock yourself out. My brain is too tired to remember all the details today."

With a nod to Copper, he rubbed a hand up and down Makenna's back as though he had as much right to touch her as these men did their ol' ladies. When she didn't protest, he left his hand at the base of her spine as he began. "Mav and I were there to scope shit out. We were working on getting closer to the clubhouse when I heard someone come out a back door. It was Mak. She had an incident that left her shaken and came out for some air."

On the drive home, she'd finally fessed up to what went down with Crank. Thunder had almost cracked her steering wheel in half with the force of his grip. He itched to be left alone in a room with that fucker. Seasoned enforcer or not, he'd tear Crank apart with his bare hands for daring to lay a finger on Mak.

"Are you okay?" Shell asked with concern scrawled across her face. Not the obligatory kind, but the genuine kind one has for a true friend.

"Yes," Mak said. "I'm fine. It was just a very long night, which is why I've been a little off today."

Thunder draped his arm across Mak's shoulders. When Screw raised an eyebrow, he diverted his gaze to the others. They could think whatever they wanted. He owed no explanations for his actions toward Mak. If he wanted to give the woman a comforting touch, he'd damn well do it. Didn't mean he'd be putting a ring on it anytime soon, or ever.

"She overheard Crank and Blade planning an attack for today"—his eyes shifted to Jazz then back to the group at large—"on Jazz."

"What?" Jazz straightened in her seat, gaze bouncing between Screw and Gumby, who sat on either side of her. "S-seriously?"

"Yes," Mak said with a nod. She leaned forward, resting her forearms on the table.

Nice to see her gaining some confidence and finding her voice amidst all the dominant personalities.

"They planned to be waiting here, out back for when you took out the trash. Seems like they've been watching for a while, learning your patterns. The plan was to, uh, beat you up to send a message to the club. They wanted you all to remember they're still out there, and they haven't forgotten about you."

"Holy shit," Jazz whispered on an exhale. Screw and Gumby both turned in, speaking low into her ears. She nodded and managed to keep her emotions in check.

With Mak tucked against him, Thunder kept his gaze on the loving threesome. Of all his brothers, the last one he'd have predicted to enter into a committed relationship was Screw, the biggest man-whore around. But he had, and Thunder would be lying if he said it didn't suit the man.

A weird feeling twisted in his chest.

"So, that's why I was forbidden to set foot outside the building, huh?" Jazz eventually asked.

"Yes." Now that the cat had escaped the bag, Copper would be honest and blunt with his answers.

"Um," Mak said, her gaze on the prez. "Are they…out there? Now?"

"We're taking care of it."

Honest and blunt, but not overly informative.

The vague answer had Mak tensing beside him, so he squeezed her shoulder.

"Are they going to figure out it was me? Who told you, I mean. I have um, some younger siblings who live with me. I need to know if they might not be safe."

Shaking his head, Copper rubbed his chin. "As of now, we have no reason to believe they'll suspect you. You said Crank didn't realize you'd heard him, correct?"

Mak nodded as she drummed her nails against her coffee mug. Caffeine probably wasn't the smartest move right now. She needed to go home and sleep, not be artificially awake for the next few hours running on jittery nerves and chemicals. Thunder wrapped his hand around hers, stilling the motion.

"Sorry," she whispered. "No, he didn't realize I'd heard him speaking. And he has no idea I have any kind of connection to your club. He thinks I'm just a friend of Kristy's."

"Good." Copper smoothed a hand down the back of his wife's head before resting it on her neck.

Screw jumped in. "We all drove here in cages today, so there aren't any bikes out front. We've got it set up, so some of our guys just happen to wander out back and find the Disciples. They'll have no reason to think anyone informed us beforehand. Just dumb bad luck that Rocket stumbled upon them and fucked them up."

With a nod, Copper brought the focus back to Mak. "If at any point you feel unsafe, let us know, and we'll have someone keep an eye on your house. Does that help?"

"Yes," she said. "Thank you."

Thunder had every intention of making that happen whether she admitted to feeling unsafe or not.

"Hey, Mak, why don't you let us take the kids tonight?" Shell reached across the table and covered Mak's hand with her own. "We can have a giant sleepover party and give you a little time to yourself."

It was clear in the way her eyes lit up and she sucked in a small breath that Mak loved the idea. How long had it been since she'd had any time to take care of herself?

"Shell, I can't ask you to do that. It's…it's a lot. Too much."

"Well, first off, you didn't ask, Thunder came up with the incredible idea. And second, I would not offer if I didn't want to. Beth would be over the moon, and between Mama V and myself, we got it under control."

"The older ones can come stay with us," Toni added. "I know Rissa and Lindsey have hit it off. I bet Amy would have fun with them as well. Then you just have to get rid of Lee for the night and, you can have some time alone."

Mak chewed her lower lip, most likely at war in her head between the teeny tiny part of her that thought she deserved some quiet time and the ruling part that felt selfish and as though she'd be taking advantage of Shell's kindness.

"Let them do this for you, Mak. You deserve some time to relax. You need it," he said, as though the rest of them weren't staring. He leaned in close. "Think about it. A whole night to yourself. You can eat whatever you want. You can drink an entire bottle of wine. You can sleep for twelve straight hours if it makes you happy."

Mak groaned, and lust shot straight to his cock. Fuck, that was a sexy sound.

"All right." She turned to Shell. "Thank you. Thank you so, so much."

"It's my pleasure. Trust me when I say we've all needed a little help from time to time."

"Oh, and Thunder has something for you," Copper said. "From the club."

"Shit, that's right." He pulled the thick envelope out of his back pocket and pressed it into her hand. "Don't even think about refusing this."

Mak's forehead scrunched in the most adorable way, and he had to clench his fists to resist rubbing a thumb across the lines. He'd already given the guys enough to interrogate him over the moment she left. No need to pour gas on the fire.

"What is it?"

"Open it."

With a wrinkled nose, she opened the envelope and gasped at the sight of twenty-five crisp twenty-dollar bills. "What? No, I ca—"

He slid a palm over her mouth, shaking his head. "No. Just say thank you, Copper."

Mak sagged, and he removed his hand. "Thank you, Copper," she said, emotion bleeding through.

The big man nodded. "Trust me when I say it is the very least we can do. I wanted to put more in there, but Thunder told me you'd never accept it."

Her cheeks flushed red. "He was right."

Something about those three words had his chest filling with warmth. In the short time since he'd met her, he'd come to know her in a way he'd never bothered to understand other people. To predict how she'd respond to a gift showed a level of intimacy he didn't let himself find with women.

But Mak was different.

"Okay, we'll let you ladies finish closing up and Shell, you and Mak can work out the details. Rest of you need to be at the clubhouse for church tonight at six."

"Mak, you're done for the day. Go home and chill. That's an order," Toni said, pointing a finger at Mack.

Everyone fled the table, leaving him alone with Makenna. She turned to him with a troubled expression. "You shouldn't have done that."

How did he know this conversation was coming? "Done what?"

Her frown deepened. "Any of it. I could have made up the money with extra shifts here. And I'm used to being tired, Thunder. It's just a fact of life."

Christ, she broke his heart. "But you don't have to be. You're one of the crew here, Mak. And we take care of our own. Why suffer through it alone when we're all willing to help?"

She didn't so much as crack a smile. In fact, she looked utterly confused by the question. "Because I've always had to do it alone, and I will again, only next time, I'll be so much worse off because I'll know what I'm missing." She shook her head. "I sound so ungrateful. Thank you, Thunder. Thank you for thinking of me." She leaned in, pressed a chaste kiss to his cheek, then got up from the table, taking a large chunk of his heart with her as she went to gather her belongings.

Chapter Fourteen

Makenna trailed her hand along the wall as she strolled through the empty house. This was the first time since she'd moved in, hell, this was the first time since leaving the community, that she could remember being alone at home.

It was nice. The quiet, the peace, the…uncertainty as to what to do with herself. Sure, the laundry had backed up days ago, and there were those pictures she'd picked up at the thrift store she'd meant to hang, and the floor hadn't been mopped in an embarrassingly long time, but those were all chores.

Using her precious and rare solo time on housework felt like a waste of a precious gift, but she had no idea what a prudent use of the time would be. In the hour since Copper and Shell had picked up the little kids, she'd realized one depressing fact.

I have no life.

She didn't have hobbies.

She had no clue what music someone over the age of seven liked to listen to.

Hopes and dreams were a luxury she'd never indulged in, so she had nothing to strive for.

So much of her life, the entirety of her adult life, had been spent first on survival, then caring for and focusing on others. It had never been a problem until she met the women of the

HHMC. It still wasn't a problem, she loved her siblings and cherished the opportunity to provide them with a childhood she'd never had, but meeting women like Holly, Shell, and Toni had shown her something was missing from her life.

An identity.

Part of her resented them for it. Before them, she'd been ignorant of what her life lacked. Now it was at the forefront of her mind at least ten times daily. Until Emmie turned eighteen, she needed to keep the focus on her family, not turn it inward. She shouldn't even be having these selfish thoughts.

She walked into her bedroom and let out a sigh.

Now what? So far, she'd eaten some leftovers, opened all the windows to let in the incredible crisp evening air, and had tried to find something to watch on Netflix, but hadn't been able to settle on anything. She should have asked the girls at work for a recommendation.

As her gaze scanned the room, she wondered if she might as well go to bed and catch up on years' worth of neglected sleep. Again, it felt like a waste. She paused, zeroing in on the shabby nightstand next to her bed.

Hmm…

Maybe tonight, only tonight, she could indulge in something just for her. Something completely selfish. Something she'd been way too timid to test out while the kids were sleeping one thin wall away.

With a shaky hand, she opened the drawer and peered down at the hot pink vibrator as though it would spring out and bite her. It had been a present from Kristy, of course. The wind blew, wafting her curtains, and Makenna slammed the drawer shut with a yelp.

Shit! What the hell was wrong with her, acting like a teenage boy caught with his mom's lingerie catalog?

"I'm gonna need some wine for this," she muttered, as she stalked back out of the room. In the kitchen, she poured herself a third of a glass full of Pino Grigio then gulped it down in three large swallows. Wincing at the tart bite, she refilled it with twice as much wine.

"Blech. Now I know why you're supposed to sip wine instead of chugging it. Too much." She headed back out toward her room, glass in hand. "And I'm already talking to myself like a crazy person."

But she wasn't used to the silence, and it made her a little nutty.

This time, she sat on the side of the bed, legs near the night table. One day she hoped to be able to get a headboard and better quality bedding; create a bit of a comforting oasis for herself. For now, she got by with a mattress and box spring stacked on a rickety metal frame and a hideous brown and orange comforter she'd found on clearance for under twenty bucks. Some things she couldn't buy at the thrift store and a comforter was one of them—a result of the time the community had been overrun with bedbugs.

She shivered, just thinking about it. It'd been horrifying.

After another sip—fine, a huge gulp—of wine, she'd worked up the courage to open the drawer again. Kristy had received it as some sort of promotional item at work and "already had like six," so she'd gifted it to Makenna as though she handled vibrators every day.

Maybe she did.

How nice for her.

This was Makenna's first vibrator, and she had no idea what the hell to do with it. Well, she knew what to do with it in a textbook sense, but that was about it. There'd been a few instances where she'd touched herself over the years, but living in tiny houses with lots of siblings never made it practical. And before leaving the community, it hadn't been an option.

Guess it was high time she introduced herself to the supposed wonders of a vibrator. Or, "a girl's best friend," as Kristy had called it.

She plucked the thing out of the drawer and held it up at eye level. Seemed simple enough, a relatively slender cylindrical shaped rod with a slight curve to a tapered end. Smooth, pink, and—she pushed the center of three buttons on the base, bringing the thing to life—yikes, powerful.

Mak depressed the little minus button a few times. Maybe a lower setting to start. As the vibrator buzzed and whirred against her palm, she scooted herself back against the wall. Next, she shimmied out of her sleep shorts and bikini panties.

"You can do this," she said aloud. The T-shirt followed the rest of the clothes, ending up in a heap on the carpeted floor. Instantly, her nipples hardened from the slight chill in the room.

Makenna blew out a breath. Nerves fluttered in her stomach as she stared at the quivering vibrator.

And what the hell was she supposed to do now? She closed her eyes, leaned her back against the wall, and blew out a breath. In the two years she spent married to a man she despised, she'd become skilled at disappearing into her head during sex. She'd faded away into an almost meditative state, allowing her mind to separate from the uncomfortable experience. Now, as she prepared to masturbate for the first time in ages, her mind started to drift away as though automatically programmed to do so.

"This is ridiculous." With her eyes closed, Mak fumbled around for the wine glass. Once she found it and somehow managed to keep from knocking it over, she finished the rest in two large swallows. She needed to chill out. Hopefully, the wine would kick in soon.

"Okay," she said aloud. "What do you feel?"

The sheets beneath her were cool and soft against her skin. Goosebumps popped up along her arms and legs as the soft breeze blew in through the windows. A slight scent of honeysuckle permeated the air from the bushes beneath her window. The only sound reaching her ears was the low buzz of her new toy.

With her eyes closed, she inhaled a deep breath and held it, focusing on the feeling of her chest expanding. Her breasts moving. She swore she felt her nipples pucker even more.

Suddenly, a buzz of energy skittered across her skin, bringing excitement along with it. All she needed now was a realistic fantasy to really get her in the mood.

Instantly, Thunder's face popped into her head. Actually, his body. Just as it had looked the night he danced on the bar at the Handlers' clubhouse. Damn, the man could move in ways she'd never even imagined. Were his hips even attached to his body? Because they sure seemed to move independently of the rest of him.

And those abs? Maybe he'd let her run her hands all over them just once. It'd probably be the only time in her life she'd be able to touch a man with such a stunning body. As she replayed the erotic dance in her mind, Makenna shifted on the bed. Whatever slight chill she'd been feeling a moment ago vanished, and she grew almost uncomfortably warm.

Her nipples remained hard, but for a different reason now. She bent her knees and planted her feet on the mattress, spreading her legs slightly. With her free hand, she reached between her thighs.

Wet.

Keeping her eyes closed, she progressed the fantasy to one involving her. One where Thunder knelt on this very bed with a knee on either side of her body, straddling her. He'd be staring down at her with desire clear in his light brown eyes. The thought of seeing a man like him want her so badly had her squirming as arousal grew to a powerful level.

Thankfully, he wasn't actually present to see the way her hand trembled, and she bit her lip with nerves. The fantasy Thunder overlooked all that, including her inexperience with an overtly sexual man like him.

As she imagined Thunder reaching between her parted thighs, she lowered the vibrator to her saturated folds. The second the toy made contact, fire shot through her body, and she lurched as though she'd been jolted with a live wire instead of a buzzing hunk of pink silicone.

"Holy shit," she whispered, nerves gone. All she wanted now was more of that incredible feeling. "That felt so damn good."

Prepared this time for the concentrated rush of sensation, Mak did it again. Her hips bucked, but she managed to keep from almost rocketing off the bed like before. This time, she let herself absorb the electric sensations pulsing from her sex out through her body. Moaning a little, she moved the toy up, brushing it over her clit. Her back arched, and she squeaked.

"Wow."

She probably looked like the biggest fool, but she sure did owe Shell and Copper big time for this reprieve from responsibility because this was fantastic. In these twenty seconds of experimentation, she found more pleasure than she'd ever had during sex with her husband.

Mak lost track of time as she pleasured herself with light touches and passes from the vibrator. A few times, she even ran it up and down her thighs, enjoying the tickle, and all the while, imagining it was Thunder's hand on her skin.

Staying quiet didn't matter, so she allowed herself to be vocal as she enjoyed the onslaught of sensation. After a while, a twist low in her belly had her sex clenching and the need for more surging in her.

With her free hand, she brushed her thumb over a nipple and gasped at the new sensation. Amazing but still not enough. She felt empty and needier than she'd ever been in her life. Feeling bold, she inserted the tip of the vibrator into her pussy. "Shit!" she cried out, nearly arching off the bed.

"Holy shit, that's good." Penetration had never felt like this before. Maybe it was the wetness or the daydream involving Thunder, but whatever it was that eased the vibrator's entry, she needed more of it in her life.

Thrusting the toy in and out at a quick pace, she began to pant. Each time she pushed it a little deeper and loved it a little more. The intense vibrations combined with the stretching fullness and friction, had her racing toward orgasm.

God, she needed it. She'd had one. One in her entire life, given to her by herself as she'd huddled in the corner of the shower and held a fist over her mouth.

Now she planned to be loud and proud about it.

She kept going, fucking herself with the toy while moaning loud and thumbing her nipple. After a few minutes, the sensation of rushing toward a crescendo began to fade. "No!" she shouted as disappointment crashed over her. What the hell was going on? This felt good. Felt incredible. How could it disappear?

"No!" she yelled again as the erotic throbbing between her legs became almost painful in its intensity. It wasn't going to happen. She'd wasted all this time to be left unsatisfied. Disappointment sat on her chest like a two-thousand-pound elephant. Was it her? Was she broken? Damaged by—

The door to her bedroom flew open, and Thunder burst in, screaming, "Makenna!" The second his eyes landed on her, he stopped dead in his tracks. "What the fuck?" he shouted as his jaw hit the floor.

Makenna froze, vibrator lodged halfway inside her, fingers pinching a nipple. "Oh, my God," she squeaked.

Kill me now.

Chapter Fifteen

Thunder tapped his booted foot beneath the enormous table in the chapel. Copper wasn't exactly droning on, but still, he couldn't wait for his prez to wrap it up so he could get the hell outta there and swing by Makenna's.

His original plan had been to pick up some takeout and surprise her with dinner, but church started nearly an hour after it had been scheduled, so by the time he made it out to her place, she'd probably have eaten.

No matter, he could be flexible. Dessert worked just as well. An image of Mak with a can of whipped cream popped in his head. Dessert could be even more promising than dinner.

"Everybody got that? We're all on the same page, right?" Copper asked as he folded his arms across his chest and glanced around the table at the nodding heads.

Yes, we fucking get it!

"We sent the two CDMC fuckers back home bruised and bloodied. Made it look like a total coincidence that we found them behind the diner." Rocket had dressed like a civilian and wandered behind the diner, looking for a quiet place to smoke where his wife wouldn't find him. When he bumped into the CDMC guys, he got mouthy about how he hated bikers. "Should come as no surprise to anyone, they took the bait and attacked.

Rocket is a scary motherfucker and sent them running back to Crank bruised, and bloody as fuck."

You told us this shit already.

Thunder shifted in his seat for the thousandth time.

"You good, brother?" Jigsaw asked.

"Yeah, just got some shit to take care of. Cop's talking more than usual."

The scarred side of Jigsaw's face twitched as he resisted the urge to smirk.

"Anyway, they have no reason to suspect we were on to them. Just dumb fucking luck, they ran into a ballsy fucker who hates bikers. Regardless, they accomplished their mission. We remember they're out there and that they have a hard-on for us." He unfolded his arms. "Remain vigilant, guys. Don't want the ol' ladies alone at any time. You need help covering yours, let me know. Okay?"

"Izzy's gonna fucking *love* his."

"Yeah," Thunder whispered with a snort. "Don't envy you there, brother." Of all the women, Izzy was the most kick-ass by far and had the hardest time accepting club protection.

Everyone voiced their agreement, and Copper rapped his meaty fist on the table. "Okay. Dismissed. Get the fuck outta here."

"Wanna grab a drink?" Jig asked, as Thunder stood.

He side-eyed his brother. "You afraid to go home, man?"

With a laugh, Jig stretched his arms overhead. "Nah, man. Izzy and the nugget are hanging with Chloe at the shop. Something about some new ink for Chloe. A surprise for Rocket's birthday, so don't fucking blab it." As he lowered his arms, his shoulder let out a bone-chilling crack. "Shit, getting too fucking old, brother."

"Seriously, you're what? Sixty-one? Two?"

"You're a funny fucker." Jig took a swipe at him but missed when Thunder jumped back, laughing.

"Appreciate the offer, but I gotta split."

Of course, that was the moment Screw wandered over. "You heading out to your girl's place?"

Jig raised an eyebrow. "You got a girl?"

With a roll of his eyes, Thunder said, "No. Just checking on Makenna since she's alone."

Jig's face turned serious, and he nodded, but not fucking Screw. No, that joker said, "Well, aren't you a selfless little fucker?"

After sitting through a long-ass church while fighting his mind to stay present, Thunder had no patience for this shit. "Yeah, yeah. We done here? I gotta roll."

With a slap to Thunder's back, Jig said, "Yeah, brother. Catch ya tomorrow."

"Thanks." He turned and started toward the exit at a near jog. Shit, when the hell had he ever been this fucking eager to see a woman?

"Hey!" Screw yelled just as Thunder had one foot out the door. "Make sure you wrap your shit up. She may be your queen, but that don't mean she's clean!" His voice lowered. "See what I did there?" he said, probably to his poor lover, Gumby.

Thunder didn't bother turning back around. He just lifted his hands and gave Screw the double bird. Classic and on point.

Laughter followed him out the door, and his own continued until he reached his bike. Bunch of crazy motherfuckers, but, damn, he loved his brothers.

Forty-five minutes later, armed with three different gallons of ice cream and a crap-ton of sugary toppings, Thunder cruised to a stop in front of Makenna's place. No, he had no intentions of downing that much dessert between the two of them, but there were a lot of kiddos in this house, and who knew how often Mak was able to splurge on a treat for them? Shelling out a few bucks for extra ice cream wouldn't put him in the poor house, and it might bring a smile to that cute face of Emmie's or the other kids to return home to a freezer full of ice cream.

As he dug the dessert out of his saddlebags, a loudly shouted, "No!" rent the night air.

He froze. "What the fuck…" Did that come from Mak's place?

Another shout followed by what could only be called a tortured moan had him racing toward the front door.

Christ, that was Mak, for sure. What the hell had they been thinking, leaving her alone? Had the CDMC seen through their bullshit story? Did they know Makenna had ties to the Handlers? Were they in there fucking torturing her right now?

The smart thing would be to call this into Screw, but another of those moans had him charging the front door without backup.

Of course, she'd left the goddammed thing unlocked.

"Fuck," he muttered as he entered the house. He dropped the bags at the door and sprinted down the hallway toward the one room with a strip of light shining at the bottom. Backup wouldn't be necessary. He'd tear apart whoever was in there, hurting Makenna with his bare hands.

"Makenna!" Without bothering to announce his presence, he rammed into the door, busting through the flimsy lock only to come to a complete stop.

"What the fuck?" His dick hardened before his brain processed what his eyes were seeing.

Splayed out on the bed, in the most erotic picture he'd ever seen, lay Makenna. A totally naked, mid-masturbation, clearly loving it Makenna.

She squeaked and even that had his dick twitching.

He should leave. Hell, at the very least, he should offer to leave, but he couldn't fucking move. His dick throbbed and probably fucking leaked in his jeans.

Her body was flushed pink with exertion, and a light sheen of perspiration made her silky-smooth skin fucking glow. Her chest heaved, and her tight little nipples pointed out as though reaching for him. Her lower lip was red from where she'd no doubt been biting it, and her eyes had that pleasure-drunk look that meant one thing.

She'd been close.

She was so damn sexy, he could have come from the tight fit of his jeans against his still growing erection.

Between her spread legs, a thick pink vibrator penetrated her, still buzzing away. It was slick and shiny, as was her pussy and upper thighs. Thunder's mouth fucking watered. It'd been ages since he'd tasted a woman in that way. He'd fucked, clients mostly, and they never had time for him to go down on them. They either wanted to suck him off or be fucked roughly. Not that he ever had any desire to eat those women.

But Makenna?

Fuck the ice cream; a much more tempting treat had presented itself.

He took two steps forward, and her eyes began to dart around the sparsely decorated room, but when he reached the bed, she made eye contact.

"I-I..." Breathless, the words barely audible, she gaped at him with wide eyes and parted lips. But still, she hadn't shifted. Hadn't removed the toy.

As they stared at each other, the buzzing and Mak's heavy breathing were the only sounds in the room. He couldn't help but ogle her small but perky breasts with their pink nipples puckered so nicely for him. All they needed was a glossy shine from his tongue to make them picture-perfect.

Without speaking, he lifted one foot to the bed, removed his boot, then did the same with the other. Mak never took her eyes off him. Not even when he crawled onto her bed and right up to her bent legs.

The moment grew so charged, so tense with sexual need, there was only one way this would end. It'd been so long since he felt this genuine and all-consuming desire for a woman. Getting off was one thing. Coming was easy as fuck in his line of work, but finding one who made him want to fuck her all night long was quite another. The women he fucked didn't even register beyond the physical release. It was the same from their perspective. They didn't want *him*. They wanted ammunition. For the moment they found out their husband of fourteen years was banging his secretary. Perfect opportunity to fire back with the time—or times—they had their mouth full of twenty-five-year-old stripper dick. Or the time the dirty biker fucked them senseless.

This scenario here was entirely different, and quite the mind fuck. Christ, he wanted to see Makenna's face contort with pleasure as he made her come again and again. And he wanted to be inside her while she did it. Feel her nails score his skin. Her pussy milk his cock. Hear his name on her lips. Feel that rush of pride at being the man to bring her pleasure. That shit did as much to a man as the actual orgasm.

"Take it out," he said, voice deeper than ever before.

He gave her a beat to comply. Indecision flashed in her eyes before they took a quick peek at the tent in his jeans.

Yeah, baby, that's all for you.

Her throat worked in a delicate up and down motion as she swallowed and then slowly, so slowly he'd have thought she was trying to torture him if he didn't know her better, she began to draw the vibrator from her pussy.

It'd take a bullet to the brain to keep him from watching as each millimeter of the toy became exposed. It was wet, shiny, slick with her juices. When nothing but the tip remained, he gripped above her fingers and pulled it the rest of the way out himself.

Makenna gasped then bit her lower lip. The unconscious move was so damn sexy he nearly blew his load right there. This look of curious innocence on her face, so in contrast with the drenched vibrator he held.

"I heard you scream," he said as he lifted the toy. "Heard loud moans like you were being hurt."

Her mouth popped open, and her cheeks became as pink as her vibrator. "No," she whispered.

With one push of a button, the noise stopped, and Mak's breathing became the only sound. Still faster than average, still making her tits quiver. Lifting the toy to his face, he inhaled then smiled at her loud gasp. "No," he said in agreement. "You weren't being hurt. You are being naughty." Then he met her gaze and took a long lick up the side of the vibrator before tossing it on the bed.

"Oh, my God," Mak whispered as the sweetness of her pussy hit his taste buds. "Y-you didn't just..."

He laughed, the sound low and smoky. She shivered.

"Oh, but I did. And it was fucking delicious." He reached out and circled her ankle with his hand. "Do you have any idea how sexy you are, Makenna?"

She shook her head.

Thunder hefted his denim-covered erection. "This oughta give you some clue." He tilted his head. "I've spent most of my life around dancers dressed in nothing more than ribbon and glitter, and none of them got to me like this."

"I—you're serious?"

Ugh, her lack of confidence hit him straight in the ticker. "Fuck, yes, I'm serious. Babe, I've had a hard-on for you since the first time I saw you in your diner T-shirt. Now..." He lifted the toy up again. "You want this back, or you want to replace rubber with a real live cock?"

She was quiet for so long, he almost didn't believe she'd answer when she finally said, "You," in the softest voice imaginable.

It was all he needed to hear to have him catapulting his body forward until he hovered over her. "You fucking scared me," he said, hands on either side of her head, holding his weight. "Thought something was wrong."

Her face softened, and for the first time, she seemed to find her voice. "I was taking advantage of the alone time." Her shy smile nearly killed him.

"Maybe next time...close the windows? Yeah?"

She giggled then slapped a hand over her mouth, but it was too late. More giggles bubbled out. "Oh shit," she finally said between laughs. "I didn't even think of that."

"Yeah. Though I can't say I'm mad about it right now." He rocked his pelvis into her, making her eyes flare.

"C-can you take your clothes off?" she asked.

"You wanna see some skin?" he asked as pushed off the bed and up onto his knees.

"I do," she whispered. "I want to feel it, too."

"Fuck, yes."

As he drew his T-shirt over his head, she spoke again. "I was thinking about you."

His movement stuttered, making her laugh. She was gonna be the death of him. "When? While you fucked that toy into your pussy?"

She nodded. "You were dancing."

Where the hell was this confidence coming from, and how did he keep it going? He tossed his shirt on the floor. "Ballet? I do a mean Swan Lake."

Another laugh. Damn, he could live off those elated noises for weeks. It was the lightest she'd sounded since he'd met her. This woman needed more enjoyment in her life. Someone had to remind her there was fun to be had among the mountains of responsibility.

And he was the man for the job. He was the fucking master of fun.

"It was something a little less, uh, refined," she said, mischief twinkling in her eyes.

Yeah, he fucking bet it was. He lowered the zipper of his jeans, tooth by tooth, noting the way her gaze tracked the movements. When his cock spilled out, hard as a fucking spike, she sucked in a breath.

That's right, baby. Commando.

He gripped his length, then gave a few rough strokes.

Mak licked her lips. Licked her fucking lips like she was trying to lap up the precum escaping from the slit.

"Unrefined, huh?" He asked as he continued to pleasure himself. Watching her watch him was as good as any sex he'd had in the last few years. "You sure it wasn't just plain fucking dirty?"

"Thunder?"

"Yeah?"

"Can we stop talking now?"

Now, he was the one laughing. "Somebody's getting hungry for my cock, huh?" he asked as he released said cock then worked his jeans off. Over his shoulder they went, but not before he snagged the condom out of the back pocket.

Mak was ready, more than ready. She squirmed as she watched him roll the latex down his weeping dick. The damn thick twitched in protest of the condom. First time in his life, he regretted the need for one. How fucking unreal would it feel to push into her scorching wetness without a barrier?

Damn, his eyes rolled back, just imagining it. Maybe someday…if this continued.

And if unicorns flew out of his ass.

Once the condom was secure, he grabbed her thighs and pushed her legs even wider, exposing her soaked pussy to his ravenous gaze. He'd be eating that sometime soon, but not tonight. Tonight, foreplay wouldn't be necessary, not with how far gone she'd been when he busted the door down.

But shoving into that willing pussy would be rude without at least a kiss first, so he crawled up her body until their lips aligned. He rarely kissed the women he fucked. Kissing was an intimate act that spoke to connection and he had none with other women.

Mak breathed heavily, and each time her chest expanded, those pert little nipples brushed against his smooth chest, sending a series of shocks through his system.

"Gimme your lips and I'll give you my cock," he whispered, barely grazing her mouth with his.

Mak lifted her lips in offering and he wasted no time taking a taste. She'd been drinking wine before he'd arrived. The acidic tang, combined with her intoxicating flavor, got him drunker than he'd ever been. He eased into the kiss, teasing her lips with flicks of his tongue and gentle nips. Each time he brushed his mouth over hers, her lips parted on a soft sigh as though waiting to admit him, but he kept the contact light. Soon she was chasing him with her mouth, lifting her head to prolong contact.

"Please," she whispered, eyes shut.

"Please, what?"

"Please kiss me."

He chuckled. "I am kissing you," he murmured against her lips.

A small growl rumbled from her, making him smile.

"Kiss me for real."

"Yes, ma'am." He captured her lips with firm pressure this time. As before, her lips parted on a blissful sigh. This time, he slipped his tongue inside, tasting her sweetness. When she whimpered, he kissed her harder.

They made out for long minutes, sampling every corner of each other's mouths. Thunder swallowed her mewls and she did the same to his groans of pleasure. Need for more ramped up, and he found himself crushing her into the bed as he began to rock his needy cock against her.

She wrapped her arms around him, forcing their bodies even closer, but it was the way she thrust her hips up that undid him. The heat of her sex stroked along the length of his cock, eliciting a rolling tremor that started in his balls and shook him to his core.

All he felt after that was the driving need to fuck. To be buried inside her and experience her pleasure from the inside out. Somehow, he managed to rein in the animalistic need and slowed things down.

He snuck hand between their bodies and down to the neatly trimmed thatch of dark hair hiding her pussy. One finger found its way to her sex. He teased her with light touches and rims of her opening.

Fuck, the look on her face. Excitement, wonder, bliss.

She was soft and soaked, prepared by the toy. He should probably play for longer, draw this out, and make her come a few times before fucking her, but seeing her splayed out, fucking herself on the vibrator had him unable to ignore the need to replace that damn toy.

"Ready?" he whispered, panting as he hovered an inch above her. If she changed her mind, he'd go, but the effort might annihilate him.

She nodded fast. "So ready." Beneath him, she shivered.

Nerves? Excitement? Cold?

No, not cold. They'd nearly burned down the house, and they weren't even fucking yet.

Time to change that.

Thunder reached between them, fisting his latex covered cock. The damn thing was so hard, it stuck out like a barb, and the contact of his hand made his entire body seize up. He met Mak's gaze as he positioned it at her slippery opening. Her eyes darkened, glazed and needy but with a hint of trepidation.

Some anxiety could be expected as it didn't seem she messed around like this often. He couldn't wait to chase away the uncertainty and replace it with a come-drunk haze.

Ever so slowly, he pressed forward, breaching her.

Mak gasped, arching her neck as her eyes widened. Then she bit her lower lip in a way he'd have sworn was practiced seduction were she any other woman. It was so inherently erotic.

Innocence and invitation tangled, hot as hell.

With every fraction of an inch he burrowed deeper, rational thought disappeared. "Fuck me, you're so goddamned tight," he ground out, as he fought to keep his eyes from crossing.

Finally, after what felt like an eternity tunneling through the tightest pussy he'd ever felt, he bottomed out.

Mak moaned and squirmed beneath him. Each movement caused intense shocks of pleasure to shoot up his spine. "Thunder, please."

Shit, he could listen to her beg for hours. But there was no way his cock would be put off for that long. "Please, what? Tell me what you want."

"More," she said as she curled her short fingernails into his sides. "I don't know...something...more. It's not enough."

His hair flopped against his forehead as he stared down at her. "You want me to fuck you now?"

She nodded. That lip was back between her teeth, and if he wasn't careful, he'd unload inside the condom from the sight alone. She nodded again.

"My pleasure." This time he thrust harder, making her back arch off the bed.

She cried out.

Thunder bent down and kissed her until she released the abused flesh. "Don't keep it in," he said against her mouth, already breathing hard. "I want to hear you. I fucking love your sounds."

"O-okay," she said, eyes wide and glassy. Their gazes met, and he swore at that moment she saw past all his bullshit straight to the man he was. The man who feared getting crushed by love and had no idea what to do with all these churning emotions.

"Thank you." He kissed her again, then talking ceased as he powered into her over and over. Beneath him, Makenna mewled and whimpered with every hammer of his hips. She gripped him like he'd disappear if she let go.

Would he bear ten small round bruises from the force of her fingers clinging to his sides? She'd probably turn beet red with embarrassment, but fuck, he hoped she'd marked his skin.

It'd been so damn long since he found this much pleasure in a woman. Since he wanted one to mark him, fuck him up in the best way, and do the same to her. Even longer since he wanted to see one again after he fucked her. But he wanted more than just core-shaking sex. He wanted the way she looked at him with a combination of shyness, need, and curiosity. He wanted her smiles and laughs. And he wanted her to want him just as much.

Within minutes, his balls had drawn up tight, nearly pulsing with the need to come. Makenna was close too.

She planted her heels on the bed, lifting her hips. Thrust for thrust, she met him with her brand of desperation. Her eyes were screwed shut, but her mouth hung open as she sucked in deep, gasping breaths. Her dark hair clung to her damp forehead, and a sheen of perspiration covered her chest, beckoning him. He licked the side of her neck, unable to resist a taste. That fucking salty-sweet was dammed delicious.

Thunder picked up the pace. With each thrust of his hips, his orgasm drew closer until holding back became nearly imposing. He stared down at her. For sure, she'd be right there with him, ready to explode.

But what he saw almost made him stop. No longer did her face look contorted in pleasure, but in fierce concentration. Maybe she needed a little clit action. Why the fuck hadn't he thought of that before? With a gentle touch, he used his thumb to stroke a circle around the firm nub.

Makenna jolted.

"That's the spot, isn't it, baby?"

She nodded, but didn't relax, didn't open her eyes, didn't come. Her groan wasn't one of pleasure, but of frustration.

What the hell?

"Mak?"

She didn't answer but continued to pump her hips against him as though working with a single-minded focus to get herself off. Gone was the intimate connection that had crackled between them. She'd severed the link with her fierce determination. He might as well have been that pink vibrator for all the attention she paid him. Typically, that was fine by him, preferred even, but something about this wasn't working for her, and that wasn't acceptable. He wanted the soft, mewling woman who'd stared up at him with adoration.

"Mak," he said again, with tenderness. He slowed his hips until they rocked in and out of her with small gentle movements.

"N-no," she said on a groan. Her eyes were screwed so tight, she'd give herself a headache. She bucked as though trying to fuck herself on him, so he pressed his weight into her to hold her still.

"Makenna, look at me," he said before pressing a kiss to each of her eyes.

She shook her head. "I c-can't."

"Sweetheart," he said as softly, and with as much care as he could manage, despite the fact he was still buried inside her tight heat. "Look at me."

On instinct, he wrapped a hand around the front of her throat, squeezing with slight pressure. Not enough to restrict her breathing, but enough to snatch her attention.

Her eyes flew open, and she met his gaze. Then she moaned. Not another of those frustrated ones, but a straight-up sex moan. Pure lust shone in her gaze.

He squeezed again with the same light pressure. This time her pussy clenched around him, and she shuddered.

Holy fuck, his Makenna liked this.

Chapter Sixteen

Oh, my God, he's choking me.

Just as she was about to screech at him to get off, her insides spasmed with a need so violent, it almost stole her breath. There wasn't anything she could do to keep the throaty moan from escaping.

They stared at each other, both seeming shocked by this discovery. Thunder flexed his hand and she swore her entire body lit up like a neon sign.

In actuality, he wasn't choking her. Not at all. But he could be. One crush of his hand and her air would vanish. He held her life in his hand. She was his to do with as he pleased. There was no option to break free, as he had so much more strength and bulk than she did. Powerless and without an ounce of control, she couldn't think, only lie there and wait for his next move, which happened to be a slow, torturous roll of his hips that made her whimper.

God, that felt incredible.

He did it again, and she trembled as the charged sensations came to life inside her.

How could this feel good? How could she want more? She'd been controlled by violent men all her life. Men who told her what to wear, what to say, who to marry. Her husband had been the most domineering of all, ordering her to spread her legs whenever he wanted an attempt at knocking her up.

She'd hated every second of that life.

But this? This was different. She was under him by choice, and Thunder used his hands for *her* pleasure.

As rational thought fled, physical sensation filled up the vacated space. No longer did she worry about the kids sleeping at Cassie's. Stress over their financial situation vanished. Fear of being discovered by her father or husband dissipated like smoke in the wind. Thunder and pleasure assumed command over her mind and body, leaving room for nothing else.

He owned her with complete authority as he thrust into her again and again. Within seconds, she was right back to where she'd been, hovering at the precipice of an incredible cliff. Before, she'd been stuck there, working like a madwoman to fling herself over the edge, but never tipping forward enough to take the plunge.

The hand around her throat tightened as the exact moment his hips ground into her, rubbing her clit, and that was all it took. Makenna shattered with a sharp cry. Blinding light flashed behind her closed eyes, her muscles seized, and her entire system flooded with overwhelming ecstasy. If she could have lived in that moment forever, she would have.

How had she gone so long without experiencing it?

She'd known her life was lacking, but now she knew exactly how much. Not only the physical but the intimate connection they'd shared. The way he'd been able to read her and provide what she'd needed.

"Yes, baby, that's it," Thunder said as he continued to fuck her. "God, you're so beautiful when you come." His hips flew, propelling her through the orgasm. Within a minute, he shouted her name as his muscles bunched and flexed beneath her fingertips. "Fuck, fuck, fuck," he yelled, hands moving to her shoulders. He held himself deep, pushing down on her shoulders to maintain the connection.

Thunder

The sight of him lost to his pleasure fascinated her. She'd done that to him with her body. She'd made him feel as good as he'd made her feel.

"Fuck," he mumbled one last time before collapsing on top of her.

With the weight of him compressing her chest, she couldn't catch her breath, but she wouldn't have changed it for the world. Their sweaty bodies mashed together with their runaway hearts beating side by side. It was life-changing,

"I'm moving," he grumbled. "In a second."

She stroked her hands up and down his damp back. "Don't."

Now he laughed. "You could barely say the word because you don't have any air."

The statement had her freezing up. God, had she really come like that while his hand was wrapped around her throat?

What the hell was wrong with her?

It was crazy, right? Depraved and sick. She was a freak.

Her limbs still zinged with pleasure and a pleasant heaviness. Now wasn't the time to worry about her reaction to his manhandling. She had Thunder in her bed and planned to enjoy every second of it. Once he left, she could freak out.

With a groan, he pushed up until he hovered over her. Then he kissed her. It was so tender and full of unexpected sweetness, her chest constricted. After, he rolled off her and onto his back. One arm flopped above his head on the pillow, and the other rested on his ridged stomach. Mak couldn't help but risk a glance at what had been inside her seconds ago.

Spent, his cock lay against his thigh, still covered in the condom, but slick now with the evidence of her desire. The craziest thought crossed her mind and had she been braver and experienced, maybe she'd have given into it and snapped a picture of him with her phone. One to remind her of the time a man brought her to life in a brand-new way.

"Like what you see?" he asked, humor lacing his tone.

Her face heated as she jumped.

Busted. "How did you know?"

Eyes still closed, he shrugged. "I can feel those pretty blue eyes."

"Guess you're used to women looking at you." Oh, my God. She nearly slapped her forehead. Had those words really left her mouth? How insensitive. There he was, basking in the afterglow of what she thought was world-changing sex, and she brought up his job as a stripper.

Smooth, Mak.

But Thunder just laughed. "True," he said. Then he turned her way.

She watched, entranced, as he pulled the condom off, tied the end, then tossed it in the small trash can next to her bed.

"Come here," he said, once finished. His voice thickened, sounding heavy with the need for sleep. "Much as I like those pretty eyes on me, I'd rather feel your skin on mine." He nearly slurred the words.

At that point, Mak was nearly giddy with excitement. This night was already so far out of her realm of experience, she'd had no idea what to expect now that they'd had sex. His leaving seemed the most probable outcome, at least based on conversations she overheard when serving other single members of his club at the diner. None of them seemed keen on spending the night with a hook-up. At least that's what she assumed when Screw had been telling a story about a time he'd "rocked the box then changed the locks." Unfortunately for him, Jazz had also overhead, and he'd earned himself a slap to the back of his head.

Mak scooted until they were chest to chest, then inhaled his intoxicating fragrance. The cologne, aftershave, deodorant... whatever it was he used, it drew her in to the point she wanted to rub all over him like a needy cat.

Wait...she just had.

Her face heated, and she peeked up at his face. The man was out cold. Oblivious to her private smile and internal euphoria. The strong arms anchoring her to an equally strong chest were a luxury she'd never experienced in her years of marriage. Not only were her husband's arms those of a sixty-plus-year-old man who'd never taken care of himself, but they belonged to a man who didn't give two shits about her beyond her incubation ability and mothering skills. Lying with a man who seemed not only to want her sexually but enjoy her company was a novel experience that could easily become addicting.

She'd be a fool to let that happen, wouldn't she? Thunder hadn't expressed any desire for a relationship. He hadn't taken her on a date, spoke of a future, or expressed an interest in knowing her on a deeper level.

But he had come to her house to apologize. He'd spent an evening with her siblings. He'd held Emmie while the toddler slept. Then there was the way he'd helped her at the CDMC clubhouse and stayed with her the entire time Copper interrogated her.

If it was true, what they said, and actions did speak louder than words, maybe he was interested in more than just this night. He was sleeping in her bed after all, instead of running for the hills.

Argh, and there went her head again, full of ridiculous, unobtainable fantasies.

Her eyes grew gritty, and the steady beat of his heart against her ear began to lull her into a sleepy state. Maybe, only for tonight, she could pretend this was her real life. Imagine she didn't have hundreds of pounds of baggage, siblings to take care of, more expenses than funds, and fantasize that Thunder wanted to fall asleep this way every night and wake together each morning.

She couldn't wait to see what he looked like in tomorrow's early morning light.

THUNDER BLINKED THROUGH the darkness of the unfamiliar surroundings.

Fuck me, did I fall asleep at a client's place?

The night came crashing back to him in a rush of pleasure that had his dick thickening against the ass cradling it.

Makenna's sweet ass.

He'd never experienced anything like the expression of wonder on her face when she came with his hand wrapped around her neck. Fuck, it'd been hot as hell. He'd never been much for exerting control in the bedroom; hell most of the women he fucked around with got off on bossing him around, but this shit with Makenna ramped him up like nothing else.

Knowing she'd been struggling to climax, unable to fucking grab it until the moment he'd forced her to submit hit his blood like a drug. It'd sent him on a high he'd kill to chase again and again.

And it'd caused him to come so hard, every ounce of his energy had been zapped to the point he didn't even remember pulling out. Certainly didn't recall falling asleep, which was rule number one.

Never fucking fall asleep. If a guy wanted a clinger on his hands, one-night snoring in her bed would do it.

Mak was soft, warm, and smelled like a fucking vanilla cupcake, and he was ready for another sample.

Fatigue still pulled at the edges of his mind, which made sense, considering it was still dark as hell outside. What the fuck time was it?

He craned his neck to see the numbers on a clock next to Mak's bed. Three-fifteen in the morning. Damn, he'd slept half the night away.

Though the temptation to say fuck it all, curl himself back around Makenna and pass the rest of the night next to her was tempting—extra tempting if he let himself think about having her again in the morning—he forced himself to roll away.

Once sitting at the edge of her bed, he scrubbed a hand over his face. Reluctant nerve endings woke as blood flowed north. He glanced down. Well, some of the blood anyway. Plenty still pooled in his cock. Fuck, he could go again right now, gladly. Time to leave before it grew into a craving he couldn't ignore.

As quietly as he could, he gathered his clothes and tiptoed toward the door. Before leaving, he succumbed to the urge to take one last look at a sleeping Makenna.

Immediately, he wished he hadn't. She'd shifted to her stomach since he'd left her bed, drawing one leg up toward her chest. The move caused the sheet to slip down, revealing the smooth curve of her back, leading to her pert little ass.

Damn, now he wanted to bite it.

"Fuck," he whispered on a low growl.

Staying would be the stupidest idea he'd ever had, so he forced his legs into action and walked out of the house without another backward glance.

It'd be depressing to go back to fucking rich housewives after the night of real passion in Makenna's bed. But he'd do it.

Because what the fuck was he supposed to do with a sweet, hardworking girl like Makenna who put everyone in her life before herself?

He was far too fucked in the head for that kind of woman. For any woman, really. Who wanted a man whose entire childhood example of relationships consisted of brothels, abuse, and monetary exchanges? Surprisingly enough, his mother had been married for the past seventeen years—not to his father, of course, or the husband after his father, but the same man for seventeen years.

Who the hell knew who'd provided the sperm for his egg? His mother and her current husband ran an illegal cat house in Kentucky where he'd grown up. Marriage hadn't kept his mother from selling her body through his entire childhood. Nor had it made his father treat her with respect. By the time he'd been six, he'd known what sex was and about fifty different ways to execute it. He'd also learned the manipulative powers of the human body, for financial gain, political advantage, and a host of other unscrupulous and selfish reasons.

Ethics? Morals? Selflessness? They hadn't existed in his upbringing. The concept of love, of people choosing to be monogamous and treat sex as something special had been so foreign to him as a teen, the idea boggled his mind. All he'd witnessed were couples taking what they claimed was love and using it to tear each other to shreds.

He wanted no part of that kind of pain.

Even the few examples of solid relationships he'd seen recently weren't exempt from pain and heartbreak. Look at Cassie. Though she and Viper did everything right, Cassie had been left behind broken hearted, her husband ripped from her.

Time to get out of there before he began to consider something insane. Something that would end with both of them broken and bleeding from the heart.

Mak would thank him for it if she knew what was good for her.

Chapter Seventeen

"Thanks again, Shell," Mak said as she stood in the foyer of Copper and Shell's beautiful, enormous home. "You too, Cassie. I can't tell you how much this meant to me."

As she spoke the words, her face heated. She couldn't tell them why it meant so much to her because then she'd have to admit she had crazy, and mind-blowing sex with Thunder. And after that, she'd be forced to think about how she'd woken up alone, confused, and feeling like an utter fool.

"Honey, it was our pleasure," Cassie said, as she balanced Emmie on her hip. "Seriously, I might just steal this little one if you're not careful."

Mak reached out to take her sister. "Let me have her. She's heavy." Cassie had recently completed a course of chemotherapy for cancer. While Shell told Mak the older woman was in full remission, she still had a way to go to regain her pre-treatment strength. Having also lost her husband within the past few months, she'd basically been through hell. Despite it all, she always had a smile and seemed to be in remarkable spirits. The entire club had jumped in to support Cassie. She'd recently moved in with Copper and Shell to help with childcare and be surrounded by her chosen family.

Witnessing all the love and support Cassie had never failed to astound Makenna. What would it be like to have a whole huge group of people willing to do anything to help at the drop of a hat? It'd be extraordinary. And humbling. Makenna couldn't imagine it.

"Nonsense," Cassie said, swatting Makenna's outstretched arms away. "I'm not letting her go until I have to."

With a big smile and a thumb in her mouth, Emmie rested her head on Cassie's shoulder. The thumb-sucking habit needed to go, but with everything else on her plate, Mak had let it slide. If the poor little girl needed it to soothe herself for a little longer, it wouldn't be the end of the world.

"Come on in. Sit a while. Have some coffee," Shell said, waving Mak into the room. "You've been on your feet all morning."

Exhaustion pulled at her even though she'd slept like the dead in Thunder's arms. Today's five-hour shift at the diner had been particularly grueling and hectic.

Ugh, why had he left? When had he left? Had she done something wrong?

She'd woken to discover a shopping bag full of melted ice cream on the floor by the front door. In his mad dash to rescue her from her vibrator, he must have dropped it.

The humiliation never ended.

More shameful was the fact he didn't stop to pick the bags up on the way out. Did that mean he was in as much of a rush to escape as he'd been to get inside? Thank God, she'd been asleep and spared the disgrace of having to listen to excuses as he fled.

"Mak?" Shell tilted her head as she held the door open.

"Sorry. Zoned out there for a second." She stepped into the cozy home with a smile.

"I don't know how you do it," Shell said. "I'm terrified of how I'll manage two, and I have Copper and Cassie for backup. You're Superwoman." The words came across as completely sincere, yet a little sad.

She got it. It was sad, from others' perspectives. There she was in her early twenties with no life beyond working and raising siblings. No time for dating, love, even a night of fun. Last night had been the first ever. She shrugged off the weight of despair that occasionally snuck in. No point in lamenting reality. "When you don't have a choice, you just do what you have to. Trust me, I am far from Superwoman. I'm way too messy for that title."

Shell stepped closer and opened her arms. "You look like you need this."

As Shell's arms closed around her, Mak shook her head. "Sorry. I didn't mean to sound snarky or whiny." She returned the embrace. How long had it been since someone had hugged her with the sole purpose of comforting her? God, it felt crazy good, and the urge to cling to Shell while she had a minor breakdown hit hard. If she'd known sharing a little of her struggles would make her feel so needy, she'd have kept her mouth shut.

Mak released Shell and stepped back.

Getting used to comfort from others would be foolish and make it so much harder to move on when she inevitably left.

Cassie set Emmie down. The toddler immediately charged into the den with the other girls. With a welcoming smile, Cassie took Mak's hand and led her to the kitchen. As they walked, Kara came running up for a quick hug, followed by Emmie, then the kids wetn into the den to finish watching their movie.

"Okay, honey," Cassie said as she guided Mak to a chair in the sunny kitchen. Everything looked so new and fresh, as though it'd only been a short time since the home had been remodeled. The counters were littered with papers, a few toys, and cooking utensils, giving the space a comfortably disorganized look. Like the rest of what she'd seen of the house. Not messy by any means, but a home lived in by real people who were comfortable in their space.

Cassie placed a mug in front of her and filled it with coffee. A plate of cookies also appeared on the table. This home was straight out of a Disney movie. All they needed was for someone to break out in random song, and her youngest few siblings would be more than happy to crush that task. "We've known each other long enough now that I hope you consider Shell and I friends. I know I speak for her when I say we think of you as a friend, a good one."

Good friends? Really? Was Makenna so socially stunted she hadn't realized they thought of her in that way? A burst of warmth spread through her body. She hadn't been looking for friendship; hadn't wanted it, but apparently, she'd found it. Her mental reflex was to deny Cassie's words and keep their association on a professional level, but something inside of her craved this connection.

Would it really be that awful to claim them as friends? She'd started over from nothing before and knew how difficult the experience was. But she also knew she could survive it again if they left. So maybe she should soak up the gift and use the memories to help her through dark times later.

Mak straightened in her chair. "I do think of you guys as friends. And I value that friendship so much." It'd been so long, she worried she didn't express her feelings well enough. It was impossible not to like Cassie. The woman had barreled her way into Mak's life in the most fantastic way possible, getting her a job, babysitting, and bringing sunshine every time she came around.

"Good," Cassie said, pushing the plate of cookies Mak's way. "Then tell us what has you stressed out when you should be... dare I say, satisfied today." One of her thin eyebrows rose in an arc above her eye. They'd only begun to grow back in recent weeks.

"Satisfied?" Shell's gaze bounced between the two of them. "Huh? What am I missing?"

Oh, my God, could the floor just open up and swallow her whole? Her face burned.

Cassie's grin was positively smug. "A little birdie told me Thunder went to your house last night and didn't come home until almost four this morning."

Four, huh? So he'd stayed for a while. Slept even. But why had he left?

"Monty?" Shell asked, gaze on Cassie. "I heard he was rooming with Thunder for a few months until he found a place."

"Yep. That boy is the worst of the bunch when it comes to gossip." Cassie's eyes sparkled with mirth. "That's why I love him."

Both women stared at Mak. "I…uh…well, he…can I plead the fifth?"

"No!" They said in unison, making Mak laugh.

Shell leaned forward. "Hmm." She strummed her nails on the tabletop while studying Mak's face. Then her jaw dropped. "Holy shit! You slept with him," she whispered as though Thunder sat in the next room.

"I, wha—how do you know that?" Was the woman a psychic?

Shell sat back with a mischievous smile while Cassie chuckled. "I didn't. But thank you for confirming it."

Well, shit, she'd been had. "You're evil." Despite her embarrassment, Mak couldn't help but smile. She bit into the cookie Cassie practically forced into her hands. It was then she realized how much she was enjoying herself. When the hell had she ever done this? Girl talk, gossiping about her sex life, laughing. Damn, it was fun!

"You know you're the first," Shell said around a mouthful of cookie.

"First?" Mak sipped her coffee. Caffeine was precisely what she needed—lots and lots of caffeine. "You can't possibly mean the first woman he's been with," she said with a laugh.

"No, I mean the first who has a connection to the club. Usually, he just sleeps with clients." She waved a hand as though it was common knowledge and no big deal.

Mak's stomach dropped. "Clients?"

"Shell..." Cassie's voice held a note of warning.

"Oh, uh, I assumed you knew." Shell's hand stilled midway to the plate of cookies. She let it fall to the table before shaking her head. "You know what. Never mind. Forget I said anything."

Like that would happen. "No, tell me, please."

Shell shot a pleading look Cassie's way.

The older woman just sighed. "Thunder grew up in a bit of an unconventional way. His mother was a...well she was a sex worker in a cat house. He doesn't talk about it, so I don't know much, but he grew up there and has a bit of a skewed view of relationships. From what I gather, he only has sex with women who...hire him, I guess you'd say."

"He's a prostitute?" Mak squeaked. She sure as hell knew about unconventional upbringings, but prostitution wasn't something she'd never have guessed. Or had any idea how to handle.

"Not really," Shell cut in. "He doesn't specifically hire himself out for that purpose." She frowned. "It's a little hard to explain. You know he's a stripper. Many times, the women will offer him extra for...other things." Her cheeks turned pink. "He's never hooked up with anyone at a club party or had a girlfriend that I'm aware of. I think he views sex as a form of currency. It's... well, it's a little sad."

"Wow, I had no idea." She slumped back against her chair as her thoughts whirled. So why her? Why did he break his pattern for her?

"He must really like you," Shell added, beaming.

"I like him too." Whoops, she hadn't meant to admit that aloud. But the cat was out of the bag now.

Shell clapped. "This is awesome. I love you two together. He's so fun, and you need some fun in your life, missy."

Cassie smiled, but it didn't portray the same enthusiasm. Older and with more life experience, she probably realized nothing would come of this, but still, Mak couldn't help the buzz of excitement at being something more to Thunder.

Bits of the previous night replayed in her head, making her nearly dizzy with the thrill of it. Until she recalled the moment Thunder had grasped her neck. Then the uncertainty, confusion, and even shame came rushing back. So much about what happened made no sense to her. If only there was a way to unbox and sort the feelings.

Cassie and Shell claimed to want to be her friends, said they were her friends, and, so far, acted as though they meant it. Girlfriends shared their problems and went to each other for advice, right? Who else did she have to talk to? For years she'd kept her fears, troubles, and stresses confined inside her head. Sure, Lee was an excellent sounding board, but not for something like this.

Maybe, just maybe, opening up to these women would provide some clarity. A quick peek over her shoulder into the den revealed the kids still absorbed in the movie while Shell's daughter Beth built a tower of blocks with a chattering Emmie. "Can I ask you guys something?"

"Of course," Cassie said. "Anything. And if you need, nothing leaves this table."

Shell reached out and took her hand. It seems the women could sense her internal struggle. "We have a powerful bond with our sisters in the club, Makenna. It's one we take seriously, and one that can be trusted."

The words chased away any lingering doubt with regards to opening up. "Okay, well, I um, also grew up in a bit of an unconventional way." She waved a hand in front of her face. "I don't want to get into it all right now, but I was married at nineteen, to a man older than you, Cassie."

Both women gasped.

"It wasn't my choice; it was just how they did things where I grew up. Anyway, it was a very controlling relationship." She stared at her hands as she spoke. The women may be friends, but embarrassment still kept her from making eye contact. "I had no independence, no ability to say no…if you get where I'm going with this."

Shell scooted her chair closer then wrapped an arm around Mak's shoulders. "Take your time."

"Thank you. I hated being with him…uh, you know."

"You hated having sex with him," Cassie said. "Pretty sure anyone would feel the same way, sweetie."

"Right. Since my siblings and I left, I've been extremely independent. A complete one-eighty from how I grew up. It's the most important thing to me. Having control over my life, never living under anyone's thumb again. Choosing for myself."

"Understandable," Shell said, squeezing Mak's shoulders.

"Right, so uh last night when we were…"

"Fucking?" Shell supplied.

They all laughed. Tension dissipated, and Mak was able to nod. "Right. It was good…really, really good."

"I can imagine," Cassie said, making Shell hoot with laughter.

"You dirty girl," Shell said to Cassie, who just winked.

Mak smiled. The banter went a long way toward making this admission easier. "Okay, so it was good, but I couldn't…finish. It just wasn't happening, no matter how incredible it felt. No matter how hard I concentrated. And then Thunder…" Oh, God, she couldn't say it.

"Hey, whatever it is, it's okay. If you both consent, anything is fair game," Shell said.

"Um, he put his hand around my throat. Not enough to choke me," she rushed on, lifting a hand to her neck. Last thing she wanted was to make them think he hurt her in any way.

But both women just nodded. "Hot, right?" Cassie asked, making Mak's jaw drop.

"Honey, Viper and I weren't vanilla. We liked to have fun."

"Ugh," Shell said with a laugh. "You're like a second mom. TMI, woman."

"So, I'm guessing you liked it?" Cassie asked, voice soft. "And it's confusing you?"

"Liked it is an understatement," Mak mumbled. When her friends giggled, she continued, "It's kinda freaking me out. I mean, I should have panicked. I should have pushed him away, smacked him, anything but…"

"Freakin' love it?" Shell asked with a half-smile.

"Right."

"It makes perfect sense to me," Cassie said, which had Mak and Shell turning her way. She shrugged as though the maddening puzzle baffling Mak for hours was the simplest thing to solve. "No one would mistake Thunder for an overbearing, controlling asshole, right?"

"Oh yeah, he's not like that at all. The man is super chill," Shell said while Mak nodded.

"And, you trust him," Cassie added.

Well, she did, but… "Okay…"

"Why couldn't you come last night?"

Ugh, could her face get any hotter? Why the hell did Cassie have to be so blunt?

Because you're all adults and friends.

"I don't know. I was trying to but—"

"Exactly!" Cassie said, slapping her hand on the table as though Mak had just made her point. Even Shell nodded along now.

"I don't get it."

"You were trying too hard." Shell grabbed another cookie. "I'm gonna gain ninety pounds this pregnancy, and it's all your fault, Cas. Anyway, you couldn't shut your brain off. You probably have a million things pinging around in there at all times. Having an orgasm just became one more thing for you to stress about."

Without thought, Mak reached for a cookie as well. "Okay, yes, that makes sense, but what does it have to do with me liking…the thing."

"You didn't just like it," Shell said before biting her cookie. She smirked, crumbs and all. "You needed it to get off. You consented, but Thunder took control, which actually gave you some control. You trusted him to stop if you asked, and I guarantee he would have. Even though you could still breathe, the threat of not being able to—and I say threat lightly—took away your stress. Since you were no longer driving the bus, your mind let go, and your body followed straight into orgasmic goodness."

"Hmm." She sat back, nibbling on the delicious cookie as she processed. It made sense. The moment his hand had closed around her throat, all her concerns disappeared. She was able to be present in the moment because she had nothing to worry about. Thunder had her.

She'd trusted him, and he'd given her something she hadn't known she'd needed. An outlet. A safe place to fly with someone to watch over her, protect her, and take the reins while she did so.

The sound of the front door opening saved her from having to respond further.

"Daddy!" Beth screamed before the thumping of little footsteps pounded across the wood floor.

"There's my big girl," Copper's voice boomed into the house. "Where's my *really* big girl?"

"Hey, I heard that," Shell called out with a laugh as she rubbed her growing baby bump. "We're in the kitchen."

"We?"

Copper strode into the kitchen with Beth on his shoulders, followed by Zach, Jigsaw, Izzy, and...oh shit, Thunder.

Mak's heart fluttered in the most ridiculous way. Her stomach did some weird flip-flop as well.

"Ladies," he said before his gaze landed on Makenna. Once it did, his steps faltered, but he played it off and kept walking as though nothing had happened.

"Hey, Mama," Copper said, as he walked up and placed a lingering kiss on Shell's upturned lips while Beth laughed and squealed at him not to drop her.

If Mak wasn't a realist who knew such a connection would never be in the cards for her, she would have sighed, all schmoopy and starry-eyed from witnessing this picture-perfect family.

"Good to see you, Mak," Copper said once done kissing on his wife.

"You too. Thanks again for letting my wild beasts invade your house last night."

With a laugh, Copper snagged a cookie. "Pretty sure I can't take a lick of credit for any of it."

"It's true," Shell said with a snort. "He can't. You guys want anything?" she asked the other men. "Coffee, cookies? Izzy, sit and give me that baby!"

"Don't mind if I do," Thunder said, reaching over Mak's head for a cookie.

Her heart pounded so hard, she'd be amazed if no one called her out on it. Her skin felt hot and tingly just being near him. What the hell was happening to her?

"So Mak," Shell asked with a smirk. "What are you up to for the rest of the day?"

What was she up to? What the hell was Shell up to? "Just gonna hang out with the kids. I promised Emmie and Kara I'd take them to the park if it was a nice day."

"How about you, Thunder? Didn't you say you were looking for something to do this afternoon?"

Mak widened her eyes and glared daggers at Shell. "Seriously?" she mouthed. That had to be the worse, most unsubtle *hint* ever.

Shell shrugged, not an ounce of repentance in sight.

With a laugh, Thunder shook his head. "Nah, I'm laying low this afternoon. Got a gig tonight." He waggled his eyebrows. "Bachelorette party." He executed a sexy little dance move that no doubt would be making an appearance tonight only with much fewer clothes.

Mak's stomach dropped through her seat. A bachelorette party? Did that mean just dancing, or…more? God, how she wished she didn't know about what he got up to for extra cash. Would he be sleeping with another woman tonight? Though she had no claim on him, the thought of it made her want to sink through the floor.

The dramatic change in Shell's facial expression would have been funny had Mak's smile not felt fake as hell. "Oh," Shell said, forehead scrunched. "I thought you were backing off on those?" She cut a glance at Mak, who gave her friend a sharp shake of her head.

"Nope. Why would I? I'm not dancing at the club anymore because the hours fucked with my club obligations, but the private gigs bring in some serious bank and are usually earlier in the night. Why would I give that up?"

Again, Shell cut her gaze to Mak. "Oh, uh, I don't know. Guess I misunderstood."

It felt as though every eye in the place bored into her even though most had no idea about the undercurrent of the conversation. Still, she felt like a bright spotlight shone over her head with a neon sign flashing the word *naïve*.

As Mak made plans to never show her face in Townsend again, Emmie toddled into the kitchen.

Perfect timing, kiddo.

An adorable distraction was precisely what the room needed. She began to rise so she could snatch up her sister, but Emmie noticed Thunder before Mak had a chance to lift off the seat.

Emmie's high-pitched squeal would have been obnoxious from any of the older children, but when combined with her chubby cheeks, bouncy pigtails, and ear to ear smile, no one minded one bit.

"Under!" she yelled so loud most of the adults in the room winced. In an instant, her short arms were reaching up to him. He scooped her up, settled her on his hip, and blew a raspberry on her cheek as though he spent his life making children laugh.

Emmie giggled and yelled, "Again!" as she patted his scruffy face with enthusiasm.

Of course, Thunder obliged; who could resist such a cutie?

"My turn!" Emmie said as she mashed her mouth against Thunder's face, blowing with far more slobber than necessary.

Mak winced and held her arms out. For sure, he'd be ready to pass her off. But Thunder just laughed and held up a hand for a high five, which Emmie happily delivered. Then, as though he seemed to finally realize he and Emmie had an audience, he scanned the room. "What?" he asked the group staring at him with various expressions of surprise.

Izzy, who Mak had learned wasn't one for subtly, snorted. "I can think of a few reasons to cancel. A few damn good ones." She folded her arms across her chest and raised an eyebrow.

Thunder's face screwed up, and he shook his head. "Huh?"

These people were way too far up in each other's business. Izzy clearly meant reasons to give up on the stripping gigs, and she was referring to Mak and Emmie, a fact everyone else in the room seemed to pick up on. Thank God Thunder remained oblivious, though it sure did hit her square in the ego.

And it hurt.

Shit, now the tip of her nose was tingling the way it did before she cried. She blinked rapidly.

Don't cry. Do. Not. Cry.

Things were better this way. After just one night, she'd begun to spin fairytale fantasies she had no business drumming up. Already, he'd taken up too much of her headspace. Her neurons needed to focus on bettering her family's situation, not daydream about a man who would never be hers. Thunder being clueless about how his job taking his clothes off for women and possibly having sex with them might make a significant other feel helped her remember her place.

Significant other? The only thing significant was that orgasm she'd had.

God, she had to get out of there before she did something ridiculously stupid like begging him to cancel his gig.

Or cry.

She stood, shoving her chair back so fast, Emmie shrieked. "Well, we should probably get going." Nothing like depressing introspection and supreme mortification to get someone moving. "Don't want to wear out our welcome."

"Pretty sure that will never happen. You're welcome here any time. In fact, I insist on babysitting more, so please keep me in mind." Cassie rose as well, putting a hand on Shell's shoulder to keep her sitting. "I'll walk you out."

"I got it, Mama V," Thunder said, still holding a very content Emmie. "You sit and chat."

Cassie nodded and sent Thunder a narrow-eyed look. What was that about?

He was walking her out? Why? What did that mean?

And why was she such a cliché with the mental questions?

"Thank you again, ladies." Mak gave Cassie a long hug then moved on to Shell, who stood as well, her bump making the embrace a bit awkward.

"Give him some time," she whispered. "This is new for him."

"Not necessary," Mak whispered back. "Much better this way." Stepping back, she gave Shell a grin. Hopefully, her friend bought it. The pressed set of Shell's mouth didn't have her feeling too optimistic about her acting skills.

A solid fifteen minutes were eaten rustling up the kids, getting shoes on, and collecting all their belongings. Thunder kept Emmie entertained and having a blast the entire time. Then, he followed them outside to Mak's beat-up old car. She'd bought the thing for five hundred dollars and said a prayer of thanks every time the engine turned over.

"No Lee today?" he asked on the way.

Mak shrugged. "He's still at his friend's house." Or at least she assumed he was. He hadn't answered her texts that morning and was supposed to return home more than an hour ago. She refused to let herself freak out. Lee was secure with his friends. He knew how to play the game and keep himself safe. Knew to be cautions. He was well aware of what would happen to all of them if their father or her husband located them. He wouldn't be reckless.

Please let that be true.

Lee wasn't the best at making wise decisions these days. He could easily let something personal slip if he'd had too much to drink. There were a million things she should have done differently, could have done better to guide him through his teen years. Now she could only hope she hadn't done him a disservice, and he had the tools to make wise choices.

"Everything good with him?" As though a seasoned parenting pro, he put Emmie in her car seat and fastened the five-point harness. Anything he did, he made seem effortless. It'd taken Mak a solid twenty minutes to figure out how to put one of the kids in a car seat the first time. He did it so fast, too fast, as it only gave her a minute to stare at his ass bent over the carseat.

"Yeah, all good. Just typical teenager stuff." She may not have started the day as a good actress, but she'd be an Oscar nominee by sundown.

Or maybe not.

Thunder frowned. "Let me know if you need me to talk to him about anything. I was a teenage boy once." Then he winked and flashed her the grin that made her knees jelly. Why did he have to be so nice at the same time he rejected her? Not one reference to their night together. Not a single comment about it happening again, or grabbing a cup of coffee, maybe dinner.

Those are dates. You don't have time for a date. This is for the best.

"All set there, princess," he said to Emmie before pulling his head out of the car. "I'm rolling out too. Gotta get ready for work." Another wink and a wave and Thunder took off, jogging toward his bike.

If this was all for the best, why the hell did the thought of him taking his clothes off for other women make her feel so shitty?

Chapter Eighteen

Thunder watched Makenna's old car rattle down the road before turning back toward the house. After taking two steps, he drew up short at the sight of Mama V strolling toward him. "Cassie," he said. His brain screamed at him to run, but it was as though his boots had cemented to the ground.

"Take a walk with me?"

Instantly, his entire body broke out in a cold sweat. He hadn't been alone with her since Viper's death. Couldn't be alone with her. What if she asked questions? What if she found his actions lacking? What if she thought he should have let Jeremy escape and stayed with Viper?

"Thunder?"

"W-what?" A metallic taste filled his mouth.

She offered him an understanding smile. "Would you like to take a walk with me?"

She'd posed it as an offer, but Thunder wasn't stupid enough to think it wasn't a command. "Sure." He held his elbow out to her.

She giggled like a schoolgirl as she threaded her arm through his. "Thank you, sir."

"Of course."

Thunder

They walked about thirty feet down the road in silence. Each step filled him with more dread.

Finally, she spoke. "You've been avoiding me."

He could deny it, but they'd both see his lie for what it was. The coward's way out. Much as it wrecked him, she deserved this conversation. She deserved to ask him any questions she had about that day. It was her husband's life for fuck's sake, and in dodging her, he'd been selfish too long. "I have." He stopped walking and faced her. "Cassie, I'm so sorry. Ask me anything about that day. I'll be completely honest, and I'll accept however you feel about me afterward."

Her forehead scrunched as she frowned, and then as though the light went on, she tilted her head and sighed. "Thunder," she admonished.

Christ, he was going to throw up.

She reached up to cup his face between her hands. He had no choice but to look down into her thin face and slightly sad eyes. The hair she'd lost was slowly growing back. Now she had a silvery mop cropped close to her head.

"Oh, my sweet boy," she said in the loving, maternal way that had earned her the nickname Mama V. "Have you been avoiding me because you think I have a problem with how you handled yourself that day?"

He tried to look away, but she held his face firm, forcing eye contact. "I'm not sure I did the right thing." Goddammit, his eyes began to water. "Maybe I should have grabbed the bomb on my way out. Or I shouldn't have chased down Jeremy. Or—"

"Shh!" She said with a strength he hadn't realized she still possessed. "Enough of that nonsense. Do you hear me?"

Despite being near fucking crying and all torn up inside, he chuckled. While Cassie dished out motherly love like no other, the woman could scold with the best of them as well. "I hear you."

"You helped your club that day, Thunder. Maybe even saved your club. If Jeremy had escaped, who knows how much more harm he would have done to Jazz or the rest of your brothers? If Viper was standing here right now, he'd smack you upside the head for questioning your actions that day, and you know it." She dropped her hand and whacked him on the arm for emphasis.

Her words were a balm to his injured soul, stopping the bleeding, but not closing the wound. Now that he'd opened the floodgates, he couldn't hold back from expressing the worry he'd felt every day since Viper died. "I keep thinking I should have been able to do both. To make sure Viper and Jazz got out alive and chased down Jeremy."

"Oh, well, look at you," she said, voice heavy with sarcasm and eyes sparkling. "Didn't realize you had a cape and bodysuit under that cut. Superman, in an MC. Who'da guessed?"

"I know," he said, shaking his head. "I know I'm thinking irrationally. But…" He shrugged.

"But you wish Viper hadn't died. Simple as that."

With one hand, he pinched the bridge of his nose to fight off the tears while tugging Cassie to him with the other. "Yeah," he said as he hugged her close. "Simple as that."

"So do I, honey—every second of every day. But I do not for one second think you could have done anything differently. Had you tried, we might have been burying two or even three people we love. So please, Thunder, please release yourself from this burden. If you need to hear me say it, fine. I absolve you of any and all misguided and misplaced guilt. You're just as much a hero as my husband, and you need to remember that. Your club loves you. I love you. It's time to let yourself off the hook."

With each word she spoke, a bit of weight lifted from his shoulders. "Thank you," he whispered against the top of her head as he held her tight. "I should be the one comforting you."

"It's always a mom's job to comfort her kids when they're hurting."

After walking Mama V back home, he said his goodbyes and took off. Between this conversation and constantly thinking of

Makenna since he'd woken up, his brain felt like mush. What he needed was an afternoon of mindless fun, and he knew just the man to give it to him.

"The fuck's wrong with you, man?" Screw asked two hours later, as he tossed his PS4 controller on the large ottoman in front of the couch. "You're usually kicking my ass by now, and I'm mopping the floor with you. You hit your head or something?"

Or something.

"Nah, just off my game today." He chucked his controller next to Screw's with a huff as he sagged into the couch.

Gumby and Jazz went out for a little one-on-one time. Screw'd been feeling sorry for himself in his solo state, so he'd begged Thunder to come over for a few hours of *Call of Duty* before his gig.

Too bad his head was too scrambled to concentrate.

"This funk have anything to do with a responsible little dark-haired beauty who is in desperate need of some excitement in her life?" Screw lifted his beer to his lips as he spoke but didn't sip, just stared at Thunder over the lip of the bottle.

"What? The fuck you talking about? No. Who, Makenna? Pfft, you're fucking crazy. No."

Oh, Christ.

Screw burst out laughing. "Yeah, good job convincing me, brother."

"Can we not talk about this right now and just go back to you kicking my ass?"

With a shake of his head, Screw took a long pull from his beer. "Nope. This is more fun."

"For who?" Thunder muttered.

"For me, obviously. Spill it. You fucked her, didn't you?"

"Screwball." Thunder tried to growl it out in as menacing a tone as he could muster. Too bad it had no effect on Screw, who snorted.

"Thunder," he mocked back in the same tone. "You fucked her, and now you're the one who's fucked. In the noggin." He twisted his body until his head propped against the armrest, and his long legs rested on Thunder's thighs. "Come one, tell Dr. Screw all about it. Let me shrink your head."

"Uh, aren't I supposed to be the one lying on the couch, asshole?"

Screw shrugged. "Fuck if I know. Besides, I'm comfortable, and it's my house, so I get to make the rules. Now, start talking."

With a snort, Thunder shoved Screw's nasty feet off him and stood. "Ain't nothing to talk about. Yeah, I fucked her, but that's it. Since when are you one to talk about everyone you fuck?"

"Well, I only fuck two people these days, but I'll give you all the details you want. Say the word."

Ugh. "No, thanks."

After dropping his feet to the floor, Screw sat up again. "So nothing's going on? Just some straight-up tension relief? One and done?"

"Yep," he said, popping the *p* as he sat back down. "What do you care who I'm fucking and how I'm doing it?" he asked as he looked over at his brother, who used to be the biggest man-whore around. Hell, the guy still couldn't settle for monogamy, having to find an unconventional relationship with a man and a woman.

As he lifted both hands in surrender, Screw laughed. "Hey, I'm not judging. I'm all for fucking any way you can get it. Just trying to help out a friend."

"Yeah, well, I don't need help with this. There's nothing there to help."

"Wasn't talkin' about you."

A prickle of unease had Thunder narrowing his gaze at his club brother. "What?"

"Monty's got a real hard-on for her. You should hear him. Sounds like a lovesick puppy dog, all slobbery and awkward." With a wink, he shook his head. "Figure since you're not gonna be tapping that on the regular, I might as well give her a nudge in his direction."

Thunder

It's a trap. It's a trap. It's a trap.

The sliver of rationality in his brain screamed at him, but it was too fucking late. Screw's words had bypassed his logic and hit him straight in the possessive, caveman portion of his mind. "The fuck you will," he shouted as he hopped to his feet. Rage was instant, flowing hot and wild in his blood. The thought of Monty taking her out, touching her, tasting her had him in a murderous state. He'd lay that motherfucker out flat before he ever got close to Makenna.

Turning toward Screw, he advanced until he loomed over the man. "You have any idea how amazing that woman is? The shit she sacrifices to take care of five younger siblings? She's working her ass off to keep them clothed, fed, buy their medications, and doing it all on her fucking own. She deserves the best there is, and you wanna push that bald motherfucking child on her? She's has enough people to take care of. Doesn't need some stupid ass prospect trying to stick it in the wrong hole and failing to find her clit. Christ!" He spun and stalked his way across the room as he raked a hand through his hair. Fucking Monty, of all people.

As his blood began to cool from the initial flash fire of rage, Thunder became aware of the fact Screw's smirk had grown with each word that flew out of his mouth.

He groaned. Goddammit, he'd been played by a master.

Now he had to face the music.

Slowly, Thunder spun until he faced his brother. If he could have gotten away with it, maybe if Screw hadn't been the club's enforcer, Thunder might have smacked that smirk right off his smug face. "You are a piece of shit."

"That I am," Screw said with a loud laugh. "But damn, that was fun. You ready to stop bullshitting me now?"

With a frustrated sigh, Thunder dragged his feet back over to the couch. After he'd plopped down and swallowed the rest of his beer, he glared at Screw. "That shit about Monty true?"

Nodding, Screw said, "Some of it. He wants your girl, but he won't step on your toes." When Thunder gave him a dark look, he added, "And I didn't encourage the kid. Swear it."

"I gotta head out in about fifteen minutes." He stared up at the ceiling, stomach cramping as it had been off and on all day. "I don't feel right about it."

"What? Makenna?"

"Nah, working tonight. Something feels fucking off, and it's been eating at me all damn day."

"Ahh. Because of Makenna."

Thunder didn't say anything, just watched the ceiling fan spin above him. Screw hadn't been asking, more stating the obvious.

"You like her."

He turned his head to look at his brother. "I like her."

"And?"

"And I left her bed in the middle of the night because I like her. Because no woman deserves my fucked-up experiences with relationships. The shit I saw growing up? The relationships I grew up around? Fuck, no one needs to benefit from those lessons. I saw her today at Copper's, and I acted like I hadn't spent my night buried inside her. I let it slip that I was working a bachelorette party tonight. She didn't say a word, but I swear to fuck it was like I'd snuffed out a light inside her."

"Whoa, okay, brother, this is a lot to unpack." Screw picked some kind of glittery ball from a bowl on the coffee table and began tossing it in the air. High energy fit the guy to a tee. Always needing something to keep his hands busy. "Let's start with the childhood shit." He winked. "As any good therapist would."

Thunder grunted. "I'll give you the short version. Mom's a whore. Dad's a john. She's remarried to my stepdad. They run a brothel. I grew up literally living in a small apartment at the back of the cat house. Saw all combinations of men and women fucking since the time I could walk. Seen normal shit, kinky shit, seriously fucked-up shit, basically women who'd do anything to get a dollar to change hands. The women there married and divorced like it was a sport. Men were abusive as fuck and high all the time. Alcohol started flowing the moment they opened their eyes in the morning. For some, it was the only way they could make it through the day. It wasn't a classy place. I don't have the first fucking clue how to make a woman happy beyond making her come. There you go, Dr. Freud. Not exactly a tough case to crack. Fucked-up childhood leads to an adult with more issues than he can count."

"Shit, brother, I knew a little bit of that, but…well, shit." Screw caught the ball then leaned forward, bracing his forearms on his knees. He stared straight ahead at the blank TV, perhaps lost in his own memories. Many unpleasant, if what Thunder had heard was accurate. "You know, you didn't grow up too far off from how I did."

"I've heard that." He and Screw were close, brothers, but they didn't typically sit around sharing their tragic pasts and crying in each other's beers. Suddenly, he found himself dying to know what Screw's life had been like prior to prospecting with the Handlers.

"My mom stripped, but not at reputable places like you have."

Thunder grunted. He'd worked his fair share of seedy establishments.

"Most of my life, she headlined at this shithole titty bar notorious at my high school for letting teens sneak in."

"Oh, fuck, brother. That must have made for one shitty adolescent experience."

"Yeah, you can imagine how much fun that shit was. Anyway, any 'relationship' she had," he continued, air-quoting relationship, "was off the charts dysfunctional. Telling you, brother, I've seen some shit as well. You think I had any idea what the hell I was doing when I hooked up with Jazz and Gumby?" He made a noise of disbelief. "I still worry I'm gonna fuck it all up on a daily basis."

"Pretty sure those two won't let you fuck it up. They love your stupid ass."

Screw shot him a lascivious grin. "They sure do. Gumby is particularly fond of my ass."

Barking a laugh, Thunder held up his hands. "Not touching that one, brother."

"You better not touch it. Both of 'em'll have something to say if you do." As Thunder rolled his eyes, Screw said, "Man, I'm on a roll." He gave himself a high five like the dork he was. "All right, I'm gonna get serious on you for a minute here, so man up and take it, 'kay?"

Ignoring his head issues and continuing a carefree life of stripping and getting blowjobs for cash was a million times easier than listening to this shit and trying to improve himself. But he wasn't a stupid, horny kid anymore. Now, as a patched member of the HHMC, he'd proven to Copper and his brothers they could trust him. He was responsible. He was a fucking adult. Maybe he needed to take the same approach to his personal life.

"All right, lay it on me."

"The fact that you're all torn up over Mak tells me she's already wormed her way in. She's different."

Yeah, she was different. Sweet, caring, dependable, intelligent. A host of attributes he'd never cared about before. And when combined with a physical package that drove his dick wild, it made for a woman he couldn't stop being drawn to. He found himself thinking of her first thing in the morning, all throughout the day, and when his head hit the pillow. And yeah, many of those thoughts centered around fucking her. The million ways he could make her lose her mind and scream his name. But sex wasn't all he thought about.

He wondered if she was tired after being on her feet at the diner all day. Whether she'd had enough to eat. If she needed help wrangling the kids.

"She's different," he said with a sigh. "In a way that's making me insane."

"I'm gonna ask you a question," Screw said as he leaned back and began tossing the ball again. "Forget all your head shit. Just answer it based on gut and dick, okay?"

Thunder watched him from the corner of his eye. "Okay…"

"Do you want her? Do you wanna fuck her again? Do you want to be the only one fucking her? Do *you* want to be fucking only her? And do you want other shit too? Meals, hanging with her family—because you know bailing on those won't be an option. Being there for her when her day sucks. Having her be there for you. Dates, good times, bad times. Do you want it?"

Did he want it? Yes. His gut, his head, and something deep in his chest resonated with everything Screw said. His dick? Well, sure, that was easy. Fuck yes, he wanted Mak to be fucking him and him alone, and he had no interest in sticking it anywhere else either. Instead of sending him for the hills, the picture Screw painted sounded…nice. Perfect, actually.

"Yes, I want it. I want her, but—"

"Nope." Screw held up a hand. "No buts. No telling me you'll fuck it up, or you don't deserve that shit. You're a good fucking guy, T. Shit, I'll owe you forever for catching Jeremy the day he blew up the diner. Who knows what he'd have done to Jazz if you hadn't caught him. You want her, take her, brother. The rest of the shit is just work. If she wants you too, you work together."

"That easy, huh?"

With a half snort, half laugh, Screw stood. "Fuck no, it's not easy. Hardest thing I've ever done some days. But I'm not afraid of hard. Neither are you. And trust me when I tell you it is so fucking worth it. Pun intended." Screw winked then headed toward his kitchen. "Need something stronger than beer to counter all these feelings. Want something?"

"Yeah, man. I'll take whatever you're having."

When Screw disappeared into the kitchen, Thunder pulled out his phone and opened a text message to a buddy of his.

Got a gig I can't make tonight. Bachelorette party with extras. Want it?

Not five seconds later, he had his answer.

Fuck yes. Send me the deets.

After texting the details, he also messaged the party's hostess, claiming illness, but letting her know he'd found an incredible replacement up for anything the ladies wanted. She'd been disappointed, and he could feel the annoying pout through the phone, but once he'd fired off a topless pic of his replacement, she'd perked right up and forgiven him.

As Screw sauntered back in with a glass in each hand, Thunder shot to his feet. "Sorry, brother, I gotta go."

"You cancel your gig?" Screw set the glasses on the coffee table.

"Yep." He stowed his phone and held his fist out to Screw, who gave it a bump. "Thank you."

"Anytime, man. Anytime. Gotta do something with all this newfound maturity and shit."

Rolling his eyes, Thunder practically sprinted out the front door. As he reached his bike, Screw stuck his head out the front door.

"Make sure she knows she wouldn't have gotten more of your dick tonight if it wasn't for me!" he shouted, neighbors be damned.

Thunder revved his engine and shot down the street, flipping Screw off in the process.

"Maturity, my ass," he muttered, unable to keep the huge grin off his face.

Chapter Nineteen

"And after we watch *Frozen*—the second one—and eat the ice cream, we can watch *Trolls World Tour* while we eat the cookies, and after that—"

"After that, you'll be passed out in a sugar coma." Mak laughed. Nothing like sweets and animated movies to get her normally shy sister running her mouth like a chatterbox. She pulled the shopping cart to a stop behind her car. "Remember, I told you ice cream or a few cookies. Not both."

"I know," Kara said in a tone that let Makenna know the issue wasn't dead. Not by a long shot.

"I yike cookies!" Emmie said from her seat in the cart.

The seven-year-old Kara would be lobbying for a second treat the moment she finished her first. Mak couldn't begrudge her the move. Whenever frustrated with the kids for classic kid behaviors, she reminded herself the annoyance was a privilege. Giving her siblings a stable and normal childhood experience had been the goal. Arguing over snacks seemed a pretty good indicator of normal when it came to children.

After loading the groceries in the trunk, while Kara continued to chatter on about the movies they planned to watch once home, Mak turned to grab Emmie. "Ready to get in your seat, Ems?"

"And eat cookies?" Emmie asked with the most hopeful grin.

"When we get home." She scooped the toddler up.

"Well, hello there, you pretty little thing, what's your name?" The slightly familiar male voice had Mak whirling around as she clutched Emmie close. Immediately, her chest constricted, and her mouth dried up. Kneeling in front of Kara was none other than Crank, the asshole who'd propositioned her in the CDMC clubhouse. The one the Handlers cautioned was as dangerous as they came.

He wore his cut with ripped jeans and worn boots. The enforcer patch on the left side of his chest might as well have been a blinking warning sign. But it was the sinister gleam in his eyes that had Mak reaching for her sister.

"I'm Kara," the little girl said, earning herself a very stern lecture about stranger danger later. "You have a vest like Thunder. Are you his friend?" She reached forward as though to finger a patch on his chest.

Shit. Mak slapped Kara's hand away, making her sister jump and stare at her with horrified eyes. "Kara, honey, why don't you get in the car, okay?" she asked, snatching her sister out of the lethal man's reach.

Forget two desserts, she'd let Kara eat the entire carton of ice cream if she'd just get the hell in the car. "Let me talk to the man by myself." Her heart raced in her chest like a stampeding elephant. Any attempt at controlling her anxiety failed; the fear was too strong.

Thank God, Kara seemed to pick up on the urgency in her tone because she obeyed without so much as a huff of annoyance.

"Here, take Emmie with you." She set the toddler on the ground, keeping an eye on Crank the whole time. He'd straightened from his crouched position and had propped himself against the trunk of her car. Whether his lips had curled in amusement or menace remained to be seen.

Kara grabbed Emmie's hand and tugged her to the car.

Thunder

"I don't wanna," Emmie said in an exaggerated whine, indicating a tantrum was coming.

"Just go with Kara now, and I'll give you two extra cookies." World's best parent right there. But the bribe worked, and this certainly qualified as extenuating circumstances. Emmie stopped fussing and climbed into the car with Kara, squealing about her upcoming cookies.

The second the car door shut, her smile flattened, and she glared at Crank.

His grin only expanded. In fact, the expression made him look like a hungry shark, teeth bared and malice in his gaze. "Thunder, huh?" He stroked his stubbled chin. "I've heard of a guy by that name. Hmm, I'm trying to remember…"

Mak clenched her teeth, breathing only through her nose. He wanted to play with her. Make her squirm. Same as the men who'd threatened her in the past. Her father, her husband, most men from the community she'd grown up in. Part of her wanted to cower in fear, but the instinct to protect her sisters trumped her memories of being at the mercy of evil men. She straightened her shoulders and forced a bored expression though inside, she shook and shivered. "What do you want?"

He snapped his fingers as though a light bulb had flicked on in his head. "Oh, now I remember. He's a Handler." The mocking tone disappeared, and he took a step into her personal space. Same as the other night, the putrid stench of cigarettes, sweat, and weed assaulted her senses. "He your ol' man? He send you to my club to fuckin' spy on us?"

"N-no." Damnit, there went fearless. All she could think of were the two children gawking at them through the rear windshield as intently as they'd planned to watch movies that evening. "I—I'm nothing to him. Or any of them. I work at the diner. It's a job. That's all. I don't know anything about their club. I needed money, and I'm friends with Kristy. That's it. Nothing else."

Stop talking! Time to go.

She took a step back only to be jerked forward when a rough hand clamped around her wrist.

Crank tugged her so close, she could see right up his crooked nose. "Maybe I should tell your boss what a shitty employee you are. Hmm? How you like to disappear without a trace in the middle of a job? What do you think? Should I swing by and have a chat with Toni?"

His stale, coffee and booze laced breath wafted over her face causing her stomach to heave in protest. Mak tugged her arm back to no avail. His grip on her tightened to the point of pain.

"I'm sorry. I had a family emergency." With each word she spoke, he squeezed her wrist until it felt as if the bones would snap. "I-I didn't get paid first. You're not out any money. Y-you're hurting me."

She bit her lower lip to keep a cry of pain from escaping. Her sisters didn't need to know how much pain she felt.

"This ain't about money. We had an agreement—four hours of work. You still owe me an hour and a half. I'm here to make arrangements." His leer left no doubt as to how he intended her to pay that time.

Bile rose up, threatening to make her hurl. "I-I—"

"Babe, I was wondering why you didn't answer your phone. You makin' new friends?" Thunder's arm circled the front of her shoulders, and he drew her toward his chest.

Crank released her hand immediately. Though she yearned to rub her tender wrist, Mak held still as a statue. Part of her wanted to sink into the comfort of Thunder's firm body pressed all along her back, but this wasn't over yet, and she had her sisters to think about. Maybe, if they survived this without bloodshed, Thunder would be willing to stick around long enough to hold her through a breakdown.

"No, not making friends, are you? Pretty sure you can't make friends with a pile of shit." Thunder turned her head with a hand on her chin. "Hey, baby," he whispered, pressing a soft kiss to her lips.

Thunder

What the hell was he doing? Linking himself to her would only give Crank and the CDMC another reason to go after the Handlers. He should have denied any connection to her.

"There a reason you're harassing my woman, Crank?" he asked after releasing her. He spoke in a voice she'd not have thought him capable of—cold, hate-filled, deadly.

"Your woman, huh?" he asked with a smirk. "You might wanna keep a shorter leash on your bitch, Thunder, was it? Either she's stepping out to party with a real club, which is your problem, or you sent her, which makes her my problem."

"No, what? No, they didn—we aren't—"

Thunder squeezed her shoulder. Then he released her. Three steps put him nose to nose with Crank.

Oh, my God. Trembling, Mak whipped her head from side to side, scanning the parking lot. Where were Thunder's brothers? Was he alone? What the hell was she supposed to do if this came to blows? A quick peek right revealed her sisters still staring wide-eyed through the rear of the car.

"Trust me when I tell you she's not your problem. In fact, I suggest you forget you've ever fucking seen her. You're alone on Handler's turf. You got five seconds to get on your bike and head outta town before I call an escort for you."

Taking two steps backward, Crank lifted his hands in surrender, but his mouth pressed to a thin line of displeasure.

Mak held her breath.

The only one who seemed relaxed was Thunder. He returned to her side and once again pulled her close. His calm demeanor helped keep her from outwardly losing her shit.

"Guess it makes sense now," Crank said as he continued walking backward.

Thunder didn't respond. His thumb stroked her shoulder in soothing circles.

"Was wondering how you just *happened* to discover my guys behind the diner last weekend." He tossed a leg over his bike then revved the engine. "Looks like your little spy did her job," he shouted over the roar.

He sped off in a cloud of dust and spraying gravel. Once out of sight, Mak threw herself against Thunder. "Oh, my God. Oh, my *God*. What the hell were you thinking?" She slapped his chest with little force. "Why did you claim me like that? He thinks you sent me to spy on him. I could have convinced him otherwise. Now he thinks we're a *thing*. What's he going to do to your club? He's going to go after you." As fast as the words fell from her mouth, her brain raced even faster with hundreds of questions and horrifying scenarios. "What do we do? *What do we do*?" She spoke against Thunder's chest, holding his sides to keep herself anchored to him.

"Shhh, Makenna, take a breath." He stroked his hands up her back once before cupping her shoulders and putting space between them.

Now that she'd gotten his club in trouble, he'd probably want nothing to do with her. How could she have been so stupid to have taken that CDMC job? Why had she ignored her gut that night? In the past, a poor choice earned her a beating and isolation, now it endangered her entire family.

"Mak, hey." He dipped his knees, bringing them eye level. Hers watered as her lower lip trembled. "Take a breath for me, babe, okay?"

She did as he asked, sucking in air and blowing it out in a long, shaky exhale.

"Good girl. You're okay, I'm okay, and the girls are okay."

Her stomach bottomed out. "Oh, God, the kids. I need to get them—"

"Mak!" This time he gave her shoulders a gentle shake before cupping her face and tilting her head back. Though light, his hold was firm.

Clearly, she was sick in the head because a flare of arousal shot through her at his controlling actions.

"Here's what we're gonna do, okay?"

Nodding, she looked at the rear of the car, where her sisters studied their every move. Their safety was their first priority. "Okay."

"Good. You're gonna get in the car and drive straight home. I'm gonna follow right behind you. When we get to your house, we're gonna take the kids inside and watch movies while we eat junk food. Just like you promised them."

"But..." Her gaze sought out the spot where Crank's motorcycle had been parked.

"No buts. You're gonna give them a totally normal night, so you don't freak them out further, okay? I'm gonna call this into Copper, and from now on, we'll have someone on you guys to make sure you're safe at all times."

"How are you so calm? I'm freaking out right now."

He pulled her close. "I know, Mak, and I'm so fucking sorry you got dragged into this mess. It's the last thing I wanted."

Oh, was he warm and solid and...hard. Yep, that was an erection nudging her in the stomach. Despite the riot of anxious feelings coursing through her, her body responded with a little shiver of delight. How could it not when she recalled what he'd done to her with that particular body part last night.

Had it only been last night? Not even twenty-four hours ago.

"None of this is your fault, Thunder. I should never have taken that job. Wait!" She lifted her head. "Aren't you supposed to be working right now? Come to think of it, what are you doing here?"

He laughed. "I canceled and swung by your house. Lee told me you and the girls came to get some movie snacks."

With a nod, she looked at the car again. Kara was now making ridiculous faces at them, which had Emmie in stitches and trying to imitate her. "You canceled?" She faced him. He was so good looking it nearly hurt her eyes. Last night wasn't nearly enough. She wanted time to get to know him, to explore him, to learn all there was to discover about him. "Why?"

He kissed her forehead. "We'll talk about it later. Let's get those girls home, okay?"

She nearly swooned from the unexpected show of tenderness. But his actions had her head spinning. Leaving in the middle of the night, taking a stripping job, canceling a stripping job, kissing her head. What on earth would he do next? "Okay, uh, yeah. You'll be behind me?"

"Right behind you. And, Mak?"

She paused. "Yeah?"

He dropped his head, so his lips rested next to her ear. "We are a thing. I don't know what that means yet, but we are definitely a thing." Then he kissed her mouth and sauntered off to his bike as though he hadn't nearly gotten into a brawl with Crank five minutes ago.

She stood there, blinking like an idiot in the middle of the parking lot, then pressed a hand to her tingling lips. They were a thing?

What did he mean?

Was he done stripping?

Did he want to date her?

Elation soared at the notion.

No, no, no.

She was not supposed to get excited over the prospect of dating him or any man. Yet she feared the prospect of being with a man like Thunder was too tempting to turn down should it be what he proposed.

On unsteady legs, Mak moved to her car. After buckling Emmie in her car seat and Kara in the booster, she slid into the driver's seat. Her hands trembled as she tried to get the key in the ignition. A few deep breaths solved that problem but not the internal turmoil.

"Who was that other man?" Kara asked from the back with a frown. "You looked scared."

"Oh, no honey. It was just—" She'd almost said a friend of Thunder's, but then the thought of Crank confronting Kara somewhere shook her to her core. "He's a man who's not very nice, so if you ever see him anywhere, you run away and find a grown up immediately. Do you understand?" As she pulled out of the space, she flicked a glance at the mirror in time to see Kara's solemn nod.

The worry on her little sister's face broke her heart. All she'd ever wanted for these children was a chance at a joyful childhood free of worry, abuse, and the hard labor she and Lee had endured. But it appeared she couldn't shield them from everything, no matter how hard she tried.

Another glance in the mirror. As promised, Thunder rode right on her tail. Relief surged followed by a moment of panic. Scary as this business with Crank was, she needed to keep her head in the game. Becoming dependent on Thunder for protection and emotional support was a no go. She hadn't busted her ass for the past two years only to rely on someone who wouldn't be there in the long term. No way in hell would she start over with nothing ever again. Continuing to rely on herself today and tomorrow would be far easier than learning how to do it again after sharing the burden with someone else.

No matter how hard her stomach fluttered in his presence.

Chapter Twenty

Flipped his shit was the most accurate description of how Copper took the news of Crank not only being in Townsend but confronting Makenna. He'd straight-up demanded Thunder bring Mak by the clubhouse so he could find out word for word what Crank had said before Thunder showed up, but he managed to put his president off until the next day. The prez had also agreed to send someone to sit on the house. Keeping an eye on all of them would be difficult, especially since pinning Lee down often proved impossible.

Mak needed to relax. She needed to spend the evening with her family, eat some sugar, then end the night with an orgasm— or three.

He sat on the couch, waiting while she got the kids to bed. Amy was staying at Toni and Zach's house that night. She'd struck up an instant friendship with Lindsey, a teen who the Handlers had rescued from the CDMC a few months back. Mak had already called twice to check up on them even though Thunder assured her there was no safer place than his enforcer's house.

That left Kara, Emmie, and Rissa, who'd overdosed on cookies, ice cream, and animated movies. Yes, he'd admittedly been on the kids' side, begging Mak to let them eat more treats than she'd approved of. But hey, they were kids. They deserved a little fun.

So did Mak.

Didn't hurt his chances of getting the kids to love him, either.

Surprisingly enough, Thunder had enjoyed himself. A lot. The fifteen apologetic glances Mak had sent his way throughout the evening hadn't been necessary. He hadn't minded the little ones snuggling all over him or their fingers leaving sticky prints on his arms. Or the hundreds of comments Rissa voiced throughout the movies. Hell, he'd even enjoyed the cartoon movies themselves. The only thing that could have made the night better would have been Mak snuggling with him. But the night wasn't over yet.

The only kid unaccounted for was Lee, though Mak had said he was due home anytime.

Sure enough, about a minute later, as Thunder rested his head on the back of the couch, the eighteen-year-old burst through the front door, coming to a stop when he spotted Thunder.

"Oh, hey, man."

"Hey, Lee. What's up?"

The teen grabbed a fistful of cookies off the coffee table. "Nothing," he said, mouth full.

"You in for the rest of the night?" Thunder asked.

The glare he received was full-on what-the-fuck-do-you-care.

As Thunder was about to give Lee a heads up to be vigilant, Mak came back into the room. "Lee, you're home. How'd the job interview go?"

"Job interview? Thought you worked at the pizza joint?" He grabbed Mak's hand, pulling her down next to him. Ahh, finally. He'd needed to feel her next to him. Actually, he needed to feel her skin on skin, but that would come later.

"He lost that job for being late too many times," she said in an accusatory tone as she stared at Lee.

Her brother shrugged as he stuffed another cookie in his mouth. "I blew off the interview. Don't wanna work at a fucking ice cream shop."

Mak straightened. "Lee! You can't do that. You need a job. What are you going to do all day?"

Thunder squeezed her thigh, which had her settling back against him with a huff. Lee looked about two seconds from unleashing some serious attitude. "Hey, how about working at a gym? That interest you at all?"

His eyes lit. "Yeah. Fuck yeah."

"It's not glamorous. Zach's looking for someone to clean equipment, help with office work, stock towels and shit like that. But you'd have access to the gym when you weren't on shift, and you could learn about becoming a trainer."

Lee rushed forward, excited about something for the first time since Thunder had met him. "I'd love that. Last place we lived, I had access to a gym through a friend. I miss it so much. You'd really give me the job?"

Resisting the urge to chuckle, Thunder shook his head. "Final decision is Zach's, but I'll put in a good word for you, and it'll carry weight. You'd have to make it, though, and not blow off your interview. Zach's a cool guy, but he won't put up with bullshit."

Straightening as though to prove how responsible he could be, Lee nodded. "Of course. Shit, man, thank you. This is incredible."

"Give me your number so I can pass it on to Zach." And have Maverick do some voodoo security shit to keep tabs on Lee's location.

Lee rattled off his number, which Thunder added to his phone then grabbed some more cookies. "I'm heading back out."

"Really? Where you going?"

He shrugged. "Out with some friends."

Mak gave Thunder a worried glance. "Hey, Lee," he said as the kid grabbed the doorknob. "You see anyone wearing a cut like me with a Chrome Disciples rocker, I need to know immediately. Okay?"

Lee raised an eyebrow and dropped his hand. His phone chimed.

"Just sent you my number. I'm not playing. You don't engage, and you tell me immediately. Got it?"

"Isn't that where Makenna worked last weekend?"

She nodded, chewing her lower lip.

"She in trouble?" Though already tall, he seemed to grow before Thunder's eyes. Good. Kid was as protective of his siblings as Makenna.

Thunder didn't want the kid to freak, just be aware. "No, I don't think so. But they hate our club and can be dangerous. Be alert."

Lee nodded. "Got it." He opened the door, stepped out, then called over his shoulder, "Don't forget to wrap it up, Thunder. We don't need any more kids in this house."

"Lee!" Mak shrieked as she covered her face with her hands.

Thunder chuckled as the door closed. "Least you know he's thinking about condoms."

"Ugh, can we not talk about how my eighteen-year-old brother is having more sex than I am?" She still spoke into her hands, so Thunder pulled them away from her face.

"Good idea. Let's give him a run for his money instead." He stood, drawing her up with him. They had a lot to talk about, and somehow he'd have to find a way to make that happen before losing himself in her softness. But that didn't mean they had to talk clothed. "Come on. I need some skin."

The way her nose screwed up in confusion was so damned adorable he couldn't help but kiss the tip. Recalling the way to her room was easy as the place was barely bigger than his apartment. Once in her bedroom, he spun her to face him. "Arms up."

"Wait, Thunder, we need to talk first," she said even as she obeyed and allowed him to strip her plain blue T-shirt over her head.

"We're going to, baby. Just wanna do it without all these clothes between us." He shucked his shirt then went to work on his boots.

"Naked? We're gonna talk while we're naked?" She drew her sweats down her legs but kept her panties on. "Who does that?"

Fine, he'd give her the panties, but the bra had to go. He shrugged then flicked the clasp of her bra. "Don't know. But ever since I saw Crank with his hands on you, I've had this driving need to feel your skin against mine. That work for you?" He pulled his jeans down.

"Yeah," Mak said in a soft voice full of wonder. "That works."

"Good." He kissed her lips then moved to her bed, drawing the covers back. "Climb on in."

"The kids…"

Shit, not something he had any experience navigating. "Do they usually come in during the night?"

"Sometimes the little ones do." She crossed her arms over her breasts, and, oh how that wouldn't do. If they were gonna do this, there'd be no hiding. "Let me lock the door. I'll still hear them if they need something." She closed the door quietly, then with a low snick, it was locked. For at least a short while, they were alone.

Mak shifted side to side as she bit her lip, watching him. He had no knowledge to go on, but she seemed to have very little experience with men, though she hadn't been a virgin when he fucked her last night. These intimate experiences seemed so foreign to her, though, and he'd be lying if he didn't admit the idea of introducing her to all the pleasures they could discover in each other excited him like nothing else.

Even something as simple as lying in bed talking. However, he was the one who lacked experience in that area.

Thunder

After a few charged seconds of observation, she climbed under the covers on the left side of the bed then lay there, holding herself stiff. A smile played across Thunder's lips. His poor girl seemed so far out of her comfort zone.

He slipped in bed then drew her into his arms. For about five seconds, she remained rigid as a board, but once he began stroking up and down her back, she melted.

"That feels nice," she whispered, big brown eyes on him.

"It does." It felt wonderful in a way he wasn't sure what to do with. Had he ever been in bed with a naked female with the goal of just being? Did he want to fuck her? Of course. Finally, getting all that silky skin pressed against his had him hard in an instant. But they would get there. The lack of pressure to dive in, get them off, and get out left him feeling relaxed and sated even with a hard-on. The paradox hinted at a deeper connection. One he'd never experienced but he found himself loving it and wanting more.

"Thank you for tonight," he said, breaking the quiet reflection they'd been engaged in.

Mak scoffed. "Pretty sure you had better things to do than hang out with children and watch princess movies all night."

The reminder of how he'd had a stripping job scheduled injected tension into the room. "Mak, look at me."

She complied, gazing up at him with soft eyes.

"I was exactly where I wanted to be tonight. Doing exactly what I wanted to do. The club has given me the brotherhood I've never had. But this? What you have here with the kids? Even in the short amount of time I've spent with you all, I see how much love, acceptance, and connection there is here. It's given me something else I've never had. And that's a desire to have more in my life now and in my future. More than stripping, more than empty hook-ups, even more than my club."

"Thunder," she said on an exhale, right before kissing him with passion. Her hands went to his head, gripping his hair, and she held him captive against her hungry mouth. Christ, she was sweet, and though they needed to talk of much more, he was powerless to resist this taste of paradise.

He cupped her tits, hefting their soft weight. When he rubbed his thumbs over her already puckered nipples, Mak yanked her mouth away with a gasp.

"You like that?" he asked.

"So much."

He sucked a warm, stiff nipple into his mouth. Her tits weren't huge, but they filled his mouth nicely, making it easy to suck while also tonguing her nipple.

"Oh," Mak squeaked. Her hands still fisted his hair, now clutching him to her tits.

Damn, she tasted so good and got him so hard. If he didn't stop soon, he'd lose his head and fuck her into the mattress instead of continuing to talk like they needed.

One more minute.

He sucked harder, and Mak's nails pricked his scalp.

Maybe two minutes…

He switched sides, going at her other tit a little rougher than he did the first. Mak moaned. Never would he have guessed she liked sex anything other than soft and gentle, but Mak clearly liked a little aggression with her lovin'.

Her hips began to move, pushing up into him. He groaned as she ground into his stiff cock. Fuck, he was gonna blow if he didn't watch it.

Again, she rocked her pelvis. His girl had a hungry pussy. Too bad it had to wait a little longer to be satisfied.

He shifted, lifting a thigh so it pressed against her center. She immediately began to rock against his firm quads, coating his leg with the arousal that had soaked through her panties.

"Shit!" He popped her tit out of his mouth to a small grunt of protest. "Gotta stop before I lose my fucking mind."

Panting, Mak nodded and released his head.

He didn't bother to move his knee, and as she tried to shift away, he caught her hips.

"I'm getting you all, uh, wet," she whispered, staring at his chest with pink cheeks.

Fuck yeah, she was. How the hell did she not know it was hot as fuck for her to cream all over his leg? What kind of idiots had she been with in the past? "I know," he said smugly, making her lift her gaze. "Why do you think I'm keeping my leg there?"

"Thunder!" Mak buried her face against his chest, making him chuckle.

"Besides, I got you wet, so it's only fair." He strummed a nipple, shiny from his mouth. Christ, he couldn't wait to get those babies back between his lips. But first... "Mak, I don't want you to worry about the CDMC, okay? My club will keep you safe. I'll have someone outside your house, the diner, anywhere you guys are. And if you need someone to watch the little ones, use Mama V. Someone is always guarding Copper's house. You'll be safe, and they will be safe. I promise you that."

She stroked her fingers over his chest, lost in thought. Then she spoke, "Is this because you...well, I mean, is it because you want to sleep with me?"

"Yes and no. I want you, Mak, make no mistake about that. I think about fucking you constantly. I dream about the things we can do to each other. You have any idea how many times I've jerked myself off thinking about you?"

Wide-eyed, she shook her head.

"You're not the only one playing with yourself at night. I just don't have fun toys." He winked as her cheeks turned pink. "But fucking isn't all I want from you, Mak. I want more. So much more, which is one of the things we need to talk about. But the club's protection stands whether you feel the same or not. I need you to understand that."

Fuck, was she merely tolerating his touch as some way to ensure her family's safety?

No. That was something his mother would have done, and he needed to learn to shift his thinking away from the shitty lessons she'd taught him. But still, a small lingering doubt poked at his brain.

He lifted her chin. "Baby, please tell me you're here because you want to be, not because you feel you owe me something."

She shook her head. "No. I would never. I want you too, Thunder. It's just…" She sighed as though resigned to broaching a subject she'd rather not discuss. "Shell mentioned some stuff to me about your, um, relationships with women."

If he'd been standing by a wall, he'd have whacked his forehead against it. He was starting this conversation in the red.

Thanks a fucking bunch, Shell.

Now he was the one sighing, only it was full of regret and frustration. "Let me guess, Shell let it slip that I fuck women for money. Usually, ones I dance for."

Face bright red, Mak nodded. "Something like that."

Thunder dragged a hand through his messy hair. "All right, I wanna tell you a little about how I grew up, but first, I need to tell you that I've never had a relationship. No girlfriend, no dates, nothing short or long term. Hell, I haven't even had a steady fuck buddy."

Mak's mouth opened and closed like a fish on land. "Wha— but, that makes no sense." Her nose wrinkled like she smelled something rancid. "You're incredible. Thunder, you're the most gorgeous man I've ever seen. But you're also intelligent, and you're sweet, and protective, and fun, and—"

"Babe…" He groaned. She couldn't make this easy on him, could she? No, she had to be all adorable and make him want to kiss every inch of her. "The relationships I witnessed growing up made me uninterested in forming any kind of bond with a woman. But I can't stop thinking about you. I want it with you. I want…this. What we did tonight. I want to hang out with your family then crawl into bed with you. I wanna open my eyes in the morning and see you next to me. I wanna take you out. I wanna make out with you at clubhouse parties, then spend all night fucking you only to do it again the next morning. I want to hold you when you're sad, help you with the kids, and be as much a part of their lives as I am yours."

He wanted to spend every moment making her smile and smiling back at her in return. The fear of having it crash and burn still in a spectacular explosion of pain and heartbreak lingered, but his desire for Makenna dominated it to the point he was willing to take the risk.

For the first time in his life, he understood why people risked it all for another.

"Holy shit," she said on an exhale.

"I just want you, Mak. And I have no idea what I'm doing, or if I can make a relationship work, or if I should even try. But I want to." He pressed his fist to his chest. "I want it so bad I ache with it. And I want it with you, only you. Shh." He pressed a finger to her lips. "Don't say anything yet. Let me tell you about where I come from. Then you can decide if you're willing to take a chance on me."

Then she'd probably run away screaming, but at least he'd have his answer.

Chapter Twenty-One

Thunder's words wrapped themselves around her soul and unearthed a powerful desire buried so deep, she'd never allowed her mind to drift there. The things he wanted, being an integral part of her and her family's life, holding her when she was down —twenty-three years, and no one had done that for her. Not once. The thought of having him as a permanent fixture to lean on, share responsibilities with, laugh with, and spend her nights tempted her beyond belief.

And that's why she should put a stop to this. If she knew what was good for her, for both of them, she'd place her hand over his mouth to keep him from spilling his secrets, get dressed, and ask him to leave.

Not because she wanted him to go, but because it would spare them both so much pain and suffering later.

He wanted to try a relationship with her.

God, he was everything she desired and more. The man was fun, funny, sweet, dependable, kind, and his body…made her eyes cross just thinking about it. And there he was not only ready to bear his soul but change his life for her. What woman in their right mind would say no to him?

Yet she had to. Because how could she bring him into her life? A life where they hid from her psychotic family. A life where the money never met the demand. A life full of responsibility from the second she opened her eyes until she finally passed out each night. Yes, Thunder had a few years on her, but he shouldn't spend the rest of his twenties shackled to someone with a mountain of baggage. Hell, she shouldn't be spending her twenties as a mom to five kids, but they were her blood.

They were her everything.

But as she looked at the sincerity and desire in her eyes, she found herself saying, "Tell me." Because she desperately wanted to know him and learn everything about this incredible man lying naked in her bed.

She couldn't seem to stop touching him, stroking her fingers over his chest, his arms, his abs. That thigh between her legs was doing insane things to her. It kept her aroused, riding the line of desire. Every so often, her hips rocked against him, completely out of her control. And it felt so damn good.

Thunder seemed reluctant to stop touching her as well. His hands roamed her back, stopping to squeeze her ass every so often.

"It's going to be impossible to concentrate on what you're saying if you keep doing that," she said as her eyes fluttered closed. Who knew having a man's hands on her backside would drive her wild?

He hummed out his agreement then slid his hands up her back. "My mother was a prostitute," he finally said.

The confession wasn't exactly a bucket of cold water on her arousal but did shift her focus to his words. Thankfully, she'd already known that much from Cassie, so the news wasn't a complete shock.

"Wow," she said softly. "That must have been difficult growing up." Her heart ached for the little boy whose parents didn't give him what he'd needed.

He nodded. "Yeah, and I'm just getting started. I have no idea who my father was. Some trick she fucked. She worked at an illegal cat house in Kentucky. The place had apartments attached, so we lived there. From as early as I can remember, I was exposed to fucking in all its forms. Some of the shit I've seen would make your eyes bleed."

"God, Thunder, I can't imagine what that was like." So different from her own upbringing, yet just as dysfunctional and emotionally scarring for a child. It strengthened the bond she already felt with him. Two souls wounded by their pasts. If her past didn't run the risk of endangering their future, this moment would be perfect. She tried not to feel angry about that fact. Now wasn't the time, but still, she couldn't help but experience some bitterness knowing she was the one who'd ruin what she had with Thunder. Either by turning him down now, or later when she had to leave.

He played with a lock of her hair, staring at the strands as they sifted through his fingers. "It wasn't pretty. I saw the working girls get eyes blackened. I saw them steal from johns. I saw men screaming, violent, drunk, high, you name it. But I never saw a healthy relationship. Not one. My mom eventually married the asshole who owned the brothel."

"Did she stop working after she got married?"

He snorted as though it meant nothing, but his eyes held the pain of painful memories. God, she understood that.

"Nah. That's when she became a cash fucking cow. You got any idea how much these pieces of shit were willing to pay for an hour or two with the owner's wife?" He whistled. "A pretty penny, and let me tell you, there were hordes of johns willing to pay. Can't tell you how many times I'd be doing homework while listening to some guy give it to my mom as my stepdad grinned and counted his fucking Benjamins."

"Oh, Thunder, I'm so sorry." Her insides bled for the boy forced into the dark side of an adult's world way before his time. Along with the heartbreak came a kind of understanding. While different circumstances, she'd not been allowed a childhood, either. She also witnessed the ugly underbelly of life before she'd been old enough to grasp the repercussions.

"All I'd ever known were men and women who made each other miserable. Who tore each other down, broke each other's hearts, and destroyed each other's lives."

She cupped his face and pulled him down for a quick kiss, trying to pour all her understanding and caring into the act. "Yet you grew up into such a good man," she whispered against his lips.

He grunted. "A good man? Makenna, I've done what I know. Treated women the same way I saw growing up. I've continued the pattern."

No, he'd told her he avoided relationships to keep from hurting and getting hurt. Sure, he may have become a stripper and, well, prostitute in some sense, but he hadn't carried on his parent's tradition of severely dysfunctional marriages. The idea of Thunder acting in a violent or even disrespectful way toward a woman almost made her laugh. "No, it's not the sa—"

"I was fourteen the first time I fucked," he plowed on as though not even hearing her. "She was another unfortunate soul who'd been raised in the brothel. A year older than me. Her name was Paris. She was awkward and painfully shy, but we were both curious about sex. It dominated everything in the house, yet we had no idea what it felt like. So we decided to find out for ourselves. For me, it was fucking awesome. But I was a hormone-fueled teenaged boy. Paris cried, but pleaded with me to just get it over with."

He shook his head, and her heart squeezed. No doubt, the memories seemed alive in his mind as though they happened yesterday instead of over a decade ago.

"I felt like such a monster. My stepfather discovered us, curled up in her bed afterward, naked, tears still staining Paris's cheeks. I got a fist bump out of the deal where Paris got a lecture about sucking it up and getting more practice, so she'd be broken in and useful by the time she started working at eighteen."

"God, Thunder…"

He nodded. "Fucked up, right? We were encouraged to keep fucking, but I was told my balls were on the line if I knocked her up. I'd loved it, hell what fourteen-year-old boy with hormones running rampant wouldn't? But Paris hadn't. She'd avoided me at all costs after that until one day when I finally cornered her. Not for sex, but to find out why my only friend wanted nothing to do with me. She'd broken down in my arms, sobbing in a way that had torn my heart in two. Turned out, that hadn't been Paris's first experience. Her father molested her throughout the years, and her head was more fucked up than mine."

He fell quiet, resting his forehead against hers as she gently traced the tattoos on his chest. When it seemed he wasn't going to continue, Mak asked. "What happened to her?"

"For months, she begged me to help her find a way to leave. Finally, I caved. I couldn't take seeing her so miserable. What the hell did I know about life? I was a stupid fourteen-year-old kid. We hatched a plan, and she ran away. Six months later, authorities found her dead on the street. She'd been working a corner." His voice caught. "All she'd wanted was to escape, and she ended up dying the same way she lived, in filth. I think I'm so superior because I strip at a club and have never worked a corner. But I'm the same."

"No. You're not the same. This conversation alone proves that." So many unhealed wounds to this man's psyche. She circled her arms around him and squeezed tight. What could she say? The story was horrifying and taught him lessons about life that drove his thinking and actions for years. So she didn't bother with fluffy words of sorry and empty sympathies. She held him and pressed her lips to his neck, where his pulse beat strong and steady.

"So yeah," he continued after clearing his throat. "I fuck in a way that ensures no one will form emotional attachments, but, Christ, Mak, I can't stop thinking about you and wanting more. I get it if this is all too much for you. And I can't make long-term promises because I don't know if I'll fuck it all up."

He wouldn't get the chance to screw anything up. She'd be the one.

"I'm a shitty bet, but I swear to God I'll give you everything I got."

He kissed her then, hard and desperate as though showing with his body how strongly he meant his words. Though she loved it, the kiss wasn't necessary to plead his case. He had her.

As foolish as it was. As hard as the crash would be when she eventually needed to leave, she found it completely impossible to turn away from him. Her heart and mind wanted him as badly as her body craved him.

When he pulled back, lust burned in his gaze, heating her blood to a simmer. As they stared at each other, she swallowed her fear. After years of keeping secrets, she was about to do the one thing she'd forbidden her oldest siblings from ever allowing to happen. Again and again, she'd coached them on keeping the details of their past a secret. Under no circumstances were they to reveal where they'd come from. No matter how much they loved their friends. No matter how hard Lee fell for a girl or Amy a boy. Over and over, she'd made them swear to keep quiet and practice a lie they'd come up with about their parent's deaths from a car accident.

And now she was about to break her most important rule for a man who'd crashed through his barriers for her. But he'd been so honest and open with her, and their shared traumas had her feeling they were kindred souls.

"I was married," she whispered.

Thunder stilled. The poor guy had to be confused, seeing as how she came across as such a sexual newbie. "Tell me," he said, giving the words back to her. "I'll keep your secrets safe, Makenna. Always."

"I grew up across the country, in a…well I guess the best word to describe it is a commune-like place. We called it the community, but it didn't have an official name. It was made of the kind of people you see documentaries about on TV. Preppers who stockpiled guns, food, ammo, and other supplies in preparation for Armageddon. They are a militia group. Violent, paranoid, bigoted. Hell, they're probably considered a domestic terrorist organization by now."

Thunder remained quiet, focused on her face as his hands stroked her back. The steady up and down trail of his hands kept her even.

"The community made their money farming. All the men farmed, but especially the male children. Long, hard days not appropriate for kids. And they participated in military-style training. Every boy was brought up to be a little soldier. Lee could shoot a rifle with more accuracy than most hunters by the time he was nine. He's also trained in hand-to-hand combat, which is pretty much the only reason I don't worry about him out on his own."

"What about women? What do they do?" he murmured, running his hand along her spine. If the conversation hadn't been so heavy, she'd have purred.

Memories of all the brainwashed women she'd grown up around had her frowning.

"They make babies. Lots of babies. And the female children and teens work as seamstresses. They pretty much had their own little sweatshop. I started working when I was three—bringing the workers fabric, putting things away. Again, long days. Few breaks."

"What about school?"

"We were educated by a select group of the women. Former schoolteachers who'd joined us. Four hours of school in the morning, then six to eight hours of work in the afternoon, depending on your age. Once we turned nineteen, we were married off. Since my father is one of the founders of the community, I was considered a prized bride. I—" The words stuck in her throat.

She hated recalling the details of this time so much, her stomach cramped.

"It's okay, baby. Take your time." His soothing tone and the stroke of his steady hand helped her continue. If he wanted to know, she'd tell him. Denying him wasn't possible.

"On my nineteenth birthday, I was married to a man in his sixties."

"Fucking Christ." He closed his eyes then ran a hand down his face as though fighting for control.

"His first wife had died a few months before. He could still produce children so…" She shrugged. "My job was to give him as many heirs as possible. He was permitted to impregnate single women outside our marriage as well. I was not allowed to stray. Those were the rules."

"Christ, Mak, that's fucked up. How long were you married to him?"

"About two years. He was…unaffectionate." Such a tame word for his lack of caring about his wife.

Thunder's jaw grew more like granite with each word she spoke. Mak stroked her fingers over his face. "Did he hurt you?"

"Sometimes," she said though the truth would only make him angrier. "I was never interested in him, so sex was often uncomfortable." Or worse. "I was considered rebellious. The black sheep who wouldn't submit to the leader's or my husband's will. I'd never agreed with that way of life and didn't always stay quiet about it, so I was frequently punished by my father, then my husband."

"How?" he asked, tone cold.

She shook her head. "It doesn't matter anymore." The punishments were in the past and needed to die there.

"How, Makenna?" he asked, voice turning deadly.

"Thunder…"

"Please," he whispered, pressing a soft kiss to her forehead. "I need to know."

Her eyes fell shut, trapping a watery sheen of tears. "Beatings," she whispered. A shiver ran up her spine as she recalled the final one that nearly did her in. "Isolation. Food and water deprivation."

No longer was he warm and comforting presence against her. Now rigid, with anger radiating off him in waves, she used her body to bring him back down. "Thunder, it's over. I'm okay. I had assistance from outside the community, and with Lee's help, we got all the kids out. We escaped. That is not my life anymore and hasn't been for two years." She cupped his face and forced him to look into her eyes.

To see she was whole.

"Is Emmie your child?" he asked without the heat of moments ago.

"No." An invisible band wrapped itself around Makenna's chest. "I couldn't do it," she choked out, as more memories assaulted her.

"Shh, it's okay," he whispered, rubbing his nose along her jaw. Whatever you had to do to survive, it's okay." Not an ounce of judgment. "None of it matters anymore."

God, she could fall for this man so easily.

So foolishly.

"I knew a woman in town. She helped us escape. But before that, she would sneak me birth control pills each month. I was such an embarrassment to my family. My father and my husband. As the daughter of the founder, I was supposed to have the most children. The place became its own twisted religion of sorts. Lee and I had been stashing money and supplies for years. We'd planned to leave, but then my father got a woman pregnant. She hated it there as much as we did but was too afraid to leave. She begged us to stay until she gave birth, and the baby was old enough to travel. We planned to wait until Emmie was about six months old and could wean."

She'd never forget the way Emmie's mother pleaded with her to give Emmie a better life. The young woman had been so scared but so brainwashed she'd refused to leave when Makenna offered to take her along. She had no idea what had become of the sad, scared woman and shuddered to imagine the punishment she'd have endured for allowing her baby to be kidnapped. Mak had to lock certain things in a box in her mind to survive and that was one of them. Opening that box had her insides twisting in agony.

"Uh," she said, clearing the thickness from her throat. "My, uh, when Emmie was two months old, my husband discovered my birth control pills. Lee gathered the kids and got everyone ready to leave. I'd been beaten so severely, I wasn't sure I could meet the physical demands of running. And Emmie was so young. Too young. It was terrifying. But we made it out of town. For the first six months, we lived in a tiny trailer in a rural area of Montana. I worked as a seamstress until we had enough money to move again. And this has been our life for the past two years."

She'd skipped over the long nights of stress and worry over how she'd feed the children. Those days were also over. She had a steady job, and though they didn't live like royalty, they lived free.

Thunder kissed her over and over—light kisses to her nose, eyes, cheeks. "I'm so sorry," he whispered between kisses. "You're incredible, Mak. So strong, loyal, loving, and beautiful. You amaze me."

"They might find us one day, Thunder." She grabbed his face to keep him from kissing her again. He needed to understand the very real risk of being with her. "You have to hear me on that. If they show up, we run. No matter what. It's happened before, and I won't let those assholes drag my siblings back to the community. Their lives wouldn't be worth living. And you have to know of the risk to you. They'd kill you in a heartbeat. Viciously. I've seen it happen."

She didn't have the energy left to delve into her mother's disappearance or the death of her mother's lover.

He scoffed. "Let them come. You don't have to run. You have me now. And the club. We'd tear them apart." He pulled her into his embrace. "They'll never touch you or any of the kids."

Though she nodded, she'd never put that burden on the club. Being with Thunder did not mean his family should inherit her problems. Her father didn't run a group of Rambo wannabees playing with guns. They were a highly trained militia with the skills and hatred to destroy the Handlers.

"Thunder," she whispered against his chest. He told her she was strong, but that couldn't be further from the truth. Strength would be walking away. Her weakness drove her now.

"Yeah, babe?"

"I can't make you any promises either. And I'm pretty sure I'll screw this up way worse than you ever could, but I want you too. For however long it can last, I want you. But you need to understand, really understand that I might have to disappear on a moment's notice."

"That won't happen. Not with my club at our back." His excitement at her declaration was evident in his shining eyes. And the erection nudging her stomach. "So we're doin' this? You and me. A...relationship?"

Mak chuckled. "It doesn't bode well for us if you can't even say it without making it sound like a bad word."

He rolled them, trapping her under his powerful body. The planes and ridges of his abundant muscles molded to her as he settled against her. Had anything ever felt so good? Who knew feeling the weight of a strong man against her would be so remarkable? If all they did was lie like this, she'd be the happiest girl in Tennessee.

"Just getting used to it on my tongue," he said, wiggling his tongue for effect. "Never had cause to say it before. I like the way it feels. Wanna feel it?" He licked up the side of her neck, making her shiver and laugh.

Actually, it was more a giggle. A light, playful chuckle. Never before had she heard such a sound come from herself. Playing and silliness went hand and hand with feeling lighthearted, and she'd never had the freedom to indulge. Responsibility, fear, and stress weighed her down daily. But at that moment, she felt... carefree. It gave her hope that she could have something she'd all but written off. It also struck a strong chord of fear deep in her heart. Already, this man had the power to hurt her in a way from which she might not recover. The longer they played this game, the further she'd fall once it ended.

But instead of doing the sensible thing and sending Thunder on his way, Makenna gazed up into his lust-filled eyes. "Yes," she said, teasing gone. "We're doing this."

His grin went from roguish to hungry in the blink of an eye. Holding her gaze, he stroked his hands down her body. One slipped between her legs to play between her slick folds.

Mak gasped at the shocking pleasure as she arched into his hand for more.

"I need to see you come." He nuzzled his nose in the spot right beneath her jaw that had goosebumps popping up all over her body.

"The kids..." she said on a quiet moan.

This time, his lips latched onto that same spot with gentle suction. The man did not play fair. Last night, when she'd come, it'd been the most incredible sensation of her life. Already, she tingled with anticipation of another explosion of pleasure.

"We'll be quiet. Please, baby," he whispered into the crook of her neck. "You're so gorgeous when you come. Let me see it. Let me feel it."

What woman in their right mind could resist Thunder rubbing all over them and begging to give them an orgasm? "Yes. Okay, yes, please make me come."

His lips curled against her skin in victory. He popped up, hovering over her for a second. "I'm gonna make you lose your fucking mind," he whispered before attacking her mouth. The kiss was deep, sloppy...it was utterly dirty. He sampled every corner of her mouth, biting at her lips, sucking on her tongue, and touching every inch of skin he could reach at the same time.

When he drew away, Makenna followed him with her lips, an automatic response.

Thunder chuckled. "Don't worry, baby. There's plenty more to come. Now be a good girl and lie back."

He crawled down her body, licking, sucking, and kissing a fiery path that had her squirming. She fisted the sheet beneath her as he tongued her bellybutton. How on earth did a belly button feel so erotic? If she'd been able to form rational thoughts, she'd have been embarrassed by the extreme wetness soaking into her panties. But she could barely even give it a thought as she tried to keep up with the sensations rioting through her body.

Holy shit, did he lick along the arch of her foot? If so, he needed to do it again because her eyes rolled back in her head at the sensation.

In the next instant, Mak was traveling down the mattress. "Wha—" she said as her feet flopped off the edge of the bed. She blinked, trying to clear her head as she propped up on her elbows.

Kneeling between her legs, Thunder gave her a downright wicked grin.

Holy shit, he looked hot down there. Her legs hung off the bed, dangling in midair. Instead of standing and grabbing a condom as she's assumed he'd do, he stared between her legs with a ravenous gleam in his eye.

"Wha—oh, my God," she shouted as he dove in and licked her sex. "Thunder!" she squeaked.

He let out a dark laugh. "Shhh, remember there are sleeping children in the house."

God, she could barely remember her name, let alone to keep from waking the kids. "What are you doing?"

He tilted his head. "It's my turn for a treat. I prefer something sweeter than ice cream and cookies."

"But...but...you don't have to. We can do what we did last night." Her face burned so hot, she'd have melted that ice cream in an instant.

Another of those laughs had her shivering. "Wish I could say I wasn't a selfish bastard, and this was one hundred percent for you, but, baby, ever since that tiny taste I had last night, I've been fucking dying to eat you."

Her breath caught in her chest. "Oh, God."

"You've never?"

She shook her head.

"Christ." He dropped his forehead to her thigh. "Fucking love that I'm the only man to eat this pussy." As he lifted his head, he shoved her thighs wide, exposing every inch of her to his gluttonous gaze.

Mak flopped back down with a hand over her eyes. If she didn't die of humiliation, it'd be a miracle.

"So fucking pretty," he murmured. He lifted his head, and the sincerity on his face slayed her.

All of a sudden, all her insecurities and embarrassment at being exposed this way disappeared. She was sharing an incredibly intimate moment with a man she adored. Not only was he making her feel things she'd only read about, but he clearly loved doing it. Her shyness morphed into a feeling of flying from the knowledge he desired her so much.

Never, in a million years, would she have expected what came next.

Thunder bit her!

Gently, but his teeth definitely sunk into the skin of her upper thigh. And what did she do? Well, she moaned shamelessly and thrust her pelvis up into his face.

"There's my greedy girl," he murmured. "Better find a muzzle, baby, I have a feeling you're gonna wanna get loud."

Oh shit.

Chapter Twenty-Two

Thunder chuckled as Mak slapped a hand over her mouth as though that would contain her screams of ecstasy once he really got going.

It'd been a damn long time since he'd gone down on a woman, and he couldn't fucking wait to break the streak with Makenna. And the fact he'd be her first...well, fuck, that was a turn-on he never saw coming. A woman's experience level never entered his thoughts in the past. He didn't give a shit if they'd been with one or one hundred men. Long as both parties got off, they were good to go.

But knowing he'd be the only man with the memory of Mak's flavor on his tongue? The only one to watch her face as he ate her to completion?

Fuck.

Mouth watering, he licked over the pink mark where he'd nipped her thigh. She jolted and began to pant in anticipation.

The sweet scent of her arousal surrounded him, making him dizzy with desire. Tonight was about her. He wanted her to know he was serious about giving this a go and didn't want to just stick his dick in her. He planned to get her off, kiss her goodnight, and let her get some much-needed sleep.

Thunder

His balls sure as fuck would hate him, but they'd survive until he could get home and rub one out. Or two. Hell, it might be a three jerk-off kinda night. Already, his dick felt strangled by his boxer briefs and his balls heavy and full. He'd be blowing a huge load tonight.

In the time he'd paused, Mak dropped her hands from her face and propped herself on her elbows again. She watched him with hooded eyes. Christ, she was gorgeous with those rosy tits, her creamy skin, and innocent yet curious gleam in her eyes.

"Eyes on me, baby. Watch how much I love eating you."

She bit her lower lip, and he groaned.

"Gonna fucking kill me," he muttered. Then, with his gaze on her, he moved in. She stared at him as he drew closer and closer to her. "Keep those legs wide for me."

She nodded, breath coming hard now that she was in full-on anticipation mode.

Thunder licked one inner thigh, then the other, gathering the flavor he'd been starving for since last night. Then, instead of continuing with the licks, he sucked one of her pussy lips into his mouth.

Mak squeaked, never releasing her lower lip. Her eyes flared wide.

He repeated the move to the other side, following immediately with firm strokes of his tongue. Every hitch in her breath was like a pat on the back, encouraging and praising him for his efforts.

With two fingers in a V-shape, he spread her lips and fucked his tongue into her. Her soaked pussy clenched around him as her thighs closed in on his shoulders, hard. He kept at it for a few minutes, loving the way she tried to crush him with her slender yet surprisingly strong legs.

She tasted fucking delicious. He could have died there, gorging himself on her pussy and listening to the ragged sounds of her breathing.

"Thunder," she whispered in a desperate plea for relief.

"Hmm?" he hummed against her, earning a firm bump of her sex against his face.

"It's so good," she whispered. "I can't...I don't even know."

With a chuckle, he lifted his head to find her loopy gaze still fixated on him. His lips and chin had to be shiny with her juices because he'd gone all in there like a fucking animal. But he wasn't done yet.

Keeping their gazes locked, Thunder slid two fingers into her. Her head fell back on her shoulders with a soft gasp.

"I love feeling full of you. Whatever you put in me makes me feel so full. It goes through my whole body."

"Christ," he whispered. Her reactions were honest, so real and unpracticed. Something about the authenticity made him even hotter. No overdone moaning, fake shouting, or Oscar-worthy production. Just a genuine response to extreme pleasure.

Damn, it was something to witness.

And now he got to watch her fly to the moon.

He moved his fingers, fucking into her as he curled them forward. Still clamped around his shoulders, her thighs began to shake.

With a smile, he tongued her clit. Mak reacted as though she'd been struck by lightning, gasping loudly as her body bucked. Her thighs nearly crushed him. He did it again, and again reveling in the whimpers and tremors as the climax took her.

After a few seconds, Mak could no longer hold herself up. She collapsed to the bed with a whispered, "Oh, my God." Another few seconds of fingering and lashing at her clit with his tongue had her thrashing on the bed.

His dick ached, probably leaving a mess in his underwear.

One more time, he curled his fingers at the same time he sucked her clit with force. Mak bowed, shoving her fist in her mouth. Her pussy pulsed around his fingers, and her thighs clenched and unclenched in a rhythmic pattern. This went on for a good forty-five seconds before she sagged limp into the mattress.

He crawled up and over her, dragging her up the bed with him. Once positioned on the pillow with his weight on top of her, she opened her eyes.

"Hi," he said, with what had to be the smuggest grin of all time.

Mak gave him a shy smile. Flushed cheeks, glassy eyes, and a sweat-dampened brow made her the cutest damn thing. "Hi. That was...um...well..."

Thunder laughed. "That good, huh?"

She shook her head. "No, a hundred times better." She reached up and stroked his face. "I never could have imagined."

He kissed her and she froze beneath him, probably shocked by the taste of herself on his tongue. But it only lasted a second, then she was tangling her tongue with his and sighing into his mouth.

"So, um, what's next?" she asked in a shy voice.

He shouldn't have laughed, but the question was so Makenna. Innocent yet to the point. "Next, you're gonna go to sleep. Someone's sitting outside your house for the night just to keep an eye on things. I'll be back in the morning to drive you to work."

"Wait, you're leaving?" Her nose scrunched.

"Figure you're not ready to have me here all night yet. Not until you figure out what to tell the kids."

"Well, yeah, that makes sense, but... You didn't...I mean, I'm the only one who..."

"Came?" He laughed. "We gotta work on your dirty-talk, babe. How you gonna beg me to fuck you harder or suck your clit if you can't even say the word come?"

Her face flamed so red, he couldn't help but laugh before kissing the tip of her nose.

"You didn't answer my question."

"You had a rough day. This was for you," he whispered. "I'll get my cock in you next time. Sleep. I'll lock up behind me."

"Wait," she said, wrapping a hand around his wrist, or as much around as she could get. "Thank you."

"Baby, believe me, it was my pleasure."

She giggled. Actually freaking giggled, and the sound lit him from the inside. Incredible to hear her sounding lighter than air.

"That's not what I meant. Though I do appreciate you making me *come* so spectacularly."

"Hey! We'll make a dirty-talker of you yet." Shit, this playful side of her was as captivating as the rest of her.

"I meant thank you for sharing your story with me. And listening to mine without judgment."

"Shit." He rested his forehead against hers. "I like having you know me in a way no one really does. And I love knowing you. But don't think we're done talking about you running. That's not happening."

When she went to argue he kissed her. They made out for a few minutes, until his cock throbbed, and his control threatened to snap. Going against his word and fucking her senseless right now wasn't smart. She needed to know she could rely on him to do as he said. To be responsible so she'd share some of her burdens with him.

Because he planned to teach Makenna that she didn't have to be an island. Not anymore. Now she had a big, rowdy, biker family at her back.

Chapter Twenty-Three

"Come on, Lee," Mak said as she unplugged the crockpot a few days later. "I'm not asking you to babysit, I just need you to pick Amy up from her friend's house and drive her to Cassie's."

"At eight o'clock on a Friday night!" Lee huffed out a pissed off growl as though she'd asked him to give up a month of his life to stand guard twenty-four-seven over his younger sisters. Oh, how she missed the days of responsible and unselfish Lee where he'd anticipate what help she needed and jump in without argument or attitude. Still, she found it difficult to get mad at the kid. Growing up in the community robbed him of so much. Didn't he deserve a little fun?

Don't you?

"Yes. At eight on a Friday night. But that's it. You have the rest of the night to do whatever it is you do on Friday nights."

He waggled his eyebrows, and Mak made a mock wrenching sound.

"Gross, Lee. I do not need to know about whatever girl you're disappointing for the night. Just promise me you're being safe." The thought of Lee having sex made her cringe. Wasn't he just a little boy?

No, he was a man now, and one who hadn't had any male role models through his late teen years. And shitty ones the beginning of his life. Hopefully, working with Thunder and some of the other club members at the gym would refresh his memory on how to be dependable. Maybe some of the guys could take him under their wings.

His jaw dropped. "Did you just make a sex joke?"

"What?" Her face heated. "Oh, shut up." Damn Thunder, rubbing off on her.

Oh…there was another joke in there somewhere.

Lee laughed and walked up next to her, where she stood at the counter. He slung an arm across her shoulders. "Okay, fine. I'll do it."

Thank God.

"But I want it on the record that I'm not happy about it." He snagged a tortilla chip from the bowl she'd filled a few moments ago.

"Hey!" Mak slapped his hand. "Can't you wait five minutes? Thunder will be back with Em and Kara, then we'll eat." He'd gone on a quick run to the store to grab a few things she'd run out of. The girls insisted on going with him, and he'd been more than up for the task.

Poor guy had no idea what he was in for. Emmie liked to touch *everything* in the store while Kara tried to add extra items to the cart.

With a grunt, Lee wandered across the kitchen. He rested his back against the refrigerator and folded his arms across his chest. Was it her imagination, or was her brother getting seriously buff? Maybe this gym job would work out after all.

One could hope.

"So, this is like an official thing now?" He asked as he raised an eyebrow.

"What's a thing?" Okay, she knew full well what he was asking.

"Thunder. *You* and Thunder." His voice took on a protective edge.

Thunder

In the days since she and Thunder had decided to give this thing between them a go, she'd not yet worked up the courage to talk to Lee about it. The only man Lee had ever seen her with had been her husband, and that hadn't exactly been healthy. She had no idea what reaction to expect from him. At first, he hadn't seemed too fond of Thunder, but perhaps that had changed with the assist in securing a job he'd enjoy.

"Yes," she said, propping her backside against the counter. "I'm not sure where it will go, or where it can go, but we are a thing."

"Hmm." He pursed his lips.

"Go ahead."

"What?"

She rolled her eyes. "Say your piece. Since when do you hold back your opinions?"

With a shrug, he stared out the window for a solid minute. As she was about to resume dinner preparation, he turned back to her. "I don't get it," he said. "Okay, some of it I get. You had a shitty sham of a marriage to a geriatric. You're young. You want some hot, wild sex, and I'm sure the biker gives it to you."

"Lee!" Not where she wanted this to go.

"But he's a biker, Mak," he said with true concern in his voice. "I know I'm a dude, but we left one male-dominated controlling-as-fuck situation. Why the hell do you want to stick yourself in the middle of another one? MCs aren't exactly known for treating women well, Mak." He was riled now, practically shouting at her as he advanced.

"Lee…" She kept her voice even and calm though her insides shook. He'd never yelled at her before, and even though it was out of fear for her, it brought back memories that shook her. She'd be lying if she didn't admit she frequently worried Lee would inherit their father's temperament. "He's not like that."

He threw his hands up. "Seriously, Mak? You're the last person I'd expect to fall for bullshit, but you're doing it. The fuck are you gonna do when this goes bad, huh?"

When it goes bad. Her heart clenched in her chest. Lee knew it wouldn't last.

He took another step toward her. "You've got the kids to think about, Mak."

Oh, hell no, he did not just go there. "I have the kids to think about? Seriously, Lee? Everything I do is for the kids. I've given up my life to take care of everyone."

"Huh." He lowered his voice and took a step back. "Didn't know you saw us all as such a burden."

A pounding in her temples had her rubbing the sides of her head. "That's not what I meant, and you know it. I'm just saying that I do think of the kids. I think about all of you in everything I do."

"Look, all I know is we left to get a better life for all of us. That means you too, Mak."

Couldn't he see that's what she was trying to do? Get a better life for herself? One she enjoyed. One where she could grab a little slice of happiness. Even if only for a short time.

"You deserve more than some biker who's gonna treat you like a piece of property."

"Lee, that's not fair. You barely know him. I thought you trusted me. We're a team, Lee." Her voice broke. "We've always been a team. I'd never do anything to hurt any of you. He's a good man."

"Yeah, well, I guess that remains to be seen."

The words sliced through her heart, proving that despite all they'd been through, he didn't trust her. They stared at each other across the kitchen, hurt and accusations making the distance seem like miles instead of feet. If there'd been one person she could always count on to have her back, it'd been Lee. How had they drifted so far apart? And what on earth did she do to mend the rift?

"Uh, everything all right in here?" Thunder's voice had both their head whipping to where he stood in the entryway to the kitchen.

"Fine," Mak said, plastering on a smile. "Where are the girls?"

He strode in, tall and confident. "Getting washed up for dinner. I'll tell you, those two are a trip. Got everything you asked for." He set the bags on the counter then moved to her, winking. "And maybe a few things you didn't."

"Thanks." Sure it was childish, but she glared at Lee over Thunder's shoulder as if to say, *See, he's helpful and reliable, and your sisters love him.*

Thunder captured her face between his hands. He gave her a long, slow kiss, not seeming to care that Lee looked on. "You're a shit liar," he whispered when the kiss ended.

With a chuckle, she just shook her head. "Just some sibling drama. Nothing to worry about."

"Hmm." Thunder didn't look convinced, but he let it drop.

"Everything go okay?" she asked. Now that they were home, safe and sound and the tension bled from her body, she realized how uptight she'd been about this trip to the grocery store.

"Yeah, babe, all good." Thunder kissed her again. "Told you we got it covered. Crank isn't stupid enough to show his face in town again so soon. We've got eyes all over."

With a nod, Mak leaned into him. Whenever he engulfed her in his strength, it seemed nothing could touch her.

"I'm heading out," Lee announced without so much as a hello to Thunder.

Her heart sank. "What? Lee, I promised the kids you'd eat with them tonight. They'll be crushed." Was this how it'd be now? Lee would disappear whenever Thunder came around. He'd been fine when the man was getting him a job.

He shrugged. "They'll be fine."

"You start work tomorrow, right? Morning shift?" Thunder circled her waist and gave a reassuring squeeze.

Eyes narrowed to slits, Lee nodded.

"Sweet, I'm on the same shift. Probably be the one training you."

Oh, fantastic.

That wouldn't be awkward at all.

"Why don't you stick around? I'll fill you in on how some of the shit works. Even tell you about the time I caught my brother Maverick doin' his ol' lady in the locker room."

Mak snorted. What did it say that she wasn't shocked by that news?

Lee fell quiet, and she held her breath.

Come on, stay.

When she'd been certain he was about to refuse, Lee nodded. "Yeah, I guess I could do that. Might help to have a leg up."

Thunder kissed her cheek then moved toward Lee. "That's the spirit," he said, slapping her brother on the back. Footsteps pounded down the hall a few seconds before the four absent siblings piled into the kitchen.

"When's dinner? I'm starved," Rissa announced with a loud stomach growl. "See?"

Mak giggled. "You finish your schoolwork?"

"Yep."

"Great. We're having chicken tacos. Everything is out on the counter. Grab a dish and bring it to the table, please. I'll carry the meat over."

Chaos ensued as all the kids scrambled to grab a dish. The sooner the food got to the table, the sooner they could eat.

Thunder snatched a stack of paper plates off the counter then crouched down in front of Emmie. "Hey, baby doll, I got a really important job for you. Can you handle it?"

Her light blue eyes lit up, and she seemed to grow two inches. "Yes! I can do it by myself."

"All right. I need you to carry these plates to the table. But don't drop them because we won't have anything to eat on! Okay?"

With her little face screwed up in concentration, Emmie nodded and held out her arms. After depositing the paper plates in her arms, Thunder began to stand up.

"Wait!" Emmie shouted. "Kiss!"

"What?" He dropped back down just in time to receive a big old kiss on his cheek from Emmie. The plates mashed between their bodies as she plastered herself against him.

Mak swore her ovaries did backflips. She glanced over her shoulder at Lee, who observed with an assessing gaze. "See?" she mouthed.

He rolled his eyes and turned to the refrigerator.

Mak plucked the giant bowl of shredded chicken off the counter and made for the table at the same time, Lee turned back from the fridge, beer in hand. Had there not been other impressionable teenage and pre-teen kids in the house, she probably wouldn't care if he drank it, but there were. "Lee—"

"Oh, thanks, man," Thunder said as he snatched the beer from Lee's hand. "Appreciate you grabbing that for me. Been dying for one tonight." He used his keychain to pop the cap then took a long drink. "Ahh, hits the spot." With a wink, he lifted the bowl from her hands and made his way to the table, whistling.

Lee stood in the same spot he'd been, blinking, with his hand curled as though the bottle still resided there.

Mak burst out laughing at the slack-jawed expression on her brother's face.

"What the hell just happened?" he asked as his arm dropped to his side.

Still chuckling, she strode past him, bumping his hip with hers. "You got outplayed, brother."

With a loud scoff, Lee trailed behind her.

Thunder caught her gaze and winked. She gave him a smile he hopefully understood was thanks for the smooth way he'd not only gotten Lee to stay for dinner but relieved him of the alcohol. Was there anything the man couldn't do without making it appear effortless?

Twenty-five minutes later, the table resembled a war zone. Empty plates piled high with crumpled and stained napkins sat in front of each person. Chip crumbs, shreds of lettuce and cheese, as well as drips of salsa splattered across the vinyl tablecloth, making a gigantic mess. At a volume of about nine out of ten, everyone chattered, laughed, and tried to one-up each other with the worst jokes she'd ever heard.

"Okay, I've got one for you," Thunder said as he leaned back in his chair. Mak hadn't stood a chance of sitting next to him as Emmie and Kara fought over that honor the second they'd entered the small dining room. Ever the lady's man, he'd seated himself between the arguing duo with a tug for each of their ponytails. Both girls had beamed, clearly thinking themselves the winner of that competition.

Sitting across from him had come with its own set of perks as she'd had a full view of his face and the enjoyment he seemed to derive from their simple family dinner. Laughter and fun came so easy for the man who'd quickly stolen her heart.

What? No. No, no, no. Not her heart.

Her body. Just her body.

"Lay it on me," Kara said, making her siblings laugh.

"Why did the teddy bear say no to eating dessert?" Thunder rubbed a hand over his stomach as though thoroughly satisfied with the meal.

"Cookies!" Emmie called then dissolved into a fit of toddler giggles.

"What? Cookies?" Thunder tickled her belly. "Girl, that doesn't even make sense."

"What's the answer?" Kara tugged his sleeve, far more serious than her little sister.

"Because he was stuffed! Ohhh!" Thunder slapped his palms on the table in a ba-dum-dum fashion.

Lee groaned. "That's the worst one yet, man." But he was smiling and interacting with them all more than he had in months.

Mak sat back and scanned the table. All around her, with their bellies full and wide smiles on their faces, her siblings fell under the spell of Thunder. They were all happy. Truly happy. Even Lee, for the moment, seemed satisfied to be right where he was.

Thunder

Thunder sent her a wink across the table before turning back to a joke Rissa was telling. It made absolutely no sense, but that didn't seem to matter to any of them. They all hooted and hollered as though she was a comedian with a Vegas special.

Warmth filled Makenna. This was it. This was the moment she'd wished for her entire life. Why she'd stolen away in the middle of the night, taking her siblings from everything they knew. This moment of pure happiness and childhood joy.

And she had Thunder to thank for it. They all loved him just as much as she—

As though an icy hose sprayed her in the face, Makenna froze.

Oh shit.

No, it wasn't love. Not for her or her siblings. For them, it was the novelty of a new face around the house. A fun man, who brought something light and different from their lives. That's all it could ever be.

The only person she could truly rely on to have her family's best interest at heart was herself. One day they'd have to leave Townsend, not by choice but as a product of circumstance. And on that day, the inevitable would be so much easier to swallow without having the devastation of severing emotional connections. Leaving a town that had become home was hard enough. She and Thunder could connect, could have fun, could have a relationship, but she needed to guard her heart and her siblings' so they didn't become reliant on Thunder as a permanent fixture in their lives.

But as she gazed around the table, Mak's heart sank. Truth whispered to her, getting through, no matter how hard she symbolically covered her ears.

It's too late.

Chapter Twenty-Four

Thunder had *plans* for tonight.

Epic plans.

Tonight's mission, which he'd already accepted, was to ensure Makenna forgot she was responsible for raising her five siblings. Forgot her money troubles. Forgot she had an abusive ex-husband out there searching for her.

They were going to drink, dance, and have fun with his family. Once they'd had their fill of socializing, he planned to take her back home and spend the rest of the night worshiping every inch of her delectable body.

Epic plans.

He jogged up to Mak's door then gave it a knock, which he'd given up doing days ago. The house was about a hundred times quieter than usual, and Thunder felt an odd disappointment at not being able to say hi to the kids tonight. Cassie had all of them. Lindsey was joining the older girls in helping Cassie take care of the younger ones.

A solid few seconds ticked by before a "Coming!" came from inside. He frowned. That didn't sound like Mak. It sounded more like—"Kristy," he said, as she pulled the door open.

"Well, hey there, hot stuff." She propped her curvy hip against the door frame as she folded her arms across her chest, plumping her tits up until they nearly spilled from her skimpy tank top. The move seemed so practiced, yet it probably had most men slobbering and making fools of themselves to get a taste of her.

Thunder's dick didn't so much as twitch. "I'm almost afraid to ask what you're doing here."

"Why, I'm helping your lady get ready," she said in an exaggerated southern belle accent.

"Jesus," he grumbled. "She better not have on some shit that shows off what's mine alone to see."

Though annoying, the interaction had been worth it to witness the shock on Kristy's face.

"Well, fuck me with a giant cock," Kristy said.

"I'll pass," he muttered under his breath.

"Never in a million years did I think you'd become a possessive ape." She rolled her heavily made-up eyes. "If the girl wants to show off her bangin' body, I'm not the one who's gonna discourage her, sweet thang."

"Kristy, who is it?" Mak yelled from the back of her house, probably her bedroom.

"It's your *boyfriend*," she called back in a singsong voice.

"Thunder?" Mak appeared in the hallway visible from the door. "Why'd you knock?"

Well, shit. His face grew warm.

The glee forming in Kristy's eyes had him wanting to wring the woman's neck. "Oh, aren't you just the cutest. Mak, I think he wanted to pick you up all formal-like for your date."

"Will you please get the fuck out of here?" he growled through clenched teeth.

Of course, she wasn't remotely offended by the tone or the request. "Sure, sure. I can tell when I'm not wanted." She pushed off the door frame and stepped outside, allowing Thunder into the house.

"Thanks, Kristy," Mak said, waving to her friend.

"Anytime, honey. And don't just spread your legs for this one here. Make him work for it. It's good for his soul."

Thunder slammed the door, which did nothing to hide Kristy's victorious laughter. "That woman is a bad fucking influence," he said as he turned around. "Holy shit." Finally, he got a good look at Makenna.

Forget his former remarks. If this was Kristy's doing, he owed the woman a bottle of her favorite champagne.

With her cheeks pink, Mak smoothed her hands down her short, very short, shimmery black shorts. "Too much? Kristy promised me I wouldn't stick out like a sore thumb, but I don't know…"

"Jesus, Mary, and Joseph, every man in the room is gonna get hard the second they see you." He'd be sending death glares all night at this rate.

"What?" she squeaked. "I'm not wearing this."

"Babe," he said as he rushed forward and caught her hand before she took off. "How do you feel in this?"

She looked down at the black crop top. He imagined Kristy had to force the garment over Mak's head. It wasn't risqué, but it was sexy with thick, black shoulder straps, a fine black mesh covering her chest, and it revealed a fair yet not obscene amount of cleavage. The lower part of the top molded to her body, leaving a two-inch strip of skin peeking out.

He wasn't even going to try to keep from stroking that tease of flesh all night. On her feet were spiky black heels that gave her an extra few inches. That would make kissing even more fun than usual.

"I feel good. Sexy, even," she whispered, as though afraid someone would overhear the confidence.

"You look hot as fuck, Mak. You will never stick out like a sore thumb, but you will stand out because you're beautiful."

"Thunder…" She gave him a sweet smile. "You haven't kissed me yet." She spoke against his lips.

"A serious lapse in judgment." He took her mouth in a hard kiss meant to mess up her lipstick and mark her as his.

As always, she opened for him immediately, but this time, she fought him for control of the kiss. His cock filled, and he walked them to the side. Mak's back hit the wall, giving him something to brace against as he deepened the kiss.

"Shit." He ripped his mouth away from her. "I want you to come out to the club and have fun tonight."

She brushed a thumb over his lower lip, and he couldn't help but sneak a nip.

"If we keep this up, we're never gonna make it there."

"We can be a little late—"

"Ahh! Enough outta you, naughty girl. There'll be plenty of time to ravage me later on." When she colored, he laughed. "Go fix your lipstick. I fucked it up good."

He slapped her on the ass as she walked by, laughing when she yelped and scurried faster.

Though she planned to be away from him for nothing more than a minute or so as she reapplied her lipstick, the ache he experienced when she left the room had him following. It was as though he couldn't bear to be physically separated from her.

When he reached the open door to her bedroom, he found her leaning over the dresser to get her face closer to the mirror as she swiped a glossy wand over her peachy lower lip. An image of her mouth wide and shiny taking his cock hit him hard as he advanced toward her. Shit, they needed to make that fantasy happen.

"Can't fucking wait to get you dancing with me tonight," he said as he came up behind her and lined himself up against her pert ass.

With a laugh, she met his gaze in the mirror. "Uh, yeah, I don't think so." She stuck the wand back in the tube and gave it a quick twist.

"What?" Pulling her up, he spun her around. "What do you mean, no?"

"I mean, I don't dance. Aside from fooling around with kids, I've never danced in my life, and I'm not about to start tonight. Making a fool of myself in front of your family isn't what I want."

It was as though she'd socked him in the gut. Dancing was hands down his favorite activity. "Oh, we're dancing, baby." He stepped toward her, arms out as he wiggled his hips in the most unsexy manner he could imagine. "No one will think you're a fool."

A bark of laughter bubbled out of Mak as she slapped his hands away. "Not happening. The first time I dance, it's not going to be with a professional in front of all his people."

"Excuse me?" Pressing a hand to his chest, he gasped as though offended. "I'll have you know, I'm an excellent lead. I'd never let you look bad."

"Not happening." Her silky black hair swished back and forth as she shook her head.

"All right, that's it." He gripped her shoulders and steered her toward her bed. "Sit that sexy ass down. You're about to get your first dance lesson."

As she sank down to the edge of the bed, she rolled her eyes. "My first dance lesson isn't going to be a lap dance, is it?"

Oh, this girl just did it for him. Her particular brand of sass, sweetness, innocence, and curiosity drove him wild. "It sure as fuck is, baby. It sure as fuck is. Want you to be able to feel it as well as see it."

"Oh, Jesus."

Laughing hard, he dug his phone out of his pocket, pulled up his current favorite playlist, and hit play. This was gonna be a fucking trip.

Two seconds later, a heavy hip-hop base beat filled the room.

Mak's jaw dropped into the most adorable face of disbelief. "Please tell me this isn't—oh, my God it is. It's WAP." She buried her face in her hands.

Too funny. "I'm shocked you even know this song."

Thunder

"I live with an eighteen-year-old boy. I know this song."

Thunder moved so he stood directly in her line of sight—or he would have been were she not hiding behind her hands. "All right. Step one, loosen up."

Mak snorted.

"A few drinks will help with this. Close your eyes and let your body feel the beat. Let it take on the rhythm of the music." He demonstrated as he spoke, softening his knees and beginning to bounce with the beat. For him, it came as naturally as breathing. As though the pumping of his blood changed to match the pulse of the music. When he opened his eyes, Mak had her fingers spread and peeked through the openings. He had to bite his lower lip to keep from smirking.

"Next, hips. You got some sexy ones, baby, and they're gonna drive the train here. Move them first, and follow with the rest of your body." He gave her a sexy example of a body roll, making sure to add an extra pump of his hips at the end.

"I can't do that!" she whined as her hands dropped to the bed. "My body does not move that way."

Shit, this was more fun than he'd thought it'd be. "Babe," he said, dancing close to her. "I'm intimately acquainted with how well those hips can move and trust me, you have no problem workin' 'em."

"Whew." She fanned herself. "Why's it so warm in here."

He winked. "So, we're loose, and our hips are poppin', now we're gonna move." He spun and shuffled around the room, letting the music take him as it always did. This was his happy place. "You're not a tree rooted to the ground; let yourself travel."

The song switched over, another hip-hop beat changing his moves a bit.

"How'd you learn to do this? It seems to come so effortlessly to you."

He executed a move that took him to the ground and had him twerking his ass. Mak laughed and whooped. Now she was loosening up and getting into the fun of it. "Some of it comes naturally. I've always loved it. It was an escape for me as a kid. When shit got fucked up, I'd get angry sometimes. Slapping on some headphones and dancing gave me an outlet for energy that could turn ugly otherwise."

She tilted her head. "It's hard to imagine you angry. You always seem so...light."

"Been getting laid a lot lately. There's this sexy waitress at the diner who can't keep her hands off me."

Mak laughed. "True."

Time to kick this show into high gear. He danced closer to her, dipping his hips into a sensual sway as the music slowed. As he drew close, he widened his legs until he basically straddled her. Then he lifted the hem of his tee, giving her a peek of the abs he worked very hard to maintain.

As though on autopilot, Mak reached out to touch.

"Nuh-uh." He waggled a finger. "Keep your hands off the dancer, please. This is not that kind of establishment."

With her eyes twinkling, Mak smirked and raised her hands to head height. "Won't happen again."

One swoop had his shirt up and off his body. He swung it around before tossing it behind him. As Mak giggled, he lowered until he was an inch above her lap. Then, he gave her his best lap dance skills, poppin' his hips, teasing her with near touches of his hard cock, and flexing as many muscles as possible.

"Seriously?" Mak asked in a droll tone though her eyes darkened with lust. "This is how you want me to dance at the clubhouse?"

Thunder's head fell back as he let out a loud laugh. "Fuck, no! You do this, and you'll be getting your first spanking."

He froze. Shit. How the hell could he have been so insensitive? If she'd expressed interest in a little sexual spanking, he'd have been all for it, but the woman had a history of abuse. Fuck, had he just ruined the evening?

But Mak didn't react with horror or revulsion. Instead, she disobeyed the rule he'd just given her and ran her fingertips over the ridges of his stomach. He shivered as sparks of electricity zinged through his blood.

"Pretty sure that's not a deterrent."

"Fuck." He straightened his knees, putting his cock at face height.

Eyes fixated on the bulge behind his fitted black boxer briefs, she licked her lower lip, and he swore to Christ he felt that curious tongue stroke his cock.

"So," she said, her voice taking on a smoky quality he'd yet to hear from her. "You said no hands on the models, but you didn't say anything about lips."

Never in a million years would he have guessed Mak was about to lean forward and mouth his stiff dick through his underwear, but fuck, that's exactly what she did. Thunder clenched his fists as the urge to grasp her head and shove his cock in her face hit him like a sledgehammer.

"Hmm, haven't been kicked out of the place yet." She brushed her nose against him then lifted her head, capturing the band of his boxer briefs in her teeth. The scape of them over his lower abs, combined with her hot breath on his skin, had him jerking. The band slipped from her teeth, snapping against his stomach.

"Fuck."

"Not sure the security at this place is up to par." Mak giggled. "Sure I can't put my hands on my dancer?"

Christ, he'd die if she didn't get her hands on him. "Yes," he said in a hoarse croak. "Put your fucking hands all over me."

She shifted her gaze upward, meeting his. "Thank you."

Then the goddammed siren snuck her fingers in the sides of his shorts and tugged them down. His cock sprang free with a bounce, ending up pointing straight out toward her face.

Thunder's eyes rolled heavenward. "Mak..." Christ, it sounded like someone had run over his vocal cords with a truck.

"Yes?" she asked, all syrupy sweet.

He felt like a rubber band stretched to failure, one tug, and he'd snap. "You want me in your mouth?"

She nodded. "Yes." It came out as a whisper. "I want to feel you come down my throat."

"Jesus fucking Christ." He gripped his hair. It was either that, or do it for her, ramming his cock down her throat. Maybe someday, but he had a feeling she didn't have much experience in this art. Instead, he settled for bossy. "Suck me."

Her little pink tongue slid past her lips to take a quick lap of his cockhead. Thunder gritted his teeth. Fuck, how the hell did that one lick feel better than any blow job he'd had in the past?

Easy answer. It came from a woman he'd grown obsessed with.

Chapter Twenty-Five

His erection felt different against her tongue than she'd expected. For some reason, she'd only considered the hardness of his cock, not the silky-smooth skin surrounding it. Who would believe she'd been married for two years but had never given a blowjob? Probably no one.

But her role hadn't involved pleasure, giving or receiving. She'd been cast as nothing more than a human incubator.

Again, she licked him, this time curling her tongue around the tip. From the corner of her eye, she spotted his fisted hands clench as a harsh groan left him. A glance up revealed his ticking jaw, corded neck muscles, and piercing gaze. Veins popped in his forearms from the tension.

Power surged through her. A few licks of her tongue and the man appeared wrecked. With that power came bold confidence and desire to make him lose his mind in the way he'd done to her so many times.

She sucked the head into her mouth, still tonguing him. Hadn't she read somewhere the underside was particularly sensitive? She pressed her tongue to it, and Thunder jerked as though she'd struck him.

Yep, sensitive.

Excitement flared as she scooted forward on the edge of the bed. Her mouth slid down his length, stretching wide to accommodate his girth. Even once she felt full of him, Mak continued to see how far back she could tolerate. His dick hit the back of her throat, making her gag a bit. But she didn't even mind. The low grunts and gasps pouring from him made up for any small amount of discomfort.

Wringing more of those desperate noises from him became a craving. Each time he groaned in pleasure, she sucked harder, moved faster, and reveled in her power. Within minutes, she'd found a rhythm that seemed to drive him wild. Her tolerance for deep throating improved as well. Sure, she wasn't a master midway through one blowjob, but hopefully, her enjoyment overrode her lack of experience.

"Fuck, baby," he said as she took him deep, deeper than she had before.

"Mmm," she hummed, without any realization of how the vibrations of her throat would affect him.

Thunder shouted, and his hands moved to her head. It was the same as when he'd held her throat. This knowledge that if he wanted, he could take this beyond her tolerance. He could ram down her throat, cut off her air, and cause fear. But he didn't. He let her set the pace and just held on to her hair.

But if he wanted, he could dominate her in an instant, and for whatever reason, that made her wet and needy every time. At first, it'd freaked her out, but she trusted him to know her limits and decided to enjoy the intense pleasure.

"You like this baby? My cock in your mouth?"

"Mm-hmm." Liked it enough to not even want to pull off to answer him.

"You wet?"

Wet? If she could, she'd have snorted. The lacy pink thong she'd purchased on impulse yesterday felt like she'd worn it straight from the washer, it was so damn wet.

"Yes," she managed around his girth.

"Fuck." He moaned loud, totally unabashed.

A quick flick of her tongue under the tip had his hips bucking and his cock hitting the back of her throat.

Curling her hands around his thighs, she sucked him in again. A subtle salty flavor hit her tongue as his cock seemed to expand in her mouth.

"Fuck, I'm close already," he rasped. "Your mouth is destroying me."

His words might as well have been a physical caress for the way her body reacted. Her nipples ached, and she rocked her pelvis on the bed in an attempt to grind against the mattress—anything to relieve the intensity of the needy ache.

"Oh, Christ," he shouted. "Pull off now if you need to." Even as he suggested she back off, he tightened his grip on her hair.

She wouldn't have released him for anything.

Grasping his thighs as tight as she could, Mak let the slight sting in her scalp wash over her. She jammed him as far as she could manage and rocked her hips against the mattress with wild abandon. It wasn't nearly enough to get her off, but she'd grown so desperate for relief she'd take anything.

Thunder's hands clasped hard, and he hollered a string of filthy words as he filled her mouth with his cum. His abdominals flexed and practically spasmed while the thighs she clung to trembled like a tree in a hurricane.

Satisfaction flared deep inside her. She'd done this, taken this experienced man, and reduced him to a screaming mess.

With a self-satisfied smile, she relaxed her jaw and let his softening cock slip from her mouth. Before she had the chance to so much as glance at his face, she was being yanked to her feet.

"You fucking wrecked me," Thunder said, one second before he captured her mouth, not seeming to care that she still had his flavor on her tongue.

The next thing she knew, her shorts were being ripped open, and Thunder's hand was in them. Two fingers entered her without warning, making her shout against his mouth and clutch his arms for support.

"Christ, you really did like having your mouth full of my cock, didn't you? So goddammed wet, I could drown in you."

She shook and trembled as he finger-fucked her without mercy. Already, fifteen seconds in, she was close to coming. Wait, had he just asked a question?

"Oh, God, oh, God," she said again and again. "I'm gonna come. Thunder!" She planted her forehead against his chest as she worked her hips in time with his fingers.

"That's right, baby. Get it. Take it."

"Yes...yes."

His fingers moved with crazy speed, stroking the walls of her pussy with a rough touch. Mak panted, gripping him firmer with each passing second. The tips of her fingers and toes began to tingle. The sensation traveled through limbs, collecting in a tight coil low in her belly.

And then, as she screamed his name, it burst outward. The orgasm came on so fast and so hard, it made her head spin, stole her breath, and buckled her knees. Thunder caught her as she wobbled and rode out the violent storm.

Eventually, she sagged against him, and his fingers slipped from her body.

Mak blew out an unsteady breath as she straightened away from him. Her legs still felt like jelly, and her insides flowed warm and sated.

"Not how I was expecting dance class to go, but I'm not mad about it," Thunder said with a wink, as he pushed her hair behind her ears. Probably looked like a bird had been nesting in there.

"Yeah...that was..."

"Incredible? Hot? Erotic? Fucking amazing?"

She grinned at him. How could she not? His playful nature infected her in the best way. "E, all of the above."

"Damn straight." Wrapping his arms around her, he pulled her close and kissed the hell outta her.

"Let me just fix my hair and makeup, then we can go." With warm cheeks, she glanced down at her open shorts. "Guess I need to change my panties, too."

"Fuck no. Fix the hair and face if you must, but don't even think about taking off that thong."

"Seriously?"

He nodded. "I want to spend the entire night with the knowledge that you're wearing the same thong you just drenched."

Why was that so hot? "Okay," she whispered.

Fifteen minutes later, they stood outside her house, next to his bike. Yeah, she should have assumed he'd want to take the bike, but it'd never crossed her mind.

"I don't know…"

Thunder's head fell back as he laughed. "Babe, your man's a biker. You gotta ride."

Mak's mouth turned down. Weren't they dangerous? She had so many people depending on her. What if something happened?

A strong arm tagged her around the waist then yanked her flush against an equally strong chest. "You're worrying so hard, I can practically hear it. Don't you trust me to keep you safe?"

"Yes," she answered without needing to consider the question. "Absolutely. It's the other idiots I don't trust. It just seems a little scary." God, what a buzzkill she was.

"I can promise you with one hundred percent certainty, you'll love it." He still hugged her close. "And I have a secret to tell you."

"What?" She inhaled. Oh, he smelled good. Some subtle cologne, whatever made Thunder Thunder, and… and a little bit of sex. It would have embarrassed her if it wasn't so intoxicating.

"You are going to be the first woman I've ever had on the back of my bike."

Her eyebrows drew down. "Okay…that's cool."

Chuckling, Thunder squeezed her ass. "Having a woman on the back of your bike is a big deal in MC culture. You don't just let anyone hop on. It means you're my woman. *My* woman. Not my nightly hook-up, not my fuck buddy, not my friend. My *woman*. Get it?"

Wow. Mak nodded. "Yeah." So, it was a claiming. An announcement of their relationship to the world.

With a smile full of promise, he held out a hand. All the fear and uncertainty she'd been experiencing faded into the background. She not only trusted Thunder to get them to the clubhouse safely, but she also trusted his promise she'd enjoy the ride.

Mak grabbed his hand, but instead of using it as leverage straight away, she brought it to her mouth and kissed the back. His eyes smoldered, and a host of heavy unspoken emotion traveled the space between them.

As usual, her overactive worrywart brain wanted to dissect every look, every glance, every touch, but for tonight, she vowed to put everything on the back burner and enjoy each second with Thunder and her new friends.

Of course, as promised, she fell in love with his motorcycle. Nothing in her experience compared to the feelings of freedom, flying, and joy she experienced on the seventeen-minute ride to the clubhouse. If they weren't already late, she'd have worked to convince Thunder to ride all night.

Another time. Because they were a couple now, which meant they'd have time in the future for all kinds of adventures.

The entire night passed in a blur of fun and excitement. Mak drank far too much, as did Thunder. They laughed with his club brothers and their women. They danced for hours. Thanks to his very detailed dance lessons, Mak held her own. Okay, maybe it was more the copious amounts of alcohol making it so she didn't care how foolish she appeared. They'd even made out on the dance floor. Sloppy, drunk kisses that turned out to be so much fun.

Since Mak couldn't control the bike and Thunder couldn't get them home safely at the end of the night, they ended up crashing in an empty room at the clubhouse.

Laughing, groping, and kissing, they'd fallen into bed sometime after two in the morning. Thunder had been keeping her on edge all night with dirty promises whispered in her ear. Anticipation had been high, but so had their blood alcohol level, and though they made it to the naked stage, both passed out before anything more than flopping on the bed next to each other happened.

Mak woke early, just as the sun peeked through the slats in the blinds. Though nude, she'd never been warmer and more comfortable in her life. Due, of course, to the also unclothed man wrapped around her back.

Thunder slept soundly. With each exhale, his breath tickled the back of her neck. At some point, he's slung a leg over both of hers, trapping her against him. His arm had curled around her torso, resting between her breasts.

Mak closed her eyes and let the incredible feelings of safety and warmth travel through her. They had a busy week ahead of them, so the downtime felt amazing—calm before the storm.

Kara had an appointment with her neurologist in Knoxville on Monday. She'd been seizure-free for a solid year, which was fantastic. This appointment was merely a checkup and medication adjustment, still, it stressed Mak to no end. Especially when she had another commitment with Rissa at the same time. Thankfully, Thunder had offered to step in and help out with Rissa.

She'd be lost without him and his big crazy family these past few weeks.

The thought made her eyes fly open and her heart lurch to a stop. Nausea curdled in her stomach. Shit, it had happened already. He'd entwined himself in nearly every aspect of her life.

To the point she depended on him for help, comfort, and safety. The kids loved him.

Hell...she loved him.

What a freaking disaster.

A tear rolled down her cheek.

Safety was an illusion she'd begun to fall for. Dangerous and stupid. One day her husband and father would find her. And she'd have to leave. Then she'd be on her own again with her siblings. Already, she couldn't imagine not only being separated from Thunder, but how she'd survive without him in her life.

This was exactly what she'd feared would happen. In just a few short weeks, she'd failed miserably. Failed herself and failed her siblings.

The relationship would have to end. With each passing day, she fell for him harder and soon the pain of leaving would be unbearable.

It was best to do it now. Today. As soon as possible.

With silent tears soaking the pillow, Mak closed her eyes and willed herself to relax.

Just a few more hours of bliss, then she'd do what she had to for her family. She'd put on a smile, pretend everything was okay, and press forward.

Alone.

Chapter Twenty-Six

"All right, guys, head on in," Mak said as she nudged the front door open. As though she'd released a herd of bulls, the kids charged in the house, loud as ever despite her many attempts to keep them quiet throughout the morning.

Last night, she'd consumed more alcohol than ever before, and and now she understood why she hadn't indulged like that in the past.

Hangovers sucked.

She'd emerged from a deep sleep about an hour ago to find a sweet note from Thunder on his pillow. Copper had needed him for some task, so he'd taken off, letting her know he'd meet up with her at the house as soon as he'd finished. The note concluded with a lopsided heart and a sentence about how much fun he'd had the night before.

And he'd called her beautiful.

Ugh.

Ending their short relationship was going to destroy her.

And possibly him.

Everyone in the club would view her as a bitch, deservedly so. A shrew, who'd strung along a man they love for no good reason.

How would she show her face at the diner tomorrow morning? Would she have to find a new job?

Hopefully not. The thought sent a shiver of fear through her. It had been hard enough to find this one.

"Mak, why are you still standing out there?" Amy yelled from the hallway.

"I'm coming." Poised to step into the house, a car door slammed behind her, making her jump and turn on reflex. Someone from the club sat across the street in a truck, but it was Kristy's arrival that drew her attention. "Morning, Kristy," she said with a wave as her friend and neighbor climbed out of her car.

Mak narrowed her eyes. Was she walking with a limp? And why the hell did she have enormous oversized sunglasses on? Dark gray clouds loomed overhead, announcing the impending arrival of a predicted storm.

When all Kristy did was lift a hand in response, Mak grew worried. When the hell had that extroverted woman ever missed an opportunity to share some gossip? "You okay?" she called out as she jogged across the narrow strip of grass separating their houses. "Oh, my God, Kristy! You're hurt."

Despite the sunglasses engulfing the majority of Kristy's face, they weren't large enough to hide extensive bruising. Without asking permission, Mak reached up and snatched the glasses off Kristy's face. She sucked in a breath at the sight of the dark purple, near black, bruising around her friend's right eye. Deep purple and bluish bruises mottled the right side of her jaw as well. Dried blood crusted in the corner of her mouth.

"Shh," she said, glancing over her shoulder at the Handler's prospect on protective duty that day.

Thankfully he seemed more interested in his phone than their conversation.

Some bodyguard.

"I'm okay, honey. Nothing some Motrin, vodka, and a bed won't fix. And not necessarily in that order."

How could she be so calm? The way she held herself stiff and limped with each step meant more damage in areas not visible. Someone had beaten her and done a hell of a job of it. "Who did this? I can call Thunder. The club will help you. You know that."

Kristy reached out and squeezed Mak's hand. If Mak hadn't been paying such close attention, she'd have missed the slight tremor in Kristy's fingers. She'd thought her friend unshakable, but being on the receiving end of an angry man's fists could crush even the most impenetrable rock.

"Thank you, Mak, you're sweet, but it's not necessary. This sometimes happens in my line of work." She shrugged then flinched as though the simple movement pained her a great deal.

With a shake of her head, Mak said, "No, that's not acceptable." Memories of being in Kristy's exact position had her unable to ignore the problem. Mak knew firsthand the pain her friend was experiencing. Not only physical pain but fear, shame, disbelief, despair. The moment she escaped community property, she'd vowed never to let another man put his hands on her in anger, and that promise extended to every woman she knew. "I'm calling Thunder."

"Don't," Kristy said, her voice cracking. She cleared her throat. "Please. It'll just make it worse. They've already had enough trouble with the CDMC. I'm not going to be the cause of more. The Handlers have always been good to me."

A cold rush of terror shot up Makenna's spine. Leaning close, she whispered, "This was the CDMC?" She swallowed a lump rising in her throat as a thought made her dizzy with dread. "Was it...did it have to do with me?"

"What? No." Kristy shook her head. Her high ponytail sagged to the side, flopping with the motion. "Crank wants me to spy on the Handlers. I refused. He didn't take it well." She dropped her voice low though they didn't run the risk of being overheard. Mak's bodyguard couldn't hear from his position and hadn't lifted his gaze from his cell.

"Shit, Kristy. Are you in danger now? Will they come after you?"

With a huff, she shrugged. "No. I don't think so. Crank got his message across loud and clear. I've been banned from their property, and I won't be able to work anywhere for weeks, thanks to all this." She gestured toward her battered face. "Even if I could cover this with six pounds of makeup, I'm too sore to do much more than shuffle around for a while."

Gnawing on her lower lip, Mak handed the sunglasses back. Kristy immediately slid them on her face. She ignored the rising discomfort from her memories of doing the same. This was about Kristy.

"You need to tell Copper what happened. You know they'll help you cover your expenses until you can work again. They're good men."

Kristy looked off into the distance as she nodded. "I know. I just don't want to be the one to bring more trouble to their doorstep. The club's been through a lot in the last few years."

"They can handle it. They're strong." Mak smoothed a gentle hand up and down Kristy's arm. Her friend may be brash, inappropriate at times, and over the top, but she had a heart of gold. Without her, Mak wouldn't have adjusted as well to life in Townsend as she had. She owed Kristy for free babysitting, fashion advice, and general friendship.

"Yeah," her voice hitched. Mak would bet if Kristy lifted those glasses, she'd have tears shining in her expressive eyes.

Drawing attention to the show of emotion wouldn't serve any purpose, so they both pretended not to notice.

"I'll stop by their clubhouse later on. I just need some time to…" She shrugged.

"Of course. They'll be there when you're ready. And let them come to you. You shouldn't be doing more than lying around the house right now."

As Mak turned to join her siblings in the house, Kristy grabbed her hand. "Thank you, Mak. It's not always easy for me to keep girlfriends." She half smiled as though it didn't bother her, but Mak caught the subtle sadness in her tone. "Just want you to know your friendship means something to me."

That was the second time recently that she'd been called a friend and told of her value. God, she liked it. Really liked having connections, putting down roots, bonding. "Same, Kristy," she said, fighting to keep her voice from cracking. "Now, go get some rest." She squeezed her friend's hand. "I'll stop by later and bring you something to eat."

Once in her house, Mak spent the next hour or so getting the kids lunch, then starting on the mountain of unfolded laundry. Every few minutes, her mind drifted to Kristy. As soon as she finished the current chore, she'd make her friend a meal. Lost in her thoughts, she never heard Thunder as he came up behind her in the den.

"Hey, beautiful." He leaned in and kissed her neck, causing her to yelp and drop the shirt of Kara's she'd been folding.

"Holy crap," she said in a breathy voice as she pressed a hand to her racing heart. "You scared me."

"Sorry," he said, flashing her his famous smile.

The plain black T-shirt he wore molded to his chest as he moved. Even the cut over top couldn't disguise his insane physique. God, the man made her stupid with lust.

"Couldn't resist." He plopped down on the floor next to her and grabbed a pair of pants from the basket.

"What are you doing?"

"Helping you fold."

She blinked, eyes prickling. This would not go well if she already felt near tears and she hadn't even spoken yet. Why couldn't he be an asshole, just for today? "Please don't. You do not want to fold laundry."

His chuckle made her smile despite her sadness. "I'm a selfish bastard. The quicker you're done here, the quicker we can fool around," he said, waggling his eyebrows.

Argh, why did the man have to be so perfect? It made what she had to do ten times harder.

"Where're the kids? It's too quiet around here."

"Too quiet?" She placed the folded shirt on a pile of others. "I'm pretty sure that's called perfection. The younger two passed out after lunch. I don't think they slept much last night. Too much partying with Beth and Cassie. The others are hiding in their rooms. Lee's at the gym."

He frowned at her. "Why do you seem weird? You're not meeting my eyes."

"Hm? I'm not weird." Anxiety twisted her stomach into dozens of knots and had her hands trembling. She squeezed the shorts in her hand to stem the shakes, then forced herself to meet his gaze.

The look he gave her was one of disbelief, but he let it go. "Hey, I was thinking maybe later we could go talk to Copper, clue him in about your ex-husband."

When her jaw dropped, he held up his hands in surrender, Emmie's pants dangling. "You don't have to give him any details, but it'd be good for him to know a little of what we're dealing with in case the fucker ever shows up."

Her arms dropped, and she blinked to keep the tears from falling.

"What?" Thunder's eyebrows drew down in concern.

"You said we."

Thunder curled a hand around her thigh and pulled her close. "Baby, I told you, you have the protection of the club. And of course, I said we. Your shit is my shit now, which means it's the club's shit."

She shook her head so hard, the room spun. "No. My problems can't be the club's problems. They're...my father and husband are extremely dangerous. And crazy when confronted. They're well trained and have access to an armory of weapons. I can't put that on you or your club. I *won't*. I'd never forgive myself if something happened to one of you."

"Babe, *we're* dangerous." He winked. "And crazy."

It was probably meant as an attempt to lighten the mood, but the joke failed. Somehow, she needed to convey the severity of this to him and get him to agree to keep her personal problems away from his club. "Look, if my father or my husband connect you to us, they won't ask questions. They did it to my mother." She sighed. "My mom had an affair with a man outside our community. When my father found out, my mom 'disappeared' and the man she slept with was killed. Brutally and publicly. They beat him to death in the center of our compound. I was a kid. It was—"

"Shit, Mak." He yanked her close and held her tight. "I am so sorry that happened to you, but we aren't your mom. We're a strong group. You wouldn't believe some of the training and experience our guys have."

He wasn't listening. He didn't get it.

She gripped his upper arms and shook. "They'll burn down your clubhouse or something insane like that. All they care about is the people of their community. Everyone else is expendable to them. My husband is crazy and my father is crazier."

He didn't appear remotely fazed by her impassioned plea. "Ex."

"What?"

"Ex-husband."

Oh shit.

They stared at each other. Mak wrung her hands, twisting the shirt she still held. "Um, Thunder, he's not my ex-husband. I'm still married." The last part came out in a whisper.

He stiffened. "Excuse me?"

"I—w-we ran. Literally ran in the middle of the night. Divorce wasn't possible. Technically, I'm still married. This is why the club can't get involved. It's too messy. Too complicated." She had to steer this conversation back around to what was important.

"You're still fucking married?" He shoved to his feet and stormed into the kitchen. "I need a fucking drink."

"Um, all I have is beer and wine," she called as she rushed after him.

"Fucking married," he mumbled as he yanked a beer out of the fridge. He flipped the cap off with his keychain then downed the entire thing in five swallows.

Mak stood there, shoulders slumped and chest heavy. Now what?

"This bullshit is pretty much exactly why I avoid relationships," he spat out as he slammed the empty bottle on the counter. "People just fucking lie and cheat and tear each other apart." He gripped the edge of the small island, head hanging between his shoulders. "You know how many times angry wives showed up at the brothel crying and shattered because they found out their husbands were our customers?"

The threat of impending tears thickened her throat. "I'm so sor—"

"You know," he went on as though she hadn't spoken. "I was gonna tell you I fucking loved you today."

Oh, God, her heart pulsed with a deep ache.

He lifted his head, staring straight at her. The anguish in his gaze tore her heart in two. Hurting him cut her worse than she'd imagined.

The first tear fell free.

"My whole life has been full of cheaters and liars. They came to fuck my mom. They come with a fist full of cash to fuck me. It's all a big game to them. They don't give a shit about anyone but themselves." He shook his head, then in a mocking voice, said, "'Look at me, I'm married but, I can still blow the stripper.' It's not like I'm gonna fucking tell. I'm an immoral stripper. Stuff a few hundred in my shorts, and my mouth is sealed tight. I refuse to let that poison into my personal life."

No. Those situations were nothing like hers. How could he not see that?

But he seemed lost to his rage, now pacing the kitchen. Then he stopped dead in his tracks and faced her. "Why the fuck didn't you tell me?" he snarled with hatred.

Honestly, it hadn't even crossed her mind. In her head, she sure as hell wasn't married. She had never been. There hadn't been any truth to her "vows" or loyalty between her and her husband. It'd been a business deal, one she'd never wanted and escaped from at the first chance she could.

He had to recognize that.

"It wasn't a real marriage, Thunder," she said, defeat weighing her down.

"Is it legal?"

"Yes, but—" She wanted to go to him, soothe him with her touch, beg for forgiveness, plead with him to look at things from her perspective, but maybe this was the catalyst she'd been looking for. Even though it sliced into her soul, here was her out.

And she needed to take it.

"M-maybe..." Oh, God. She pressed a hand to her queasy stomach. The words stuck in her throat like a sharp shard. "M-maybe, this is a sign we should c-cool things down for a while." She stared at her feet, like the coward she was, unable to make eye contact.

"Seriously? You're fucking dumping me?"

"Y-yes," she squeaked around constriction in her throat. "I-I just think we're getting in over our heads. It's too much right now. Too much with all my other responsibilities."

"So, being with me is just another responsibility on your long, long list, huh?" His voice was so dark and ugly, full of disgust, it made her cry harder.

She wanted to scream that he could never be a responsibility. He was the one thing in her life just for her. The one thing she'd chosen for herself. The one thing that made her happier than everything else. But she choked back the words. "I just can't divide myself like this anymore. I'm neglecting my family."

Liar. Liar.

"You know what? That's fucking fine." He threw his hands in the air. "I don't need this horseshit anyway. Only fucking fools fall in love." As he stormed toward her, he slapped a box of cereal on the counter, sending Lucky Charms flying to every corner of the room.

Mak flinched but didn't budge as he stomped past her. The forceful clomp of his boots on the linoleum floor echoed in time with her battered heart. Her chest grew tighter with each passing second, and when the door slammed so hard it rattled the walls, she doubled over on a painful exhale.

Air whooshed from her body as she wrapped her hands around her middle. A sob tore from her throat. Then another. And another. After a few seconds, her legs gave out, and she sank to the floor, a weeping, hyperventilating mess.

The agony of watching Thunder walk away from her made all the beatings she'd taken in the past feel like hugs.

She'd done the right thing.

As horrible as it was and as long as it would take her heart to recover—maybe it never would—she'd done the right thing for her family.

"Mak?"

Amy's tentative voice cut through her intense sorrow.

"I heard shouting. Are you okay?"

"Uh, yes." She kept her back to her sister and quickly swiped at the tears. Over the years, she'd become a pro at keeping her true emotions from her siblings. First, when living in their father's house, she'd never let them discover the bruises from her punishments for rebellious behavior. Then, once married, she kept a smile plastered on her face so they'd never know her misery. Even in the years since they'd escaped, she shouldered the financial burdens and fear of being discovered without a peep.

The kids would have a better childhood than she did. One without constant fear, worry, and unhappiness.

Thunder

"I just, uh, tripped. Landed hard on my knee," she said as she began to rise from the floor. Before she had a chance to stand, thin arms circled her from behind.

"I love you, Makenna," Amy whispered in Mak's ear. "It's okay if you need to cry sometimes. I'll still think you're the strongest and most amazing person I know."

Her eyes fell closed as she curled her arms over the ones hugging her. Tears continued to leak out and stream down her face, but she didn't wipe them this time. This was all she needed. The love and connection of her incredible family. For a moment, she'd forgotten that and had gotten greedy.

But a romantic life wasn't in the cards for her.

That knowledge had never hurt before Thunder came along, but now it nearly crippled her.

Chapter Twenty-Seven

By the time he stepped outside, Thunder was convinced he was having a heart attack. An elephant sat on his chest, cutting off the blood flow to the rest of his body. His hands tingled. His feet weighed a ton. And he was seconds away from—

Thunder ran to the grass, dropped to his knees, and hurled up everything he'd drank the night before.

"Shit, man." Tex's voice did nothing to improve his mood. "Want me to get your girl?"

Thunder sat with his ass on his heels, shaking his head while he wiped his mouth. "No," he rasped through a throat burning with acid. "Fuck no. I'm good."

With a frown, Tex glanced over his shoulder at Mak's house then back at Thunder. "Uh, okay. Something happen with you two?"

As he pushed to his feet, Thunder cleared his throat. "Yeah. It's fucking done." He started for his bike only to be called again by Tex.

"The fuck do you want now, prospect?"

Tex's eyes flared wide. It was probably the first time he'd seen Thunder in anything but a fun and playful mood. "Uh, just, I think something's wrong with Kristy. She was walkin' funny when she got home, then she chatted with Mak for a while. They were trying to be all stealth, but I could see fucking bruises on Kristy's face."

Thunder frowned. Dealing with Kristy's drama was the last thing he had tolerance for today. But she was a friend of the club. And a good friend to Mak—not that he cared.

Not anymore.

He blew out a heavy breath, then spun on his booted heel and trudged toward Kristy's door. No rest for the fucking weary.

The door opened before he'd even lifted his fist to knock.

"Shoulda known she couldn't keep a secret from you," Kristy said as she gestured for him to enter.

Thunder winced. That quip hit a little too close to home. Like, right smack on the bullseye.

Fuck.

Forget her.

He shoved thoughts of Makenna aside and stepped into Kristy's house. The place was decorated as he'd have predicted. Bold colors, unique, modern furniture, and artwork that could double as porn.

He'd have chuckled if he didn't want to throw himself off a building.

"Shit, Thunder, you smell disgusting."

"Yeah, well, I just tossed my cookies all over the grass, so…"

"That much fun of a night, huh?"

He snorted. "Something like that. And it wasn't Mak who clued me in. It was Tex."

"Little rat," she mumbled under her breath.

Thunder folded his arms across his chest and leaned against the closed door. You gonna turn a light on and take the shades off, or do I gotta guess what happened?"

Kristy's spine straightened as though she was preparing to argue, but instead, she sighed and slumped as she reached for the sunglasses.

"Oh fuck," Thunder said as he moved closer. With a gentle hold, he grasped her chin and moved her head side to side to get the full effect. Someone had worked her over good. "How's the rest of you?"

"Sore as fuck," she said with a harsh laugh. "Don't think anything's broken. Just a shit ton of bruising on my ribs. Enough to make it impossible for me to work anytime soon."

"This a disgruntled customer?"

She tilted her head and pursed her lips. Thunder's stomach dropped. Whatever she was about to say wouldn't be good.

"Well, the cat's poking his head outta the bag, might as well let him all the way out."

"The fuck?"

She sighed. "This was Crank. He wanted info on your club. Info I wouldn't pony up. Guess I do have my loyalties after all, huh?"

"Shit, hon. I am so sorry." Thunder scratched his stubbled face as he ran through his options. Copper needed to know and fast.

She just shrugged. "Want something to rinse out your mouth?"

"Yeah," he said absently. "Mouthwash would be great if you got it."

With a soft snort, Kristy slowly made her way down the hallway. "Of course, I got it."

Anyway he looked at it, Kristy couldn't stay here. Not until the club was confident, she didn't have a target on her back.

He turned as he shot off a text to Copper, letting him know he needed a sit down at the clubhouse in a bit.

While waiting for a response, he stared out the window. Mak and her siblings piled into her piece of shit car.

Where were they—oh, right. The daughter of one of Toni's Diner's waitresses turned eight this weekend and invited Kara to her birthday party. Being homeschooled, the kids didn't often have the opportunity to make friends. Kara had been talking about the party non-stop. Mak had promised to take the other kids to an afternoon movie to keep them happy.

He'd been planning to join them.

"Here."

He turned to find Kristy standing with her arm outstretched, a small cup of blue liquid in her hand. "Thanks."

"You wanna tell me what's going on with you and Mak?"

"Nope."

Her perfect eyebrows arched high into her forehead. "Hmm."

Thunder's phone chimed. "Copper wants you to stay at the clubhouse a few nights. He'll have some of the Honeys take care of you until you're moving better, and we can make sure Crank's not coming back for more."

"I like how you say this as though you're giving me a choice." She rolled her eyes. "All right. Give me a few hours to get my shit together."

He nodded. "I'll send someone to pick you up around six tonight. That work?"

"Yep."

"All right. See you later." He walked toward the door.

"Hey, Thunder?"

He glanced over his shoulder.

"Thank you. And I know you might not want to hear this right now as something clearly went down between you and Mak, but I'm pretty sure that girl is head over heels in love with you. So before you walk away, think about that."

"Appreciate it, Kris, but you're dead wrong."

He stepped outside, swigged the mouthwash, spit in the grass, then jogged to where his bike waited in the street. Tex was long gone, having followed Mak and the kids.

It didn't take Thunder long to get to the clubhouse.

Copper was waiting in his office with Zach. "Come on in and shut the door," he said after Thunder knocked.

"Thanks." He took the empty seat next to Zach, across the desk from Copper.

"How bad is it?" Copper asked, his eyes holding the promise of retaliation.

"You know Kristy, she's tough, but she's hurting. Her face is all fucked up. Black eyes, bruised jaw, says her ribs are busted but not broken. She's hobbling around but staying in good spirits."

As Thunder gave Copper the run down, the prez stroked his fiery beard. "I'm done," he said with a definite note of finality in his voice.

Beside Thunder, Zach nodded. "It's time, prez."

Thunder cleared his throat. "Time for what, exactly?"

The glare Copper laid on him would have had him shitting himself if the anger had been meant for him. "Time to end the CDMC. The Feds aren't watching them any longer, and we've been dicking around for too long." He glanced at Zach. "We do this for Viper. Exec meeting tonight at six. Church tomorrow morning at nine. I want a solid plan by then. Tired of fucking around."

Fuck yes. A taste of blood was just what Thunder needed.

Thunder preceded Zach out the door. "Shit's about to get real, isn't it?"

With a nod, Zach checked his phone. "Yeah, we may be looking at a lockdown. Might wanna prepare your woman."

Thunder's stomach lurched. "Uh, yeah. I'll do that." Christ, was it possible to miss her already?

"Can you do me a favor?" Zach asked.

"Of course. Name it."

"I'm supposed to head to the gym and run the front desk for a few hours. Do you mind taking my place? I wanna call in the exec board and get some ideas flowing before we have to meet with Copper this evening." Even as he spoke, he typed away on his phone.

"No problem. I got it." A few hours of work would help keep his mind off Makenna.

Hopefully.

Zach slapped him on the back. "Thanks, brother. Owe you one."

With a snort, Thunder shook his head. "Pretty sure you don't."

Turned out, a few hours at the gym did nothing to keep his mind off Makenna. What it did was plant his ass in a seat behind the front desk and give him the perfect opportunity to stew and obsess. Every so often, Lee walked through his line of sight, bringing thoughts of Makenna back to the forefront of his mind.

With each passing hour, his heart grew heavier, and doubt settled deeper into his bones. By the time he was getting ready to leave, he full-on hated himself for losing his shit over Makenna being married. His fucking issues exploded all over her when she didn't deserve it in the least.

"Hey man," Lee said, as Thunder walked outside. He stood by the piece of junk car he drove.

Shit. Had Makenna told him what happened? Thunder really wasn't in the mood to be torn a new asshole by an eighteen-year-old kid, especially not when he'd been ripping himself apart for the last five hours. "Hey."

"Just wanted to say thank you for getting me the job." Lee stuck his hands in his pockets and shuffled back and forth as though unused to expressing gratitude. "And, uh, sorry if I've been a bit of a dick to you."

Thunder nodded. "Appreciate it, man, but I think you might have been more of a dick to Mak than me."

Lee grunted a half laugh. "Yeah. It's just...I worry about her, you know?" He shrugged. "She's been through some shit."

Thunder glanced around. They were the only two in the lot. No one to overhear. "She told me all about where you guys come from."

Lee's eyes nearly fell from his head as he laughed. His dark hair stuck out in spikes, a new style he'd been trying apparently. "Shit. You have no idea how many lectures I've sat through about not telling anyone, even girlfriends. She always told me she didn't care if it was true love, the info stayed secret. Too dangerous otherwise. Then she goes and blabs. Well, man, guess she's the one in love."

Fuck. Lee was the second person to mention that to Thunder, which only had him feeling worse.

"It was bad, huh?"

"Oh yeah. Really fucking bad. I worked the farm and had military training. Long, hot as fuck days, starting when I was way too young for hard labor. The girls worked as seamstresses. Also, insanely long days way too young. But it was the marriage that changed her. The light just...died. I try not to think about it much. It's fucking over. But, uh, Mak never fully came back to who she was. Since then, she's been single-minded in her focus on taking care of everyone but herself. She forgot how to have fun. Won't rock the boat. Refuses to do anything that makes her happy unless we're right along with her. Until you." Lee tapped Thunder on the shoulder with his fist. "So, thanks for that, man. It's good to see her smile."

He just might vomit all over again.

Lee's phone started to ring. He frowned at the number then answered. "Hello? Yes, this is Leif."

Right before Thunder's eyes, Lee paled to the color of death. "W-what?" he said, gripping the phone so hard his knuckles whitened. "Uh, y-yes. I-I'll be right there."

He lowered the phone then searched out Thunder with teary eyes.

"Lee, what's wrong?" When Lee's mouth opened and closed without sound, Thunder grabbed his shoulders and shook. "Lee! What the fuck is wrong? Is it Mak?"

He shook his head. "No. K-kara. That was the hospital. She had a seizure, and they can't get a hold of Mak."

"Fuck!" He pulled up Mak's number as fast as his fingers would fly. "Straight to voicemail. Dammit."

"I have to—I have to go to the hospital." Lee's hand shook, and he breathed as though he'd run a mile. "Oh, God, I don't think I can drive. I'm dizzy."

"Gimme your keys. I'll take you." Together they jogged toward Lee's car.

Thunder's bike would be safe in the gym lot for a few more hours. If need be, he'd text a prospect to get it to the clubhouse.

He rang Tex.

"What's up, brother?" the prospect answered.

"You with Mak?"

"I'm outside. She's in with the kids. Kristy just lef—"

"She's not answering her damn phone. I need you to go inside and tell her Kara is in the hospital. She had a seizure. I don't have any details. Just that she needs to get to the hospital. I'll be there with Lee." He steered out of the parking lot as he spoke.

"Fuck," Tex said.

Thunder heard Tex's truck door slam, then the pounding of his boots as he ran to the house. "Have her call me, and I'll tell her where to find us."

"Got it, brother."

The line went dead.

Thunder drove like a fucking Indy racer, his heart pounding with absolute terror. He could only imagine what Mak would feel when she heard the news. He'd do anything to spare her unnecessary moments of fear. The faster he got to the hospital, the faster they could get answers and set Mak's mind at ease.

Of course, they'd have to set his mind at ease too. Because he just realized that he not only loved Makenna, he loved those kids too.

And he wanted to be a part of their family more than he wanted his next breath.

Chapter Twenty-Eight

Makenna poured herself a hearty glass of wine—hey, she'd broken up with her boyfriend, and it was five o'clock somewhere in the world—grabbed an unopened bag of tortilla chips, then padded into the den.

Kara wasn't due home for an hour or so. Thankfully, her friend's parents would be giving her a ride home, which meant Mak could down as many glasses of wine as necessary to block out the day.

Toni had picked Rissa up a few moments ago so she could hang out with Lindsey. Emmie was back in Amy's room watching her sister with rapt attention while she tried some new makeup technique that was "fire." Whatever that meant.

Teenagers.

Regardless, watching her big sister slap goop on her face would keep Emmie fascinated for hours and gift Mak some time to herself. On a normal day, she'd soak up any free time, even it if was five minutes. Today, well…today, she needed to self-medicate in order to tolerate her own thoughts.

Sitting through the adorable animated princess movie at the theater had been torture. Of course, that damn perky princess with her perfect hair and ever-present toothpaste-ad-smile overcame all her mountain of troubles and found true love in the span of ninety-two minutes.

As if.

Mak had been stewing for days over what to do about Thunder, and now that she'd followed through on breaking up with him, she felt wrecked. Ending things hadn't come as a result of a problem with their relationship. Thunder was... everything.

And she was the genius who destroyed their relationship out of fear.

Already, mere hours after he'd walked out of her house, a Thunder-sized hole remained in her heart and her home. At least five times, she'd pulled out her phone to shoot off a quick and flirty text before remembering she no longer had the right.

Emmie had asked when he'd be over no less than ten times.

And Mak found a T-shirt of his balled up on her bed.

She pressed a hand to the left side of her chest.

The pain surpassed what she'd mentally prepared herself for. How long would this last? Would the emptiness ever be filled again?

With a sigh, she shoved the glass of wine across the coffee table. Getting drunk had seemed like a stellar idea until she'd taken her first sip, and her stomach protested. Great, now she had no way to dull the suffering.

A loud knock at the door had her groaning. Who the hell was it? To say she wasn't in the mood to deal with people would be the understatement of the year. "Coming," she called out, not bothering to hide her enthusiasm.

"Kristy," she said as she pulled the door open. "Come in! If you needed something, you should have called instead of coming all the way over here." She ushered her friend into the house. "What—"

"Makenna," Kristy said, voice ultra-serious. She grabbed Mak's arms.

Instantly, the back of her neck began to tingle. "What? What is it? Is it Crank?"

Shaking her head, Kristy said, "There were two men here looking for you. At least I think it was you. They were looking for someone named Delilah with a bunch of kids."

Mak stumbled backward as her entire world went up in flames. "Oh, my God. I have to go. We have to leave." She turned and rushed to her bedroom. This was going to kill the kids, but it had to happen.

"Lee," she said out loud, then muttered, "I have to call him." She started searching her room, tossing blankets and pillows off the bed in a frantic rush. "Where the hell is my phone?"

From behind her, Kristy said, "Hey, take a breath, Mak. You're gonna freak out the kids."

"Oh, I gotta get Kara too." She grabbed a handful of her hair. "I think I'm having a panic attack."

Kristy's hands landed on her shoulders. "Breathe in slowly."

Doing as asked, Mak inhaled. The air stuttered as it filled her lungs.

"Now out, very slowly."

She tried, really did try, but it came out more as a choppy forceful expression of air. "You're safe for now. There's a prospect outside. The men that were here said they knew you'd hooked up with a motorcycle club. They knocked on my door when you weren't home asking about the club. I gave them false information to throw them off track. They won't be back here for a while."

"Okay." She wrapped her hands around Kristy's forearms as her mind whirled with all that had to happen in order to leave. "Okay, that's good. Thank you, Kristy. You should go. You don't want to be involved in my mess."

With a snort, Kristy shook her head. "Honey, have you met me? I live for drama. Now, what can I do to help?"

"Uh…" She raked a hand through her hair.

Get it together, Mak. Think.

Thunder

"Help me look for my phone while I grab our go-bags."

Kristy raised an eyebrow, which couldn't have felt good considering how bruised her eye was. "Go-bags? You knew this day would come."

"Yes, I did." She turned and dropped to her knees in front of her open closet. "Those men were my husband and father. We escaped from them years ago and have been running ever since," she called over her shoulder as she dove through the shoes and fallen clothes to find the backpacks stashed deep in the closet.

"Shit," Kristy said. "That's a story we should have talked about earlier.'

"I've never told anyone," Mak said. She yanked out two of the bags and tossed them over her shoulder before grabbing a third."

"Not even Thunder?"

God, she'd broken his heart, and now she was going to vanish from his life forever. Never again would she get to see that sexy smile, or hear his laughter, or hold his hand, or be touched by him. The despair threatened to crush her. She had no choice but to compartmentalize it away into a little box. Later, when she and the kids were safe, she could open it and free the pain.

"I'll take your silence to mean you did tell him. You know, you don't have to run. You could go to the Handlers."

"No, I can't," she muttered before grabbing the final bag and standing. "Thunder and I broke up."

Kristy snorted. "I don't see your phone. Could it be in a different room?"

"Shit, I don't know. Maybe. My thoughts are a mess right now. I'll find it. You should go."

The sound of her front door slamming open had both women freezing and Mak's heart stopping dead in her chest.

"What was that?" Amy shouted from her room a second before a male voice shouted, "Makenna!" in an urgent tone.

She met Kristy's gaze. "That's Tex." Rushing out of the room, she yelled back, "It's fine, Amy, just Tex."

"Makenna!"

"Tex?" She almost collided with him in the hallway between her room and the door. "What's wrong?"

He gripped her upper arms. "Christ woman, why aren't you answering your fucking phone?"

Oh, God, her father and husband found the clubhouse. Kristy's diversion didn't work. "Is everyone—"

"Kara is in the hospital. She had a seizure at the party."

"What?" Mak whispered as her knees buckled.

Tex's grip on her arms tightened, keeping her from collapsing. "They've been trying to reach you for an hour," he said, gentling his voice. "Finally, they got a hold of Lee. Thunder drove him to the hospital and called me."

Everything fled her mind but the burning need to be with her little sister. "Why?" she whispered. "It's been so long." Then she inhaled a sharp breath. "I have to get to the hospital."

"I'll drive you," Tex said, already turning for the door.

She scrambled to grab his arm, halting his progress. "No! The kids, you need to stay with the other kids." Her father could come back at any time.

"Babe, I've got it covered. Copper is on his way. He's less than five minutes out. He'll take the kids back to his house."

"Good. That's good. They'll be safe there, right?"

Tex looked at her like she had ten heads. "Of course."

"Okay, let's go." She looked over her shoulder to find her friend standing there with a look of sympathy.

"Go!" Kristy said, waving her hands toward the door. "I'll stay here until Copper arrives. We'll be fine. It's a few minutes. I'll text you as soon as he leaves with them."

It was like being torn straight down the middle. If only she could clone herself so one Makenna could be at the hospital and the other could prepare the children for their next move. Iowa. That's where they'd be going next. A small town she'd been researching since they arrived in Townsend. "You sure that they won't—"

"Makenna," Kristy said. "I promise you the kids will be safe. They will not be back anytime soon. Go to the hospital." It came out as a command.

"Okay." She gave Kristy a quick and gentle hug, then hurried toward the door.

"Who won't be coming back?" Tex asked as he rushed after her.

"No one."

"Christ," he muttered under his breath. "I'm driving. You're too worked up."

She opened her mouth to argue but thought better of it. He was right, she was far too distraught to operate a car safely. As she jogged to his truck, she stopped next to her vehicle and peered in the window. Sure enough, there sat her entire purse on the passenger's seat.

How had she been so careless? With the threat of her father discovering them always looming overhead, she made it the number one priority to have her phone charged and on hand.

Always.

The breakup with Thunder had screwed with her head to the point of making dangerous mistakes.

She grabbed the purse then ran after Tex, who'd reached the truck. "Guess that explains the radio silence," he said, pointing to her bad.

"Mmm." Would it be rude to ask him to shut up and drive? Probably, but she was seconds from the request. Talking took more energy than she had right now. Not when all her strength was going toward not losing her shit completely. When they reached the hospital, she'd need to be calm and collected, so Kara didn't feed off her anxiety.

Thankfully, Tex seemed to pick up on her need for silence and didn't try to make small talk. She stared out the window for the entire drive, bouncing her knee and drumming her fingers on the window frame.

Couldn't he drive any faster?

It felt like hours had passed when they arrived at the hospital.

Tex rolled to a stop outside the Emergency Department entrance. "I'll be—"

"Thank you!" she yelled as she threw open the door and jumped to the ground. A quick sprint had her bursting into the lobby of the ED. The only thing that kept her from screaming out, "Where is my sister?" was the immediate sight of Thunder striding her way.

A sob broke free as she charged toward him. He caught her as she practically flew into him. Two strong arms wrapped around her in a fierce hug, and for the first time in hours, she felt she could breathe, even with the threat from her family and her worry over Kara's health. One second of being back in Thunder's arms had her realizing it was where she belonged.

Forever.

"She's okay," he whispered in her ear, causing a choked sound to erupt from her and a torrent of tears to soak into his shirt. "Shhh, baby, she's okay. She was conscious and talking when we got here. They've taken her for tests. Lee is with her. He's been amazing."

"I forgot my phone in my car," she practically wailed against his chest. At least it better be in the car. She couldn't afford yet another phone, cheap as hers was.

"Huh," he said, pressing a kiss to the shell of her ear. "So, you are human, after all."

"God, Thunder, I was so scared. Are you sure she's going to be okay?"

"I know you were terrified. And yes, baby, she's all right."

"Why did it happen now? Did they say anything?"

Without breaking his tight hold, he rubbed an arm up and down her back. "They won't let me in since I'm not family."

God, she wanted to change that. She'd been through some hard experiences in her life but leaving him would be the toughest by far.

"But they said they think it's just the medication adjustment the doctor made last week. He lowered it because she'd been doing so well for so long. Remember, he told you if this happened, they'd just go back up on the dose."

She sagged in his arms as the conversation with the neurologist from a week ago came to the forefront of her mind. "I completely forgot."

"Here, come sit. They'll call us as soon as she's back from the MRI." He guided her to a plastic chair in the back of the waiting area where a few people sat. Then he took a seat and drew her onto his lap.

She should refuse, get up and claim her own chair, but his warmth and strength felt incredible seeping into her anxiety ridden body. "How could I have forgotten that? I didn't even think of it when Tex told me she'd had a seizure. I went straight to the worst-case scenario."

Thunder rested his chin on her shoulder. "It was a huge shock, Mak. It's okay for you to have freaked out. You've got to learn to cut yourself some slack."

And he didn't even know the information came only seconds after learning her father and husband were nosing around. If she had her way, he wouldn't find out until they were long gone. Otherwise, he'd insist on getting the club involved and she couldn't face the possibility of one of them being harmed.

As she sat there staring at the door to the patient care area, Mak's entire body began to shake. "W-what's h-happening?" she asked as she clenched her fists to stem the quiver.

"It's adrenalin, baby. Put your head on my shoulder, close your eyes, and try to relax. I promise I'll let you know the very second someone comes through that door."

It was then she realized she trusted him with her life and the lives of her children. Still trembling, she did as he requested and rested her head against his bulging shoulder. "Thank you," she whispered though what she wanted to say was three words that would make leaving impossible.

"Always," he whispered back. "I will always be here for you."
If only that could be true.

Chapter Twenty-Nine

Kara's physician insisted on keeping her in the hospital overnight for observation. The news had seemed to distress Makenna almost as much as finding out her sister had had a seizure at the birthday party. Thunder sat in the corner of the hospital room watching her fret and work to convince the doctor she didn't need to stay.

Her reasoning hadn't worked, and Kara would be a Blount Memorial Hospital guest for the evening.

The moment Lee said Kara was in the hospital, Thunder knew what a terrible mistake he'd made walking out of the house that afternoon. Emotion had been running high, which was never the right time for life-altering decisions. He should have stayed and fought for her, fought for them. He hadn't just wanted to be at the hospital for Makenna, he'd needed to be there with every cell in his body. The thought of her at the hospital, stressed, scared, and without him by her side was unimaginable.

Somewhere around two hours after they arrived, Mak hit a wall. Her movements grew sluggish, her eyes heavy, and her anxiety increased tenfold. He'd have thought seeing how well Kara was doing would appease Mak, but she only grew more agitated by the minute. The woman needed to rest, and she needed it yesterday before she broke down.

For the past twenty minutes, Lee had been sending him imploring glances, but for what reason, Thunder had no idea.

Finally, the eighteen-year-old said. "Mak, you need to go home. I'll stay with Kara tonight. You can come back in the morning to pick us up."

"What?" She snapped to attention staring at her brother as though he'd asked her to dance naked on the hospital bed. "No! I'm not leaving. And you should go stay at Copper's."

"What?" Lee laughed. "Why the hell would I do that?"

When Mak flicked a glance his way then returned her attention to Lee, he frowned. Was there something she didn't want him knowing? Sure, they'd technically broken up earlier that day—Christ, it seemed like months ago—but the way he saw it, that was over.

Soon as he got Mak alone, he'd be rectifying the situation. Her reasons for breaking up were bullshit, as were his reasons for going apeshit about her marriage. His past hit him full in the face as soon as she'd said she was still married. Of course, her situation wasn't anything like he'd seen in the past, but he'd let the discovery fuck with his head and lost it before the rational side of his brain kicked in. He'd get on his knees and apologize until she forgave him. Then it was just convincing her he loved her and refused to let her break up with him. He'd take her to see Copper. If anyone could do it, the prez could convince her the club could handle her family and keep Mak and the kids safe.

Simple.

Or it would be, if his woman wasn't so damn stubborn.

"So you don't have to be alone. There's no way I'm leaving."

Exhausted from an afternoon of being poked and prodded, Kara slept just a few feet away. It seemed as though a marching band could parade through, and it wouldn't wake the fatigued girl—poor kiddo. The doctor said she might experience extreme fatigue for a few days. According to the neurologist, it'd been a whopper of a seizure.

Lee shot him another of those beseeching looks, which he now understood. "Makenna," he said, using his most commanding tone. "You look worse than Kara, and you're running on fumes," he said, gathering her hands in his.

"Gee, thanks." Her hair was a mess, falling from a sloppy bun, and the bags under her eyes could carry a week's worth of supplies. In truth, she looked adorably sleepy, but the woman needed to get horizontal before she crashed and ended up in a bed next to Kara.

"You know I think you're the most beautiful woman I've ever seen. But that doesn't take away from the fact that you are seconds away from collapsing. How about this, you go home and sleep for a few hours while Lee stays. When you wake up, you can relieve him, and he'll go to Copper's."

"I'm no—" Lee's mouth snapped shut as Thunder shot him a murderous glare. "That sounds good, Mak. Please let him take you home for a while."

She stared at Kara for a few moments before saying, "I don't know…"

Thunder moved in close and slid an arm around the back of her shoulders. Even now, in this uncertain situation, he couldn't help but savor the way she fit just right against him. "Baby, she is fine. They are only keeping her to be overly cautious. Even the neurologist said so."

"Yet they still wouldn't let me take her," Mak grumbled.

"Come on. You know this is a smart decision." He started to gently tow her toward the door.

With a sigh, Mak nodded. "Okay, fine." Then she turned and pointed a finger at Lee. "But I'm coming back in a few hours at most, okay?"

Lee nodded though he trained his eyes on Thunder over Mak's shoulder who shook his head and mouthed, "In the morning." He had a few tricks up his sleeve to ensure she was too drained to do anything but pass out for the night.

She pulled away from him and moved to press a soft kiss to Kara's head. After whispering something to her sleeping sister, Mak rejoined him.

He extended his hand to her, and she gave him a startled look before interlacing their fingers together.

Ahh, that's where you belong.

In silence, they walked to Lee's car. And in complete silence, they drove home. Mak stared out the window, lost in thought. Every so often, her eyes would drift shut, then pop back open as though she fought the battle of her life to remain awake.

That was fine. They didn't need to talk right then. He'd give her time to collect herself and her thoughts, but he'd be taking over once they got inside her house.

When he killed the engine after pulling into the driveway, Makenna jumped as though surprised they'd arrived home. "Thank you," she said, opening her door. As though she were a zombie, she trudged up to the front door and stuck the key in the lock.

Thunder trailed right behind her, but she didn't notice his proximity or even the fact he'd left the car. She just opened the front door and stepped into the house as though on autopilot. When she turned and moved to shut the door, Thunder slapped his palm against the wood.

Mak started again and met his gaze. "Oh, uh, do you need something?"

"I sure as fuck do," he said, shoving the door open.

"No!" she said in a panicked tone. "Don't come in."

But it was too late.

He was in the house and couldn't tear his gaze away from the row of backpacks lined up by the door. Kristy must have done it after she left.

"What the fuck?" he whispered before turning on her. "You're leaving?"

Shaking her head, she took a step away from him. Her back hit the door.

"No? You're not leaving?" He planted his palms on either side of her head.

"I-w-we are. We have to," she whispered, as though the admission broke her heart.

"No, you don't, Mak."

With a nod, she said, "They found us. They came here looking for us. Kristy sent them on a wild goose chase, but it's only a matter of time before they realize and come back. It's not safe. We have to leave."

"Oh, baby," he said as he rested his forehead against Mak's. "You really don't get it, do you?"

"Thunder, I-I have to put the bags in the car and go." Fat tears rolled down her cheeks. Her hands landed on his chest, but instead of pushing away, she curled her fingers into the fabric of his shirt. Despite her words of dismissal, the idea of leaving him killed her as much as it did him.

That simple over-the-clothing touch had him shuddering in pleasure. "You don't have to go anywhere, Makenna. You have a big, tough, family ready to fight your battles at any time."

"I can't. It's too much. The club already has the CDMC to deal with. Thunder, you don't understand how dangerous my father can be. He wouldn't think twice about hurting or even killing any of you."

"We can handle it," he whispered in her ear.

"No."

"Makenna…"

"No."

"I love you."

"No!" she shouted, shoving him hard. Her push barely nudged him a few inches back.

"I love—"

"No!" she whispered in a desperate plea. Her hand landed on his mouth while tears coursed down her face. "Please don't say it. Please." Her eyes were closed, and her head shook back and forth. "No." This time her voice cracked.

Thunder circled her wrist and peeled her hand away then anchored it to the door above her head. "I love you," he said again.

Instantly the other hand pressed to his mouth.

"No." Her voice grew weaker with each denial.

He kissed her palm before joining this hand with her other. "I love you."

"Thunder...you can't love me. I'm a mess." Her eyes opened. "I've already fucked this up by not telling you I was still married. I'm a guardian to a bunch of kids. I have no money. My sister is in the hospital. My father and *husband* are after us. And then there's the CDM—" She sucked in a sharp breath.

He shifted her wrists to one hand then used the other to circle her throat much as he'd done the first time they'd fucked. Mak's watery eyes stared into his, but the panicky outburst ceased.

The tears still fell, but slower.

He kissed her then, soft and seeking. Her mouth stayed firm for a few long seconds, but she softened under him and parted her lips. A tiny whimper left her when his tongue met hers. After kissing until his dick was an iron beam in his jeans, he drew back. "I love you," he said, looking her in the eye.

"I-I love you too. Damn you, Thunder, I love you so much."

Fuck, those words. Words he'd never imagined he'd hear from a woman. Hell, he'd never wanted them and now couldn't imagine another day passing without hearing it a dozen times. "That's better."

"But—"

"No," he said, giving her neck a gentle squeeze. He swore she thrust her pelvis into him as though seeking his dick each time he did that. "No buts. Kara is safe and monitored round the clock. The rest of the kids are safe. Copper took them to the clubhouse. You are safe. Right here and right now, the only thing you are allowed to think about is us."

She nodded, her soft neck flexing beneath his fingers.

Thunder

"Here's how this is gonna go. Since it seems to be the only way to get you out of your head, I'm gonna fuck your brains out right here against the door."

Her breath hitched, and he swore her eyes darkened with need.

"Then, we're gonna grab your bags and head to the clubhouse to meet with my brothers and come up with a plan to get rid of the motherfuckers hunting you."

When she bit her lower lip, he knew she wanted to argue, but she kept it in.

"Two rules. One: you will not run. Not now, not tomorrow, not ever. And two: you will not argue with any plan we come up with." As he spoke, he stroked the pulse point now rapidly fluttering in her neck. Goosebumps erupted under his fingers, and she shivered with each upstroke of his thumb. "You with me so far?"

As she nodded, she squirmed beneath his hold. He made sure to keep the grip on her hands light enough to avoid damaging her delicate skin but firm enough to remind her who had control at the moment. The way she wiggled indicated her need was growing.

Christ, his dick was hard and needed inside her in the next few moments.

"Then when we've dealt with the problem of your family, you and I are gonna start something for real this time. Something where we fall asleep together at night and wake up together. Something where you allow me to share your responsibilities and burdens. I want us to be a team, Mak. You don't have to do it all alone anymore."

"Thunder," she whispered.

"Nuh-uh. Forget all the challenges, and the bullshit, and the fears. Just tell me if you want it, too. If you want me, too." With a soft kick, he nudged her legs apart then pressed his thigh to her mound.

A soft whimper left her. Without an ounce of shame, she began to grind her hips against him with slow rocks. "I want it, Thunder. I need it…so bad."

Her words washed over his soul, bringing him a combination of peace and anticipation that shouldn't have been possible. How could he simultaneously feel so settled and excited? He wanted to give Makenna the world. Wanted her happiness over his own. And that's when he understood without a doubt this would work between them. They both cared about the other above themselves. It's why the relationships he'd witnessed growing up didn't work. It's why the women who paid to be with him in recent years would never be content in their marriages. They were selfish and not truly in love.

"But I'm so afraid to take it," she whispered as he pressed their foreheads together. "What if it disappears? What if I fall deeper and deeper in love with you and you—"

He kissed the words out of her mouth and didn't stop until she was desperately humping his leg and moaning. "Makenna," he said, needing to pause to suck in air. "I. Love. You."

"God, Thunder, I love you too." She panted, fast puffs of air drifting against his lips. "And I want it. I want it all. Yes, I am scared, but that's never stopped me from doing anything before."

Fuck no, it hadn't. She'd run from a cult in the middle of the night to save herself and her family. The woman may not be fearless, but she was courageous as fuck.

"Thunder, please," she whined as he went in for more of her sweet lips. She captured his lower lip between her teeth and gave a tug. The pinch of her bite bordered on painful. His cock twitched at the unexpectedly bold move.

"Kick off your shoes."

She did as he asked, toeing them off and sending them flying.

Though he hated to do it, he released her wrists and her neck. His hands went back to the wall on either side of her head. "Undo your pants. Shove 'em down with your panties."

He gazed between their bodies as she scrambled to do his bidding. Trembling hands fumbled with the button more than once before finally finding success. As she lowered the zipper, revealing a swatch of pale blue fabric, Thunder's pants grew so tight his dick was in serious danger of death by strangulation. And if his buddy was going to go out, he'd much rather it be asphyxiated by Mak's pussy than some denim.

After Mak shoved her pants and panties down then kicked them away, she met his gaze with a shy look, waiting for his next directive. Damn minx was playing the game well.

"Now, do mine." Fuck, he could barely speak. His throat felt raw and tight.

Those nimble fingers made quick work of his button and fly. With a mischievous grin, she slid her hands down the back of his jeans, squeezing his ass.

He gritted his teeth through a hiss of hot pleasure.

"Get them the fuck off me now, Makenna."

She shoved them down, and he stepped out. The second his dick sprung free, she hummed in approval and he almost shot his load all across her stomach and tits right then and there.

Just from a fucking sound.

But that wasn't all she did. Nope, she wrapped those silky fingers around his cock and stroked how he liked it. A little rough, a little manhandling. "You're fucking devious," he rasped as his hips shoved forward of their own accord.

When Mak chuckled and squeezed his dick, he reached his fucking limit. "Enough," he growled, grabbing her wrists and slamming them above her head. Again, he secured them in place with one hand.

The other he used to grab a handful of her ass and draw her close. As if it were the most natural impulse in the world, Mak hiked up her leg and wrapped it around his back. The position put her dripping pussy directly in line with his cock.

He groaned. "Fuck, you're hot and wet and I don't have a motherfucking condom."

"I'm clean," she said. "Been tested and haven't been with anyone since…"

"I got tested last week," he said. "I was hoping you'd—oh, Christ."

She pumped her hips, dragging her wetness up the length of his dick.

"Thunder?"

"Yeah," He clenched his teeth so hard they squeaked.

"We're done talking. Fuck me."

"Yes ma'am," he growled, as he slammed himself into her with one thrust and nearly passed out from the pleasure.

Chapter Thirty

Mak's eyes fluttered closed as Thunder plunged into her with little finesse.

Overwhelming.

It was the only word she could drum up to adequately describe the moment. Her heart was full. Her body was full of Thunder in a now familiar and delicious way. She kept her eyes shut tight, trying to absorb every single sensation.

His hand clutched her ass as he held her flush against him, allowing him to bottom out inside her. The other hand held hers above her head. He had full control, and she trusted him with not only her body, but her heart.

"Christ, I never get used to how tight you are." He attacked her neck with his lips, making her moan and tilt her head to the side. "It's like fucking heaven, baby."

She turned her head, and their noses bumped. Both of them froze. The clock ticked as they stayed still, gazes locked. Everything Thunder had claimed, his love, the desire to blend into her family was all shining at her through his eyes.

"Thunder…" The moment felt so significant, so huge, she had no way of capturing the strength of her feelings with words. Even love seemed too small.

"I know," he whispered back. "Me too."

She smiled then squeezed her internal muscles.

With a harsh groan, Thunder's head fell back. He snapped his hips forward, yanking her toward him with the grip on her ass at the same time. Now she was the one groaning except it came out as more of a mewl. He did it again, and again. Sharp, hard thrusts, controlling both their bodies.

Mak's head hit the wall. "God, you feel so good."

"That's right, baby. You love that fat cock fucking you, don't you?"

"Yes," she hissed. With him at the helm and her hands still trapped, she couldn't do anything but be a puppet at his mercy. And it was mind-blowing.

They panted in time with each other as Thunder moved even faster inside her. Sweat rolled down her back to her ass, making him need to tighten his grip to keep from slipping. She'd bet tomorrow her ass would be full of finger-sized bruises.

"It's yours whenever you want it. Whenever you need it. As is the rest of me." He released her wrists. "Leave them up there."

Mak linked her fingers. Her elbows drooped a bit, and her hands slid down the wall to rest on her head. Thunder continued to pound into her. "I'm close," she whispered. Still, after all the orgasms he'd given her over the past few weeks, she felt a sliver of anxiety each time. Fear it would fade, and she'd be left hanging on the precipice.

He grunted then ran a finger down the front of her throat. "You need it?" he asked.

No longer ashamed of what her body and mind craved, she nodded. "Yes. I need it."

"So fucking hot." His hand ringed her throat again and grasped just enough to quiet the last of the outside world, threatening to break through her happiness.

"Thunder," she said on a gasp.

"I got you, baby. Let go."

Their gazes met and held.

Thunder

He increased the pressure on her neck, and she couldn't have held back the climax if she wanted to. A scream ripped from deep in her gut, slightly breathy due to her constricted airway. Pleasure flooded every cell in her body, weakening her knees and making her muscles contract and relax in an uncontrollable rhythm.

Thunder spoke, but she couldn't make out anything more than "fuck" and "tight" over the rush of blood in her ears. Then he was kissing her—hard, as though he wanted to steal the rest of the air from her body.

He didn't stop the assault on her mouth, even as his fingers clenched against her ass and he undulated against hers. A long, satisfied groan filled the quiet room.

Thunder released her throat but buried his face in the crook of her neck. Every few seconds, he took a little lick or pressed a kiss to her skin. They stayed there, lingering against the door for what felt like hours. With their damp bodies plastered against each other, breathing came in choppy puffs. Neither spoke as they let their bodies slowly calm.

Though her shoulder blades dug into the unforgiving wood of the door, and Thunder's weight against her chest kept her from sucking in a full breath, Mak prayed the moment would never end. She slipped her hands under the hem of his T-shirt, stroking up and down his smooth back.

The long, corded muscles running the length of his spine fascinated her. The man knew exactly how to use each and every one of those muscles to his advantage, not only when dancing but also when driving her out of her mind with pleasure.

"I'm crushing you," he eventually murmured into her neck.

"Mmm." Real words took too much energy.

He pushed off the wall, causing the last inch of his semi-soft cock to slip from her body. She didn't even try to hide the groan of disappointment, which only made his eyes flare with renewed desire.

"Insatiable," he said before pressing a hard kiss to her swollen lips. Anyone who saw her over the next few hours would know what they'd been up to. "Let's clean up quick then head to the clubhouse. Okay?"

Her knee jerk reaction was still to reject the idea of involving his club, but she clamped down the urge. Blowing out a breath, Mak said, "Yeah. Let's do it."

"Good girl." Thunder winked and pulled her toward her room.

Forty-five minutes and one very stress-relieving shower later, they found an unexpected surprise waiting for them at the clubhouse. Three police vehicles with lights flashing blocked the entrance.

"What the fuck?" Thunder said as he removed his helmet.

"T-thunder," she said, completely failing at removing the quiver from her voice. Suddenly, she wished she hadn't devoured a muffin while running out the door.

He turned and rested one hand on her shoulder where she still sat astride the bike. As he worked the strap of her helmet open, he said, "We don't know anything yet, babe. Don't panic."

"My father—" What if they walked in there to find someone injured, or God forbid killed by her father or husband?

Oh, God. She pressed a hand to her stomach. If she were responsible for harm coming to Thunder's club, she'd never be able to set foot on this property. Hell, she wouldn't be able to look at her own face in the mirror ever again.

"We don't know anything. Let's get inside before you think the worst. Sometimes the cops have nothing better to do than swing by and harass us." He flashed her his famous grin, but tension simmered beneath it in the stiff set of his shoulders. "Maybe they're just arresting one of my brothers."

That had a whole new spool of anxiety unraveling in her gut. "Seriously? Is that supposed to make me feel better?"

He winked.

Bless the man for working so hard to keep her from melting down while he had to be as worried as she was.

"Come on. We won't know until we go in."

He gripped her hand, helped her off the bike, then on stiff, wooden legs, she walked at his side into the clubhouse.

The place was a hundred times quieter than the few instances she'd been there in the past. Normally rowdy and full of activity, the place had the soundless and strained feel of a mausoleum. Copper, Zach, and some of the other Handlers sat scattered throughout the main room. A few of the ol' ladies were present as well, seated together at one table as though they'd been hanging out before the cops showed up.

No one lay face down with their arms cuffed behind their back, so she'd consider that a win. And the place wasn't riddled with bullet holes from her father, which counted as a victory. Mak blew out a breath she hadn't realized she'd been holding.

"See," Thunder whispered. "Everyone's good. Everyone's safe."

Well, everyone in that room, anyway.

"Thunder," a man in uniform said as he watched their entrance. He stood with his thumbs hooked in his standard-issue belt. The belt that boasted an enormous silver buckle. Mak had heard the town's sheriff moved from Texas less than a year ago.

"Slow day, Sheriff?" Thunder asked as he guided Mak to the closest table.

The man snorted, making his bushy blonde mustache rise and fall. "Not exactly. Why don't you and your lady friend have a seat. I was just about to tell your president why we're here."

"Sounds like a plan." He pulled out a chair for Mak, and she sat, unable to take her eyes off the sheriff. Where she'd come from, the police were dirtier than shit. They'd lived in her father's pocket as long as the money kept coming. Once, when she'd been ten, she'd snuck away from her family on an outing to town. She'd run straight to the police station and blabbed about a plot she'd overheard to terrorize a town council member's family. This particular official happened to be an outspoken critic of the community. The cop had laughed, called her father, and she'd spent the next week alone in a shed with one meal a day and a host of bruises.

Once she situated herself, Thunder sat as well, then dragged her chair directly next to his. "Shoot," he said, also focused on the sheriff.

After nodding to one of his deputies, who moved to stand by the door, the sheriff turned to look at Copper. "I need a formal account of everyone's whereabouts for the afternoon," the sheriff said.

With a scoff, Copper frowned. "Gonna need more than that before my men tell you shit."

The sheriff rolled his eyes. "Look, Copper, I'm still new in town, and I get that my predecessor caused a shit load of trouble for your club, but I've yet to hassle you or arrest a single one of your members, so cut the big bad biker act."

Copper folded his arms across his massive chest. The man really was a giant. "Sheriff, since you're new, I'll clue you in as to how we work around here. You give it to me straight, and I'll do the same for you."

If it benefits my club.

Those words weren't spoken aloud, but everyone in the room heard them anyway.

"Fair enough." The sheriff took a few steps forward, then planted his palms on a vacant table and leveled a glare at Copper. "A group of heavily armed men attacked the CDMC clubhouse about an hour ago. Wrecked the fuck outta the place. I'm talking Swiss cheese walls all around. It's a total loss. That club gave as good as they got though, and now my department is dealing with a bloodbath. I got almost a whole club of dead bikers and about ten cowboy crusaders who I've never seen also fucking dead."

All around the room, shocked gasps and harsh curses sounded.

Thunder

Mak remained silent, her body frozen solid. Every hair on her body stood straight on end. No one needed to confirm anything. She knew in her bones exactly who had launched a violent attack on the Chrome Disciples clubhouse.

Probably sensing the drastic change in her energy, Thunder placed a hand on her thigh and squeezed.

She turned her head, staring straight into his eyes. Her bleak expression must have conveyed her thoughts because he gave her the subtlest of head shakes, which she took to mean she should keep her mouth shut. As if she was about to announce her father and husband's role in a gruesome assault.

Copper ran a hand down his face, pausing to scratch his beard. "You fucking with me?" he finally asked, voice full of disbelief.

The sheriff dropped his head. "Fuck," he whispered. "I'm pretty damn good at reading people, and you all seem genuinely shocked as fuck. Suppose it woulda been too easy a case if you'd been the ones to do it."

With a snort, Zach shook his head. "We wouldn'ta done something so fucking obvious."

"What's the actual damage?" Screw asked from across the room. "They really all dead?"

Straightening, the sheriff smoothed a hand down his tan uniform. "It was a fucking bloodbath. When we arrived on scene, one of the Disciples was lying out front in the parking lot, gut shot. We were able to get a few things outta him before he died. He said the club got an anonymous call about ten minutes before the assailants showed up claiming an attack was coming. Whoever was inhouse, which seems to be most of them, armed up and fought back. I'm talking bullets, bombs, Molotov cocktails, you name it, all these fuckers used it. As far as we can tell, only one or two of the attackers managed to survive as well. We know from a blood trail that someone escaped, we just don't know if it was CDMC or one of the other guys."

"You said you don't recognize any of the assailants," Zach said. "Were you able to identify any of them yet?"

The sheriff shook his head. "None of them carried ID. I've got a deputy working on prints right now from the guys who still had 'em. Rest are gonna have to be teeth by the ME."

"Well…" Copper's grin stretched across his face. "Can't say this news darkens my day, but I can say we didn't have a fucking thing to do with it. Sheriff, you and your buddies can see yourself out. I'll send my guys to the station a few at a time to give formal statements since I'm assuming you won't let that drop."

"All right." The sheriff tilted his head the nodded, seeming resigned to that being Copper's best offer. "I can work with that. Have a good day, gentlemen." He tipped his hat. "Ladies."

When he was halfway to the exit, he snapped his fingers while turning back around. "Oh, one more thing. Any of you happen to know a woman named Delilah?"

Oh, my God. Oh, my God.

Mak sucked in a breath before her brain could warn her to keep quiet. Then she bit her lower lip so hard, the metallic taste of blood oozed onto her tongue.

The sheriff's head whipped her way and his gaze locked with hers. She held her breath until the room started to spin.

It'd been excess of two years since she'd been called by that name. The suffocating sensation of existing in the community came rushing back in a flood of nausea and terror.

The only thing keeping her from flying apart was Thunder's touch, but even that couldn't erase the brutal memories.

Chapter Thirty-One

They'd never discussed it, but after hearing Mak's story, Thunder assumed Makenna wasn't the name given her at birth. He hadn't bothered to ask because, to him, it didn't matter. She was Makenna. His Mak.

But clearly, the name she'd gone by throughout childhood had been Delilah.

She sat so still and stiff he feared her leg would shatter beneath his palm if he squeezed too hard. Unfortunately, this sheriff didn't appear to be the same kind of fucking moron they last one had been. His shrewd gaze assessed Makenna with open curiosity and suspicion.

Thunder cleared his throat and spewed out the first bullshit that came to his mind. "Sorry," he said. "This is my ol' lady, Makenna. Her mother passed last week in Ohio. Her name was Delilah. Kinda hard to hear you say it since it's still so fresh."

"Hmm," the sheriff said, still studying Mak.

Had he bought it?

His woman played her part to a tee. "I'm sorry," she squeaked. "I didn't mean to interrupt. Just shocked me is all. It was a heart attack. U-unexpected."

After clearing his throat, the sheriff nodded. "Sorry for your loss, ma'am."

"Thank you."

Copper shot the sheriff a raised eyebrow then grunted. "None of us know any Delilah around here. Why?"

Even if Copper suspected, it helped that he didn't have to lie. None of them did know a Delilah. At least not that they were aware of.

"The disciple we spoke to said this group of psychos came roaring up in two Jeeps. They busted into the clubhouse, mowing down anyone they crossed. Hollering and opening fire at the clubhouse. One of them was screaming for the CDMC to send Delilah out. According to the disciple, they had no clue who the group was looking for. Then the battle began."

Thunder's lips wanted to curl into a smug fucking grin. The fuckers took care of the two sharp thorns in the Handlers' side with one idiotic move.

Perfection.

But he kept his mouth set in a thin line. Once the sheriff left, they could celebrate with a huge fucking party. First, they needed to get rid of the man in uniform.

"Well, like I said. We got no clue." Copper stood. "Forgive me if I don't walk you out."

The room stayed quiet until the door slammed shut behind the sheriff. Then every head in the place swiveled in Mak's direction.

Copper lifted a meaty paw. "Not yet." He waited a few minutes for the sounds of the police cars to leave before nodding. "Okay. Who the fuck is Delilah? And how do we thank her for getting rid of the CDMD?"

"Fuck yeah!" Screw yelled.

Maverick pounded his fist on the table, and the rest of the men started stomping their boots. Relief and the desire to celebrate were palpable.

Beside him, Mak sagged in either reprieve or utter exhaustion. The day had been absolute insanity, and she needed sleep more than a wild party.

Copper raised his hands. "All right, all right. Simmer the fuck down." He directed his attention toward Thunder and Mak. "Anything you two wanna tell us?"

When Thunder opened his mouth, Mak put a hand on his shoulder. "It's okay. I got it."

As he nodded, he lifted her hand and pressed a kiss to her palm. Though he hated to have to put her through the difficulty of revealing her identity, he was damn proud of her for her bravery.

She stood. "I was born with the name Delilah into a militant community that used children for labor and women for breeding. I don't want to get more into it than that right now, but I escaped with my younger siblings about two years ago. We've used different names a few times, but the ones we have now are what we are hoping to stick with. I have all the necessary documents even if they aren't exactly…legal." She winced.

Not one of them would even blink at the thought of a woman, or anyone obtaining an illegal identity to save themselves. Hell, his club wasn't exactly keen on following the rules in general.

"My father runs the community and has been hunting for me ever since we left. I…" She took a deep breath and blew it out."

Across the room, Jaz nodded, and Toni yelled out, "You got this, honey. We're all behind you one hundred percent."

Thunder coulda kissed her at that moment. You know, if her boyfriend's baseball bat, affectionally named Louie, wouldn't bust his head open like a watermelon.

"At nineteen, I was married off to a man in his sixties. I'm assuming my father and…and my husband led the men who attacked the CDMC."

"Well fuck me sideways," Screw said, wide-eyed.

"Anytime," Gumby shot back, making everyone laugh as he tended to be the most subdued of the triad. Thank Christ, Makenna laughed as well. The tension reliever hit at the perfect time.

"I take it this is what you two were coming to talk to me about?" Copper continued once the commotion subsided.

"Yeah," Thunder said as he drew Mak onto his lap. She didn't resist; in fact, she rested back against him as though wanting and needing the support of his arms around her. Of course, he obliged her immediately, wrapping her in a firm embrace. "We got wind that they'd discovered where she was living."

"Okay." Copper stroked his beard. "Until we catch word of who died in the attack and who might be alive and looking our way for revenge, no one is to be alone. That includes us. No riding solo until we're sure no one will mistakenly retaliate against us. Anyone who needs to is welcome to stay here. Mak, the kids are here and upstairs with Cassie already."

"Thank you," she said. "Is it all right if I run up and see them?"

Copper nodded. "Of course. This is your home as much as it is my wife's now."

"Thunder, what about Kara and Lee?" Anxiety bled through her tone.

"I'll have Copper put a few guys at the hospital. I'm guessing there's no way to keep you away from there, huh?"

Her head shook violently. "No. I need to be there in the morning to pick her up. But Lee can stay tonight."

Arguing would be pointless. She'd given him more than he'd expected, which was her demanding he drive her straight to the hospital. Now that he knew more about Lee's upbringing, he felt confident he could be trusted to protect his little sister. Especially once he had the back up of a few Handlers.

Thunder pressed a lingering kiss to Mak's forehead. "Okay, babe, you run up and get the kids settled while I figure out protection for the hospital. Later, when it's just us, we're gonna talk about all this cuz it's gotta be fucking with your head."

"Yeah, right now I'm afraid to believe it's real. That we might be safe. I'm sure it'll sink in later, and you'll have a mess on your hands."

"I'll happily clean you up," he said, waggling his eyebrows.

Mak laughed, as he'd hoped, then she kissed him and hopped off his lap.

Copper wandered his way over and landed in an empty seat. "How's she holding up?"

With a shrug, he accepted a beer from his prez. "Think it's all a little surreal right now."

Copper tipped up his bottle, took a long sip, then smacked his lips together. "Yeah. I imagine so. She's a strong one, huh?"

Pride swelled in Thunder. "Sure as fuck is."

"Makes a good addition to our family, brother."

Fuck, he felt like his chest would burst. His prez's approval meant the world to him. "Thank you."

Copper just nodded in response.

"Her sister is in the hospital, set to be released in the a.m. Think you can spare me a few guys to keep an eye on us? I promised her I'd bring her over for the night."

"Consider it done. Take whoever you want."

"Thanks, Cop. Hey, Kristy ever show up here?"

With a nod, Copper pointed toward a hallway leading to a back door. "Tex brought her a bit ago. Last I saw her, was right before the sheriff showed up. She was heading out back to have a smoke."

"Thanks, man." Thunder rose, returned the fist bump Copper offered, and wandered toward the back exit.

As predicted, Kristy sat out behind the clubhouse in one of a few camping chairs they kept outside. The things had long faded from sun and rain, but no one really gave a fuck what they looked like. Long as they supported some biker asses, they could be pink and sparkly for all he gave a shit.

The orange glow of her cigarette traveled through the air as she lifted it to her mouth, took a drag, then held it up. "Share?" she asked without turning to see who'd joined her.

"Nah, quit that shit a while ago." He sat in an empty chair next to her, joining her in the peace and quiet that one could only find when staring at nature.

"Hmm, me too," she said with a chuckle.

"You're gonna have to stay here a few days." He propped an ankle on his knee and relaxed back into the chair.

"I was planning on it."

"Well, it's more important now than it was a few hours ago. Someone attacked the CDMC clubhouse tonight. From what the sheriff said, they decimated the place. Left very few survivors, and the ones that are alive are in bad fucking shape."

"Huh, you don't say?" She took another drag from the cigarette, attention fixed on the gently blowing trees in the woods.

"Yep. Crazy, huh?"

"It certainly is."

Nothing flickered across her face. Not shock, surprise, pleasure, fear. The woman brought stoic to a new level.

"Turns out the men who attacked were looking for a woman named Delilah. No one seems to know who she is, but uh, it sounds like she's damn lucky they didn't find her."

"Sounds like it."

"Hold on, the story gets crazier. Someone made an anonymous call warning the CDMC of the attack. Majority of the attackers were killed too. The CDMC gave as good as they fucking got." The smell of her cigarette brought back memories of sitting with his fellow dancers in just this way after a night of shaking his ass and having tips stuffed down his briefs. He didn't experience even a flicker of desire to return to that lifestyle.

"You don't say?"

"That's what the sheriff told us. Anyway, seems anyone who might have been in the CDMC's crosshair is now a free woman...or man. At least they will be after we have official ID confirmation that they're all dead."

"Good news for your club." Each time she lifted the cigarette to her mouth, the glow illuminated her battered face.

"Sure is."

They fell silent, soaking up the tranquil quiet of the evening, so in contrast to the carnage that occurred just twenty miles away.

After a while, Thunder stood. He dropped his hand to Kristy's shoulder and gave a squeeze. "Thank you."

Finally, she turned her head to look up at him. "For the chat? We're friends, Thunder. Anytime."

Their gazes stayed locked for a few seconds. Though the words would never be spoken aloud, neither of them were under the false impression he'd been referring to this little heart-to-heart. Kristy had purposefully steered Makenna's family toward the CDMC. No, she couldn't have known exactly how it'd play out, but she'd seen an opportunity to help herself and her friend, and she'd taken it.

This would be the one and only time he acknowledged it. The secret would die with them because Kristy would be in a world of trouble should the cops catch wind of her involvement. A woman beaten by the CDMC's enforcer happened to *accidentally* send a deadly pseudo-militia to their doorstep—even the cops weren't dumb enough to buy that horseshit. So she'd play dumb, and he'd keep his trap shut.

And Makenna would now be free to live her life without fear for herself or her siblings.

After giving Kristy's shoulder a final affectionate squeeze, Thunder made his way back inside only to find Makenna chatting with Izzy at the bar.

"There he is," Izzy said, pointing toward him. "Thunder, take your woman home, she can't keep her eyes open."

Mak's drowsy gaze met his, and his stomach flipped. Even though they'd do nothing more than pass out the moment they got to her house, he was as excited as ever to be in her bed. "Shit, babe, you look like you went a few rounds in the ring with Iz here."

With a weak chuckle, Mak stood. "Feels like it, too." Swaying on her feet, she leaned into him.

Her soft weight against him brought up all these possessive, caveman feelings. Though everyone in the club already knew she belonged to him, he couldn't help but grab her face and kiss with the intensity of a brand.

Mak moaned into his mouth at the same time Izzy whistled.

Rolling his eyes, he released his woman. She gave him a glassy-eyed, slightly dopy smile.

"Hey!" Izzy said. "Who said you could stop? I was enjoying the show!"

Thunder snorted. "Here's an idea. Why don't you take your man home and put on your own show?"

"Hmm…" Izzy tapped her chin. "You know, Thunder, that is a damn good idea." She rose and winked. "You are more than just a hot ass and killer smile, you know that?"

He flipped her off, making Izzy feign offense as Mack giggled.

He slung his arm around her shoulders and tugged her toward the stairs. "Come on, let's grab the kids and get you guys home."

"They're actually all sleeping upstairs. Cassie said she'd stay so we can just go home and get some sleep before we have to pick Kara up in the morning."

He raised an eyebrow at her. "You sure you're cool with that? With leaving the kids here and with letting Lee stay at the hospital?" He looked down into her soft, loving gaze.

Nodding against her chest, she said, "Yes. Haven't you heard? I have a big, crazy MC family now that I can lean on when I need them." She rose on her tiptoes. "I don't have to do it on my own anymore," she whispered before kissing him as passionately as he'd kissed her moments ago.

Groaning, he nipped her lip then rested his forehead against hers. "Let's get the hell outta here. I need to spend the next ten or twelve hours wrapped around you."

Pleasure lit her eyes. "That sounds absolutely perfect."

And it was. After they arrived home, and she'd checked in with Lee at the hospital, hearing all good things, they stumbled to her bed. Neither bothered to put away their clothes, tossing them in a pile on the floor.

If someone had asked him a month ago if he could ever imagine himself crawling into bed next to a naked, sexy woman and not fucking her, he'd have called them insane. But not only was that the case tonight, but he was more satisfied than he'd ever been in his life.

Makenna and the kids were free to live without fear of being discovered and dragged back to a life of abuse and dread.

The Handlers could return to business as usual without threat from the CDMC.

And Mak was his.

What more could he ask for?

Chapter Thirty-Two

"Do you really think we still need a guy guarding the house?" Mak asked Thunder, as she peered out the front window. Poor Monty had been out there for hours, and it probably wasn't even necessary any longer.

"Probably not," Thunder said as he stuffed his foot into his boot. "But Copper's orders are non-negotiable. And I'd much rather be safe than sorry. Once we have ID confirmation of exactly who died at the CDMC clubhouse, we'll be able to let up on it. But until I'm one hundred percent sure Crank and Blade are dead as well as your father and husband, I'm not taking any chances. I'm not risking one hair on your gorgeous head or any of your siblings."

Well, when he put it that way...

He cupped the back of her neck and gave her a lingering kiss. "I'm gonna go pick up Kara and Lee. Copper will be here with the other kids in a half hour or so."

Her heart swelled with warmth and love. "You sure you don't want me to come with you?"

He shook his head. "I'm good, babe. You stay here and make us some cookies." He opened the front door.

"Ahh, now I see why you volunteered to pick them up," she said as she rolled her eyes. The man was incorrigible.

He winked. "You know it."

Laughing, she slammed the door in his face. "While you're driving, think about ways to thank me for the cookies!" she shouted through the closed door.

His laughter made her grin stretch so wide, her cheeks ached. In all her life, she hadn't known she could feel so light. So carefree and excited for the future.

Now that she was alone in the house, she took a breath and let the events of the previous night wash over her. So much had happened in a twenty-four-hour span. She hadn't had a chance to begin processing. The fight with Thunder, Kara's seizure, Kristy's injuries, her father's arrival in town, and the most life-altering incident, the attack on the CDMC clubhouse. Just listing the occurrences had her head spinning. No wonder she hadn't begun to internalize the overwhelming day.

"My father is dead," she said aloud. "My husband is dead."

She stood there in the hallway, letting the words sink in.

Nothing. No sorrow, no elation—nothing. Okay, relief. She did feel relief, but she'd expected...more, somehow. Maybe it just hadn't resonated yet. Perhaps once the sheriff confirmed the names of the dead, she'd have a stronger reaction, but for now, all she felt was the strong desire to move forward with her life and forget where she'd come from.

Thirty minutes later, she had the dough for chocolate chip cookies chilling in the refrigerator when there was a knock on the door. Assuming it would be Copper, she jogged to the door and pulled it open with a flourish. "Oh, Kristy, hey." She took a step back. The club had agreed it'd be safe enough for Kristy to be home since Monty had no problem keeping an eye on both houses.

Her friend laughed as she stepped into the house. "Don't sound so excited to see me."

Laughing, Mak waved her into the kitchen. "Sorry, I was expecting Copper with the kids. Come on into the kitchen. I'm just about to throw some cookies in the oven."

"Well, that was good timing on my part." Kristy followed her through the house into the kitchen.

"How are you feeling?" Mak asked over her shoulder. Her friend's face looked even more colorful this morning.

"Not terrible. Sore, but..." She shrugged. "Suppose it'd be weird if I wasn't."

After pulling the large bowl of cold cookie dough from the fridge, Mak asked, "How do you feel about the news?"

The grin on Kristy's face could be described as elated, but with a bit of evil pleasure thrown in there. "Pretty damn good. You?"

"'Bout the same. Not that I wish death on people, but..." These deaths freed both Makenna and the MC from so many potentially deadly problems. And the men who'd died were the worst of humanity.

"Trust me, I get it," Kristy said. "Mind if I grab myself a cup of coffee?" she asked, indicating the coffee pot."

"No, of course not. Help yourself to anything." Mak scooped a hunk of cookie dough, rolled it into a ball, and placed it on the lined sheet, giving a little press to flatten it a bit.

As Kristy prepared herself a mug of coffee, Mak filled the cookie sheet then popped it in the oven. "Drink that slowly, and you can have a cookie to go with it in about ten minutes."

"Perfect."

This time, there was no knock, just the thwack of the door bursting open as the kids came barging in.

"I smell cookies!" Emmie yelled as she barreled into the kitchen with the force of someone three times her size. "Kwisty's here!" She threw herself at Kristy, who caught her practically in midair with a wince.

Mak flinched right along with her. She'd been on the receiving end of a child's boisterous love when her own body had been battered, so she knew firsthand it didn't feel great. But being the sweet friend she was, Kristy didn't so much as make a peep of protest. She scooped Emmie up and planted a noisy smooch on her cheek.

"Hey!" Copper's voice came from the front door. "I'm telling Thunder your door was unlocked."

Mak walked toward his voice. He stood in the doorway, head peeking in. "Ahh, I'm sorry!" Mak called as she reached him. "I wasn't thinking. Thank you for dropping off the kids." The older two had gone straight to their rooms.

He propped a massive shoulder against the doorframe. "No problem. Thunder at the hospital?"

She nodded. "Yeah, he should be back with Kara and Lee any time."

"Sounds good. I'm out. Lock the door!" Copper said, giving her a scowl that had her shivering. How did Shell deal with that mountain of a man? The woman deserved a medal. He was one scary dude when riled.

The moment the door shut, she clicked the lock and deadbolt into place. "Good girl," she heard through the door.

Once all the cookies were finished baking, they all piled into the den, munching, laughing, and sipping coffee—well, milk for the kiddos.

Mak was about to bite into a second—fine, third—cookie when a succession of *pops* sounded from outside.

She froze, gaze meeting Kristy's equally stunned one.

"What was that?" Rissa, mouth full and eyes wide. "It sounded like gunfire."

"It was," Amy said, voice extra high.

They were right. It was a sound Mak knew well but hadn't heard in over two years. The rapid-fire of a semi-automatic machine gun. An AK-47 if she had to guess. It'd been the daily soundtrack to her childhood.

"We need to move," Mak barked as she jumped to her feet. Years of repressed training kicked in. Her brain moved on autopilot, not allowing time for fear. "Take Emmie and hide in a closet. Do not go outside until we know what's going on."

Amy snatched Emmie off the ground and started for her bedroom with Rissa two steps ahead, but before they had a chance to leave the den, the front door crashed open, torpedoing a shower of splintered wood across the room.

Amy and Rissa screamed while Emmie began to cry with loud, frightened shrieks.

Kristy sprung from the recliner, landing with feet spread and fists clenched as though she planned to attack their intruder.

"Run!" Mak's heart pounded against her ribs like gloved fists on a punching bag. She hadn't so much as taken a step toward the kids when her father's hulking form appeared in the den.

No!

"No one fucking move!" he shouted.

The kids froze in place.

A roaring storm rushed in her ears, drowning out the sound of Emmie's wails and Amy's useless shushing. Old enough to recognize and have horrendous memories of their father, Rissa began crying as well. Normally, Mak's priority would be reassuring her distraught siblings, but she couldn't tear her gaze from the sight of their enraged father.

She hadn't seen the man in more than two years and had hoped with all her heart she'd never come face to face with him again.

Blood crusted the entire front of his shirt, seeming to have originated from a dark stain near his right shoulder. Aside from the way his right arm hung limp at his side, he looked as strong and capable as ever, standing with the rifle braced against his uninjured shoulder and trained on Kristy. Of course, he could handle a gun with one hand, his non-dominant one no less. That rifle was practically an extension of his limbs.

"You fucking bitch," he snarled, finger on the trigger. Pulsing veins bulged in his neck and forehead. His left arm held rock steady, not a waver in sight despite the weight of the weapon and the fact he had to be in extreme pain. "You set us up. They were fucking ready for us."

"N-no," Kristy whispered, shaking her head. For the first time, Mak witnessed Kristy off her game. The woman sputtered and shook under the sight of the gun. "I-I...I had no idea."

Holy shit, the anonymous caller. Had Kristy sent them to the CDMC compound on purpose, then called to warn the club? Mak had been so focused on the fact she might be free, she hadn't given thought to the caller.

God, he'd kill her friend for sure if she didn't cut in.

"D-dad," Mak said, taking a step forward. Her knees wobbled and almost gave out, but she managed to stay upright through sheer force of will and determination to save her sisters and Kristy.

"And you," he said, disgusted voice and sneer turning her way. The gun followed, arcing from Kristy to her. "Took my fucking children." Though he kept the firearm trained her way, his gaze shifted to the frightened kids. "Girls," he said, in a tone that brokered no argument. "Get behind Daddy. Now!"

Mak had never been so helpless in her life. If she charged forward, she'd be shot, and the girls taken by their father. But how could she stand there and watch him walk away with them? And then there was Monty? Was the prospect lying in the street bleeding out? He didn't deserve to die because of her selfish inability to stay away from his club.

Emmie cried harder as Amy squeezed her tight.

Amy shook her head. "N-no," the girl said, and Mak felt so proud even while she wanted to throttle the girl. Disobeying an insane gunman was a perfect way to get killed, but her sister had guts.

"Why don't you let them go to their rooms to get packed," she said. They could escape out the window if he'd just let them go.

"You poisoned them against me. You were rotten from day one," he yelled before spitting on the ground. "Should have gotten rid of you years ago. Girls! Now!"

All three of them cried now, shaking their heads. The pleading looks in their eyes broke Mak's heart. She'd failed in her one and only goal in life.

To keep her siblings safe and out of the clutches of their father.

The urge to scream at him that she'd never let him take the kids hit strong, but it would never work. He held all the power here, and he knew it. She'd be dead, and he'd take the girls.

"A-Amy," She said, voice wavering. "It's okay." None of them stood a chance if they were dead. She'd get them back. She'd walk through hell a million times to get them away from him.

"Shut the fuck up!" her father screamed. He stormed toward her until the barrel of the weapon met her sternum with a rough jab. "She doesn't fucking listen to you anymore."

Rissa screamed, and Emmie called for her over and over. Only Kristy remained silent, moving to shield the girls with her trembling body.

Mak winced at the sharp stab in her sternum but held motionless as could be. If his attention remained on her, it'd be off the others.

"Two years! Two fucking years I've wasted searching for your selfish ass." Spittle hit her face, and her heart threatened to explode, but she stood still as a statue. As terrified as she was that a bullet would tear through her chest at any moment, relief that the girls no longer held his focus had her locked in place.

"I hope you're not expecting me to apologize," she said with a smirk. "I hear Roger is dead. We're going to be throwing a party tonight. I'm finally fucking free of that sadistic asshole."

Her father's nostrils flared. Baiting the beast might be stupid, but she didn't give a shit. Anything to keep his attention on her and off the kids.

In her periphery, Kristy ushered the girls out the front door. She whispered something, hopefully telling them to run to safety, then paused in the doorframe. Mak gave her an imperceptible nod. Kristy wouldn't be able to help her now. No one would. But Kristy would get the kids out and seek help so Makenna could focus on getting out alive.

Her father continued to rant in her face about the countless atrocities she'd committed her entire life. His tirade made him oblivious to the activity occurring behind him. "You were given everything," he snarled, bubbles forming in the corner of his mouth like foam from a rabid dog. "You could have been the queen of the fucking compound. But not only are you an insubordinate bitch, you're also a useless excuse for a woman. Couldn't even give your husband a child. And now he's dead because he spent his last years searching for his defective, ungrateful fucking wife."

Mak couldn't help it, even knowing how it would end for her. Her lips twitched into more of a sneer than a grin. "I work just fine," she said, reveling in the way his red face mottled an even deeper purple. "But for the two years I was forced to be married to an abusive man as psychotic as you are, I took birth control pills."

"W-what?" He stumbled back, though managed to maintain his hold on the gun.

Pressure eased from her chest, allowing a much-needed deep breath. It bolstered her confidence, amped up her strength, and desire to hurt him any way she could.

"Every. Single. Day." She reveled in the way his face paled and his jaw went slack. "Roger didn't tell you, did he?"

Escaping the community had been necessary but fighting back gave her a sense of satisfaction she'd never imagined she'd experience. Advancing on him, she took advantage of his momentary shock and shoved the gun away from her. "There was no way in hell I was going to let that man put a baby in me. I'd have died first."

Frothing with his rage, her father recovered control of the gun and jammed it dead center in her forehead. "Looks like you're going to get your wish."

She winced as the metal crunched the bone. It hurt like a bitch and would leave a mark for sure, though the bullet hole would take care of that.

Eyes the same blue as hers met her gaze head on. They shared so many features, hair color, nose shape; they even had the same freckle on their left shoulders. But the evil gleam in her father's eyes and the blackness of his soul was something they'd never had in common. He'd kill her right then and there without an ounce of remorse.

Mak gritted her teeth and panted through her nose. Her arms and legs shook with violent force. This was it. The culmination of her failures. Her breaths came in shallow pants, making her dizzy.

No! Please don't do this! I want to live. I have so much to live for!

Screams clawed at her throat, trying to tear their way free, but she gnashed her teeth together so hard the enamel would be dust. She refused to beg him for her life.

"Hope it was worth it," he said with a maniacal laugh.

Worth it? Her eyes fell shut as the past two years ran through her mind like a film reel on fast forward. Laughing with her siblings, watching them grow and thrive without fear, living without bruises and beatings, happy holidays full of joy and love. None of the fear, struggles, hardships, or challenges came to mind, because they'd been nothing compared to the incredible love and bond she shared with her siblings.

Thunder's face danced in her mind's eyes.

Yes, everything had been more than worth it. Just meeting Thunder made every single choice that brought her to this point worth it.

"Yes," she breathed, though he probably hadn't intended she answer. "It was so worth it."

She inhaled what would be her last breath on earth and squeezed her eyes tight.

I'm sorry, Thunder. I never meant to hurt you. I love you.

She trembled like a leaf clinging to a tree in a ferocious storm.

Thunder

Hopefully, both the kids and Thunder knew how much she loved them and hadn't wanted to leave. How she tried so hard to keep this very moment from happening. Hopefully they felt her lo—

The deafening crack of the gun had her entire body jolting and lurching backward. Her bottom hit the ground with a bone-jarring thud as wetness splattered across her arms and neck. Pain shot from her tailbone up her spine, ripping a gasp from her at the same time a loud thud crashed right in front of her.

I'm alive. I'm alive.

Her eyes flew open to find Thunder standing at the door, his pistol dangling from his hand. "Makenna!" he shouted as he rushed her.

She scrambled halfway to her feet when he reached her and yanked her flush against his body.

"Jesus fucking Christ," he said, as he squeezed her so tight, she squeaked. Then he gripped her shoulders and peeled her away. "Are you okay?" His hands roamed up and down her body, patting and trembling. "There's blood. Are you hurt anywhere?"

"I-I'm okay," she whispered, throat tight. She tried to suck in air, but it stuck in her windpipe, making a high-pitched whistle. "I'm okay. N-not hurt. I-It's not m-mine." Another whistle and failed inhalation. Her chest felt tight, head light and whirling. "Y-you s-s-saved me. T-the k-kids?" Each word became harder to pass through her lips.

"Fuck. Slow, breathe slow, baby." His hands returned to her shoulders where he rubbed in deep circles. "In, two, three, four."

She tried to follow his lead, but the air hitched and stuttered.

"Now hold, two, three, four. And out, two, three, four. Good, baby. Again."

Once they'd done it a half a dozen times, her chest finally loosened enough to draw in oxygen and chase away the dizziness. "I'm o-okay," she said, gulping air like it tasted delicious.

"You're amazing." He dragged her to him once again, smothering her in his fierce embrace. "The kids are fine. Shaken, but fine. They're outside with Kristy and Lee. Copper is on his way back." He fell silent, burying his face in her neck. Then he whispered against her skin. "I've never been so fucking scared. When I pulled up and saw Monty slumped over his steering wheel, I lost my fucking shit. Thought I was gonna have to knock Lee out to keep him from charging in here."

Mak gasped. "Monty! Is he okay?"

Nodding, Thunder wrapped her even tighter. "Yes. He was hit in the shoulder and the hip through the car door. An ambulance is on the way."

God, he'd been hurt because of her.

"I'm c-cold," she said as chills racked her body and visibly shook her.

"I know, baby." He kissed the curve of her neck. "It's adrenalin."

"My, um, my f-father." She started to turn her head, but he cupped the back and held her immobile.

"Don't look. You don't need to see that. He's dead. I shot him through the side of his head. There's no chance he's coming back. The sheriff called Copper about five minutes ago. One of the dead men is a Roger Caldwell. You're free, Mak. You and the kids are all free."

Freedom.

The most incredible word. No more looking over their shoulder. No more fear of retaliation. No more sleepless nights afraid to drift off only to be woken by the sound of gunfire.

Mak's eyelids fluttered shut as she blew out a choppy breath. "Thank you," she whispered.

He tilted her face up and kissed her. "I love you."

A strangled sound left her throat. As her body came down from the height of terror, she was losing control of her emotions. "I l-love you too," she said as the battle to remain tearless became a futile one.

"Shhh, it's okay." He rubbed her back. "Let it out, babe, and know it's the last time you'll ever have to cry like this."

Everything came pouring out of her at that moment. All the fear, stress, anxiety, struggling, and now elation. The emotions jumbled together in an overwhelming attack on her system. The intense feelings had nowhere to go but streaming from her eyes in a torrent of hard-earned tears.

Thunder held her through it, rocking side to side and whispering sweet nonsense in her ear. After long minutes, she began to settle, with only the occasional hiccup or choked breath.

The distant whir of sirens had her stiffening in his arms. She lifted her head. Her face had to be an absolute disaster. "T-They're going to link me to them." Panic gripped her throat. "Oh my God, what do I do?"

"Shh, babe, leave it to Copper. He's got it under control. Your identity should hold up, and you've said no one ever reported you or the kids missing, right?"

Oh, yes, he was right. The community refused to involve outside law enforcement or authorities in their governing process. Even if the cops investigated her father, husband, or the men they'd brought with them, they'd never hear about a woman and five children disappearing in the dead of night two years ago. And she'd paid a pretty penny for their identities. They were the real deal and should hold up to an investigation by a small-town police department.

"Right. You're right." She pressed a hand to her head. "I'm panicking."

"You just tell the cops they came here looking for club members. Okay? We're gonna spin it to relate it to the CDMC massacre."

"But, won't this bring trouble or your club?"

He shook his head.

The shrill wail of sirens reached a level so piercing, she was tempted to slap her hands over her ears. The kids had to be miserable, though the thrill of seeing an ambulance up close might be enough to distract the younger ones.

"No," he shouted to be heard over the din. "My kill was justified. He was about to shoot you." His eyes flared with renewed rage.

All of a sudden, the noise cut off, plunging them into silence. All she could hear was the beating of her own heart, which seemed even louder than the ambulance.

"You ready?" he asked, extending a hand.

She grasped it tight. Thank God for his strength and support. "Ready to speak to the cops? No. Not ready at all."

His famous smile, the one that charmed everyone in a mile radius, broke out across his handsome face, warming her soul, and heating her blood. "No, baby, ready to walk out that door and start the rest of our lives? Together."

"Oh, yes. I'm ready for that." She returned his smile then planted a quick but hard kiss right on those upturned lips.

She was so ready for that.

Epilogue

"I THINK THAT'S the last of it," Thunder said as he set the final box from the moving van on top of some others.

Mak moved to him with a soft smile on her face. She wrapped her arms around his waist and tipped her lips up for a kiss. "Finally," she whispered.

"You're a brave woman."

Her nose wrinkled, and she shook her head at him. "Why?"

"Because I'm sweaty as fuck and probably smell damn rank right about now." He brushed his lips over hers. Once, then again. He could do this all day, planned to sometime soon, now that they were officially living together. No amount of touching, kissing, fucking was ever enough when it came to his woman. "But you came on to me, so you're stuck with it now."

"I like you sweaty," she said against his mouth. "Reminds me of when we're naked."

He groaned and kissed her with intent this time.

Another groan hit her ears, this one full of annoyance and disgust.

"Is this my life now? Every time I walk in a room where the two of you are, I'm gonna have to see this?" Amy asked in a voice conveying her revulsion.

"Sorry," Mak said, wiping her mouth as she drew away at the same time, Thunder said, "Yep. This is it, kiddo."

Hell yeah, he planned to be kissing on his woman every chance he got.

"They sucking face again?" Kara asked. She walked in the room lugging her pillow and favorite blanket. The helmet she hated with a passion sat on her head, fastened beneath her chin. Since the neurologist adjusted the medication back up, she'd been seizure-free, but he wanted her to keep the helmet on for six weeks, just in case. The news had devastated Kara and stressed Mak out, but with only a week left, they'd all survived.

"Excuse me?" he asked, charging her. He scooped her up and slung her over his shoulder. The pillow hit the floor, and her squeals of joy nearly deafened him, but he'd take it to see her having so much fun. "What do you know about sucking face?"

"Seriously!" Mak said with a frown. "Where did you even hear that?"

"From Lee!" Kara said, hanging upside down. "And I know it's super gross."

Rissa strode in carrying a small box labeled with her name. "What's gross? Oh, were those two kissing again?"

Thunder bit his lip to keep from laughing while Mak threw her arms up in the air. He set Kara down and snagged his ol' lady around the waist. Those he'd worked with for years wouldn't recognize him, nor would they believe it if he told them how much he fucking loved the new turn his life had taken. The laughing, the loving, the playing, even the fighting that went on in this family made him thankful each and every morning he woke up. Life was chaotic, messy, and full of more love than he'd thought possible. No matter what drama happened during the day with the kids, he and Mak not only managed to sneak in time for themselves, but they fell asleep sated and wrapped in each other's arms each night.

And now they'd officially be living together.

Life didn't get much more perfect than this.

"Better get used to it, guys. I plan to do this all the time. Close your eyes if you can't handle it." He tugged Mak's hair, tilting her head back, then planted a wet one on her.

The girls all shrieked their horror then scattered to their new rooms.

"Mmm," he said against her mouth. "Alone at last." Then he went back for more of her sweetness. She'd long ago lost any shyness and now took what she wanted, meeting his tongue with bold strokes and teasing flicks.

"Ewwww, gross!" Emmie giggled then barreled into their legs, almost taking them both out. "You're *bisgusting*!"

Lee chuckled as he walked in, then scooped up the youngest of the bunch. "She has a point, guys. You have a room. With a door. That locks."

Thunder snorted. "I'll tell you what I told the rest of em." He hugged Mak close, plastering her back to his front. "Get used to it."

"So that means I get to act the same way when I bring my girlfriend over, right?"

Thunder shrugged. "Sure. Why not?"

Mak's palm hit his chest in a less than gentle slap. "Uh, no! You cannot."

"Ow!" What was that for? He rubbed his sore nipple.

She scowled up at him, then turned it to her brother. "That was for suggesting Lee can make out with his girlfriend around the house where all the kids can see. It's not appropriate."

Lee snorted. "But it's appropriate for you."

Thunder kissed the top of her head then nodded at Lee over her.

"Uh, yes. We are in a committed relationship, and we love each other," she said, voice full of the sass he loved.

Lee snorted. "I'm committed to my girl."

"Yeah, for this week," Mak shot back.

Thunder would have given her a high five for the quick comeback if they were in the right position for it.

"Plus, we pay for the house, so we make the rules."

Thunder rested his chin on Mak's head as the two of them went back and forth with their sibling bickering. He stuck his tongue out at Emmie, who mimicked the move with another round of those sweet giggles. He'd do just about anything for that sound, not that it was hard to elicit from her. The girl laughed at anything and everything.

Crossing his eyes, he did it again. Emmie clapped and tried to copy it, but her cute little baby blues just went in all different and wacky directions.

As he chuckled, the rest of the clan made their way into the room.

"I'm hungry!" Rissa announced.

Mak snorted. "What else is new?"

Rissa shrugged. "I'm growing. Plus, we did a lot of work today."

"Seriously," Lee agreed. "I'm freakin' starved."

As a heated argument over what to eat for dinner erupted, Thunder remained quiet and took it all in. He didn't give a fuck what they ate.

Instead of joining in the debate, he absorbed the reality of his new life. A complete one-eighty from how he'd been living only a few months ago, he now felt full in ways he'd never thought possible.

His heart nearly burst whenever one of the kids came to him for help or gave him a spontaneous hug. Last night Emmie refused to hear a bedtime story from anyone but him, and he'd nearly melted on the spot. Never had he imagined himself a family man, but it turned out to be exactly who he was. He had as much fun staying in and watching a cheesy movie with the little girls as he did partying with his brothers.

Though nothing compared to the nights he had Makenna to himself. Those passion-filled evenings were everything, and he'd never take them for granted. He'd never take one second of his time with her for granted.

Witnessing her almost lose her life ensured he would cherish every single second with his woman and his new loud, crazy, loving family.

Mak looked up at him with a half-grin. "Regretting your life choices yet?" she asked. It came out with a chuckle, but he could tell she half worried he'd find living with all of them too much.

"Never," he whispered. Who would regret the best thing to ever happen to them?

IT'D TAKEN A very lengthy and heated debate to settle on pizza for dinner. Then, of course, once that had been decided, they needed to figure out what kind of pizza they wanted.

This bunch could turn anything into an argument and seemed to do so with pleasure. Mak was used to it but always worried the reality of living with a hoard of unruly kids and teens would prove to be too much for Thunder.

Izzy had given her a slightly hard slap upside the head and scolded her when she'd mentioned it at a girls' night. "You're not being fair to him," she said, eyes narrowed. "Actually, you're kinda being a bitch." The woman did not mince words.

Thankfully, Shell had been there, too, and had a better way with words than Izzy did. "What she means," Shell said, whacking Izzy's arm, "is that you need to trust him and what he's telling you. Does he act like he wants out? Like being around your siblings bothers him?"

"No, not at all," Mak had said. "He loves them."

"Then stop waiting for disaster and enjoy what you've got," Izzy had said.

Toni had rolled her eyes at that. "She speaks like she had no issues when she and Jig got together. Trust me, Mak, she was as hardheaded as anyone." She'd sipped her wine. "Though she does have a point."

So Mak had taken their advice and stopped looking for disaster around every corner. Listening to their counsel had brought her here. To a home where the kids had more space both indoors and out to live and play. To a carpet picnic complete with four pizzas, garlic knots, her salad, and a circle of happily munching family members.

To sharing a home with the man she loved and who she truly believed loved her back.

And loved her crazy family as though they were his own.

Of course, she hadn't been able to sit next to him. As usual, Emmie and Kara monopolized him during the meal, sitting on either side of him and vying for his focus. He took it in stride, as he always did, expertly juggling their bids for attention and affection.

"This house is awesome," Amy announced around a giant mouthful of pizza.

Mak didn't bother to remind her she shouldn't speak with food in her mouth. Moving day had proved to be too special to mar it with everyday scolding.

"I know!" Kara butt in. "We can all fit in a circle on the floor! It's so great."

With a chuckle, Thunder used his napkin to wipe sauce from Kara's mouth. "This house is bigger, but once we get the furniture set up, we may not be able to sit like this. There are a lot of you." He tweaked her nose.

"That's okay," Kara said, undeterred. "We can do it outside instead."

"Now that we can definitely do," Mak said. "We'll have to get a grill so we can make hotdogs out there."

"I *lub* hotdogs," Emmie called out.

After her father's death, the club had a contact monitoring channels for her name. Some computer whiz named Acer out in Arizona who knew Gumby, apparently. Copper had explained to her how they wanted to make sure she or the kids weren't listed on any missing person lists or police reports.

They hadn't been, thank God. But there had been an attorney searching for her. Apparently, her mother had some money in an account set up by her family. They'd tried for years to get her to leave the community to no avail. Somehow and at some point, someone, maybe the grandparents she'd never met, had listed her as a beneficiary.

Well, they'd left it to Delilah.

Acer had been able to perform some sort of internet magic, most likely of the highly illegal variety, and got the money to her. It'd been enough to make a really sizable dent in the cost of a huge house with six bedrooms, a huge backyard, and a kitchen that had made her weep when she first saw it. And one of the best parts—she could see Shell and Copper's place from the front yard.

It was perfection and she had to pinch herself daily to make sure she hadn't gotten lost in a beautiful dream.

Thunder glanced up from his food as though he'd sensed the serious direction of her thoughts. He winked and smiled the smile that still charmed her every time he flashed it her way.

Her heart swelled until her chest felt full to the max. This man had come to mean everything to her. He'd taught her how to enjoy her life, to be playful, and how to find pleasure in every day. He loved her and never failed to show it.

Thunder was a priceless gift she tried to repay in her own actions each day.

His grin disappeared and he tilted his head as though to ask if she was all right.

Holding his gaze, she nodded.

"I love you," he mouthed.

Emmie patted his leg with greasy fingers leaving an oily handprint on his jeans. He didn't even seem to notice, let alone mind. The man truly loved her family as much as he loved her.

Suddenly, overcome with emotion, Mak's eyes watered. She pressed a hand to her heart and mouthed, "I love you, too," back at Thunder.

His own eyes looked suspiciously wet as if he felt the significance of the simple moment as well.

But then every minute spent with him was important. Because they'd chosen each other and against some pretty impressive odds, found a perfection neither of them had dared to wish for.

Bonus Epilogue

Fifteen years later

COPPER NARROWED HIS eyes as though he could use the orbs as lasers to vaporize the problem playing out before him. When nothing happened, he settled for another sip of scotch and a growl.

"You know," Shell said, as she stepped up behind him and wrapped her arms around his neck. "I'm pretty sure the birthday girl shouldn't have to spend twenty minutes searching for her sexy ol' man at her party. But I am over the hill now, so maybe my memory isn't serving me as well as it used to."

With a grunt, Copper pulled his wife around from behind him, tugging her down to his lap. She looked even more gorgeous than usual tonight in a form-fitting black dress he couldn't wait to peel off her later on. With her sunny hair straightened sleek and glossy and subtle makeup, she looked fresh, young, and happy. "Over the hill, my ass," he said, palming *her* ass. At forty, well thirty-nine and three-hundred-sixty-four days, Shell didn't look a day older than she did at twenty-four when he'd finally pulled his head out of his ass and admitted his love for her. If there were lines around her eyes, and a softness to her middle, he sure as hell didn't notice it.

Making the woman his had been the best fucking move of his entire life. Soon to be the second-best because eliminating this problem in front of him might top everything, even his decision to marry Shell.

"You seeing this shit?" he asked, nudging his chin for Shell to follow his gaze.

She did, but her giggle didn't seem appropriate for how fucking bad the situation was. "Do I see our daughter flirting with a handsome man? Yes, Copper, I do. Those two have been sniffing around each other for about six months now."

He straightened, nearly dumping Shell off his lap. "Excuse me? How the fuck did I not know this?"

Rolling her eyes, his sassy wife swatted his chest. "Could you not break my hip on my birthday? And seriously, what's the big deal? Beth has been dating for years."

"Yeah, but not him. Not one of *my* guys." He shot his daughter another glower.

Shell giggled again.

Even at his expense, he loved the damn sound of his wife's happiness.

"Copper, you love Lee. He went through a bit of a rough period in his late teens, but once Makenna and Thunder got him in therapy and he dealt with his upbringing he really turned his life around. He's a good man and you know it."

He was a good man. One of the best Copper knew. Responsible, self-assured without being a cocky fucker, and damn smart, he'd make a great Sergeant at Arms in the future. None of that meant Copper wanted him dating his eldest daughter.

Makenna's brother had prospected at twenty-one and been a great addition to the club. But there was one big problem here Shell seemed to be overlooking. "Baby, Beth is twenty. And Lee is thirty-fucking-three. He's robbing the goddammed cradle. It's fucking wrong."

Uh-oh.

Shell no longer wore a playful smile. Now, her eyes were narrowed, and fire shot from the orbs. "Uh, you do realize that's three years closer in age than we are, right?"

Shit. He swallowed. How did she not see the rules were different for their daughter? "Yeah, I know, but—"

She tsked. "No buts, babe. Beth is an adult, and Lee is a great guy. I'd be happy to see them together. And she's pretty smitten, so you better get on board, big guy."

Smitten? Seriously? Had they purposefully gone behind his fucking back? "Maybe I need to send him away for a while."

Shell's jaw dropped. "Copper! Don't you dare. Shush, here they come." She whacked his chest again. "Behave."

He grunted but snatched her hand and pressed a lingering kiss to her palm. As usual, her eyes went misty, and she gave him a love-filled smile. After so many years together, he knew precisely how to worm his way back to his wife's good side.

With a sigh, Copper watched his daughter meander their way. Christ, he loved that girl. Beth wasn't his biological daughter; but not for one minute had that ever mattered to him. She was his, plain and simple. As was her mother.

"Hey, Mom! You enjoying your birthday party?" Beth asked, as she took an empty seat at their table."

Lee remained standing, eyes on Copper, and posture stiff.

That's right, asshole. She's my *daughter. You wait for my permission.*

"I am," Shell said with a bright smile for the pair. "I was just trying to get your father here to dance with me."

Copper snorted. Little liar. His snort turned into a grunt when her bony elbow landed on his ribs.

"Goddammit, woman," he muttered, rubbing his side. Those elbows were fucking lethal.

"Lee, come sit with us. How are things going with you? I hear you're thinking of buying into Zach's gym."

As the three of them chatted, Copper rested against the back of his chair and let his gaze drift to his daughter. Somehow in the past decade and a half, the adorable girl with the chubby cheeks and strawberry-blond pigtails had turned into an independent, strong, and beautiful woman. Aside from the red tinge in her hair, she looked so much like her mother, yet had a temper in her that clearly came from his bloodline.

Shit, he must be in a mood because as he scanned the room, his chest swelled and tightened with powerful emotions. This club, this rag-tag piecemeal family he'd created over the years meant more to him than they could ever know. He'd give his life for anyone of his brothers and knew without a doubt they felt the same. Blood didn't make family, choice did, and the bonds his chosen family had created were unbreakable.

Around him, kids of all ages ran amuck, laughing and having a blast. His club brothers and their ol' ladies danced, ate, and drank in celebration of his wife's fortieth birthday. So many times over the years, he'd wondered if the club would ever get to this point of prolonged peace and happiness.

But it seemed they'd made it. The years hadn't been all sunshine and rainbows, but his family had prevailed, and life was pretty damn close to perfect now. His gaze shifted back to his daughter, who practically shot hearts from her eyes to Lee.

Close, but not quite perfect.

Another elbow ramming his gut had him grunting. "Watch those bony wings, babe."

"Oh, that wasn't an accident." She gave him her sweetest, most innocent grin, and he had no choice but to kiss it off her face.

Beth groaned. "You'd think my parents would be over making out with each other every chance they get, but nope. They're just as gross now as they were when I was little."

With a snort, Copper drew away from his red-faced wife. "Go get your mother a refill," he said, shoving Shell's wine glass toward Beth. "I wanna make a toast."

"You sit, babe. I got it." Lee put his hand on Beth's shoulder as he stood and reached for the empty glass.

Hmm, gentlemanly. Fine, he got one point for that.

"Thanks, Lee." Beth gazed up at him with fucking dopey eyes.

"You're scowling," Shell whispered.

Goddammed right he was.

"Can't help it. You got any idea what an unmarried thirty-three-year-old biker gets up to in his spare time?" he whispered back.

Shell's head fell back, and a loud laugh left her. The smooth line of her throat called to him. He had a sudden urge to run his wife upstairs and celebrate the rest of her birthday in private.

"No, Copper, I don't know anything about bikers. Please fill me in." Her eyes leaked tears from laughter.

"Smartass," he said, giving her firm ass a pinch. She squealed and laughed harder.

Across the table, Beth rolled her eyes as she tossed her long reddish blond hair over her shoulder. Nothing new for her.

A few moments later, Lee returned and set the glass in front of Shell.

"Thank you so much, Lee," she said, wiping her eyes. "Whew, that was good."

Copper grunted. "Keep laughing, woman. We'll see how well that turns out for you later."

His wife's eyes darkened with lust and he couldn't resist kissing her again. Fuck. Whose idea was this party anyway? And how rude was it for the guest of honor to leave less than an hour in? Because he really wanted to get his wife home for a private celebration.

Oh, right, it'd been Beth's idea. The daughter across the table currently making vomiting noises. He turned his head. "You shut your trap," he said, pointing at his daughter. "Or your boyfriend will be spending the next month on the road."

Her jaw dropped. "You wouldn't."

Finally, Copper had a leg up. "Oh, but I would, daughter of mine."

Lee didn't look the least bit concerned as he whispered something in Beth's ear.

Copper stood, taking Shell with him. He set her on her feet and wrapped an arm around her shoulders. "Listen up!" he called out. "This won't take long."

The DJ cut the music, and everyone partying began to return to their tables to retrieve their drinks.

"We are so lucky," Shell whispered, voice cracking.

He glanced down at his wife, who was staring up at him with so much love in her gaze, his chest ached. Lucky didn't begin to cover it.

Together they looked out over their kingdom. Over the people they loved. How had they—how had he—gotten so goddammed fortunate in his life? He didn't deserve this wonderful family life he had, but the urge to make sure each and every one of his family members knew how important they were hit strong.

He cleared his suddenly thick throat. "Just want to take a quick second to thank you all for coming out to celebrate the woman who—" Shit, his throat clogged again, and he wasn't sure he could finish.

Shell squeezed his waist. "I love you," she mouthed.

He'd get it out. He'd do anything for his woman. After clearing his throat again, he spoke. "To celebrate the woman who is my entire world. It seems like only yesterday that I was a fucking idiot with my head in the sand when it came to Shell. I know you all love her almost as much as I do. She's at the very center of this club. The heart of our family. She's kept me smiling in good times and sane in the rough ones."

"You don't deserve her!" someone called out, probably Maverick. He sat with his wife Stephanie, and their twelve-year-old twin boys.

"You think I don't know that?" he yelled back. "Pretty sure I don't deserve any of you."

He paused, taking in all the love around them.

Thunder

Toni and Zach sat with their five-year-old daughter and their adopted daughter Lindsey, who'd just turned twenty-eight. They'd been the last of the crew to get married. Even Screw and Gumby had their version of a commitment ceremony with Jazz before Zach proposed to Toni. The triad was one of the few relationships in the club that hadn't produced children. They loved playing aunt and uncle to the hordes of kids in the club. They also had about ten foster animals at their house at all times.

Even Thunder and Makenna had gone on to have one boy despite always joking about their too-full house. Their boy was only seven right now, one of the younger kids.

Jig and Izzy had blown everyone out of the water, having four children. Who'd have thought the badass, MMA fighting, tattoo artist would take to motherhood like a duck to water? But she had, and within a year of having her first child, Jig had knocked her up again. They were by far the MC's coolest parents with little kick-ass kiddos set to follow in their mother's footsteps.

Rocket and Chloe, as well as Holly and LJ, had also added to the kid's club with a couple of rug-rats each. He and Shell had Beth, Lana who was fifteen, and Paige, their twenty-five-year-old in a four-year-old's body. She'd been a bit of a surprise, but very welcome addition to their crew.

What could he say? He couldn't keep his hands—or other parts of his body—off his wife.

Paige sat across the room on Cassie's lap. At seventy-three, Cassie still lived with them, and neither he nor Shell would have it any other way. They both viewed her as the mother they'd both been denied by nature. He loved her fiercely and hoped Viper would be pleased she'd come to live with them and had stayed for so long.

Copper cleared his throat again. "We've been through a lot as a club. Some really fucking high times and some devastating lows." His gaze met Cassie's, who gave him a watery smile and a nod. Still, after all these years, the hole in his heart caused by Viper's death remained gaping. It always would.

Cassie had found happiness, diving into her new role of club grandmother with both feet. She had more love in her life than almost anyone he knew.

"I'm proud to call each and every one of you, my chosen family. A lot is changing and will continue to change as the younger generation grows into adulthood and begins to take over the club."

His gaze shifted to Beth, who watched him with a smile and his chest filled with warmth. Fuck, he loved his family with everything he had.

Beth's hand rested on the table, linked with Lee's. As much as he wanted to protect his eldest daughter and keep her close, Shell was right. Lee couldn't be a better choice. Even if it chapped his hide. "I'll be proud to welcome each of our children into the club as they come of age." Then he cleared his throat again. "I'm getting off track. Tonight's a celebration." He lifted his glass. "Let's raise 'em up for Shell. Heart and fucking soul of our club, and the woman who deserves a whole room full of awards for putting up with my grumpy ass for so many years."

The room erupted in cheers, shouts, and whistles as everyone called out their birthday wishes. The music kicked back up, and everyone returned to partying even louder than before.

Shell turned in his arms and gazed up at him. All the love she felt for him shone bright in her eyes, hitting him right in the gut.

"You know," she said. "Every one of those people out there are just as lucky to have you in their life. You've given all of them purpose, a place to call home, and a family when they needed it most. But no one is luckier than me," she said as she placed her hand over his heart.

"Baby," he whispered, pressing her hand even closer.

"I'm the only one who has every single piece of the most remarkable man in the world."

"Shell, you are my everything. I love you so much." The words seemed weak in comparison to how he felt about her, but her eyes let him know she knew exactly how he felt about her.

"I love you, Copper."

He leaned down until his lips were a breath away from Shell's. "Happy birthday, baby," he whispered right before he placed a kiss on that smiling mouth.

And to think of how easily he could have missed out on this life…

Acknowledgments

And that's a wrap on the Hell's Handlers series.

It's hard to find the right words to express my gratitude for every person who's played a part in this series. Even more than four years into publishing, I feel such a giddy joy at the thought of people enjoying my books. I've always been an avid reader, so I completely understand the wonder of getting lost in a book. It's such a gift to be able to provide that feeling to other readers. So thank you to every one of you who have given my books a chance. I can't wait for you to see what's coming next!

This series would never have happened without the help of so many incredible and talented individuals.

To the editors at Words Between Pages (formerly Red Pen Coach), especially Nancy, Shirley, and Donna, you've kept me from publishing a hot mess each time. I've learned so much from you and owe my growth as a writer to you amazing ladies.

To Leah Suttle, thank you for all the gorgeous covers you've created for me over the years. They have never failed to make readers swoon!

To Gel from Tempting Illustrations, thank you for the countless teasers, banners, and promotional items you've designed. Not only are they beautiful every time, but they also represent me and my books in a fantastic way.

To Ena and Amanda from Enticing Journey Book Promotions, thank you for making cover reveals and book releases a breeze. Your hard work takes so much stress off every release.

To Carli, thank you for always being willing to listen to my ideas and help me when I'm stuck, which is often. Thank you for being willing to proofread at the drop of a hat. But most of all, thank you for allowing me to turn you into a heinous character. Miss you.

And finally, the most heartfelt thank you goes to my husband. Without your support and help, I wouldn't have published a single word. There isn't anyone else I'd be willing to take this journey with. Let's get ready for more.

Thank you so much for reading **THUNDER**. If you enjoyed it, please consider leaving a review on Amazon or Goodreads.

Other books by Lilly Atlas

No Prisoners MC
Hook: A No Prisoners Novella
Striker
Jester
Acer
Lucky
Snake

Trident Ink
Escapades

Hell's Handlers MC
Zach
Maverick
Jigsaw
Copper
Rocket
Little Jack
Joy

Lilly Atlas

Screw
Viper
Thunder

Audiobooks
Audio

Join Lilly's mailing list for a **FREE** No Prisoners short story.
www.lillyatlas.com
Facebook
Twitter
Instagram

Join my Facebook group, **Lilly's Ladies** for book previews, early cover reveals, contests and more!

About the Author

Lilly Atlas is an award-winning contemporary romance author. She's a proud Navy wife and mother of three spunky girls. Every time Lilly downloads a new eBook she expects her Kindle App to tell her it's exhausted and overworked, and to beg for some rest. Thankfully that hasn't happened yet so she can often be found absorbed in a good book.